**Praise for *New York Times* and *USA TODAY*
bestselling author Brenda Jackson**

"Brenda Jackson writes romance that sizzles
and characters you fall in love with."
—*New York Times* and *USA TODAY* bestselling
author Lori Foster

"Jackson's trademark ability to weave multiple
characters and side stories together makes
shocking truths all the more exciting."
—*Publishers Weekly*

"There is no getting away from the sex appeal and
charm of Jackson's Westmoreland family."
—*RT Book Reviews* on *Feeling the Heat*

"Jackson's characters are wonderful, strong,
colorful and hot enough to burn the pages."
—*RT Book Reviews* on *Westmoreland's Way*

"The kind of sizzling, heart-tugging story Brenda
Jackson is famous for."
—*RT Book Reviews* on *Spencer's Forbidden
Passion*

"This is entertainment at its best."
—*RT Book Reviews* on *Star of His Heart*

* * *

The Real Thing is part of
The Westmorelands series:
A family bound by loyalty…and love!
Only from *New York Times* bestselling author
Brenda Jackson and Mills & Boon® Desire™!

THE REAL THING

BY
BRENDA JACKSON

Published in Great Britain 2014
by Mills & Boon, an imprint of Harlequin (UK) Limited,
Eton House, 18-24 Paradise Road, Richmond, Surrey, TW9 1SR

© 2014 Brenda Streater Jackson

ISBN: 978 0 263 91461 0

51-0314

Harlequin (UK) Limited's policy is to use papers that are natural, renewable and recyclable products and made from wood grown in sustainable forests. The logging and manufacturing processes conform to the legal environmental regulations of the country of origin.

Printed and bound in Spain
by Blackprint CPI, Barcelona

Brenda Jackson is a die "heart" romantic who married her childhood sweetheart and still proudly wears the "going steady" ring he gave her when she was fifteen. Because she believes in the power of love, Brenda's stories always have happy endings. In her real-life love story, Brenda and her husband of more than forty years live in Jacksonville, Florida, and have two sons.

A *New York Times* bestselling author of more than seventy-five romance titles, Brenda is a recent retiree who now divides her time between family, writing and traveling with Gerald. You may write Brenda at PO Box 28267, Jacksonville, Florida 32226, USA, by e-mail at WriterBJackson@aol.com or visit her website at www.brendajackson.net.

To the love of my life, Gerald Jackson, Sr.

To my readers
who continue to inspire me to reach higher heights.

To my family—
the Hawks, Streaters and Randolphs who continue
to support me in all my endeavors. I couldn't ask
to be a part of a better family.

For we cannot but speak the things
which we have seen and heard.
—*Acts* 4:20 NKJV

One

"I understand you're in a jam and might need my help."

In a jam was putting it mildly, Trinity Matthews thought, looking across the table at Adrian Westmoreland.

If only what he'd said wasn't true. And…if only Adrian wasn't so good-looking. Then thinking about what she needed him to do wouldn't be so hard.

When she and Adrian had first met, last year at his cousin Riley's wedding, he had been standing in a group of Westmoreland men. She had sized up his brothers and cousins, but had definitely noticed Adrian standing beside his identical twin brother, Aidan.

Trinity had found out years ago, when her sister Tara had married Thorn Westmoreland, that all Westmoreland men were eye candy of the most delectable kind. Therefore, she hadn't really been surprised to discover that Thorn's cousins from Denver had a lot of the same traits—handsome facial features, tall height, a hard-muscled body and an aura of primal masculinity.

But she'd never thought she'd be in a position to date one of those men—even if it was only a temporary ruse.

Trinity knew Tara had already given Adrian some details about the situation and now it was up to her to fill him in on the rest.

"Yes, I'm in a jam," Trinity said, releasing a frustrated breath. "I want to tell you about it, but first I want to thank you for agreeing to meet with me tonight."

He had suggested Laredo's Steak House. She had eaten here a few times, and the food was always excellent.

"No problem."

She paused, trying to ignore how the deep, husky sound of his voice stirred her already nervous stomach. "My goal," she began, "is to complete my residency at Denver Memorial and return to Bunnell, Florida, and work beside my father and brothers in their medical practice. That goal is being threatened by another physician, Dr. Casey Belvedere. He's a respected surgeon here in Denver. He—"

"Wants you."

Trinity's heart skipped a beat. Another Westmoreland trait she'd discovered: they didn't believe in mincing words.

"Yes. He wants an affair. I've done nothing to encourage his advances or to give him the impression I'm interested. I even lied and told him I was already involved with someone, but he won't let up. Now it's more than annoying. He's hinted that if I don't go along with it, he'll make my life at the hospital difficult."

She pushed her plate aside and took a sip of her wine. "I brought his unwanted advances to the attention of the top hospital administrator, and he's more or less dismissed my claim. Dr. Belvedere's family is well known in the city. Big philanthropists, I understand. Presently, the Belvederes are building a children's wing at the hospital that will bear their name. It's my guess that the hospital administrator feels that now is not the time to make waves with any of the Belvederes. He said I need to pick my battles carefully, and this is one I might not want to take on."

She paused. "So I came up with a plan." She chuckled

softly. "Let me rephrase that. Tara came up with the plan after I told her what was going on. It seems that she faced a similar situation when she was doing her residency in Kentucky. The only difference was that the hospital administrator supported her and made sure the doctor was released of his duties. I don't have that kind of support here because of the Belvedere name."

Adrian didn't say anything for a few moments. He broke eye contact with her and stared down into his glass of wine. Trinity couldn't help but wonder what he was thinking.

He looked back at her. "There is another solution to your problem, you know."

She lifted a brow. "There is?"

"You did say he's a surgeon, right?"

"Yes."

"Then I could break his hands so he'll never be able to use them in an operating room again."

She stared wide-eyed at him for a couple of seconds before leaning forward. "You're joking, right?"

"No. I am not joking. I'm dead serious."

She leaned back as she studied his features. They were etched with ruthlessness and his dark eyes were filled with callousness. It was only then that Trinity remembered Tara's tales about the twins, their baby sister, Bailey, and their younger cousin Bane. According to Tara, those four were the holy terrors of Denver while growing up and got into all kinds of trouble—malicious and otherwise.

But that was years ago. Now Bane was a navy SEAL, the twins were both Harvard graduates—Adrian obtained his PhD in engineering and Aidan completed medical school—and Bailey, the youngest of the four, was presently working on her MBA. However, it was quite obvious to Trinity that behind Adrian Westmoreland's chiseled good looks, irresistible charm and PhD was a man who could return to his old ways if the need arose.

"I don't think we need to go that far," she said, swallowing. "Like Tara suggested, we can pretend to be lovers and hope that works."

"If that's how you prefer handling it."

"Yes. And you don't have a problem going along with it? Foregoing dating other women for a while?"

He pushed his plate aside and leaned back in his chair. "Nope. I don't have a problem going along with it. Putting my social life on hold until this matter is resolved will be no big deal."

Trinity released a relieved sigh. She had heard that since he'd returned to Denver to work as one of the CEOs at his family-owned business, Blue Ridge Land Management, Adrian had acquired a very active social life. There weren't many single Westmoreland men left in town. In fact, he was the only one. His cousin Stern was engaged to be married in a few months; Bane was away in the navy and Aidan was practicing medicine at a hospital in North Carolina. All the other Westmoreland men had married. Adrian would definitely be a catch for any woman. And they were coming after him from every direction, determined to hook a Westmoreland man; she'd heard he was having the time of his life letting them try.

Trinity was grateful she wasn't interested. The only reason she and Adrian were meeting was that she needed his help to pull off her plan. In fact, this was the first time they had seen each other since she'd moved to Denver eight months ago. She'd known when she accepted the internship at Denver Memorial last year that a slew of her sister's Westmoreland cousins-in-law lived here. She had met most of them at Riley's wedding. But most lived in a part of Denver referred to as Westmoreland Country and she lived in town. Though she had heard that when Adrian returned to Denver he had taken a place in town instead of moving to his family's homestead, more for privacy than anything else.

"I think we should put our plan into action now," he said, breaking into her thoughts.

He surprised her further when he took her hand in his and brought it to his lips while staring deeply into her eyes. She tried to ignore the intense fluttering in her stomach caused by his lips brushing against her skin.

"Why are you so anxious to begin?"

"It's simply a matter of timing," he said, bringing her hand to his lips yet again. "Don't look now but Dr. Casey Belvedere just walked in. He's seen us and is looking over here."

Let the show begin.

Adrian continued to stare deep into Trinity's eyes, sensing her nervousness. Although she had gone along with Tara's suggestion, he had a feeling she wasn't 100 percent on board with the idea of pretending to be his lover.

Although Dr. Belvedere was going about his pursuit all wrong, Adrian could understand the man wanting her. Hell, what man in his right mind wouldn't? Like her sister, Tara, Trinity was an incredibly beautiful woman. Ravishing didn't even come close to describing her.

When he'd first met Tara, years ago, the first thing out of his mouth was to ask if she had any sisters. Tara had smiled and replied, yes, she had a sister who was a senior in high school with plans to go to college to become a doctor.

Jeez. Had it been that long ago? He recalled the reaction of every single man at Riley's wedding when Trinity had showed up with Thorn and Tara. That's when he'd heard she would be moving to Denver for two years to work at the hospital.

"Are you sure it's him?" Trinity asked.

"Pretty positive," he said, studying her features. She

had creamy mahogany-colored skin, silky black hair that hung to her shoulders and the most gorgeous pair of light brown eyes he'd ever seen. "And it's just the way I planned it," he said.

She arched a brow. "The way you planned it?"

"Yes. After Tara called and told me about her idea, I decided to start right away. I found out from a reliable source that Belvedere frequents this place quite a bit, especially on Thursday nights."

"So that's why you suggested we have dinner here tonight?" she asked.

"Yes, that's the reason. The plan is for him to see us together, right?"

"Yes. I just wasn't prepared to run into him tonight. Hopefully all it will take is for him to see us together and—"

"Back off? Don't bank on that. The man wants you and, for some reason, he feels he has every right to have you. Getting him to leave you alone won't be easy. I still think I should just break his damn hands and be through with it."

"No."

He shrugged. "Your call. Now we should really do something to get his attention."

"What?"

"This." Adrian leaned in and kissed her.

Trinity was certain it was supposed to be a mere brush across the lips, but like magnets their mouths locked, fusing in passion so quickly that it consumed her senses.

To Trinity's way of thinking, the kiss had a potency that had her insides begging for more. Every part of her urged her to make sure this kiss didn't end anytime soon. But the clinking of dishes and silverware made her remember where they were and what they were doing. She slowly eased her mouth away from Adrian's.

She let out a slow breath. "I have a feeling that did more than get his attention. It might have pissed him off."

Adrian smiled. "Who cares? You're with me now and he won't do anything stupid. I dare him."

He motioned for the waiter to bring their check. "I think we've done enough playacting tonight," he said smoothly. "Ready to leave?"

"Yes."

Moments after taking care of their dinner bill, Adrian took Trinity's hand in his and led her out of the restaurant.

Two

"So how did things go with Trinity last night?"

Adrian glanced up to see his cousin Dillon. The business meeting Dillon had called that morning at Blue Ridge Land Management had ended and everyone had filed out, leaving him and Dillon alone.

He'd never thought of Dillon as a business tycoon until Adrian had returned home to work for the company his family owned. That's when he got to see his Denver cousin in action, wheeling and dealing to maintain Blue Ridge's ranking as a Fortune 500 company. Adrian had always just thought of him as Dillon, the man who'd kept the family together after a horrific tragedy.

Adrian's parents, as well as his uncle and aunt, had died in a plane crash more than twenty years ago, leaving Dillon, who was the oldest cousin, and Adrian's oldest brother, Ramsey, in charge of keeping the family of fifteen Westmorelands together. It hadn't been easy, and Adrian would be the first to confess that he, Aidan, Bane and Bailey, the youngest four, had deliberately made things hard. Coming home from school one day to be told they'd lost the four people who had meant the most to them had been worse than difficult. They hadn't handled their grief well. They had rebelled in ways Adrian was now ashamed of. But Dillon, Ramsey and the other family members hadn't given up on them, even when they truly should have. For that reason and many others, Adrian deeply loved his family. Especially Dillon, who had taken on the State of Colorado when it had tried to force the youngest four into foster homes.

"Things went well, I think," Adrian said, not wondering how Dillon knew about the dinner date with Trinity even when Adrian hadn't mentioned anything about it. Dillon spoke to their Atlanta cousins on a regular basis, especially Thorn Westmoreland. Adrian figured Tara had mentioned the plan to Thorn and he had passed the information on to Dillon.

"Glad to hear it," Dillon said, gathering up his papers. "Hopefully it will work. Even so, I personally have a problem with the hospital administrator not doing anything about Dr. Belvedere. I don't give a damn how much money his family has or that they have a wing bearing their name under construction at the hospital. Sexual harassment is sexual harassment, and it's something no one should have to tolerate. What's happening to Trinity shouldn't happen to anyone."

Adrian agreed. If he had anything to do with it, Trinity wouldn't have to tolerate it. "We'll give Tara's idea a shot and if it doesn't work, then—"

"Then the Westmorelands will handle it, Adrian, the right way...with the law on our side. I don't want you doing anything that will get you in trouble. Those days are over."

Adrian didn't say anything as he remembered *those* days. "I won't do anything to get into trouble." He figured it was best not to say those days were completely over, especially after the suggestion he'd made to Trinity about breaking Belvedere's hands...something he'd been dead serious about. "Do you know anyone in the Belvedere family?" he asked Dillon.

"Dr. Belvedere's older brother Roger and I are on the boards of directors of a couple of major businesses in town, but we aren't exactly friends. He's arrogant, a little on the snobbish side. I heard it runs in the family."

"Too bad," Adrian said, rising from his chair.

"The Belvedere family made their money in the food industry, namely dairy products. I understand Roger has political aspirations and will announce his run for governor next month."

"I wish him the best. It's his brother Casey that I have a problem with," Adrian said, heading toward the door. "I'll see you later."

An hour later Adrian had finished an important report his cousin Canyon needed. Both Canyon and another cousin, Stern, were company attorneys. So far, Adrian was the only one from his parents' side of the Westmoreland tree who worked for Blue Ridge, the company founded by his and Dillon's father more than forty years ago.

At present there were fifteen Denver Westmorelands of his generation. His parents, Thomas and Susan Westmoreland, had had eight kids: five boys—Ramsey, Zane, Derringer and the twins, Adrian and Aidan—and three girls—Megan, Gemma and Bailey.

His uncle Adam and aunt Clarisse had had seven sons: Dillon, Micah, Jason, Riley, Canyon, Stern and Bane. The family was a close-knit one and usually got together on Friday nights at Dillon's place for a chow-down, where they ate good food and caught up on family matters. Dates had kept Adrian from attending the last two, but now, since he was *supposedly* involved with Trinity, his dating days were over for a while.

He tossed an ink pen on his desk before leaning back in his chair. For the umpteenth time that day he was reminded of the kiss he'd shared with Trinity last night. A kiss he had taken before she'd been aware he was about to do so. Adrian didn't have to wonder what had driven him. He could try to convince himself he'd only done it to rile Belvedere, but Adrian knew it was about more than that.

It all started when he had arrived at Trinity's place to pick her up. She must have been watching for him out the window of the house she was leasing because after he'd pulled into her driveway, before he could get out of his car, she had opened the door and strolled down the walk toward him.

He'd had to fight to keep his predatory smile from showing a full set of teeth. Damn, she had looked good. He could say it was the pretty, paisley print maxi dress that swirled around her ankles as she'd walked, or the blue stilettos and matching purse. He could say it was the way she'd worn her hair down to her shoulders, emphasizing gorgeous facial bones. Whatever it was, she had looked even more appealing than when he'd seen her at Riley and Alpha's wedding.

Adrian sucked in a sharp breath as more memories swept through his mind. Never had a woman's mouth tasted so delectable, so irresistibly sweet. She had been pretty quiet on the drive back to her place last night. Just as well, since his body had been on fire for her. Big mistake. How was he supposed to stop Belvedere from getting his hands on her when all he could think about was getting his own hands on her?

He stood and stretched his tall frame. After shoving his hands into the pockets of his pants, he walked over to the window and looked out at downtown Denver. When Tara had called him with the idea of pretending to be Trinity's lover, he had shrugged, thinking no problem, no big deal. A piece of cake. What he hadn't counted on was his own attraction to Trinity. It was taking over his thoughts. And that wasn't good.

Frustrated, he rubbed his hand down his face. He had to have more control. She wasn't the first woman he'd been attracted to and she wouldn't be the last. Taking another deep breath, he glanced at his watch. He was having dinner at McKays with Bailey and figured he would surprise her this time by being on time.

He had one more file to read, which wouldn't take long. Then, before leaving for the day, he would call Trinity to see how things had gone at work. He wanted to make sure Belvedere hadn't caused her any grief about seeing them together last night at Laredo's.

"So how did things go last night with Adrian?"

Trinity plopped down on the sofa in her living room after a long day at work. She'd figured she would hear from Tara sooner or later, who would want details.

"Great! We got to know each other while eating a delicious steak dinner. And Dr. Belvedere was off today, which was a good thing, given that he saw me and Adrian together last night at dinner."

"He did?"

"Yes."

"Coincidence or planned?"

"Planned. It seemed Adrian didn't waste time. Once he had agreed with your suggestion he found out where Belvedere liked to hang out and suggested we go there. Only thing, Adrian didn't tell me about his plan beforehand and when Dr. Belvedere walked in, I was unprepared."

"I can imagine. But you do want to bring this situation to a conclusion as quickly as possible, right?"

"Yes. But…"

"But what?"

"I hadn't counted on a few things."

"A few things like what, Trinity?"

Trinity nibbled on her bottom lip, trying to decide how much information she should share with her sister. Although there was a ten-year difference in their ages, they had always been close. Even when Tara had left home for college and medical school, Trinity had known her sister would return home often. After all, Derrick Hayes—the man Tara had dated since high school and had been engaged to marry—lived there.

But then came the awful day of Tara's wedding. Her sister had looked beautiful. She'd walked down the aisle on their father's arm looking as radiant as any bride could look. Trinity had been in her early teens and seeing Tara in such a beautiful gown had made her dream of her own wedding day.

But then, before the preacher could get things started, Derrick had stopped the wedding. In front of everyone, he'd stated that he couldn't go through with the ceremony because he didn't love Tara. He loved Danielle, Tara's best friend and maid of honor.

Trinity would never forget the hurt, pain and humiliation she'd seen in her sister's eyes and the tears that had flowed down Tara's cheeks when Derrick took Danielle's hand and the two of them raced happily out of the church, leaving Tara standing behind.

That night Tara had left Bunnell, and it had been two years before she had returned. And when she had, motorcycle celebrity Thorn Westmoreland had given her a public proposal the town was still talking about ten years later. Trinity's brother-in-law had somewhat restored her faith in men. He was the best, and she knew that he loved her sister deeply.

"Trinity? A few things like what?" Tara repeated, pulling Trinity's concentration back to the present.

"Nothing, other than I wish Adrian wasn't so darn attractive. You wouldn't believe the number of women staring at him last night."

She decided not to mention the fact that he had kissed her right in front of a few of those women, although he'd done it for Dr. Belvedere's benefit. She hadn't expected the kiss and she had gone to bed last night thinking about it. Today things hadn't been much better. Burying herself in work hadn't helped her forget.

"Yes, he is definitely handsome. Most Westmoreland men are. And don't worry about other women. He's single, but now that he has agreed to pretend to be your boyfriend, he's going to give you all his attention."

Trinity sighed. In a way, that's what she was afraid of. "Adrian doesn't think Dr. Belvedere seeing us together once will do it."

"Probably not, especially if the man is obsessed with having you. From what you've told me, it sounds like he is."

Trinity didn't say anything for a minute. "Well, I hope he gets the message because Adrian is serious about making sure the plan works."

"Good. I think you're in good hands."

Trinity wasn't so sure that was a positive thing, especially when she remembered the number of times last night she had thought about Adrian's hands. He had beautiful fingers, long and lean. She had wondered more than once how those fingers would feel stroking her skin.

"Trinity?"

She blinked, realizing she had been daydreaming. "Yes?"

"You're still keeping that journal, right?"

Tara had suggested she keep a record of each and every time Casey Belvedere made unwanted advances toward her. "Yes, I'm still keeping the journal."

"Good. Don't worry about anything. I wouldn't have suggested Adrian if I didn't believe he would be the right one to help handle your business."

"I know. I know. But…"

"But what?"

Trinity breathed in deeply. "But nothing. I just hope your idea eventually works."

"Me, too. And if it doesn't we move to plan B."

Trinity lifted a brow. "What's plan B?"

"I haven't thought of it yet."

She couldn't help but laugh. She loved her big sister and appreciated Tara being there for her right now. "Hopefully, there won't have to be a plan B."

"Let's keep hoping. In the meantime, just enjoy Adrian. He's a fun guy and you haven't had any fun lately. I know how it is, going through residency. Been there. Done that. You can only take so much and do so much. We're doctors, not miracle workers, Trinity. We have lives, too, and everybody needs downtime. Stress can kill—remember that."

"I will."

A few moments later she had ended her call with Tara and was about to head for the kitchen to put together a salad for dinner when her cell phone rang again. Trinity's heartbeat quickened when she saw it was Adrian.

What was that shiver about, the one that had just passed through her whole body? She frowned, wondering what was wrong with her. Why was she reacting this way to his phone call? It wasn't as if their affair was the real thing. Why did she feel the need to remind herself that it was only a sham for Dr. Belvedere's benefit?

She clicked on her phone. "Hello?"

"Hello, this is Adrian. How did things go at work today?"

She wished he didn't sound as good as he looked. Or that when he had arrived to pick her up for dinner last night, he'd not dressed as though he'd jumped right off the page of a men's magazine.

She had been ready to walk out the moment his car had pulled into her driveway. So there had been no reason for him to get out of his car to meet her halfway down the walkway. But he had done so, showing impeccable manners by escorting her to his car and opening the door for her. However, it wasn't his manners the woman in her had appreciated the most. He was so tall she had to look up at him, into a pair of eyes and a face that had almost taken her breath away.

She sighed softly now as the memory rushed through her mind. Only then did she recall the question he had asked her.

"Today was okay, probably because Dr. Belvedere is off for the next two days so I didn't see him. I'm dreading Friday when he returns."

"Hopefully things won't be so bad. We'll keep up our charade until he accepts the fact that you already have a man."

A pretend man but, oh, what a man, she thought to herself. "Do you think after seeing us together last night he believes we're an item?"

"Oh, I'm sure he probably believes it. But for him to accept it is a whole other story. It's my guess that he won't."

Trinity nibbled on her bottom lip. "I hope you're wrong."

"I hope I'm wrong, as well. Enjoy tomorrow and we'll see what happens on Friday. Just to be on the safe side, let's plan a date for the weekend. How about a show Saturday night?"

"A show?"

"Yes, one of those live shows at the Dunning Theater. A real casual affair."

She thought about what Tara had said, about Trinity getting out more and not working so hard. Besides, she and Adrian needed to be seen around town together as much as possible for Dr. Belvedere to get the message. "Do you think Belvedere will be attending the show, as well?"

He chuckled, and Trinity's skin reacted to the sound. Goose bumps formed on her arm. "Not sure, but it doesn't matter. The more we're seen together by others, the more believable our story will be. So are you good for Saturday night?"

"Yes. It just so happens I'm off this weekend."

"Good. I'll pick you up around seven."

Three

This is just a pretend date, so why am I getting all worked up over it? Trinity asked herself as she threw yet another outfit from her closet across her bed.

So far, just like all the other outfits she'd given the boot, it was either too dressy, not dressy enough or just plain boring. Frustrated, she ran her hands through her hair, wishing she had her sister's gift for fashion. Whenever Tara and Thorn went out on the town they were decked out to the nines and always looked good together. But even before Tara had become Mrs. Thorn Westmoreland, people had said she looked more like a model than a pediatrician.

Trinity glanced at her watch. Only an hour before Adrian arrived and she had yet to find an outfit she liked. Who was she kidding? A part of her was hoping that whatever she liked he would like, as well. She seldom dated and now, thanks to Casey Belvedere, it was being forced upon her.

Maybe she should call Adrian and cancel. Immediately she dismissed the idea from her mind. So far the week had been going smoothly. Dr. Belvedere had been off, even on Friday. It seemed everyone had breathed a lot easier, able to be attentive but relaxed. No one had had to look over their shoulders, dreading the moment when Belvedere showed his face. She wasn't the only one who thought he was a pain in the rear end.

Deciding she would take Tara's advice and have fun for a change, Trinity settled on a pair of jeans and a green pullover sweater. Giving both a nod of approval, she placed them across the chair. It was the middle of March and back home in Florida people were strutting around in tank tops and blouses. But in Denver everyone was still wearing winter clothes.

Trinity doubted she would ever get used to this weather.

"Which is why getting through your residency is a must," she mumbled to herself as she headed for the bathroom to take a shower. "Then you can leave and head back to Florida where you belong."

A short while later she had finished her shower, dressed and placed light makeup on her face. She smiled as she looked at herself in the mirror, satisfied with what she saw. No telling how many dates Adrian was giving up by pretending to be her man. The least she could do was make sure she looked worth his time and effort in helping her out.

She glanced at her watch. She had twenty minutes, and the last thing she had to do was her hair. She was about to pull the curling iron from a drawer when her cell phone rang, and she saw it was Adrian. She wondered if he was calling to say something had come up and he couldn't take her out after all.

"Hello?"

"Trinity?"

She ignored the sensations floating around her stomach and the thought of how good he sounded whenever he pronounced her name. "Yes?"

"I'm here."

She lifted a brow. "Where?"

"At your front door."

"Oh." She swallowed. "You're early."

"Is that a problem?"

She glanced at herself in the mirror. "I haven't done my hair yet."

"I have three sisters, so I understand. I can wait…inside."

Trinity swallowed again. Of course he would expect to wait inside. To have him wait outside in the car for her would be downright tacky. "Okay, I'm on my way to the door."

Glad she was at least fully dressed, she left her bedroom and moved toward the door despising the tingle that continued to sweep through her body. "Get a grip, girl. It's just Adrian. He's almost family," she told herself.

But when she opened the door the thought that quickly went through her mind was, *Scratch the thought he's almost family.*

As her gaze swept across him from top to bottom, she willed herself not to react to what she saw and failed miserably. She was mesmerized. If she thought he'd looked good in his business suit days ago, tonight his manliness was showing to the nth degree. There was just something about a tall, handsome man in a pair of jeans, white shirt and dark brown corduroy blazer. The Stetson on his head only added to the eye-candy effect.

"Now I see what you mean, so please do something with your hair."

His comment had her reaching for the thick strands that flowed past her shoulders. When she saw the teasing smile on his lips, she couldn't help but smile back as she stepped aside to let him in. "That bad?"

"No. There's nothing wrong with your hair. It looks great."

She rolled her eyes as she led him to her living room. "There're no curls in it."

He chuckled. "Curls aren't everything. Trust me, I know. Like I said, I have three sisters."

And she knew his sisters and liked them immensely. "Would you like something to drink while you wait?"

"Um, what do you have?"

"Soda, beer, wine and lemonade."

"I'll take a soda."

"One soda coming up," she said, walking off, and although she was tempted to do so, she didn't look back.

When she opened the refrigerator, the blast of cold air cooled her somewhat; she couldn't believe she'd actually gotten hot just looking at him. Closing the refrigerator, she paused. Some sort of raw, erotic power had emanated off him and she inwardly admitted that Adrian Westmoreland was an astonishing specimen of masculinity. The kind that made her want to lick him all over.

"Nice place."

She jerked around to find the object of her intense desire standing in the middle of her kitchen. For some reason he appeared taller, bigger than life and even sexier. "As you can see there's not much to it. It was either get a bigger place and share it with someone or get this one, which I can afford on my own."

He nodded. "It suits you."

She handed him the drink and their hands touched slightly. She hoped he hadn't noticed the tremble that passed through her with the exchange. "In what way?"

His gaze gave her body a timeless sweep and she felt her heartbeat quicken. His eyes returned to hers as he took his glass. "Nice. Tidy. Perfect coloring with everything blending together rather nicely."

Was she imagining things or had Adrian's eyes darkened to a deep, rich chocolate? And was his comparison of her to her home meant to be flirtatious? "Enjoy your soda while I work on my hair."

"Need help?"

She smiled as she quickly headed out of the kitchen. She

didn't want to imagine how his hands would feel on her head. "No, thanks. I can manage."

Adrian took a long sip of his drink as he watched Trinity leave her kitchen. Nice-looking backside, he thought, and then wished he hadn't. Tara would skin him alive if he made a play for her sister. And if Tara told Thorn, there would be no hope for Adrian since everybody knew Thorn was a man not to toy with.

Then why did you flirt with Trinity just now? he asked himself, taking another sip. *You're only asking for trouble. Your job is to pretend the two of you are lovers and not lust after her like some horny ass. You've already crossed the line with that kiss—don't make matters worse.*

He took another sip of his soda. What could be worse than wanting a woman and not being able to have her? A smile touched his lips, thinking that Dr. Casey Belvedere would soon find out.

"I'm ready."

He turned slightly and almost choked on the liquid he'd just sipped. She'd used one of those styling-irons to put curls in her hair at the ends. The style looked good on her. She looked good. All over. Top to bottom.

"You look nice."

"Thanks. You look nice yourself. You didn't say what show we'll be seeing."

"I didn't? Then I guess it will be a surprise. I talked to Tara earlier today and asked her about your favorite dessert. She told me about your fascination with strawberry cheesecake, so I made arrangements for us to stop for cheesecake and coffee on our way back."

"That's thoughtful of you."

"I'm a thoughtful person. You ready to go?"

"Yes."

He placed the empty glass on the counter and crossed the room to link his arm with hers. "Then let's go."

"You're driving a different car tonight," Trinity noted when they reached the sleek and sassy vehicle parked in her driveway. The night he'd taken her to dinner he'd been driving a black Lexus sedan. Tonight he was in a sporty candy-apple-red Lexus two-seater convertible.

"And I own neither. A good friend owns a Lexus dealership in town and when I returned to Denver he sold me a Lexus SUV. But he figures as much as I'm seen around town with the ladies that he might as well let me use any car off his lot whenever I go out on a date. He's convinced showcasing his cars around town is good publicity. And it has paid off. Several people have come into his dealership to buy his cars."

"And I bet most were women."

He chuckled as he opened the door for her. "Now why would you think that?"

"A hunch. Am I right?"

"Possibly."

"Go ahead and admit it. It's okay. I've heard all about your dating history," she said, buckling her seat belt.

"Have you?" he asked, leaning against the open car door.

"Yes."

"From who?"

"I'd rather not disclose my sources."

"And you think they're reliable?" he asked.

"I see no reason why they shouldn't be."

He shrugged before closing the door. She watched him sprint around the front to the driver's side to get in. He buckled his own seat belt, but before pressing the key switch he glanced over at her. "There's only one reliable source when it comes to me, Trinity."

She lifted a brow. "And who might that be?"

He pointed a finger at his chest. "Me. Feel free to ask me anything you want…within reason."

She smiled. "Then here's my first question. More women have purchased cars from your friend than men, right?"

He returned her smile as he backed out of her driveway. "I'll admit that they have."

"I'm not surprised."

"Why not?"

"Several reasons," she said, noticing the smooth sound of the car's engine as he drove down her street.

"State them."

She glanced over at him. He had brought the car to a stop at a traffic light. "I can see where some women would find you persuasive and lap up anything you say as gospel."

A smile she wouldn't categorize as *totally* conceited touched his lips. "You think so? You believe I might have that much influence?"

"Yes, but mind you, I said *some* women."

"What about you? Are you ready for a new car?"

She held his gaze. "Unless it's free, I'm not interested. A car payment is the last thing I need right now. The car I presently drive is just fine. It gets me from point A to point B and if I sing to it real nice, it might even make it to point C. I can't ask for anything more than that."

"You can but you won't."

His comment was right on the money but she wondered how he'd figured that out. "Why do you say that?"

The car was moving again and he didn't answer until when they reached another traffic light a few moments later. He looked over at her. "You're not the only one with sources. I understand that beneath those curls on your head is a very independent mind."

She shrugged as she broke away from his look to glance out the window. "I can't handle my business any other way. My parents raised all of us to be independent thinkers."

"Is that why you didn't go along with Tara's plan at first?"

She looked back at him. "You'll have to admit it's a little far-fetched."

"I look at it as a means to an end."

"I just hope it works."

"It will."

She was about to ask why he felt so certain when she noticed they had pulled up for valet parking. The building was beautiful and the architecture probably dated back to the eighteen hundreds. Freestanding, it stood as an immaculate building with a backdrop of mountains. "Nice."

"Glad you like it. It was an old hotel. Now it's been renovated, turned into a theater that has live shows. Pam's group is working on a production that will be performed here."

Trinity knew Dillon's wife, Pam, used to be a movie star who now owned an acting school in town. "That's wonderful."

"I think so, too. Her group is working hard with rehearsals and all. It will be their first show."

When they reached the ticket booth the clerk greeted Adrian by name. "Good evening, Mr. Westmoreland."

"Hello, Paul. I believe you're holding reserved tickets for me."

"Yes sir," the man said, handing Adrian an envelope. Adrian checked the contents before smiling at her. "We're a little early so we might as well grab a drink. They serve refreshments while we wait."

"Okay."

When they entered the huge room, Trinity glanced around. This area of the building was nicely decorated, as well.

"What would you like?" Adrian asked her.

"What are you drinking?"

"Beer."

"Then I'll take one, as well."

Adrian grabbed the attention of one of the waiters and gave him their order. It was then that a couple passed and Adrian said, "Roger? Is that you?"

A man who looked to be in his late thirties or early forties turned and gave Adrian a curious glance. "Yes, I'm Roger. But forgive me, I can't remember where we've met."

Adrian held out his hand. "Adrian Westmoreland. We've met through my brother Dillon," he lied, knowing the man probably wouldn't remember but would pretend that he did.

A huge smiled appeared on the man's face as he accepted Adrian's handshake. "Oh, yes, of course. I remember now. And this is my wife Kathy," he said, introducing the woman with him.

Adrian shook her hand. He then turned to Trinity and smiled. "And this is a very *special* friend," he said. "Roger and Kathy, I'd like you to meet Dr. Trinity Matthews."

Trinity couldn't help wondering what was going on in that mind of Adrian's. She soon found out when he said, "Trinity, I'd like you to meet Roger and Kathy Belvedere."

Trinity forced herself not to blink in surprise as she shook the couple's hands. "Nice to meet you."

"Likewise," Roger said, smiling. "And where do you practice, doctor? I'm familiar with a number of hospitals in the city. In fact," he said, chuckling and then bragging, "my family is building a wing at Denver Memorial."

"That's where I work. I'm in pediatrics, so I'm familiar with the wing under construction. It's much needed and will be nice when it's finished," Trinity said.

Roger's smile widened. "Thanks. If you work at Denver Memorial then you must know my brother Casey. He's a surgeon there. I'm sure you've heard of Dr. Casey Belvedere."

Trinity fought to keep a straight face. "Yes, I know Dr. Belvedere."

"Then I must mention to him that Kathy and I ran into the two of you."

"Yes, you do that," Adrian said, smiling.

After the couple walked off, the waiter approached with their beers. Trinity looked over at Adrian. "You knew he was going to be here tonight, didn't you?"

He looked at her. "Yes. And there's no doubt in my mind he'll mention seeing us to his brother."

Trinity nodded as she took a sip of her beer. Tonight was just another strategic move in Adrian's game plan. Why was she surprised…and sort of disappointed?

At that moment someone on a speaker announced that seating for the next show would start in fifteen minutes. As they finished their beers, she decided that regardless of the reason Adrian had brought her here, tonight she intended to enjoy herself.

Four

As he'd planned, after the show Adrian took Trinity to Andrew's, a place known in Denver for having the best desserts. While enjoying strawberry cheesecake topped with vanilla ice cream, Adrian decided he liked hearing the sound of Trinity's voice.

She kept the conversation interesting by telling him about her family. Her father owned a medical practice and her mother worked as his nurse. Her two older brothers were doctors, as well, living in Bunnell.

She also talked about her college days and how she'd wanted to stick close to home, which was why she'd attended the local community college in Bunnell for two years before moving to Gainesville to attend the University of Florida. Although it was a college town, the city of Gainesville provided a small-town atmosphere. She'd enjoyed living there so much that she'd remained there for medical school.

She also told him how she preferred a small town to a big one, how she found Denver much too large and how she looked forward to finishing up her residency and moving back to Bunnell.

He leaned back in his chair after cleaning his plate, admitting the cake and ice cream had been delicious. "Aw, come on," he joked to Trinity. "Why don't you just come clean and admit that the real reason you want to hightail it back is because you have a guy waiting there for you."

She made a face. The way she scrunched her nose and pouted her lips was utterly cute. "That is totally not true... especially after what Derrick did to Tara. The last thing I'd have is a boyfriend that I believed would wait for me."

He had heard all about the Tara fiasco from one of his cousins, although he couldn't remember which one. He couldn't believe any man in his right mind would run off and leave someone as gorgeous as Tara Matthews Westmoreland standing in the middle of some church. What a fool.

"What happened to Tara has made you resentful and distrustful of giving your heart to a hometown guy?"

She shrugged her shoulders and unconsciously licked whipped cream off her fork. In an instant his stomach tightened. Sexual hunger stirred to life in his groin. He picked up his glass of water and almost drained it in one gulp.

"Worse than that. It taught me not to truly give my heart to any man, hometown or otherwise."

He studied her, seeing the seriousness behind the beautiful pair of eyes staring back at him. "But things worked out fine for Tara in the end, didn't they? She met Thorn."

He saw the slow smile replace her frown. "Yes, she did, and I'm glad. He's made her happy."

Adrian nodded. "So there are happy endings sometimes."

She finished off the last of her cake before saying, "Yes, sometimes, but not often enough for me to take a chance."

"So you don't ever intend to fall in love?"

"Not if I can help it. I told you what I want."

He nodded again. "To return to Bunnell and work alongside your father and brothers in their medical business."

"Yes."

He took another sip of his water when she moistened the top of her lip with the tip of her tongue. "What about your happiness?" he asked her, shifting slightly in his chair.

She lifted a brow. "My happiness?"

"Yes. Don't you want to have someone to grow old with?"

She turned the tables when she asked, "Don't you?"

He thought about the question. "I intend to date and enjoy life for as long as I can. I'm aware at some point I'll need to settle down, marry and have children, but at the moment there're enough Westmorelands handling that without me. It seemed every time I came home for spring break, I would have a wedding to attend or a new niece, nephew or second cousin being born."

"Speaking of cousins…mainly yours," she said as if to clarify. "I've heard the story of how the Denver Westmorelands connected with the Atlanta-based Westmorelands, but what about these other cousins that might be out there?"

He knew she was referring to the ongoing investigation by Megan's husband, Rico, who was a private investigator. "It seems my great-grandfather Raphel Westmoreland was involved with four women before marrying my great-grandmother Gemma. Three of the women have now been accounted for. It seemed none were his wives, although there's still one more to investigate for clarification."

He paused and then said, "Rico and Megan found out that one of the women, by the name of Clarice, had a baby by Raphel that he didn't know about. She died in a train derailment but not before she gave the child to another woman—a woman who'd lost her child and husband. A woman with the last name of Outlaw."

He could tell by the light in Trinity's eyes that she found what he'd told her fascinating. He understood. He was convinced that if there were any more Westmoreland kin out there, Rico would find them.

Adrian glanced at his watch. "It's still early yet. Is there anything else you want to do before I take you home?"

She glanced at her own watch. "Early? It's almost midnight."

He smiled. "Is it past your bedtime?"

"No."

"Then plan to enjoy the night. And I've got just the place."

"Where?"

"Come on and I'll show you."

A half hour later Trinity was convinced she needed her head examined. She looked down at herself and wondered how she had let Adrian talk her into this. Indoor mountain climbing. Seriously?

But here she was, decked out with climbing shoes, a harness, a rope and all the other things she needed to scale a man-made wall that looked too much like the real thing.

"Ready?"

She glanced over at Adrian who was standing beside her, decked out in his own climbing gear.

Ready? He has to be kidding.

She saw the excitement in his eyes and figured this was something he liked doing on a routine basis. But personally, she was not an outdoorsy kind of girl.

So why did you allow him to talk you into it?

It might have had everything to do with the way he had grabbed hold of her hand as he'd led her out of Andrew's and toward his car. The tingling sensation that erupted the moment his hand touched hers had seemed to pulverize her common sense. Or it could have been the smile that would creep onto his lips whenever he was on an adrenaline high. Darn, it was contagious.

He snapped his fingers in front of her face, making her realize she hadn't answered his question. "Hey, don't start daydreaming on me now, Trinity. You need your full concentration for this."

She looked over at the fake mountain she was supposed to climb. He claimed this particular one was for beginners, but she had serious doubts about that. She glanced up at him. "I don't know about this, Adrian."

His smile widened and she felt the immediate pull in her stomach. "You can do this. You look physically fit enough."

She rolled her eyes. "Looks are deceiving."

"Then this will definitely get you in shape. But to be honest, I don't see where there needs to be improvement."

She swallowed. Had he just flirted with her for the second time that night? "So, have you ever climbed an outdoor mountain? The real thing?" she asked, rechecking the fit of her gloves.

"Sure. Plenty of times. I love doing it and you will, too."

She doubted it. Most people were probably in bed and here she was at one in the morning at some all-night indoor mountain climbing arena.

"Ready to try it?" Adrian asked, breaking into her thoughts.

"It's now or never, I suppose."

He smiled. "You'll do fine."

She wasn't sure about that, and did he *have* to be standing so close to her? "Okay, what do I do?"

"Just grab or step on each climbing hold located on the wooden boards as you work your way to the top."

She glanced up to the top and had to actually tilt her head back to see it. "This is my first time, Adrian. There's no way I'll make it that far up."

"You never know."

She did. She knew her limits…even when it concerned him. She was well aware that she was attracted to him just as she was well aware that it was an attraction that could get her into trouble if she didn't keep her sense about her.

Trinity moved toward the huge structure and proceeded to lift her leg. When she felt Adrian's hands on her backside, she jerked around and put her leg down. "What are you doing?"

"Giving you a boost. Don't you need one?"

She figured what she needed was her head examined. Had his intention been to give her a boost or to cop a feel? Unfortunately her backside didn't know the difference and it was still reacting to his touch. Heat had spiked in the area and was spreading all over.

"No, I don't need one, and watch your hands, Adrian. Keep them to yourself."

He gave her an innocent smile. "I am duly chastised. But honestly, I was only trying to help and was in no way trying to take advantage of a tempting opportunity."

"Whatever," she muttered, not believing him one bit. However, instead of belaboring the issue, she turned and started her climb, which wasn't easy.

Beginner's structure or no beginner's structure, it was meant to give a person a good workout. Why would anyone in their right mind want to do this for fun? she asked herself as she steadily and slowly moved up one climbing hold at a time. After each attempt she had to take a deep breath and silently pray for strength to continue. She had made it to the halfway point and was steadily moving higher.

"Looking good, Trinity. Real good."

It wasn't what he said but rather how he'd said it that made her turn slightly and look down at him, nearly losing her footing in the process. Climbing this structure was giving her backside a darn good workout. She could feel it in every movement, and there was no doubt in her mind that he could see it, too. While she was struggling to get to the top, he was down below ass-watching.

"That's it." Frustrated with him for looking and with

herself for actually liking the thought of him checking her out, she began her descent.

"Giving up already?"

She waited until her feet were on solid ground before she stood in front of him. Regarding him critically, she answered, "What do you think?"

Dark lashes were half lowered over his eyes when he said, "I think you're temptation, Trinity."

Whatever words she'd planned to say were zapped from her mind. Why did he have to say that and why had he said it while looking at her with those sexy eyes of his? The last thing she needed was for heat surges to flash through her body the way they were doing now.

"Considering the nature of our relationship, you're out of line, Adrian."

He leaned in closer and she got a whiff of his manly scent. She watched his lips curve into a seductive smile. "Why? And before you get all mouthy on me, there's something you need to consider."

"What?" she asked, getting even more frustrated. Although she would never admit it, she thought he was temptation, as well.

"I'm *supposed* to find you desirable. If I didn't, I couldn't pull off what needs to be done to dissuade Belvedere. My acting abilities can only extend so far. I can't pretend to want a woman if I don't."

Trinity went still. Was he saying he wanted her? From the way his gaze was darkening, she had a feeling that assumption was right. "I think we need to talk about it."

"At the moment, I think not."

When she opened her mouth to protest, he leaned in closer and said in a low, sexy tone, "See that structure over there?"

Her gaze followed his and she saw what he was referring to. It was huge, twice the size of the one she'd tried to scale, designed to challenge even the best of climbers. "Yes, I see it. What about it?"

The look on his face suddenly changed from desire to bold, heated lust. "I plan to climb all over it tonight. Otherwise, I'll try my damnedest later to climb all over you."

Five

Some words once stated couldn't be taken back. You just had to deal with them and Adrian was trying like hell to deal.

He had taken his climb and had done a damn good job scaling a wall he'd had difficulty doing in the past. It was amazing what lust could drive a man to do. And he was lusting after Trinity. Admitting it to her had made her nervous, wary of him, which was why she was hugging the passenger door as if it were her new best friend. If he didn't know for certain it was locked, he would be worried she would tumble out of the car.

"I won't bite," he finally said as he exited the expressway. *But I can perform a pretty good lick job,* he thought, but now was not the time to share such information.

"Pretending to be lovers isn't working, Adrian."

"What makes you think that?" he asked, although he was beginning to think along those same lines. "Because I admitted I want you, Trinity?"

"I would think that has a lot to do with it."

Adrian didn't say anything for a minute. Watching Trinity's backside while she'd climbed that wall had definitely done something to him; had brought out coiling arousal within his very core. And when the crotch of his jeans began pounding like hell from an erection he could barely control, he'd known he was in trouble. The only thing that had consumed his mind—although he knew better—was that he needed to have some of her.

"I thought I explained things to you, Trinity. You're a sexy woman. I'm a hot-blooded male. There're bound to be sparks."

"As long as those sparks don't cause a fire."

"They won't," he said easily. "I'll put it out before that happens. I'm no more interested in a real affair than you are. So relax. What I'm encountering is simple lust. I'll be thirty-one in a few months so I think I'm old enough to handle it." And he decided, starting now, he would handle it by taking control of himself, which is why he changed the subject.

"So what are your plans for tomorrow?" he asked.

He heard her sigh. "You mean *today,* right? Sunday. It's almost two in the morning," she said.

"I stand corrected. What are your plans for today?"

"Sleep, sleep and more sleep. I seldom get the weekends off and I can't wait to have a love affair with my bed. It will be Monday before you know it."

A love affair with her bed. Now why did she have to go there? Images of her naked under silken sheets were making his senses flare in the wrong directions.

He could imagine her scent. It would be close to what he was inhaling now but probably a little more sensual. And he could imagine how she would look naked. Lordy. His body throbbed at the vision. His fingers twitched. When he had touched her backside while giving her that boost he had actually felt the air thicken in his lungs.

"What about you? What do you have planned?"

If he was smart, he would go somewhere this weekend and get laid. Maybe that would help rid his mind of all these dangerous fantasies he was having. But he'd said on their first date that he would see her and only her until this ordeal with Belvedere was over. "Unlike you I won't be sleeping late. I promised Ramsey that I would help him put new fencing in the north range."

"I understand from Tara that you're not living on your family's land, that you lease a place in town."

"That's right. I'm not ready to build on my one hundred acres quite yet. Where I live is just what I need for now. I have someone coming in every week to keep things tidy and to prepare my meals, and that's good enough for me."

A short while later he was walking her to her door, although she'd told him doing so wasn't necessary. She had told him that the other night, as well, but he'd done so anyway.

He watched as she used her key to unlock the door. She then turned to him. "Thanks for a nice evening and for walking me to the door, Adrian."

"You're welcome. I'd like to check inside."

She rolled her eyes. "Is that really necessary?"

"I think so. After what happened with Keisha last year, I would feel a lot better if I did."

He figured she had heard how his cousin Canyon's wife, Keisha, had come home to find her house in shambles.

Trinity stepped aside. "Help yourself. I definitely want you to feel better."

Ignoring the sarcasm he heard in her voice, Adrian moved past her and checked the bedrooms, kitchen and bathrooms. He returned to the living room to find her leaning against the closed door, her arms crossed over her chest.

Her gaze clashed with his. "Satisfied?" she asked in an annoyed tone.

Suddenly a deep, fierce hunger stirred to life inside him. That same hunger he'd been hopelessly fighting all night. He told himself to walk out the door and not look back, but knew he could no more ignore the yearnings that were rushing through him than he could not breathe. She had no idea how totally sensuous she looked or the effect it was having on him.

He walked toward her in a measured pace. When she turned and reached for the door to open it for him to leave, he reached for her. The moment he touched her, fiery heat shot straight to his groin.

Before she could say anything, he pressed her back against the door and swooped his mouth down on hers with a hunger he needed to release. He couldn't recall precisely when she began kissing him back—all he knew was that she was doing so, and with a greed that equaled his.

He pressed hard into her middle, wanting her to feel just how aroused he was, as his tongue tangled with hers in a duel so sensuous he wasn't sure if the moans he heard were coming from her or from him.

No telling how long the kiss would have lasted if they hadn't needed to come up for air. He reluctantly released her mouth and stared down into the fierce darkness of her dazed eyes. She appeared stunned at the degree of passion the two of them had shared, which was even more than the last time they'd kissed.

He leaned in close to her moist lips and answered the question she'd asked him moments ago. "Yes, I'm satisfied, Trinity. I am now extremely satisfied."

He then opened the door and walked out.

Trinity stood there. Astonished.

What on earth had just happened? What was that sudden onslaught of intense need that had overtaken her, made her mold her mouth to his as though that was how it was supposed to be? And why did her mouth feel like it was where it belonged when it was connected to his?

She shook her head to jiggle out of her daze. The effects

were even more profound than before. It had taken days to get her mind back on track after the last kiss; she had a feeling this one would take even longer.

Her brows pulled together in annoyance. Why had he kissed her again? Just as important, why had she let him? She hadn't been an innocent bystander by any means. She could recall every lick of his tongue just as she could remember every lick of hers.

She hadn't held back anything. She'd been just as aggressive as he had. What did that say about her? What was he assuming it said?

As she moved toward her bedroom to strip off her clothes and take a shower, she couldn't help but recall something else. Watching him climb that wall. He was in great shape and it showed. He'd looked rough and so darn manly. Every time he lifted a jeans-clad thigh as he moved upward, her gaze had followed, watching how his muscles bulged and showed the strength of his legs. The way his jeans had cupped his backside had been a work of art, worthy to be ogled. And when he removed his shirt, she had seen a perfect set of abs glistening with his sweat.

The woman in her had appreciated how he'd reached the top with an overabundance of virility. That was probably why she'd lost her head the moment he'd taken her into his arms and plowed her with a kiss that weakened her knees. But now he was gone and once she got at least eighteen hours of nonstop sleep, she would wake up in her right mind.

She certainly hoped so.

Six

With little sleep and the memory of a kiss that just wouldn't let go, Adrian, along with his brothers and cousins, helped his older brother Ramsey repair fencing on a stretch of land that extended for miles.

Ramsey had worked as CEO for a while alongside Dillon before giving it up to pursue his first love: being a sheep rancher. Adrian's brothers Zane and Derringer preferred the outdoors, too. After working in the family business for a few years, Zane, Derringer and Ramsey, as well as their cousin Jason, joined their Montana Westmoreland cousins in a horse breeding and training business.

Ramsey's wife, Chloe, had arrived with sandwiches, iced tea and homemade cookies. Everyone teased Adrian's cousin Stern about his upcoming wedding to JoJo, who Stern had been best friends with for years. The two had been engaged for more than six months and Stern was anxious for the wedding to happen, saying he was tired of waiting.

Adrian didn't say anything as he listened to the easy camaraderie between his family. Leaving home for college had been hard, but luckily he and Aidan had decided to attend the same university. As usual, they had stuck together.

Their careers had eventually carried them in different directions. But Adrian knew that eventually his twin would return to Denver.

Aidan's plans were similar to Trinity's, regarding returning to her hometown to practice medicine. He could understand her wanting to do that, just as he understood Aidan. So why did the thought of her returning to Florida in about eighteen months bother him? It wasn't as if she meant anything to him. He'd already established the fact that she wasn't his type. They had nothing in common. She liked small towns and he preferred big cities. She wasn't an outdoor person and he was. So why was he allowing her to consume his thoughts the way she had been lately?

"So what's going on with you, Adrian? Or are you really Aidan?"

Adrian couldn't help but smile at his brother Zane. It seemed that while he had been daydreaming everyone had left lunch to return to work. "You know who I am and nothing's going on. I'm just trying to make it one day at a time."

"So things are working out for you at Blue Ridge?"

"Pretty much. I can see why you, Ramsey and Derringer decided the corporate life wasn't for you. You have to like it or otherwise you'd hate it."

Adrian liked his job as chief project officer. His duties included assisting Dillon when it came to any construction and engineering functions of the company, and advising him on the development of major projects and making sure all jobs were completed in a timely manner.

As they began walking to where the others were beginning work again, Zane asked, "So, how are things going being the pretend lover of Thorn's sister-in-law?"

Adrian glanced over at Zane, not surprised he knew. How many others in his family knew? Bailey hadn't mentioned anything the other night at dinner so she might be clueless. "Okay, I guess. I'm busy trying to establish this relationship with her for others to see. The first night I made sure the doctor saw us together and last night I went to a show that I knew one of his family members would be attending."

Zane nodded. "Is it working?"

"Don't know yet. The doctor's path hasn't crossed with Trinity's since we started this farce."

"Hmm, I'm curious to see how things turn out."

Adrian looked at his brother. "If he's smart, he'll leave her alone."

"Oh, I'm not talking about her and the doctor."

Adrian slowed his pace. "Then who are you talking about?"

Zane smiled. "The two of you."

Adrian stopped walking and Zane stopped, as well. "Don't know what you mean," he said.

Zane shrugged. "I saw her at Riley's wedding. She's a looker, but I expected no less with her being Tara's sister and all."

Adrian frowned. "So?"

Zane shoved his hands into the back pockets of his jeans. "So nothing. Forget I said anything. I guess we better get back to work if we want to finish up by dusk."

Adrian watched his brother walk off and decided that since he'd gotten married, Zane didn't talk much sense anymore.

"Dr. Matthews, I trust you've been doing well."

Immediately, Trinity's skin crawled at the sound of the man's voice as he approached her. She looked up from writing in a patient's chart. "Yes, Dr. Belvedere. I've been fine."

As a courtesy, she could ask him how he'd been, but she really didn't want to know. She tried ignoring him as she resumed documenting the patient's chart.

"I saw you the other night."

Her heart rate increased. He had come to stand beside her. Way too close as far as she was concerned. She didn't look up at him but continued writing. "And what night was that?"

"That night you were out on a date at Laredo's."

She glanced up briefly. "Oh. I didn't see you." That was no lie since she had intentionally not looked in his direction.

"Well, I saw you. You were with a man," he said in an accusing tone.

She hugged the chart to her chest as she looked up again. "Yes, I was. If you recall, I told you I was involved with someone."

"I didn't believe you."

"I don't know why you wouldn't."

Belvedere smiled and Trinity knew the smile wasn't genuine. "Doesn't matter. Break things off with him."

Trinity blinked. "Excuse me?"

"You heard what I said."

Something within Trinity snapped. Not caring if anyone passing by heard her, she said, "I will not break things off with him! You have no right to dictate something like that to me."

A smirk appeared on his face before he looked over his shoulder to make sure no one was privy to their conversation. "I can make or break you, Dr. Matthews. If you rub me the wrong way, all those years you spent in medical school won't mean a damn thing. Think about it."

He turned to walk off, but then, as if he'd forgotten to say something, he turned back. "And the next time you decide to report me to someone, think twice. My family practically owns this hospital. I suggest you remember that. And to make sure we fully understand each other, I've requested your presence in the next two surgeries I have scheduled, which coincidently are on your next two days off. What a pity." Chuckling to himself, he walked off.

Trinity just stared at him. She felt as if steam were coming out of her ears. He'd just admitted to sabotaging her time off. *How dare he!*

Placing the patient's chart back on the rack, she angrily headed to the office of Wendell Fowler, the chief of pediatrics. Not bothering to wait on the elevator, she took the stairs. By the time she went up three flights of stairs she was even madder.

Dr. Fowler's secretary, an older woman by the name of Marissa Adams, glanced up when she saw her. "Yes, Dr. Matthews?"

"I'd like to see Dr. Fowler. It's important."

The woman nodded. "Please have a seat and I'll see if Dr. Fowler is available."

She hadn't been seated a few minutes when the secretary called out to her. "Dr. Fowler will see you now, Dr. Matthews."

"Thanks." Trinity walked around the woman's desk and headed for Wendell Fowler's office.

Less than a half hour later Trinity left Dr. Fowler's office unsatisfied. The man hadn't been any help. He'd even accused her of dramatizing the situation. He'd then tried to convince her that working in surgery on her days off under the guidance of Dr. Belvedere would be a boost to her medical career.

Feeling a degree of fury the likes of which she'd never felt before, she walked past Ms. Adams's desk with her head held high, fighting back tears in her eyes. If Dr. Belvedere's goal was to break her resolve and force her to give in to what he wanted, then he was wasting his time. If she had to give up her days off this week, she would do it. She refused to let anyone break her down.

Seven

Adrian leaned back in the chair behind his desk and stared at the phone he'd just hung up. He'd tried calling Trinity from a different number and she still wasn't taking his calls. He rubbed his hand across his jaw, feeling totally frustrated. So they had kissed. Twice. Big deal. That was no reason for her to get uptight about it and not take his calls. This was crap he didn't have time for.

It had been well over a week since that kiss. Ten days to be exact. He'd heard of women holding grudges but this was ridiculous. Over a kiss? Really? And no one could convince him she hadn't enjoyed it just as much as he had. All he had to do was close his eyes to relive the moments of all that tongue interaction. It had been everything a kiss should be and more.

The text signal on his cell phone indicated he had a message. He pulled the phone out of his desk drawer and tried to ignore the flutters that passed through his chest when he saw it was from Trinity.

Got your calls. Worked on my days off. Belvedere's orders. Spent last 10 days at hospital. Tired. Can barely stand. Off for few days starting tomorrow a.m.

Adrian sat straighter in his chair. What the hell! Trinity had worked on her days off? And it had been Belvedere's orders? Adrian's hands trembled in anger when he texted her back.

On my way 2 get you now!

She texted him back.

No. Don't. I'm okay. Just tired. Going home in the a.m. Will call you then.

Adrian frowned. If Trinity thought that message satisfied him, she was wrong. Who required anyone to work on their days off? There were labor laws against that sort of thing. And if Belvedere had ordered her to do so then the man had gone too damn far.

There was a knock on his office door.

"Come in."

Dillon stuck his head in. "I'm leaving early. Bailey's watching the kids while Pam and I enjoy a date night."

His cousin must have seen the deep scowl on Adrian's face. He stepped into the office and closed the door behind him, concern in his eyes. "What's wrong with you, Adrian?"

Adrian stood. Agitated, he paced in front of his desk. It was a few moments before he'd pulled himself together enough to answer Dillon's question. "I hadn't heard from Trinity in over a week and was concerned since I knew Belvedere had seen us together that night at dinner. She texted me a few moments ago. The man ordered her to work on her days off. She's worked ten days straight, Dil. Can you believe that?"

Before Dillon could answer, Adrian added, "I've got a

good mind to go to that hospital and beat the hell out of him."

"I think you need to have a seat and think this through."

The hard tone of Dillon's voice had Adrian staring at him. And then, as Dillon suggested, he sat. "I'm sitting, Dillon, but I still want to go over to that hospital and beat the hell out of Belvedere."

"Sure you do. But I'm telling you now the same thing I told you the day you came home after whipping Joel Gaffney's behind. You can't settle anything with a fight."

Maybe not, Adrian thought. But if he remembered correctly, he had felt a lot better seeing that bloody nose on Gaffney. Adrian had wanted to make sure Joel thought twice before putting a snake in Bailey's locker again. "It was either me or Bane," Adrian said. "And I'm sure Gaffney preferred my whipping to Bane's. Your kid brother would not have shown any mercy."

Dillon rolled his eyes. "Again, I repeat, you can't settle anything with a fight. Belvedere will file charges and you'll end up in jail. Then where will Trinity be?"

"Better off. I might be in jail, but when I finish with Belvedere he'll never perform surgery on anyone again. I'll see to it."

Dillon stared at him for a long moment before crossing the room to drop down in the chair across from Adrian's desk. "I think we need to talk."

"Not sure it will do any good. If I find out Belvedere made Trinity work on her off days just for spite, I'm going to make him wish he hadn't done that."

"Fine, then come up with a plan that's within the law, Adrian. But first know the facts and not assumptions. It could be that she was needed at the hospital. Doctors work all kinds of crazy hours. You have two siblings who are doctors so you should know that. Emergencies come up that have to be dealt with whether you're scheduled to be off or not."

Adrian knew what Dillon was trying to do. Come up with another plausible reason why Trinity had been ordered to work on her days off. "And what if I don't like the facts after hearing them?"

"Then like I said, come up with a plan. And if it's one that makes sense, you'll get my support. I don't appreciate any man trying to take advantage of a woman any more than you do. In the meantime, you stay out of trouble."

Dillon stood and headed for the door. Before he could open it, Adrian called out, "Thanks, Dil."

Dillon turned around. "Just do as I ask and stay out of trouble. Okay?"

"I'll try."

When Dillon gave him a pointed look Adrian knew that response hadn't been good enough. "Okay. Fine. I'll stay out of trouble."

Trinity believed that if she continued forcing one foot in front of the other she would eventually make it out of the hospital to the parking lot and into her car. But then she would have to force her eyes to stay open on the drive home.

Never had she felt so tired. Her body ached all over. Not from the hours it had missed sleep but because of the other assignments given to her on top of her regular job…all deliberately and for the sole purpose of making her give in to Dr. Belvedere's advances. If she'd ever had an inkling of attraction to him, did he really think she would let him touch her after this? Did it matter to him that she was beginning to hate him? He didn't see her as a colleague; all he saw was a body he wanted. A body he would do just about anything to get. A conquest.

When she stepped off the elevator on the main level, Belvedere stood there waiting to get on. Her eyes met his and she gritted her teeth when he had the nerve to smile. "Good morning, Dr. Matthews."

"Dr. Belvedere," she acknowledged and kept walking.

"Wait up a minute, Dr. Matthews."

She had a mind to keep walking, but it would have been a show of total disrespect for a revered surgeon, so she paused and turned. "Yes, Dr. Belvedere?"

He came to a stop in front of her. "Just wanted to say that you did a great job in surgery the other night."

"Thank you," she replied stiffly. She was tempted to tell him just what he could do with that compliment.

"I think we should have dinner to discuss a few things," he added smoothly. "I'll pick you up tonight at seven."

"Sorry, she has other plans."

Trinity's breath caught at the sound of the masculine voice. She turned to see Adrian walking toward them. Why was her heart suddenly fluttering like crazy at the sight of him? And why did seeing him give her a little more strength than she had just moments ago?

Even with the smile plastered on his lips, his smile didn't quite reach his eyes. He was angry. She could feel it. But he was holding that anger back and she appreciated that. The last thing she needed was him making a scene with one of her superiors.

Because of his long strides, he reached her in no time. "Adrian, I didn't expect to see you here."

He slid his arms around her waist, placed a kiss on her lips and hugged her. "Hey, baby. I figured the least I could do after you worked ten days straight is be here to take you home."

She glanced over at Dr. Belvedere and swallowed. Unlike Adrian, Dr. Belvedere wasn't smiling. She figured he realized that, dressed in blue scrubs, he failed miserably to compare to Adrian, who was wearing a designer suit that looked tailor-made for his body.

Before she could make introductions, Adrian turned to Belvedere. "Dr. Belvedere, right?" he asked, extending his hand to the man. "I've heard a lot about you. I'm Adrian Westmoreland, Trinity's significant other."

From the look that appeared in Belvedere's eyes, Adrian knew the man hadn't liked the role he'd claimed in Trinity's life. It took every ounce of control Adrian could muster to exchange handshakes with Belvedere. He wanted to do just what he'd told Dillon and beat the hell out of him. Even so, the memory of Dillon's advice kept him in line. Though he couldn't resist the opportunity to squeeze the man's hand harder than was needed. There was no way the doctor didn't know he'd purposely done so.

Let him know what I can do to those precious fingers of his if I'm riled.

Adrian turned back to Trinity and inwardly flinched when he saw tired eyes and lines of exhaustion etched into her features. He needed to get her out of here now before he was tempted to do something he would enjoy doing but might regret later. "Ready to go, baby?"

"Yes, but my car is here," she said, and he noticed that like him she had dismissed Dr. Belvedere's presence. Why the man was still standing there was beyond Adrian's comprehension.

"I'll come back for it later," he said, taking her hand. He didn't even bother to say anything to the doctor before walking away. He just couldn't get the words *It was nice meeting you* from his lips when they would have been a bald-faced lie.

When they exited the building Trinity paused and glanced up at him. "Thanks."

He knew what she was thanking him for. "It wasn't easy. Just knowing he had you work on your off days made me angry." He paused. "Were you needed or did he do it for spite?"

She looked away, and when she looked back at him, he saw the anger in her eyes. "He did it for spite."

If it wasn't for the talk he'd had with Dillon he would go back into the hospital and clean up the floor with Belvedere. But what Dillon had said was true. In the end, Adrian would be in jail and Belvedere would make matters worse for Trinity.

"Come on, my car is parked over there. I lucked out and got a spot close to the entrance."

"I'm glad. I don't recall the last time I was so tired. It wouldn't be so bad if I'd been able to sleep, but Belvedere made sure I stayed busy."

"The bastard," Adrian muttered under his breath.

"I heard that," she said. "And I concur. He is a bastard. What's so sad is that he actually thinks what he's doing is okay, and that in the end I'll happily fall into his arms. He's worse than a bastard, Adrian."

Adrian wasn't going to disagree with her. "We need to come up with a plan."

She chuckled softly and even then he could hear her exhaustion. "I thought we had a plan."

"Then we need a backup plan since he wants to be difficult."

"He actually told me to get rid of you, and told me he deliberately scheduled me on my days off. I went to see Dr. Fowler, who is chief of pediatrics, and he accused me of being dramatic. It's as though everyone refuses to do anything where Belvedere is concerned."

Adrian pulled her closer when they reached his car. He helped her inside and snapped her seat belt in place. "Go ahead, close your eyes and rest a bit. I'll wake you when I get you home."

* * *

Doing as Adrian suggested, Trinity closed her eyes. All she could do was visualize her bed—soft mattress, warm covers and a firm pillow. She needed to go to the grocery store to pick up a few things, but not today. Right now she preferred sleeping to eating. She would take a long, hot bath...not a shower...but a soak in her tub to ease the aches from her muscles. She planned to sleep for an entire day and put everything out of her mind.

Except.

Except the man who had showed up unexpectedly this morning to drive her home. Seeing him had caused her heart to thump hard in her chest and blood to rush crazily through her veins. She knew for certain she had never re-acted to any other man that way before. That meant she was more exhausted than she had thought. And it was messing with her hormones.

Why this effect from Adrian and no one else? Why was Adrian's manly scent not only flowing through her nostrils but seeping into her pores and kicking sensations into a body that was too tired to respond?

In the deep recesses of her mind, she was trying not to remember the last time they'd been together. Namely, the kiss they'd shared. It had been the memory of that kiss that had lulled her to sleep when she'd thought she was too tired to close her eyes. The memory of that kiss was what she had thought about when she had needed to think of pleas-ant things to keep going.

There was no doubt in her mind that when it came to kissing, Adrian was definitely on top of his game. Even now, she remembered how his mouth had taken hers.

She had kissed him back, acquainting herself with the shape and fullness of his lips, his taste. It had been differ-ent from the first kiss. Longer. Sweeter. She had allowed herself to indulge. In doing so, it seemed her senses had gone through some sort of sensitivity training. Her head had been spinning and her tongue tingling. She'd been stunned by the force of passion that had run rampant through her.

Then there was the way he had held her in his arms. With his hands in the center of her back, he had held her with a possession that was astounding. She had felt every solid inch of him. Some parts harder than others, and it was those hard parts…one in particular…that had her fantasizing about him since.

"Wake up, Trinity. We're here."

She slowly opened her eyes. She glanced out the window at her surroundings. Slightly disoriented, she blinked and looked again before turning to Adrian. "This isn't my home."

A smile touched his lips. "No, it's mine. When I said I was taking you home, I meant to my place."

Now she was confused. She sat straighter in her seat. "Why?"

"So I can make sure you get your rest. Undisturbed. I wouldn't put it past Belvedere to find some excuse to call or show up at your place uninvited."

The thought of Dr. Belvedere doing either of those things bothered her. "Do you think he'd actually just drop by?"

"Not sure. But if he does, you won't be there. The man has issues and I wouldn't put anything past him."

Trinity hated saying it but neither would she. Still… To sleep at Adrian's place just didn't seem right. "I don't think it's a good idea for me to stay here."

"Why?"

She shrugged. "People might think things about us."

He chuckled. "People are *supposed* to think things about us, Trinity. The more they do, the better it is. Belvedere will look like a total ass trying to come on to a woman already seriously involved with another man. It will only show how pathetically demented he is."

What Adrian said made sense, but she was still wearing her scrubs and she wanted to get out of them. "I don't have any clothes."

"No problem. I'll loan you my T-shirt that will cover you past your thighs, and after you get a good day's rest, I'll take you to your place to get something else to put on. The main thing is for you to get some sleep. I'm going into the office once I get you settled in."

"I can't hide out here forever, Adrian."

"Not asking you to do that. I just think we need to continue to give the impression that we're lovers and not just two people merely seeing each other."

He paused a moment and then asked, "Why are you afraid to stay at my place?"

Good question.

"It's not that I'm afraid to stay here. It's just that I was looking forward to sleeping in my own bed."

An impish, feral smile curved his lips. "You might like mine better."

That's what I'm afraid of.

Why had his tone dropped a notch when he'd said that? His raspy words had resonated through her senses like a heated caress.

Quickly deciding all she wanted was to get some sleep, regardless of whose bed it was, she agreed. "Fine. Let's go. Your bed it is. And…Adrian?"

"Yes?"

"I sleep alone, so no funny business."

He chuckled. "I give you my word. I won't touch you unless you touch me first."

Then there shouldn't be any problems, she thought, because she wouldn't be touching him. At least she hoped not.

Eight

Adrian glanced around the conference room at the four other men sitting at the table. All wore intense expressions. Since joining the company and regularly attending executive board meetings, he'd discovered that they all wore that look when confronted with major decisions involving Blue Ridge Land Management.

Today's discussion was about a property they were interested in near Miami's South Beach. He'd given his report and now it was up to the board to decide the next move. It was Dillon who spoke, addressing his question to Adrian. "And you don't think a shopping complex there is a wise investment for us?"

"No, not from an engineering standpoint. Don't get me wrong, South Beach is a nice area, but there are several red flags such as labor issues and building costs that we don't want to deal with. One particular company is monopolizing the market and deliberately jacking up prices. It's not a situation we should get into right now. Besides, whatever development we place there will only be one of the same kind of complex that's already there. Even that's spelled out in the marketing report."

He knew his report hadn't been what they'd wanted to

hear. For years, Blue Ridge had tossed around the idea of building a huge shopping complex in South Beach. The timing hadn't been right then and, as he'd spelled out in his report, the timing wasn't right now.

Because he'd been taught that when he was faced with a problem he should be ready to offer a solution, he said, "There's a lucrative substitute in Florida that I'd like you to consider."

"And where might that be?" Riley asked, taking a sip of his coffee. "West Palm Beach?"

"No," Adrian replied. "Further north. It's one of the sea islands that stretches from South Carolina to Florida, right along the Florida coast. Amelia Island."

A smile touched Dillon's lips. "I went there once for a business conference. Took Pam with me and we stayed for a week. It's quaint, peaceful, totally relaxing…and—" his smile widened "—there are about six or seven beautiful golf courses."

"So I heard. And while you were enjoying your time on those golf courses, what was Pam doing?" Adrian inquired.

Dillon scrunched his forehead trying to remember. "She visited the spa a few times, otherwise she hung out by the pool reading."

"Just think of what choices she could have made if we had a complex on the island," Adrian said. "The clientele flocking to Amelia Island can afford to jet in on private planes, spend seven days golfing and dining at exclusive restaurants. They can certainly afford the type of luxury complex we want to build."

Adrian could tell he had their interest.

"What about labor issues and building costs?" Stern asked.

"Nearly nonexistent. The only problem we might run into is a few islanders not embracing change, who might want the island to remain as it is. But the person I spoke with this morning, who happens to be a college friend of mine who lives on the island, says that segment of the population is outnumbered by progressives who want the island to be a number-one vacation spot."

Providing everyone with the handouts he'd prepared, Adrian told them why placing a development on Amelia Island would work. A huge smile touched Canyon's face. "So, I suggest we see what we can do to make it happen."

An hour later, Adrian was back in his office. Since the meeting had been scheduled for ten o'clock, that had given him time to pick up Trinity from work and get her settled into his place. By the time he'd left for the office she was in his Jacuzzi tub. He expected that she was asleep now and that's what he wanted. That's what she needed.

And because his housekeeper had just been in, his place was in decent order and his refrigerator well stocked. Trinity had even complimented him on how neat and clean his place was and how spacious it was for just one person.

He had another meeting to attend today, a business dinner. But he was looking forward to returning home. Just to check on her, he told himself. Nothing more. She wasn't his first female houseguest and she wouldn't be the last. But then there was the fact that he had been thinking of her all day, when he hadn't wanted to. So what was that about?

He was pulling a folder from the In tray on his desk when his cell phone rang. He couldn't help smiling when he saw the caller was his twin.

"Yes, Dr. Westmoreland?"

The chuckle on the other end was rich. "Sounds good, doesn't it?"

"I always told you it would. How're things going?"

"Fine. When are you going to pay me a visit?"

Adrian leaned back in his chair. "I had planned to visit Charlotte this month but—"

"You're too involved with some female, right?"

Adrian chuckled. "Should I ask how you know?"

"You're letting off strong emotions."

Adrian didn't doubt it, and he blamed Belvedere for making him want to hurt somebody. "I have a lot going on here." He told his brother about the charade he and Trinity were playing.

"Trinity Matthews? I like her. I spent a lot of time talking to her at Riley's wedding."

"I noticed."

"Oops. Someone sounds jealous."

"No jealousy involved. Just saying I noticed the two of you had a lot to say to each other." He paused and added, "But I figured you were doing it to get a rise out of Jillian."

"If I was, it didn't work."

"Now what are you going to do?"

"Move on and not look back."

"Can you do that?" Adrian asked.

"I can try." Aidan paused. "Now back to you and Trinity. Has that doctor taken the bait and left her alone?"

"No, in fact he told her to break things off with me and when she refused he made her work longer hours and on her days off. And both days were assisting in surgery."

"Is the man crazy? An exhausted doctor can make costly mistakes, especially during surgery. The man isn't fit to be a doctor if getting a woman in his bed is more important than the welfare of his patients. That disgusts me."

"It disgusts me, as well," Adrian said. "That's why I refuse to let him use her that way."

"I'm feeling your emotions again. They are pretty damn strong, Adrian. Unless you plan on doing something with those feelings for Trinity then you should try keeping them in check."

"I suggest you do the same with Jillian," Adrian chided. "Just like you feel my emotions, remember I can also feel yours."

"I guess I do need to remember that."

After Adrian ended the call with his brother he couldn't help wondering if Aidan would be able to move on from his breakup with Jillian and not look back as he'd claimed. Adrian's thoughts shifted to Trinity. Was she still sleeping? The thought of her curled up in a bed in one of his guest rooms sent strong, heavy heartbeats thumping in his chest.

When he recalled how exhausted she was, barely able to stand on her feet, a muscle jumped in his jaw. No one should have to work in that state. All because Belvedere had tried breaking her down.

Anger poured through him at the thought. He was only soothed in knowing that for the time being she was safely tucked away under his roof. He rubbed the back of his neck. Aidan was right about keeping his emotions in check where Trinity was concerned. Doing so was hard, and he didn't like the implications of what that could mean. Especially when he was in a mad rush to leave the office and go home to see her. That wasn't good. He needed a diversion.

Adrian knew the one woman he could always count on. He picked up his phone and tapped in her number. He sighed in relief when she answered.

"Bailey Westmoreland."

"Bay? How would you like to do a movie tonight?"

He smiled when she said yes. "I have a business dinner in a few hours and will pick you up afterward. Around seven."

Trinity shifted in bed and curled into another position beneath the covers. When had her mattress begun to feel so soft? She slowly opened her eyes and looked around the room. Beautiful blue curtains hung at the window, the same shade as the bedspread covering her. Blue? Her curtains and bedcoverings weren't blue. They were brown. Pushing hair back from her face, she pulled herself up in a bed that wasn't hers. She then recalled where she was. Adrian's place.

Although she had been too exhausted to appreciate the décor when she'd first arrived, she remembered being impressed with the spaciousness of his condo as well as how tidy it was. He'd told her he had a housekeeper who came in twice a week, not only to keep the place looking decent, but also to do his laundry and prepare his meals.

That was a nice setup. Although she had a fetish for keeping her own place neat, she couldn't help but think about all the laundry she had yet to get to. And as far as cooked meals, she only got those when she went home to Bunnell. Otherwise she ate on the run, and mostly at fast-food places.

This was a nice guest room, she thought. Not too feminine and not too manly. The painting on the wall was abstract and she appreciated the splash of color that went with the drapes, the carpeting and the dark cherrywood furniture. There had been a lot of pillows on the bed, which she had tossed off before diving under the covers.

She pushed those same covers back as she eased out of bed, suddenly remembering that the only stitch of clothing she wore was the T-shirt Adrian had loaned her. It barely touched her mid-thigh. The material felt soft against her skin.

Moments later, after coming out of the connecting bathroom, she slid her shoulders into a silk bathrobe Adrian had placed across the arm of a chair. Her gaze lit on the clock on the nightstand. It was a little after seven. Had she really slept more than ten hours?

Since she felt well rested, she figured her body must have needed it. What had Belvedere been thinking to make her work such long hours, which was clearly against hospital policy? She knew very well what he'd been thinking and it only made her despise him that much more.

Her stomach growled and she left the bedroom for the kitchen. As she passed by several rooms on her way downstairs, she couldn't help but appreciate how beautiful they looked. When she got downstairs to the living room, she was surprised at the minimal furnishings. Although the place was more put-together than her own, it had the word "temporary" written all over it.

Once in the kitchen she opened the refrigerator and saw that Adrian's housekeeper had labeled the neatly arranged containers for each day of the week. Did that mean he ate in every day? What if he missed the meal for that day? Did it go to waste?

If that was true, today wouldn't be one of those days. She pulled out the container labeled for today and pulled off the top. *Mmm.* The pasta dish smelled good. Recalling that Adrian had told her to eat anything she wanted—and it seemed he definitely had more than enough to share— she spooned out a serving onto a plate to warm it in the microwave. Meals cooked and at your disposal was a working person's dream. Life couldn't get any better than this.

This kitchen was nice, with stainless steel appliances. She thought about her drab-looking kitchen and figured she could get used to living in this sort of place.

She ate her food, alone, and couldn't help but appreciate how Adrian had showed up at the hospital this morning to pick her up. He'd known her body would be racked with exhaustion and he had thought about her welfare. Dr. Belvedere, on the other hand, hadn't thought of anything but his own selfish motives.

Now that she was well rested, she recalled how Adrian had looked. Already dressed for work, he had been wearing a business suit that fitted perfectly over his broad shoulders, heavily muscled thighs and massive biceps. He had walked toward her with a swagger that had nearly taken her breath away. No man should have a right to look that good in the morning. His shirt had looked white and crisp, and the printed tie made a perfect complement. The phrase "dress to impress" had immediately come to mind, as well as *mind-blowingly sexy.*

It didn't take her long to eat the meal and tidy up the kitchen after loading the dishes in the dishwasher. The clock on the kitchen wall indicated it was almost eight. Adrian hadn't mentioned anything about working late. Now that she was rested she could go back to her place. Her only problem was that she didn't have her car.

She glanced down at herself. The bathrobe covered more than the T-shirt, but still, she didn't feel comfortable parading around any man's home not fully dressed. Going into the living room, she decided to call her sister with an update on what Belvedere had done.

"Why am I not surprised?" Tara said moments later. "He reminds me so much of that doctor in Kentucky who tried forcing me into a relationship with him. But Belvedere really did something unethical by forcing you to work. And the nerve of him telling you to end your relationship with Adrian. Just who does he think he is?"

"I don't know but his actions only make me despise him more. And he saw firsthand that I won't end things with Adrian this morning. Adrian came to the hospital to pick me up."

"Adrian picked you up from work?"

"Yes." Trinity proceeded to tell her sister how Adrian had been there to drive her and, instead of taking her home, had taken her to his place to get undisturbed sleep.

"That was nice of him."

"Yes, it was," Trinity said, glancing at the clock on the wall again. "He hasn't come home yet, so I guess he's working late." She wouldn't mention that she was slightly disappointed he hadn't called to check on her. "He'll be taking me home when he gets here."

"Well, I'm glad you got undisturbed sleep."

"I'm glad, too. I honestly needed it."

Trinity had washed the clothes she'd worn that morning and was tossing them in the dryer when she heard Adrian's key in the door lock. Finally he was home. It was close to ten o'clock and he'd known she was stranded at his place without her car. The least he could have done was call to see how she was doing, even if he needed to work late.

But what if he hadn't been working late? What if he'd been with someone on a date or something? She frowned, wondering why her mind was going there. And why she was feeling more than a tinge of jealousy.

Why are you trippin', Trinity? It's not as if you and Adrian got the real thing going on. It's just a charade. How many times do you have to remind yourself of that? On the other hand, he had said he wouldn't see anyone else.

"If the rules changed, he should have told me," she muttered angrily, leaving the laundry room and passing through his kitchen. She'd made it to the living room by the time he walked inside.

She willed herself not to show any reaction to how good he looked with his jacket slung across his shoulder. But then she noticed other things: his tie was off and she picked up the scent of a woman's perfume.

Trinity took a calming breath, thinking a degree of civility was required here. But then she lost it, and before Adrian had a chance to see her standing there, she said in an accusing tone, "You've been with someone."

Nine

The moment Adrian saw Trinity a jolt of sexual desire rocked him to the bone. She was angry, hands on hips, spine ramrod straight and wearing his bathrobe, which drooped at her shoulders and almost swallowed her whole. But damn, nothing would satisfy him more than to cross the room and kiss that angry look off her lips.

But, suddenly, it occurred to him that she had no right to be angry. She was the reason he hadn't come home when he could have. Too much temptation under his roof. Too many thoughts of her had floated through his head all day. He hadn't enjoyed the movie for thinking of her.

And what had she just accused him of? *Being with someone?* So what if he had? What he did and who he did it with was his business. Period.

Tossing his jacket onto a wing-backed chair, he crossed his arms over his chest and rocked back on his heels a few times. "And what of it?"

He didn't need his PhD to know that was the wrong answer.

Her eyes cut into him like glass and she took a step toward him.

"Did you not bring me here, Adrian?"

He shrugged a massive shoulder. "Yes, I brought you here with the intent of you getting uninterrupted sleep. What does that have to do with how I spent my time this evening and with whom?"

He wasn't used to this form of inquisition, especially after having spent the past several years making sure no woman assumed she had the right to make any demands on his time. The last time he'd looked, his marital status was still *single*.

"The only reason I brought it up is because you agreed to the pretend affair with me. And in doing so you indicated you would forgo dating for a while," she said.

"And I have."

"Then what about tonight?" she asked brusquely.

He stared at her. "Why the questions, Trinity? Are you jealous or something?"

He could tell from her expression that his question hit a nerve…as well as exposed a revelation. She *was* jealous. He inwardly smiled at that. It looked as if he wasn't the only one plagued with emotions.

"Of course I'm not jealous," she said, dropping her hands from her waist. "I just thought we had an agreement, that's all."

"And we do. Like I said, I wanted you to get uninterrupted sleep, so after my business dinner, I called Bailey and invited her to a movie."

"Bailey?"

"Yes. My sister Bailey."

"Oh."

"That's all you have to say?" he asked, deciding not to let her off so easily.

"Yes, that's all I have to say…other than I'll be ready to go home when my clothes finish drying, which shouldn't be too long. I'll check on them now." She turned to head toward the laundry room, but he reached out and snagged her arm. He tried ignoring the spike of heat that rushed through him the moment he touched her, but it was obvious that she felt it, as well. "Hey, wait a minute. You owe me an apology."

She lifted her chin. "Do I?"

"What do you think? You all but accused me of lying to you. It was an unnecessary hit to my character and I feel wounded."

Trinity rolled her eyes. "Getting a little carried away, aren't you?"

If only she knew just how carried away he felt. Every cell in his body was sizzling, all the way to the groin. Especially the groin. Desire throbbed all through him, and an urgency he'd never felt before began overtaking his senses. Pushing him on. That had to be the reason he was still holding on to her arm. Something she noticed.

"Why are you touching me, Adrian?"

She was visibly annoyed and visibly turned on. He could see both in her eyes. There were frissons of heat in the dark depths staring back at him. He'd been involved with enough women to know when sexual hunger was coiling inside them. Some women tried ignoring it, pretending they didn't feel a thing. Calling Trinity out on it would only increase her anger.

"You had no right to question me just now," he said, speaking firmly, not liking the way she was making him feel. Or the way he'd been feeling all day while thinking of her.

"You're right. I didn't. But that's not giving me an answer as to why you're touching me."

No, it didn't. If she wanted an answer he would give her one. "I like touching you. I also like kissing you." He saw the way heat flared even more in her gaze, and his body pounded in response.

Then, although he knew she wouldn't like it, he added, "Probably as much as you like kissing me back."

She pulled away from his hold. "Only in your dreams."

He smiled. "Trust me, baby, you don't want to go there. You couldn't handle knowing what my dreams are like."

"I don't want to know," she said, giving him a chagrined look before walking off. Adrian was right on her heels. "About that apology, Trinity."

She turned around so suddenly, she collided with his chest. His arms were on her again, this time to steady her and keep her from falling. And not one to miss any opportunity, he tightened his hold, leaned in close to her lips and whispered, "Since you won't give me an apology, I guess I'll take this instead."

Then he proceeded to ravage her mouth.

The man was a master at kissing.

The last thing Trinity wanted was for Adrian to know how much she wanted him, wanted this. But for the life of her, she couldn't stop responding to his kiss. She was engaging in the exchange in a way that probably told him everything she didn't want him to know. How was she supposed to deal with these emotions he could arouse in her so easily? How was she supposed to deal with him period?

He fit snugly against her. She felt the outline of his body, every single detail. Especially an erection that was as hard as one could get. It was huge, pressing into her middle as if it had every right to let her know just how much it wanted her. And this kiss…

Lordy, it should be outlawed. Arrested. Made to serve time for indecency. Who did stuff like this with their tongue? Evidently Adrian Westmoreland did. And what he was doing was driving her crazy, pushing her over the edge. Goading her into wanting things she didn't need.

Trinity followed his lead and kissed him back with a craving she felt in places she had forgotten existed.

The kiss made her remember it had been a long time since she'd engaged in any type of sexual activity. There had been that one time in college—when it was over she'd sworn it would be the last time. It had been a waste of good bedsheets. It was obvious Ryan Morgan hadn't known what he was doing any more than she had.

Since then, although she'd dated from time to time, and she'd been attracted to one or two men, there hadn't been anyone who'd impressed her enough to get her in his bed. Plenty had tried; all had failed…especially some of the doctors she'd worked with. She had a rule about not connecting her personal and professional lives since doing so would only result in unnecessary drama. But it seemed Casey Belvedere didn't know how to take no for an answer. He was causing drama anyway.

But then Trinity stopped thinking when Adrian intensified the kiss, sinking deeper inside her mouth like he had every right to do so. He used his tongue to lick her into submission. What was he doing to her? Images flashed in her mind of scandalous things… all the other things he could do with that tongue. She began tingling all over, especially between her legs. When she felt something solid against her back she knew he'd somehow cornered her against the wall.

She heard herself moan and felt a tightening in her chest. Is this how it felt to desire a man to the point of craziness? Where she was tempted to tear off his clothes and go at it with no control? And all from a little kiss. Well, she had to admit there was nothing little about it, not when her own tongue was swelling in response, doing things it normally wouldn't do, following his lead. And talk about swelling… The erection pressing against her had thickened and poked hard against her inner thigh.

She instinctively shifted to direct his aim right for the

juncture of her thighs. Ah, it felt so right. Yes, there. He evidently thought so, too, because he began moving his body, grinding against her, holding tight to her hips.

He suddenly broke off and took in a slow breath. She did the same. How long had they gone without breathing? Not long enough, she figured, when he stared hard at her without saying anything. The dampness of his lips said it all. He'd gotten a mouthful and wanted more.

"You taste good, Trinity," he said huskily, reaching up to touch her lower lip with his finger.

Why was she tempted to stick out her tongue and give that finger a slow lick? Or, even worse, suck it into her mouth.

She shook her head hoping to shake off the craziness of that thought. "We've gone too far," she said in a voice she barely recognized as her own.

A seductive smile touched his lips as he used that same finger to slowly caress the area around her mouth, causing shivers to run up her body. "And I don't think we've gone far enough."

He *would* say that, she thought. She shifted her body to move away from him, but he pulled her closer. His body seemed to have gotten harder.

She squared her shoulders, or at least she tried to do so. "Now, look, Adrian—"

"I am looking," he interrupted throatily, while staring at her mouth, "And I like what I see."

The fingers that had moved away from her lips to her chin were warm and soft, long and strong. She needed all the control she could garner. Adrian was making her feel things she'd never felt before. How? Why? She was losing it. That was the only explanation for why she had gone almost eight years without wanting a man and now passion was eating away at her.

"Trinity?"

She lifted her chin, that same chin he was caressing, and held tight to his gaze. "What?" Those long, strong fingers slowly eased to the center of her neck, touching the pulse beating there.

"I do things to you."

If he thought she would admit to that, he was wrong. "Is that what you think?"

He chuckled softly, sensuously. "That's what I know. I can tell."

She was dying to ask how he could tell, but decided to claim denial for as long as she could. "I hate to crush that overblown ego of yours, but you're wrong."

He chuckled again. "Let me prove I'm right, sweetheart."

Trinity pulled back from his touch. She'd had enough of this foolishness. "If you don't mind, I need to get my clothes out of the dryer and get dressed so you can take me to the hospital to get my car."

"Not tonight. It's late." He took a step back and dropped his hands to his sides.

She frowned. If he thought they would share space under the same roof tonight, he needed to think again. "Then I'll call a cab."

"No, you won't. You're staying put until tomorrow. I'll drop you off at the hospital for your car on my way to work in the morning."

And then he had the nerve to walk off. She couldn't believe it. Steaming, she was now the one on his heels. "I can't stay here tonight."

He turned so quickly she almost bumped into him. She caught herself and moved back. He stared at her. "Why not?"

"Because I don't want to. I want to sleep in my own bed."

He crossed his arms over his chest. "And I want you in mine."

She swallowed. "Yours?"

"Yes, you have the guest room all to yourself. And if you need another T-shirt to sleep in, I'll get you one."

Although he hadn't suggested they share the same bed, she was growing angrier by the minute. She told herself it wasn't because he hadn't invited her to be his sleeping partner. That had nothing to do with it. "What I need for you to do is to take me home."

She wished his stance wasn't causing her to check out just how good he looked. Long legs, masculine thighs, slim waist, tight abs. Why did the air in the room suddenly feel electrified? Was that a crackling sound she heard? Why did his eyes look so penetrating, so piercing? Why was she letting him get next to her again?

With a mind of its own her gaze lowered to his crotch. He still had an erection? Lordy! Could a man really get that big and make it last that long?

Her gaze slowly lifted to his eyes. The moment they made eye contact she was snatched into a web of heated desire. What in the world was wrong with her?

"We can't continue to deny we want each other, Trinity. Hell, I don't like it any more than you do," he admitted, grabbing her attention.

She swallowed and went back into denial mode. "What are you talking about?" she asked softly.

He took a step forward, coming to a stop just a few feet in front of her. "I'm talking about the way you're looking at me, the way I'm looking at you. You and I have nothing in common on the outside. But…"

She didn't want to ask but couldn't help doing so. "But what?"

He took another step closer. "But on the inside, it's a different story. Point blank, what I want more than anything is to make you come while screaming my name."

Ten

Adrian believed in saying what he thought and what he felt. He had no qualms stating what he wanted. And he wanted Trinity. He had wanted her from the first time he'd laid eyes on her at Riley's wedding, and when he'd heard she was moving to Denver he'd wanted to put her on his to-do list. But her close association with Thorn had squashed that idea. Everyone knew Thorn was overprotective when it came to people he cared deeply about.

Adrian had heard stories about how Thorn had scared off guys who'd wanted to date his sister Delaney. The other brothers had been just as bad, but Thorn had been the worst. He'd had no problem backing up his threats. And Adrian didn't want to give Thorn any reason to kick his behind, family or no family.

If Adrian knew the score, then why was he willing to skate with danger? Because Trinity, standing there wearing his T-shirt and looking sexier than any woman had a right to look, made him willing to risk it all to find out what she had on beneath that cotton. He wanted her. And when a man wanted a woman, nothing else mattered.

"Scream your name? You've got to be kidding me. No man will get a scream out of me."

Her words made him study her expression. She was actually grinning as if what he'd said was amusing. "Why do you find what I said so far-fetched?"

She rolled her eyes. "I find it more than far-fetched. The notion is so ridiculous it really isn't funny. Don't you know a woman who screams while having sex is just doing it to make her partner think he's doing something when he isn't?"

He leaned back against the side of the sofa table and stared at her, his arms crossed over his chest. "You don't say?"

"Yes," she said as a smile touched her lips. "I'm disappointed. I thought you had more smarts in the bedroom."

He should have been insulted but he wasn't. Instead he was amused, especially at her naïveté. She was wrong and he would just love to prove it. But that was beside the point. He couldn't help wondering why she was convinced she was right.

"I have plenty of bedroom smarts, Trinity. But it seems you've been disappointed along the way by some man who wasn't up to snuff."

She frowned. "It's not just me. It's about women in general. We talk and at times exchange notes, and the comparison is usually the same."

"Really?"

"I wouldn't say it if it wasn't true. I'm a doctor, so I know the workings of the human body. I know about orgasms being a natural way to release sexual buildup. I get that. That's not the problem."

"Then what's the problem?"

"Men, and some women, believing it's all that and a bag of chips when it's more like a stick of gum. When they discover it's not what they heard or what they thought, then they're too embarrassed to admit it was a disappointment. They end up faking it instead of fessing up."

"And you know women who have *faked* it."

"Yes. Can you say with certainty that you don't? Are you absolutely sure that every woman you made scream wasn't doing it to stroke that ego of yours?"

If she was trying to make him doubt his ability in the bedroom, she had a long way to go. "Yes, I can say with one-hundred-percent certainty any screams I helped to generate were the real thing."

She stared at him, probably thinking his conceit had gone to his head.

"Well, believe what you want," Trinity said, rolling her eyes.

"You don't believe me?" he asked, looking at her questioningly.

"No, and before you say it, I have no intention of letting you prove I'm wrong. I'm aware of that particular game men play and don't intend to be a participant."

He couldn't help but smile. "So it's not the orgasm you don't believe in, just the degree of pleasure a woman can feel."

She shrugged her pretty shoulders. "Yes, I guess that's right. I know two people can generate passion, and they can do it to the degree that they lose control. I get that. But what I don't buy is that they can generate passion to the point where they're screaming all over the place while sharing the big O. That's the nonsense that sells romance novels. And I'm a reality kind of girl."

Adrian slowly nodded. *A reality kind of girl.* He was going to enjoy every single minute of proving her wrong, and he would prove her wrong. It wouldn't be a game for him. It would be one of the most serious moments of his life. He would be righting a wrong done to her, whatever had made her think faking it was necessary…and, even worse, that doing so was okay.

He needed time to come up with a plan. "It's late. We

can finish this conversation in the morning, *after* I've had my first cup of coffee. Towels, washcloths, extra toiletries, including an unused toothbrush are beneath the vanity in your bathroom. Good night."

Trinity tried not to stare as Adrian left the room. Sexiness oozed from him with every step he took. He had a walk that made the tips of her nipples hard. Lordy, the man had such a cute tush…. The way his pants fit his backside was a sight to behold. She could imagine her hands clenching each firm and masculine cheek. The fantasy unnerved her. Never before had she focused on any part of a man's anatomy.

Since she wasn't sleepy after having slept most of the day, she decided to stay busy. After folding the clothes she'd taken out of the dryer, she went back into the kitchen. Adrian's housekeeper was good at what she did. Trinity couldn't help looking in the cabinets, impressed at how well stocked and organized things were.

She made a cup of tea and enjoyed the beautiful view of downtown Denver out the living room window. She took a deep breath then sipped her tea, hoping it would stop her heart from pounding. Even when she'd folded clothes and messed around in his kitchen, the erratic pounding in her chest that had started when he'd walked away hadn't stopped. It was as if knowing they were under the same roof and breathing the same air was getting to her. Why?

Trying to put thoughts of him out of her mind she turned back to the view. There was a full moon tonight. Adrian lived in the thick of downtown and the surrounding buildings were massive, the skyscrapers numerous. But he still had a beautiful view of the mountains.

Her own house was on the outskirts of town in the suburbs. Adrian's condo was definitely closer to the hospital.

Adrian.

Her heart pounded even faster. The nerve of him saying bluntly that he wanted to have sex with her. Just who did he think he was? Maybe pretending to be lovers had gone to his head. Maybe it hadn't been a good idea after all. So far all she'd gotten out of it was Belvedere making her work on her days off out of spite.

That wasn't completely true. Being Adrian's pretend lover had been an eye-opener. It had made her realize how sex-deprived she was. That had to be the reason she was so attracted to him and why he was awakening passion inside of her that she didn't know she had. As she'd told him, she knew orgasms relieved sexual tension, but before meeting him sexual tension was something she hadn't worried about. Sexual urges were foreign to her. Now, with him being so sinfully attractive, her heart was overworked with all the pounding and the lower part of her body constantly throbbed.

"Trinity?"

She gasped at the sound of her name and turned from the window. Adrian stood in his pj bottoms, which rode low on his hips. He looked even sexier than he had earlier that night. "Yes?"

"Why aren't you in bed?"

Seeing him standing there almost took her breath away. And if that wasn't enough, his masculine scent reached out to her, sending her entire body into a heated tailspin, engulfing her with crazy thoughts and ideas. "Why aren't you?" she countered, trying to stay in control.

A slow smile touched his lips and her body tingled in response. That erratic pounding in her chest returned. Had it truly ever left? "I couldn't sleep," was his reply and she watched as he rubbed a hand over his face.

"You need to go back to bed. You work tomorrow. I don't. Besides, thanks to you, I got a lot of rest today."

"No need to thank me. I did what was needed."

He was getting next to her with little or no effort. She glanced down at her cup and came up with the perfect excuse to leave the living room. "Well, I've finished my tea. I guess I'll go to bed now. Maybe more sleep will come."

Her only regret was that she had to walk past him to get to the kitchen. As she walked by he reached out, took the cup from her hand and placed it on the sofa table before wrapping a strong arm around her waist and pulling her to him.

"What do you think you're doing?" she asked, making a feeble attempt to push him away.

"Something I should have done earlier tonight."

She saw his head lowering to hers and opened her mouth to protest. But he seized the opportunity and slid his tongue between her parted lips. Immediately her traitorous tongue latched on to his and before she could fully grasp what was happening, she was kissing him as hungrily as he was kissing her. Never had she wanted or needed a kiss as much as she wanted and needed this one.

Not understanding why, she molded her body to his as if it was the most natural thing, and instinctively wrapped her arms around his neck. She felt those strong, hard fingers on her backside, pressing her closer. She felt him, long, solid and erect against her.

Her brazen response prompted Adrian to deepen the kiss.

Desire felt like talons sinking into her skin, spreading through her body in a heated rush, making her moan deep in her throat. He was the first man to ever make her moan, but she still wasn't buying that screaming claim he'd made earlier.

Then he began grinding against her body. She nearly buckled over; the juncture of her legs felt on fire. She broke off the kiss and unwrapped her arms from his neck before taking in a deep breath. "You don't want this, Trinity. You don't need this. You've got self-control, girl. Use it," she muttered softly under her breath.

Adrian heard her. "What are you saying?" he asked, dipping his head low to hers.

Trinity stared up into penetrating dark eyes. Was he aware that his eyes were an aphrodisiac? Just staring into their dark depths caused crazy things to happen to her. She nervously licked her lips, really tempted to lick his instead.

"Trinity?"

She recalled he had asked her a question. She decided to go for honesty. "I'm trying to talk myself out of taking something that I want but don't need."

He lifted a brow. "Really?"

"Yes."

He placed his hand on her shoulder. "Keep talking. You might convince yourself to walk away, but I have a feeling you won't."

She sucked in a breath. A spark of energy passed between them from his touch, making her fully aware she was being pulled into something hot, raw and sensuous. "You don't think I have any resolve?" she asked him.

"Not saying that. But I know in most cases desire can overrule resolve, no matter what kind of pep talk you give yourself."

She didn't want to agree with him, but unfortunately she was living proof that he might be right. "Why? Why don't I have self-control around you?"

"Maybe you don't need it."

"Oh, I need it," she said. "But…"

"But what?"

"I'm beginning to think I need you more." She paused. "I don't want to make a fool of myself."

"What makes you think you will?"

"Because I'm not good at this."

"Good at what, Trinity?"

"Seduction."

His lips curved into a smile as he reached for her. Those penetrating eyes held hers again as the palm of his hand settled in the center of her back.

"Baby, give me the opportunity and I'll teach you everything you need to know and then some."

I can't mess this up.

That thought raced through Adrian's mind as he dipped his head to capture Trinity's lips. As soon as he was planted firmly inside her mouth he deepened the kiss, ravishing her mouth with a greed that had soaked into his bones. There was no stopping him now. He would sort out what the hell was going on with him later. Much later.

He had tried to come up with a plan for the best way to handle Trinity, but he'd decided a plan would appear too calculating and manipulative. So instead he'd decided to let desire take its course. And it had. He felt it in the way she was kissing him back, letting him know that she was as far gone as he was.

With a mind of their own, his hands moved, traveling from the center of her back to her shoulders before moving lower to cup her shapely backside. She felt good.

When he felt himself harden even more he knew it was time to take things to the next level. He ended the kiss, but kept his hands firmly planted on her backside, making sure their bodies remained connected.

"I want you," he whispered. "I want to take you into my bedroom and make love to you, Trinity."

He saw the indecision in her gaze and knew he had to be totally honest with her. As much as he wanted her, she needed to know where he stood. That was the only way he handled a woman. Trinity would be more than just a quick romp, but he wasn't making any promises of forever. Besides, weeks ago they had already established the fact that they wanted different things out of life.

"Before you answer yea or nay, I just need to reiterate that I'm not the marrying kind," he told her.

He saw the way her eyes widened. "Marry?" she asked in surprise. "Who said anything about marriage?"

"Just saying. Some women expect a lot after a roll beneath the sheets. Just wanted to make sure we're clear that I don't do forever."

"We're clear," she said with one of those matter-of-fact looks on her face. "I guess I should issue that same disclaimer since forever isn't in my future, either."

"Good. We're straight."

And before she could change her mind as to how the night would end for them, he swept her off her feet and into his arms. Quickly headed for the bedroom.

Eleven

Trinity sat cross-legged in the middle of Adrian's bed, where he'd placed her, and watched him slowly ease the pj's down his legs. He was looking at her as if she was a treat he intended to devour. And heaven help her she wanted to devour him, as well.

When he stepped out of his pajama pants, all thoughts left her mind except for one: his engorged manhood. Why did he have to be so well-endowed? No wonder he was conceited and arrogant.

She moved her gaze away from him, figuring that doing so would stop her heart from beating buck-wild in her chest. The décor of his room, like the rest of the house, was fantastic. The dominating colors of avocado and chocolate gave it a manly air. The room was a lot bigger than the guest room she'd been given. At least, it appeared that way since his furniture was positioned to give a very spacious feel.

Adrian walked toward her, completely naked, with that slow and sensual stride that he had down to a tee. Her gaze raked over him and she could imagine touching those tight abs, that muscular chest, those broad shoulders. And that flourishing manhood filled her head with all sorts of ideas.

When he reached the bed and placed a knee on it, she

figured it was time to remind him of what she'd said earlier. "I'm not good at this."

"Let me be the judge of that," he said, reaching for the hem of her T-shirt.

In a blink, he had whipped it over her head, leaving her in black panties and matching bra. But from the way he looked at her one would have thought she wasn't wearing anything at all.

With a flick of his wrist, he unsnapped the front clasp of her bra. Before she could react, he had worked the garment from her shoulders and tossed it aside. Her stomach clenched when she saw his gaze focus on her breasts and the hardened tips of her nipples. His attention made them harder.

She nearly moaned out loud when he licked a swollen nipple then sucked it into his mouth. How had he known doing something like that would make her womanhood weep? She wrapped her hands around his head to hold him to her breast. Was there anything his tongue wasn't capable of doing? She doubted it. It was made to give pleasure. No wonder Adrian was so high in demand. If this was part of his seduction then he could seduce the panties off a nun.

He released one nipple and started on the other. That was when his hand moved lower, easing beneath the waistband of her panties. As if he'd given a silent order, her legs parted to give him better access. It didn't take long for his fingers to find what they were seeking.

She groaned deep in her throat when he slid a finger inside her womanly core, finding her wet. She doubted he expected she'd be otherwise. Then, with the same circular motion his tongue was using, his finger moved likewise inside her, massaging her clitoris. There was no doubt in her mind he was readying for the next phase, but she was already there.

Then he moved his mouth to her lips, swallowing her

groan and thrusting his tongue deep. He kissed her with a hunger that he mimicked with the movement of his finger. At some point he'd added a second finger. Together the two were stroking her into a heated frenzy. Of their own accord, her hips began moving, gyrating to the rhythm of his fingers. She thought she would pass out from the sensations swamping her.

When he finally released her mouth, she gasped, and he took the opportunity to shimmy her panties over her hips and down her legs. Instead of tossing them aside as he'd done with her bra, he lifted them to his nose, inhaling deeply and closing his eyes as if he was enjoying heavenly bliss. Watching him sent sensual chills escalating through her body. She moaned again.

He opened his eyes and tossed the panties aside. He held her gaze as he lowered himself to the juncture of her thighs. And when he licked his lips, she felt her inner muscles clench. It was then that he leaned up and whispered close to her ear, "Last chance to back out."

He had to be kidding. There was no way she would back out, although her common sense was telling her that she should. Instead she'd decided based on feelings, and, at the moment she was dealing with some pretty heady emotions.

"I won't back out."

"If you're certain, now is when I tell you my technique."

"Your technique?" she asked, barely able to get the words out. Surely he wasn't into anything kinky? Although right now, he could come up with just about anything and she would go along with it.

"Yes, my technique. When I make love to you, I'm going to give you all I've got."

She swallowed slowly. "All you've got?"

"Every single inch."

Trinity swallowed again as a vision flashed through

her mind. Her skin burned for him and her womanly core throbbed.

"Ready for me?"

She wasn't sure. All she knew was that when he touched her she felt good. When he kissed her she felt even better. She figured making love to him would be off the charts.

"And, Trinity?"

She looked at him. "Yes?"

"I *will* make you scream and it *will* be the real thing."

Now that he'd given her fair warning, Adrian went about taking care of business. Wrapping his arms around her, he brought them chest to chest. The protruding tips of her nipples poked into him, and he liked the connection.

He eased Trinity onto her back while kissing her, doubting he would ever get tired of tasting her. He loved the way she kissed him, devouring him as much as he devoured her. How could any woman have so much passion and not know it?

He broke off the kiss. When her head touched one pillow, he reached behind her to grab another. Lifting her hips, he placed the pillow beneath her and then used his knee to spread her legs. He licked his lips in anticipation as he gazed at her wet womanly folds.

Adrian ran a hand up and down her thigh, loving the feel of her naked flesh. She had soft skin and the scent of a woman. She was perfectly made. He'd thought so when he'd seen her in clothes and he thought so even now that he'd seen her out of them.

"Adrian?"

He met her gaze and saw impatience. He wouldn't be rushed. If she thought he was one of those be-done-with-it kind of guys, she was mistaken. When it came to sex, he was so painstakingly thorough it was almost a shame. Before the night was over, she would discover just how wrong she was about the sexual experience for a woman. No woman left Adrian Westmoreland's bed unsatisfied; he made sure of it.

And Trinity was a special case because he could tell from their conversations that she had limited experience in the bedroom. He intended to remedy that. Tonight.

He kissed her, letting his tongue mimic what his manhood intended to do once he was inside her. But first, one taste led to another. Her scent was driving him insane.

Adrian moved his hands all over her body, loving to touch her. He trailed kisses from her mouth to the center of her throat. He sucked her, intentionally branding her. He wasn't sure why, especially when he didn't believe in giving a woman any ideas regarding possession. But for Trinity, it was necessary.

Needing to touch her again, he ran a hand over her breasts and stomach before moving lower, to her thighs, brushing his fingertips over her flesh and loving the softness of her silky-smooth skin. And he loved watching her nipples harden in front of his eyes, loved seeing her light brown eyes darken and stare back at him filled with a heated lust that mirrored his own.

"I want you bad," he muttered, putting into words just how he felt. His mouth moved from her neck back up to her lips. Down below, his fingers slid back between her legs. There was something about touching her there that he found exhilarating. And he liked the way her legs spread open of their own accord. When he stroked her nub, she threw her head back and moaned. He loved the sound and wanted to hear more.

He licked her lips, wanting more of her taste. Now. He eased his body downward to lower his head between her legs. When his tongue slid between the slippery wet folds of her womanhood, she moved against his mouth.

When it came to oral sex he was a master, and he was

about to show Trinity just what a pro he was. Doing so would be easy because she tasted so damn good.

He heard her release a deep groan and he smiled. She hadn't felt anything yet. He was just getting started. In a few more minutes she would be pulling his hair. With a meticulousness he had perfected over the years, Adrian devoured Trinity's sweetness, moving his tongue inside her from every angle.

Her legs began to quiver against the sides of his face. She dug into his scalp while bringing her hips off the pillow. But what he wanted to hear more than anything were her luscious whimpers that escalated into a full-blown moan.

She was trying to hold in what she was feeling. He wasn't having any of that. He knew the sound he wanted to hear and decided to use his *deep tongue* technique on her. Within seconds, her moans became screams. He held her as she jerked, an orgasm sweeping through her. It might have started between her legs but he could tell from the intensity of her scream that she'd felt it through her entire body.

He didn't let up. Another scream arrived on the heels of the last and it was only when she finally slumped back against the pillow that he lifted his head. Leaning back on his haunches, he looked at her. Her hands were thrown over her eyes and her breathing sounded as if she'd run a marathon.

When she sensed him staring at her, she dropped her hand and stared back.

He smiled, licked his lips and asked, "Was that the real thing or were you faking it?"

Trinity wasn't sure she was capable of answering. Her throat felt raw from her screams. Never in her life had she experienced anything quite like what Adrian had just done to her. The man's mouth, his tongue, should be outlawed.

She had screamed—actually screamed—and there hadn't been anything fake about.

"Still not sure? Then I better step up my game."

He had to be kidding. But when he shifted his body, she saw that he wasn't. His bigger-than-life manhood stood at full attention.

"Adrian," she whispered. He reached into the nightstand to pull out a condom packet. She swallowed, moistening her lips while watching him put it on. How could a woman get turned on by that? Easily, she thought, seeing how expertly he shielded himself. Thick, protruding veins ran along the sides of his erection and the head was engorged. An eager shiver raced through her.

He reached for her and she went to him willingly, not caring that he could probably see the desire all over her face. "We start off doing traditional and then we get buck wild," he murmured against her lips.

He tilted her hips toward him and entered her, inch by slow inch. She closed her eyes in sexual bliss. Her body felt tight even as it adjusted to the size of him. He stretched her, lodging himself deep, to the hilt.

"You okay, baby?"

Trinity's fingernails dug into his shoulders and she inhaled a deep breath. He had gone still, but she could feel him throbbing inside her. She held tight to his gaze as a tremor ran through her. She could tell from the look in his eyes that he felt it. He got harder, bigger.

And then he began to move. If she thought his tongue needed to be outlawed, then his manhood needed to be put in jail and the key thrown away. Something inside her ignited. He thrust in and out, going deeper. She felt him, every hard inch, with each slow, purposeful stroke.

Emotions she'd never felt before raced through her. Instinctively, her hips moved, mimicking his. Sensations overwhelmed her as he continued to pump, going fast and then slow and then fast all over again.

Something started at her womb, spreading through every part of her. Her legs began to tremble; a sound erupted at the base of her throat.

He was hitting her G spot, H spot, Q spot—every spot inside her—driving her closer to the edge with every thrust. He pumped harder, longer, the intensity of his strokes triggering hot, rolling, mind-blowing feelings.

And then the world seemed to spin out of control. An orgasm tore through her. She screamed, louder than before. Waves of ecstasy nearly drowned her in pleasure. She screamed again. This time she screamed out his name. As if the sound propelled him, he thrust inside her as another climax claimed her. Then his body bucked hard and she heard her name on his lips.

Moments later, he slumped against her and then shifted their bodies so she was on top of him. He gently rubbed his hand up and down her back. "You screamed my name," he rasped huskily.

"And you screamed mine." She raised her head from his chest to point that out.

A crooked smile touched the corners of his mouth. "So I did." He didn't say anything for a long moment. "I asked you before, Trinity. Were your screams the real thing?"

She wished she could lie and say they weren't, but to do so wouldn't serve any purpose. He had proved her wrong in the most shocking yet delicious manner. It was a lesson she doubted she would ever forget.

"Yes," she whispered softly. "They were the real thing." She placed her head back down on his chest.

She should not have been surprised about his vast knowledge of ways to pleasure a woman, but she couldn't help wondering how many women he'd been involved with to obtain that experience.

"Tired?"

She lifted her head again. "Exhausted."

In one smooth movement he shifted his body and had her on her back again so he could stare down at her. "Then I guess this time I'll do all the work."

This time? She stared at him. Surely he didn't have another round of sex on his mind. Evidently he did, she thought, watching him grab another condom from the nightstand drawer. "Time to swap out," he said, smiling at her.

He eased off the bed and trotted naked toward the bathroom. Lordy, the man had the kind of butt cheeks that made her want to rub against them all day and all night. The kind that tempted her to pinch them for pleasure.

"You can do whatever you like," he said, turning around and grinning at her.

Jeez. Did he have eyes in the back of his head? Or was he a mind reader? "I have no idea what you're talking about."

He chuckled.

"Don't let me prove you wrong again, Trinity."

Then, after winking at her, he went into the bathroom and closed the door behind him.

Twelve

Before daybreak Adrian had proved Trinity wrong in more ways and positions than she'd known existed. He'd made love to her through most of the night, guiding her through one mind-blowing orgasm after another.

Although she was one hell of a passionate woman, her sexual experience was limited. He had no problems teaching her a few things. He couldn't recall ever enjoying making love to any woman more. It had been an incredible night, which was why he was awake and had been since four that morning.

His heart was still pounding from when she had gone down on him. The first time she'd ever done so with any man, she had admitted. He had felt honored. He had no problem telling her what he liked and she had readily complied. Whether she knew it or not, she had a mouth that was made for more than just kissing.

He glanced over at her, naked and curled beside him with her leg tossed over his. She was luscious temptation, even asleep. It wouldn't take much for him to shift a little and ease inside her.

Without a condom? He blinked. What the hell was he thinking? He'd never even imagined making love to a woman without wearing protection, regardless of what form of protection she was using. That wasn't Adrian Westmoreland's way. But it also wasn't his way to let a woman spend the night at his place, either. For any reason. However, she had. And why did it look as if she belonged here, naked in his bed beside him?

Not liking the direction of his thoughts, he gently detangled her leg from his before quietly easing out of the bed. While sliding into his pj bottoms he glanced over at her. Immediately, he got hard. Trinity was too damn desirable for her own good. After making love to her, she had become an itch he wanted to scratch again and again.

Closing the bedroom door behind him, he took the stairs two at a time. He needed a drink, something highly intoxicating. But because tomorrow was a workday, he would settle for a beer instead. And he needed to talk to someone. The two people he could relate to the most were Aidan, his twin, and his cousin Bane.

Aidan was probably asleep and no telling what Bane was up to. Last time they'd talked, Bane was leaving for an assignment and couldn't say where. Adrian had a feeling Bane was enjoying being a navy SEAL.

He tried Bane's number, but when he didn't get an answer, he dialed Aidan. A groggy Aidan answered on the fourth ring. "Dr. Westmoreland."

"Wake up. We need to talk."

It took a while for Aidan to respond. "Why?"

"It's Trinity."

Adrian heard a yawn, followed by yet another one-word question. "And?"

Adrian rubbed a hand down his face. "And I might have gone beyond my boundaries."

There was another pause. This one just as long as the last. "I told you I felt your emotions and they were strong. What did you expect, Adrian?"

"Damn it, Aidan. I expected to have more control, and not to forget Thorn is her brother-in-law. He thinks of her as a sister. Tonight I've been only thinking of one thing." *To get more of her.*

"Now that your common sense has returned, what do you plan to do?"

Adrian sucked in a deep breath. He wasn't at all sure his common sense had returned. What he should be doing was hiking back upstairs, waking Trinity to tell her to get dressed so he could take her to the hospital to get her car. Then, if he really had any sense, he would tell her that pretending to be lovers wasn't working and that she should come up with another plan to get Belvedere off her back. However, he could do none of those things.

"Adrian?"

"Yes?" He took a huge sip of his beer.

"So what do you plan to do?"

Adrian wiped the back of his hand across his lips. "Not what I should be doing." He placed the half-empty beer bottle on the counter. "It's late. Sorry I bothered you."

"It's early and no bother. Just don't get yourself into any trouble. I'm not there to bail you out if you do."

Adrian couldn't help but smile. "Like you ever did. If I recall correctly, most of the time whenever I got in trouble it was because of you, Bane or Bailey."

"All right, if that's what you want to believe."

"That's what I remember."

"Whatever, Adrian. Good night"

Adrian still held the phone in his hand long moments after he'd heard his twin click off the line. He knew Aidan was dealing with his own issues with Jillian, and Adrian pitied him. He wouldn't want to be in his brother's shoes when Dillon and Pam found out Aidan had been messing around with one of Pam's sisters. Everyone knew how protective Pam was of her three sisters.

Probably the same way Tara is of hers.

Adrian picked up his beer bottle and took another swig. He didn't want to think about overprotective sisters tonight. But then, what he did want to think about was liable to get him in trouble.

Going back to bed was out of the question. Since he wasn't sleepy, he went into his office to get a jump start on the day's work. In addition to the mall complex on Amelia Island, they were looking at building another hotel and mall in Dallas.

In other words, he had too many things on his plate to be standing in his kitchen at four in the morning, remembering how great it felt being between Trinity's luscious pair of legs.

Sunlight hit Trinity in the face. She snatched open her eyes. Glancing around the room she remembered in vivid detail what had happened in this bed.

She moved and immediately felt soreness in her inner muscles, reminding her of the intensity of the lovemaking she and Adrian had shared. And she had screamed. More than once. The look on his face had been irritatingly smug. Too darn arrogant and self-satisfied to suit her.

And speaking of conceited eye candy, where was he? Why was she in his bed alone? Flashes of what had gone down last night kept passing through her mind. Actually, *she* had gone down.

She vividly recalled taking the thick, throbbing length of him in her hand, marveling at its size, shape and hardness, fascinated by the thick bulging veins. She had leaned down to kiss it, but once her lips were there, she had opened her mouth wide and taken him inside. That was the first time she'd done such a thing and now the memories set every nerve ending inside her body on fire.

A sound from downstairs cut into her thoughts. Was that

the shower running in one of the guest bedrooms downstairs? It was still early, not even six o'clock. Why was Adrian using the shower downstairs instead of the one he had in his master bath?

A part of her figured she should stay put and wait until he returned to the room. But another part—the bold side she'd discovered last night—wanted to see him now.

Refusing to question what was going through her mind, she eased out of bed. Looking around for her T-shirt, she found it tossed over a chair. Slipping it over her head, she opened the door and proceeded down the stairs, following the sound of the shower.

She opened the guest bedroom door. It was just as nice as the room she'd used. Nerves made her hesitate when she reached the bathroom door, but she didn't announce her presence. Instead she pushed the door open and stepped inside.

Adrian stood inside the shower stall as jets of water gushed over his naked body. She placed her hand to her throat. *Oh, my.* Water ran from his close-cropped hair to broad shoulders, a powerful chest and muscular legs. The area between her own legs throbbed just like the night before. Maybe worse.

She leaned back against the vanity, and continued to stare at him. She might as well get an eyeful since he hadn't detected her presence yet. His back was to her and those masculine wet butt cheeks were definitely worth ogling. She couldn't help but appreciate how they clenched and tightened whenever he raised his hands to wash under his arms.

For crying out loud, when did I begin drooling over any man's body?

Even as she asked herself that question, she knew she'd never drooled over anyone until Adrian.

He must have heard a sound—probably the pounding in

her chest—because he turned around. The moment their gazes locked, a surge of sexual energy jolted her.

He opened the shower door. With water dripping from his body, he said, "Join me."

Need spread through her as she moved toward the shower stall, pausing briefly to whip the T-shirt over her head and toss it aside.

The moment she stepped into the shower, he joined her mouth with his, burying his long, strong fingers into her hair. Water washed over them. Closing her eyes, she sighed when the taste of his tongue met with hers. Awareness of him touched every pore of her body. Her desire for him was burning her to the core.

He let go of her hair, his hands cupping her face as he kissed her as though his very life depended on it. The kiss was everything she'd come to expect from him— dominating, powerful and methodically thorough.

He dropped his hands from her face and wrapped strong arms around her, bringing her wet body closer to his as water rained down on them. He ended the kiss then reached behind him to grab the soap and begin lathering both their bodies. He ran his hands up her arms, around her back and gave special attention to her buttocks and thighs. Her heart rate escalated with every glide of his hands.

Then he lifted her and pressed her back against the marble wall.

"Wrap your legs around me."

Automatically she obeyed, feeling his hard length against her stomach. He tilted her body, widening the opening of her legs, and in one smooth sweep, slid inside her. She felt every inch of him as he drove into her deeper.

Warm water sprayed down as he pumped hard and fast. She clung to him, digging her fingernails into his back. Her body wanted even more. Somehow Adrian knew it, and he gave it to her. His hand slid under her bottom, touching the spot he wanted, right where their bodies were joined. He stroked her there.

She couldn't take any more. She sank her teeth into his shoulder. Her action drove him on, unleashing the erotic beast in him. He released a deep, throaty groan that triggered a response inside her.

She screamed his name, then sobbed when spasms took her deeper into sexual paradise. The magnitude of the pleasure made her scream again.

And even with water pouring down on them, she felt him spill inside her. Hot, molten liquid flooded her, messing with her senses and jumbling her sanity.

She met his gaze. "More."

That single word pushed him, making him hard all over again. The feel of him stretching her even more than before had her thighs and backside trembling.

Then he moved again, going in and out of her in quick, even thrusts, a sinfully erotic hammering of his hips. He stared down at her, the intensity and desire that filled his eyes more torture than she could bear.

"Adrian."

She murmured his name in a heated rush just before a powerful force rammed through her. She felt each and every sensation, the next more powerful than the last. She bit into Adrian's shoulder to keep from screaming and arched her back to feel it all.

He tossed his head back and called out her name, exploding inside her yet again. He cupped her buttocks and kept coming, giving her the *more* she wanted, what she'd demanded.

"Satisfied?" he asked against her wet lips.

Even after all of that, desire for him was still thick in her blood.

She placed a kiss on his lips as a jolt of sexual pleasure rocked her to the bone. She couldn't help but smile, and then she whispered, "Very much so."

Thirteen

"Didn't you get any sleep last night, Adrian?" Stern Westmoreland asked with a grin. "We expect you to start snoring at any minute."

Adrian blinked. Had he been caught dozing off during a meeting? He glanced around the room and saw the silly grins on the faces of his cousins Riley and Canyon, and a rather concerned look on Dillon's features. Adrian sat straighter in his chair. "Yes, I got plenty of sleep," he lied.

"Oh, then we must be boring you," Canyon observed, chuckling.

Dillon stood as he closed the folder in front of him. "I've caught the three of you snoozing a time or two, so leave him be."

Adrian knew Dillon's words were to be obeyed...for now. But he knew his cousins well enough to know that he hadn't gotten the last of the ribbing from them. He stood to leave with Dillon. He wouldn't dare stay behind and tangle with the three jokesters.

Dillon glanced over at him as they headed down the corridor to their respective offices. "So, how is that situation going with Trinity?"

If only Dillon really knew, Adrian thought, the muscles of his manhood throbbing at the memory. He'd had the time of his life last night and wouldn't be surprised if he really had been dozing during the meeting. He'd gotten little sleep, but the sex had been off the charts. He would even go on record as saying it had been the best he'd ever had. And just to think, she was still practically an amateur.

But he intended to remedy that. Last night might have been their first time between the sheets, but it wouldn't be their last. He wasn't sure how Trinity felt about it, though. She hadn't had much to say this morning during the drive over to the hospital to get her car. In fact, she had taken the time to get more sleep. He'd left her alone, figuring she needed it.

Before he could ask when they could get together again, she had muttered a hasty, "See you later," and had quickly gotten out of his car and into hers. There hadn't been a goodbye kiss or anything.

"Adrian?"

The sound of Dillon's voice cut into his thoughts. "Yes?"

"I asked how that situation is going with Trinity."

"Fine." He tried to ignore the scrutinizing gaze his cousin was giving him.

"And how did things work out a few days ago when Dr. Belvedere requested that she work on her days off?"

Anger flashed in Adrian's eyes. "It was just as I suspected. According to Trinity, Belvedere came on to her again, even mentioned the night he'd seen us out together. He told her to drop me or else."

Adrian saw a mirror image of his own anger in Dillon's eyes. "Did she report it?"

"Yes, but the chief of pediatrics accused her of exaggerating, causing unnecessary drama." Adrian paused. "I met Belvedere face-to-face."

Dillon lifted a brow. "When?"

"Knowing how tired she would be I decided to pick

Trinity up from work yesterday morning. And wouldn't you know it, he was there in her face, insinuating he would be picking her up for a date that night, after having made her work on her days off. It didn't occur to him that she might need to rest."

"What did you do?"

"Not what I wanted to do, Dil, trust me. You should have seen her. She was so exhausted she could barely stand. With self-control you would have been proud of, I introduced myself to Dr. Belvedere as her significant other and told him that Trinity had other plans for the evening. Then we left. I drove her to my place instead of taking her home. I figured Belvedere would be crazy enough to drop by her home, regardless of what I'd told him. Besides, I wanted to make sure she got uninterrupted sleep."

Dillon nodded. "Did she?"

"Yes. She slept all day while I was at work, and it was late when I got in last night after that dinner meeting with Kenneth Jenkins and a movie date with Bailey. But when I got home I could see that she'd gotten plenty of rest."

Dillon nodded again. "Then you took her home?" he asked, giving Adrian another scrutinizing gaze. It took everything Adrian had not to squirm beneath his cousin's intense examination.

"No. It was late, so she stayed the night."

"Oh, I see."

Adrian had a feeling Dillon was beginning to see too much and decided now was the time to make a hasty exit. "Well, I'll check with you later. I have that Potter report to finalize for Canyon."

He quickly walked off but stopped when Dillon called out to him. "Adrian?"

He turned around. "Yes?"

"Will you be available for tomorrow's chow-down?"

Adrian shrugged. "I'm free tomorrow night so there's no reason I won't be there."

Dillon smiled. "Good. It's JoJo's birthday and although she doesn't want to make it a big deal, you know Pam, she will make it a big deal anyway."

"Then I'll make it my business to be there."

"You can invite Trinity to join us if you like."

Adrian stared at his cousin. "Why would I like?"

"No special reason—just a suggestion. Besides, it might be a good idea to give the family an update. If Belvedere keeps it up, we might have to present a show of unity. The Westmorelands have just as much name recognition in this town as the Belvederes."

Adrian nodded. "Okay. I'll give it some thought."

He walked away giving it a lot of thought. Trinity was no longer a pretend lover. Last night he'd made her the real thing.

Trinity sat at her kitchen table finishing her dinner with a cup of hot tea. After Adrian had dropped her off at the hospital for her car, she had driven home, shivered and gone straight to bed. She'd appreciated her second day of nonstop sleep and inwardly admitted she'd been nearly as tired this morning as she had been the day before. Just for a different reason.

She had spent most of last night making love with Adrian. Now it was late afternoon and other than sleeping, she hadn't gotten anything done. Definitely not the laundry she'd planned to do today. Instead she had mentally berated herself for her brazen behavior last night. Who begs a man to ejaculate inside her, for Pete's sake? She cringed each and every time she remembered what she'd said and how he'd complied.

But while her mind was giving her a rough time about it, her body was trembling at the memory. All she had to do was close her eyes to remember how he'd felt inside her—stretching her, pounding into her then exploding inside her.

That's what she kept remembering more than anything. The feel of him exploding. He'd gotten harder, thicker… and then *wham!* His hot release had scorched, triggering her own orgasm.

She tightened her legs together when an ache of smoldering desire pooled right there.

What in the world is wrong with me? she asked herself. *I go without sex for years and then the first time I get a little action I go crazy.*

She took a deep breath, knowing it was more than just getting a little action. More than getting a *lot* of action. She was reacting to becoming involved with a man who knew what to do with what he had. Buffed, toned, sexy to a degree that couldn't even be defined, and on top of that, he knew how to deliver pleasure to the point that he'd made her scream. Lordy, she had screamed her lungs out like a banshee. It's a wonder none of his neighbors had called the police.

To think they had gotten careless and engaged in unprotected sex. Luckily she was on the pill and he had seemed quite relieved about that fact when she had told him later that night. He told her that making love to a woman without using a condom was unlike him. His only excuse was that he had lost control in the moment. She understood because so had she. Once it was established that they were both in good health, he hadn't used a condom for the rest of the night.

She stood now and gathered her dishes to place them in the sink. Then why, after behaving in a way so unbecoming, were her fingers itching to call his number, hear his voice, suggest that he come over?

She shook her head, inwardly chiding herself for letting a man get next to her to this magnitude. Besides, she had to work tomorrow and the last thing she needed was another night filled with sex.

Later she had washed the dishes, cleaned up the kitchen and tackled the laundry when there was a knock at her door. It could have been anyone but the way her body responded signaled it had to be one particular person. Adrian.

She could pretend she wasn't at home but that wouldn't stop the way her heart was beating. Only Adrian had this kind of effect on her and it annoyed her that he knew it.

She crossed the room to the door. "Who is it?" As if she didn't know.

"Adrian."

Why did he always have to sound so good?

"What do you want?"

"Do you really have to ask me that?"

Her heart skipped a beat. How on earth had she gone from a woman who didn't date to a woman who'd made a man's booty-call list? Annoyed by the very thought, she unlocked the door and snatched it open.

She also opened her mouth to give him the dressing down he deserved when suddenly that same mouth was captured by his.

This, Adrian thought as he deepened the kiss, was what he'd been thinking about all day....

She returned the kiss with the same fierce hunger he felt. It was hard to tell whose tongue was doing the most work. Did it matter when the result was so damn gratifying?

He pulled back, ending the kiss. It was either that or take her right there at her front door. A vision of doing just that immediately popped into his mind. Damn, he had it bad.

"You coming here wasn't a good idea."

"I happen to think the opposite," he said, maneuvering past her.

"Hey, wait. I didn't invite you in."

He smiled. "No, but your scent did."

She rolled her eyes as she closed the door. "My scent? What does that have to do with anything?"

He chuckled. "I'll tell you later. This is for now," he said, holding up a bag from a well-known Chinese chain. "I brought dinner."

She crossed her arms over her chest. "Thanks, but I've eaten."

"I haven't. Join me at the table. Besides, we need to talk."

Trinity stared at him and nodded. "Yes, we do need to talk."

She led him to the kitchen and he followed, appreciating the sway of her shapely hips in the cute little skirt she was wearing. He remembered how those same hips had ridden him hard last night.

And then he was drinking up her scent—a scent he remembered from last night. The scent of a woman who wanted a man—and he would admit he was just that arrogant to assume the man was him.

She took a seat at the table while he moved around her kitchen as though he'd spent time in it before. He opened cabinets and pulled out whatever he needed for his meal. From the look on her face he could tell she wasn't thrilled.

"Sure you don't want any?" he asked, emptying the contents of the carton into a bowl. When she didn't respond he glanced over his shoulder and met her gaze. He'd gained the ability to read her well and he smiled when he recalled what he had asked her. The desire in her gaze was her undoing. "I was asking if you want any of *my food,* Trinity. Not if you want any of me. Besides, I already know that you do."

"I do what?"

"Want me."

She stood and narrowed her gaze at him. "You've got a lot of nerve saying something like that."

"Then call me a liar. But be forewarned, if you do, I'll make sure before leaving here to prove I'm right."

Trinity gnawed on her bottom lip. More than anything she would like to call him a liar but knew she couldn't.

Sighing dismissively, she studied the man standing in the middle of her kitchen as if he had every right to be there. It was obvious he had dropped by his place to change clothes. Gone was the designer suit he'd worn that morning. Now he wore a pair of jeans and a V-necked sweater. Blue. Her favorite color. No matter how much she fought her drumming heart, she couldn't get a handle on it.

"Don't look at me like that, baby."

His words made her blink. It was then that she realized just how she'd been looking at him. She glanced away for a moment and then back at him. "I think last night might have given you the wrong idea."

He chuckled. "You think?" he asked, opening her refrigerator.

"I'm serious, Adrian."

"So am I," he said, turning back to her with a bottle of water in his hand. "To be honest, you didn't give me any ideas but you gave me a drowsy day. I dozed a few times in a meeting with my cousins."

Trinity could certainly understand that happening. She shrugged as she sat down. "It wasn't my fault."

"No, it wasn't your fault," he said, coming over to join her at the table with his bowl and bottle of water. "It was mine. I couldn't get enough of you."

She gave him time to sit and say grace, while her mind reeled. Did he have to say exactly whatever he thought? "Well, regardless, no matter how much you couldn't get enough, I think we need to agree here and now that what happened last night was—"

"Don't you dare say a mistake," he said, before opening the water bottle to take a sip.

"What do you want to call it?"

"A night to remember," he said huskily, taking her hand in his.

The instant he touched her, she felt it; the same sensations she'd felt last night. The same ones that had gotten her into trouble. Slowly she pulled her hand from his and looked at him pointedly. "A night we both should forget."

"Don't count on that happening." And then he changed the subject. "So how was your day?" He slid the water bottle he'd taken a drink from just moments ago over to her. "Take a sip. You look hot and it might cool you off."

Fourteen

The next move was hers, Adrian thought, holding Trinity's gaze.

She was obviously a mass of confusion, saying one thing and meaning another. He knew the feeling. He had walked around the office all day thinking he had gotten carried away last night. Nothing could have been *that* good. But by the time he'd left the office and gone home, he'd admitted the truth to himself. Of all the lovers he'd ever had, Trinity took the cake. Last night had been simply amazing. The best he'd ever had. For a man who'd had his share of lovers since the age of fifteen, that was saying a lot.

Now, since arriving on her doorstep, she had tried to make him think she hadn't enjoyed the night as much as he had. He'd listened and now it was time for action. First, he'd help her acknowledge the truth, which meant admitting they had a thing for each other. And it wasn't going anywhere.

"I don't need a drink to cool off. I'm not hot."

So she was still in denial. "You sure?" he asked, holding her gaze intently.

"What I'm sure about, Adrian, is that our little farce has

gone too far. We were supposed to only pretend something was going on between us."

"And what's wrong with making it the real thing?"

"Plenty. I don't have time to get involved in a relationship, serious or otherwise. My career is in medicine. It is my life. I told you my goal. I'm leaving here. I don't do large cities. I want to return to Bunnell and nobody is going to make me change my plans."

Adrian was thinking she had it all wrong, especially if she assumed he was looking for something permanent. He wasn't. But then, what was he looking for? A part-time bed partner? An affair that was destined to go nowhere? Both were his usual method of operation so why did those options bother him when it came to her?

"I don't want to be a booty call for any man, Adrian."

Now Adrian was confused. She didn't want an exclusive relationship nor did she want a casual one, either. "Then what do you want, Trinity? You can't have it both ways."

She lifted her chin. "Can't I be satisfied with having neither?"

The answer to that was simple. "No. Because you're a very hot-blooded woman. You have more passion in your little finger than some women have in their entire bodies. I can say that because I was fortunate enough to tap into all that fire last night. The results were overwhelming. And now that I have tapped into it, for you to go back to your docile life won't be easy. It's like a sexual being has been unleashed and once unleashed, there's no going back."

He paused, finishing the last of his meal and then pushing the bowl aside. "So what are you going to do about it, Trinity? Are you going to drive yourself crazy and try to ignore the passionate person that you are? Or will you accept who and what you are and enjoy life…no matter where it takes you? It's your life to do with it whatever you want, for as long as you want. So do it."

Adrian could see her mind dissecting what he'd said. He didn't know what her decision would be. He could see she was fighting a battle of some sort within her. For the past few years she had been so focused on her medical career that the idea of shifting her time and attention to anything or anyone else was probably mind-boggling to her. But as he'd told her, after last night there was no way she could go back.

They didn't say anything for a long moment. They merely sat staring at each other. He was certain she was feeling the sexual tension building between them. The desire in her eyes was unmistakable. It made his already hard body harder. But whatever she chose had to be her decision.

Minutes ticked by. Then, as he watched, she picked up the bottle of water and slowly licked the rim of the opening—the same place his mouth had touched earlier—before taking a sip. Then she placed the bottle down and licked her own lips as if she'd not only enjoyed the water but the taste of him left behind.

His stomach clenched. The pounding pulse in his crotch was almost unbearable. She had made her decision.

Yearning surged through his every pore and coiling arousal thickened his groin.

When the desire to have her became too strong, he pushed back in his chair and patted his lap, making his erection obvious.

"Come and sit right here."

Trinity felt the pooling of moisture between her legs. It was the way he was looking at her, was the way his huge arousal pressed against the zipper of his jeans. And he wanted her to sit on it? Seriously?

Her gaze slowly moved back to his eyes. She knew he intended for her to do more than just sit. She'd discovered last night that when it came to sex, the man came up with ideas that were so ingeniously erotic they should be patented.

He was right in saying he had tapped into something within her last night, something she hadn't known she possessed. An inner sexual being that he had definitely unleashed.

She would be the first to admit that today, upon waking from her long nap, she had felt the best she'd felt in years. Working off all that stress in the bedroom had its advantages.

So what was she waiting for? As he'd pointed out, it was her life. She could do whatever she wanted, and what she wanted at the moment was *that,* she thought, shifting her gaze back to his groin.

Pushing her chair back, she stood and while still holding his gaze released the side hook of her skirt and shimmied out of it. The look of surprise in his eyes was priceless. She fought back a smile. Did he think he was the only one who could go after what he wanted once his mind was made up?

"You look good."

A smile touched her lips. Evidently, he had no problem with her standing in her kitchen wearing only a tank top and a thong. As if not to be outdone, he stood, kicked aside his shoes, unbuckled his belt and relieved himself of his jeans.

Lordy, was it possible for him to have gotten even bigger since this morning? Her expression must have given away her thoughts because he said, "It's just your imagination."

She frowned, not liking that he knew what she was thinking.

"But why take my word for it? You can always check it out for yourself," he added.

She lifted her chin. "I intend to do just that."

Boldly, she walked over to him and cupped him. He felt engorged, thick, hard. Deciding the outside wasn't telling her everything, she fished her hand beneath the waistband of his briefs.

Oh-h, this was it. She brazenly stroked him. She needed the full length so she shoved his briefs down past his knees and he stepped out of them.

"That's better," she said in a whisper when she had him gripped in her hand once again.

"Is it?"

The throaty catch in his voice was followed by a deep moan when her fingers stroked the length of him from base to tip and back again. She met his gaze and saw the fiery heat embedded in the depths of his eyes. The tips of her nipples hardened in response. "Yes. And I still think it's bigger than last night. That's amazing," she said.

"No, you are."

She smiled, appreciating Adrian's compliment. "What's with all these flattering remarks?"

"I wouldn't say them if you didn't deserve them. I don't play those kinds of games."

So he said, but as far as she was concerned this was definitely game playing. There was nothing else to call it. They weren't having an affair. Not really. And she wasn't into casual sex. At least not the way most would define it. To keep things straight in her mind she *had* to think of what was between them as a game. That would keep her from getting too serious because with every game there were rules. And when it came to Adrian Westmoreland she needed plenty.

First of all, he was a man a woman could give her heart to, and that wasn't a good thing because he didn't want a woman's heart. For him, it was all about sex. He didn't have a problem with that since she was a willing partner with her own agenda. But she had to make sure she didn't slip and mistakenly think that since the sex was so good, there had to be more behind it.

She looked up at him as she continued to intimately caress him. If anyone had told her that one day she would be standing in the middle of her kitchen half naked, stroking the full length of a man's penis, she would not have believed them.

"Enjoying yourself?"

"Yes, I'm enjoying myself. Having the time of my life. How do you feel about now?"

"Horny."

She chuckled. "I have a feeling you were already in that state when you arrived on my doorstep. I'm not crazy, Adrian. You only came here tonight for one thing."

The smile that curved his lips made her fingers grip him even tighter. "Actually, two things," he said.

Before she could ask what that second thing was, in a move so smooth she didn't see it coming, he quickly sat and pulled her onto his lap to straddle him.

He shoved aside her thong and entered her before she could utter any word other than, *"Oh."*

Then it was on. She wasn't sure who was riding whom or who was emanating the most heat. All she knew was that her hips were moving in ways they had never moved before, settling on his length and then raising up just enough to make him growl before lowering again. Over and over. Deeper and deeper. Fast and then slow.

She managed to lean in and kiss the corners of his lips, and then she used the tip of her tongue to lick around his mouth. She got the response she wanted when he grabbed her and thrust deeper.

Then it seemed the chair was lifted from the floor as he began pounding harder and harder into her. He froze, holding his position deep inside her. Her inner muscles clenched him, squeezing him tight. That's when he exploded. She felt it, she felt him and then she came, screaming out his name.

He held firm to her hips, keeping their bodies connected

while they shared the moment. She dropped her head to his shoulder and inhaled his scent. She wrapped her arms around him and felt the broad expanse of his muscular back. Perfect. He was as perfect a lover as could be.

Lover...

Is that what he was to her? No longer a pretend lover but the real thing? For how long? Hadn't she told herself just a few hours ago that this wouldn't happen again? Then why had it?

Because you wanted it, an inner voice said. *You wanted it and you got it.*

She leaned back and their gazes locked. Before she could say anything, he lowered his mouth to hers. The kiss was slow, languid, penetrating and as hot as any kiss could be. His tongue wrapped around hers...or had hers wrapped around his?

Did it matter?

Not when he was using that tongue to massage every inch of her mouth from top to bottom, front to back. The juncture of her legs began to throb again as if they hadn't been satisfied just moments ago.

She broke off the kiss to look into eyes that were dark with desire once again. And she knew this was just the beginning.

Later, Adrian would question how Trinity had managed, quite nicely and relatively thoroughly, to get into his system. He would also question why, after making love to her at least two more times in the bedroom, he was still wanting her in a way he had never wanted another woman.

"Tell me your other reason," she asked, breaking into his thoughts.

She was spread on top of him. Her hair was all over her head, in her face. Her mouth looked as though it had been kissed way too many times. Her eyes were still glazed from a recent orgasm or two, possibly three. She looked simply beautiful.

"My other reason?" he asked, his brow rising.

"Yes, your other reason for dropping by here tonight. You said there were two."

So he had. "Tomorrow night. Do you have any plans?"

She seemed to think about his question for a quick second. "Granted I get to leave the hospital on time without Belvedere finding a reason to make me work late…no, I don't have any plans. Why?"

"I want to invite you to dinner. In Westmoreland Country."

She nervously licked her lips. "Dinner with your family?"

"Yes."

She didn't say anything for a minute. "They know about us?" she asked. "About this?"

He shook his head. "Depends on what part you're referring to. They know I've been your pretend lover, but as far as the transition to the real thing, no."

She pulled back slightly. "What would they think if they found out the truth?"

He chuckled. "Other than thinking Thorn is going to kick my ass, probably nothing."

"Why would Thorn do that?"

"He thinks of you as a kid sister."

She shook her head. "He used to. Now he thinks of me as an adult. I guess he's mellowed over the years."

He wondered if they were talking about the same Thorn Westmoreland. "If you say so. So what about it? Will you go with me to the chow-down tomorrow night?"

"Yes."

For some reason her answer made his night. "I'll pick you up around six, okay?"

"All right. I'll be ready."

Adrian gathered her close to him, thinking, *So will I.*

Fifteen

As Trinity moved through the hospital corridors checking on her patients, she couldn't help but notice she felt well-rested, although for two nights straight she'd participated in a sexual marathon. That she had left Adrian in her bed after a romp of the best morning sex ever was something she tried not to think about, but when she did she couldn't help but smile.

He'd told her he'd wanted to make sure she left for work with a smile on her face and that was one mission he'd accomplished. She was in a cheerful mood this morning and was determined not to let anything or anyone ruin her day, including Dr. Belvedere.

She had seen him when she'd first arrived but he'd been rushing off to the operating room. According to one of the nurses, he was scheduled for surgery most of the day. That only added to her cheerfulness. The less she saw of the man, the better.

She pulled her phone out of her jacket when she heard a text come through. She smiled even wider after reading the message.

Think of me today.

She smiled and texted back.

Only if you think of me.

Adrian's reply was quick.

Done.

She chuckled to herself and put her phone back in her jacket.

"I see something has you in a good mood, Dr. Matthews."

Her body automatically cringed at the sound of Casey Belvedere's voice. He moved to stand in front of her, still wearing his surgical attire. Why wasn't he still in surgery? "Yes, Dr. Belvedere, I am in a good mood."

"And you look well rested," he noted.

"I am." *No thanks to you,* she thought but said, "The nurses said you had several surgeries this morning."

"I do, but the one I just completed was finished ahead of schedule so I have a little time to spare. Share a cup of coffee with me?"

"No, thank you. I need to check on my patients."

"Not if I say you shouldn't."

She lifted her chin and fought a glare. "Surely you're not asking me to put my patients' needs on hold just for me to share a cup of coffee with you, Dr. Belvedere?"

He frowned and took a step closer under the pretense of looking at the chart she was holding. "Don't ever chastise me again, Dr. Matthews. Don't forget who I am. All it would take is one word from me and I can ruin your career before it gets started. And as far as that boyfriend of yours, I meant what I said. Get rid of him. You'll be doing yourself a favor.

"I had him checked out. He's one of *those* Westmorelands. Although he and his family might have a little money, I recall that he, his siblings and his cousin were known troublemakers when they were younger. Nothing but little delinquents. My parents sent me to private schools all my life just so I wouldn't have to deal with people like them. I come from old money, his family comes from—"

"Money that's obtained from hard work and sacrifices," she said curtly, refusing to let him put down Adrian or his family.

Belvedere opened his mouth to say something just as his name blasted from the speaker requesting that he return to the surgical wing. He glared at her. "We'll finish this conversation later." Turning quickly, he was gone.

Trinity felt shaken to the core. The look on Belvedere's face had sent chills up her spine. The man definitely had a problem. If her pretend-lover plan wasn't working and if the hospital administrators and the chief of pediatrics also refused to acknowledge his continued harassment of her, then there was nothing left for her to do but to put in a request to be transferred to another hospital, one as far away from Denver as she could get. She would start the paperwork later today.

"So what do you think?"

After having read Stern's assessment report on the Texas project slated to start in the fall, Adrian smiled. "I think you outlined all the legal ramifications nicely. We were lucky to get top bid on that property, especially since Dallas is booming."

"Yes it is," Stern agreed, dropping down into the chair in front of Adrian's desk. "So, are you joining the family tonight for the chow-down?"

"Yes, and I'm bringing Trinity with me."

Stern nodded. "How are things going with the two of you pretending to be having an affair? Has that doctor backed off yet?"

"No." Adrian spent the next ten minutes telling Stern about Belvedere's treatment of Trinity.

"I can't believe the bastard," Stern railed angrily. "Who the hell does he think he is? He better be glad he's dealing with Trinity and not JoJo. She would have kicked his ass all over the hospital by now."

Adrian fought back a smile knowing that was true. Stern's fiancée, Jovonnie Jones, was not only an ace in martial arts but she could handle a bow and arrow and firearms pretty damn nicely, as well.

"Trinity has to be careful how she handles the situation, man. The Belvedere name carries a lot of weight in this city and the administrators at the hospital refuse to do anything to stop him."

"Why wait for them? I wouldn't even be having this conversation with the old Adrian. He would have whipped somebody's behind by now. He would not allow anyone to mess with his girlfriend."

"Trinity is not my girlfriend."

"But the doctor doesn't know that and he's given you no respect. Who the hell does he think he is to hit on another man's woman? Man, you've mellowed too much over the years."

"Just trying to keep the family's name clean, Stern. You should understand that, considering my history. Besides, Dillon gave me a warning not to take matters into my own hands."

Stern leaned closer to the desk. "As far as I'm concerned, in this case, what Dillon doesn't know won't hurt him."

"I agree," a deep voice said from across the room. "So when can we go kick the doctor's ass?"

Stern and Adrian turned. Towering in the doorway, and looking more physically fit than any man had a right to look, was Bane Westmoreland.

"And you're sure that's what you want to do, Trinity?"

Trinity could hear the concern in her sister's voice and she knew she had to assure Tara she was okay with her decision. "Of course it's not what I want to do, Tara. If I had my way I would finish up my residency in Denver but that's not possible. Putting in for a transfer is for the best."

"You and Adrian pretending to be lovers didn't help, I guess?"

"No. Belvedere expects me to break up with Adrian. He's just that conceited to think I will drop someone for him."

"There has to be another way."

"I wish there was but there's not. I could go beyond the hospital administrators to the commissioner of hospitals for the State of Colorado, but then it would be Belvedere's word against mine. The case might drag out for no telling how long. Or worse yet, he might try to turn the tables and claim I'm the one who came on to him. It will take time and money to prove my case, and I don't have either. All I want to do is complete my residency, not waste time facing Casey Belvedere in court. Besides, if I pursue this, his family might stop the funding for a children's wing that's badly needed at Denver Memorial."

When her sister didn't say anything, Trinity added, "Hey, it won't be so bad. You transferred to another hospital during your residency and did fine. In fact, by doing so you were able to connect with Thorn."

"Yes, but I left Kentucky because I wanted to leave, not because I felt I had to."

"I appreciate all you tried to do," Trinity said after a pause. "Coming up with the idea for me and Adrian to

pretend to be lovers was wonderful. Any other man would
have backed off. But not Belvedere. The word *entitled* is
written all over him. He assumes he has the right to have
me, boyfriend or no boyfriend—how crazy is that?"

She glanced at her watch. "I need to get dressed. Adrian
invited me to the Westmorelands' for dinner tonight. It's
their weekly Friday night chow-down."

"That was nice of him."

"Yes, it was," Trinity agreed.

"Are you going to tell Adrian about the transfer?"

"Nothing to tell yet. I just put in for it today and it will
probably take a few weeks before a hospital picks me up.
I'll mention it when I know where I'll be going. He's been
so nice about everything." She wouldn't tell Tara how their
relationship was no longer a pretense because she knew
even that was short term.

"Well, the two of you won't have to pretend to be lovers anymore now."

No, they wouldn't, Trinity thought. Why did that real-
ization bother her? Trinity pulled herself up from the sofa.
"Okay, Tara, I need to get dressed."

"Tell everyone I said hello and I look forward to seeing
them at Stern's wedding in June."

"I will." Trinity knew if things worked out the way she
wanted with the transfer, by June she would have left Denver and would hopefully be working at some hospital on
the east coast.

After clicking off the phone with Tara, Trinity headed
for the bedroom. She refused to question why she was anxious to see Adrian again.

"When did you get home?"

"Does Dillon know you're here?"

"What's been going on with you?"

"We haven't heard from you in over a year."

Bane Westmoreland grinned at all the questions being thrown at him. "I came straight here from the airport and, no, Dil doesn't know I'm here. I've been busy and you haven't heard from me because of assignments I can't talk about. All I can say is it's good to be home, although I'll only be here for a few days."

Adrian studied his cousin and noted how much Bane had changed over the years. When Bane had left home to join the navy he had been angry, heartbroken and disillusioned. Personally, Adrian had given the navy less than six months before they tossed out the badass Bane. But Bane had proved Adrian wrong by hanging in and making the most of it. Now Bane stood taller, walked straighter and smiled more often. Although there was no doubt in Adrian's mind his cousin was still a badass.

"So where's Dillon? All his secretary would say is that he's away from the office," Bane said.

"He had a meeting with several potential clients and won't be back until later this evening. He's going to be surprised as hell to see you," Adrian said, grinning. He couldn't wait to see Dillon's face when Dillon saw his baby brother. Of all the younger Westmorelands that Dillon had become responsible for, Bane had been the biggest challenge. Dillon was the one who had finally talked Bane into moving away, joining the military to get his life together… and leaving Crystal Newsome alone.

Crystal Newsome…

Adrian wondered if Bane knew where Crystal was or if he even cared after all this time. All the family knew was that the two obsessed-with-each-other teens had needed to be separated. Crystal's parents had sent her to live with an aunt somewhere and Dillon had convinced Bane to go into the military.

"You returned home at the perfect time, Bane," Stern

noted. "Tonight is the chow-down and we're celebrating JoJo's birthday."

Bane smiled. "That's great. How is she doing? I heard about her father's death a while back. She's still your best friend, right?"

It occurred to Adrian that because Bane had been on assignments and hadn't been home since Megan and Rico's wedding, he didn't know about any of the family's recent news—like the babies, other family weddings and the engagements.

Bane had a lot of catching up to do and Adrian couldn't wait to bring his cousin up to date.

Sixteen

Trinity watched herself in the mirror as she slid lipstick across her lips. Why had she gone to such great pains to make sure she looked good tonight when all she was doing was joining Adrian and his family for dinner? No big deal. So why was she making it one?

One second passed and then another while she stood staring at her reflection, thinking of the possible answers for that particular question. When her heart rate picked up, she frowned at the image staring back at her.

"No, we aren't going there. I am *not* developing feelings for Adrian. I am *not!* It's all about getting the best sex I ever had. Any woman would become infatuated with a man who could give them multiple orgasms all through the night, without breaking a sweat."

And she didn't want to think about the times he had sweated. *Lordy!* Those times were too hot to think about.

She turned when she heard her cell phone ring and disappointment settled in her stomach. That special ring meant it was the hospital calling because she was needed due to an emergency. That also meant she would have to cancel her dinner date with Adrian.

She clicked on her phone. "This is Dr. Matthews."

"Dr. Matthews, this is Dr. Belvedere."

Trinity stiffened at the sound of the man's voice and tried to maintain control of her anger. Why was he calling her? Typically, whenever there was an emergency, the call would come from one of the hospital's administrative assistants, never from any of the doctors. Most were too busy taking care of patients.

"Yes, Dr. Belvedere?"

"Just wanted you to know I'll be leaving town for two weeks. They need medical volunteers to help out where that tornado touched down in Texas. They want the best so of course that includes me."

She rolled her eyes. "Is there a reason you're informing me of this?"

"Yes, because when I get back I expect things to change. I'm tired of playing these silly games with you."

Silly games with her? Her body tensed. "You're tired of playing games with me? I think you have that backward, Dr. Belvedere. I'm the one who is tired of your games. I told you I have no interest in a relationship with you. I don't understand why you can't accept that as final."

"Nothing is final until I say so. I would suggest you remember that. When I get back I want changes in your attitude or you'll be kicked out of the residency program."

She wanted to scream that he didn't have to waste his time kicking her out because she was leaving on her own, but she bit back the words. She would let him find that out on his own. Hopefully it would be after the approval for a transfer came in.

"Do whatever you think you need to do because I will never go out with you. Goodbye, Dr. Belvedere."

"We'll see about that. You've got two weeks."

Refusing to engage in conversation with him any longer, she clicked off the phone, closed her eyes and sucked in a deep breath. He had ruined what had started off as a cheerful day, and she simply refused to allow the man to ruin her evening, as well.

Adrian pulled into Trinity's driveway feeling pretty good about today. Bane's arrival had been a surprise for everyone and catching him up on family matters had been priceless. Bane was shocked as hell to find out about all the marriages that had taken place—Zane's especially. And for Bane to discover he was an uncle to Canyon's son Beau was worth leaving the office and sharing drinks to celebrate at McKays.

That was another thing that had been priceless. News that Bane had returned home for a visit traveled fast, and when he walked into McKays it was obvious some of the patrons were ready to run for cover. Bane's reputation in Denver preceded him and it hadn't been good. But some were willing to let bygones be bygones, especially those who'd heard Bane had attended the naval academy—graduating nearly top of his class—and was now a navy SEAL. They took the time to congratulate him on his accomplishments. Everyone knew it had taken hard work, dedication and discipline—things the old Bane had lacked. The badass native son had returned and everyone told him how proud they were of him.

Then there was Bane's reunion with Bailey. Canyon had called to tell her Bane was in town and she'd met them at the restaurant. She was there waiting and one might have thought she and Bane hadn't seen each other in years. Seeing them together, hugging tight, made Adrian realize just how the four of them—him, Aidan, Bane and Bailey—had bonded during those turbulent years after losing their parents. They'd thought that getting into trouble was the only way to expel their grief.

Getting out of his car now, Adrian headed toward Trinity's front door. He couldn't wait to get her to Westmoreland Country and introduce her to Bane. His cousin had heard enough of Adrian's conversation with Stern to know what was going on with Trinity and Dr. Belvedere. Bane agreed with Stern that Adrian should work the doctor over. Specifically, break a couple of his precious fingers. Adrian was still trying to follow Dillon's advice.

Trinity opened the door within seconds of his first knock and all he could say was *wow*. Adrian wasn't sure what about her tonight made him do a double take. He figured he could blame it on her short sweater dress, leggings and boots, all of which put some mighty fine curves on display. Or it could be the way she'd styled her hair—falling loosely to her shoulders.

But really he knew that what had desire thrumming through him was nothing more than Trinity simply being Trinity.

"Aren't you going to say anything?"

He forced his attention away from her luscious mouth to gaze into a pair of adorable brown eyes. He took her hand, entered her home and closed the door behind him. "I'm known as a man of few words, but a lot of action," he said in a husky voice as a smile curved the corners of his mouth.

He tugged her closer while placing his hand at the small of her back. They were chest to chest and he noted her heartbeats were coming in just as fast and strong as his. His gaze latched on to the lips he'd been mesmerized by just moments ago. Their shape had a way of making him hard anytime he concentrated on them for too long. And tonight they were glazed with a beguiling shade of fuchsia.

He leaned in and licked the seam of her lips. Her heart rate increased with every stroke of his tongue. When her lips parted on a breathless sigh, he took the opportunity to seize, conquer and devour. He hadn't realized just how hungry he was for her taste. How could kissing any woman bring him to this? Wanting her so badly that needing to make love to her was like a tangible force.

She suddenly pulled back, breaking off the kiss. She touched her lips. "I think they're swollen."

He smiled. "Better there than there," he said, moving his gaze to an area below her waist. His eyes moved back up to her face and he saw the deep coloring in her cheeks. Honestly? She could blush after everything he'd done to her between those gorgeous legs?

"Your family is going to know."

He quirked a brow. "What? That I kissed you?"

"Yes."

She was right—his family would know. They had a tendency to notice just about everything. But Bane's surprise visit might preoccupy them. However, his family was his family and preoccupied or not, they had the propensity to pick up on stuff. So, if she thought they could keep what was really going on between them a secret, then she wasn't thinking straight. He decided to let her find that out for herself.

He took her hand. "Ready?"

"I need to repair my lipstick."

"All right."

He watched her walk off toward her bedroom and decided not to tell her that before the night was over, she would be repairing it several more times.

A few hours later Trinity was remembering just how much fun being around a family could be. The Westmorelands, she'd discovered whenever she visited Tara in Atlanta, were a fun-loving group who enjoyed spending time together. And it seemed the Denver clan was no different.

It appeared tonight was especially festive with the return of the infamous Brisbane Westmoreland, whom everyone called Bane. Although he'd mentioned he would be home for only three days before embarking on another assignment, his family already had a slew of activities for him to engage in while he was here.

Bane mentioned he would not be attending Stern's wedding in June, saying he would be out of the country for a while. Trinity figured he would be on some secret mission. He looked the part of a navy SEAL with his height and his muscular build, and he was definitely a handsome man. His eyes were a beautiful shade of hazel that blended well with his mocha complexion. As far as she'd seen, no other Westmoreland had eyes that color. When she asked Adrian about it, he'd said their great-grandmother Gemma had hazel eyes, and so far Bane was the only other Westmoreland who'd inherited that eye color.

Everyone was sitting at the table enjoying the delicious dinner the Westmoreland ladies had prepared. It amazed her how well the women in this family got along. They acted more like sisters than sisters-in-law. Pam had told Trinity that hosting a chow-down every Friday night was a way for the family to stay connected. Earlier, they had gathered in the living room to sing happy birthday to Stern's fiancée, JoJo.

Adrian sat beside Trinity and more than once he leaned over to ask if she was enjoying herself. And she would readily assure him that she was.

"I hope you don't mind, Trinity, but Dillon mentioned the trouble you're having with some doctor at the hospital," Rico Claiborne, who was married to Adrian's sister Megan, said.

She looked down the table to where Rico sat beside Megan and across from Bane. "Yes. Adrian and I thought claiming to be in an exclusive relationship would make him back off, but it didn't. He even had the gall to tell me to end my relationship with Adrian or else." She could tell by the expressions on everyone's faces that they were shocked at Belvedere's audacity.

"Have you thought about recording any of the conversations he's having with you?" Rico asked. "Evidently the man feels he can say and do whatever suits him. There is such a thing as sexual harassment no matter how many hospital wings his family builds."

Trinity nodded. "No, I hadn't thought about it. I assumed taping someone's conversation without their knowledge was illegal."

"That's true in some states but not here in Colorado," Keisha, Canyon's wife, who was an attorney, advised. "Only thing is, if he suspects the conversation is being recorded and asks if it is, you're legally obligated to tell him yes. Otherwise it's not admissible in a court of law," she added.

"Recording his conversations might be something you want to consider, Trinity," Adrian said thoughtfully.

She nodded. It was definitely something she would consider. Although her plan now was to leave Denver and transfer to another hospital, what Rico suggested might be useful if Belvedere tried to block the transfer or give her a hard time about it. At this point she wouldn't put anything past him.

"That might be a good idea," she conceded. "At least I'll have him out of my hair for two weeks." She then told everyone about the phone call she had received earlier from Casey Belvedere and the things he had said. By the time she finished she could tell everyone seated at the table was upset about it.

"Why didn't you tell me about that call when I came to pick you up?" Adrian asked.

She could tell he could barely control his anger. "I didn't want to ruin our evening, but it looks like I did anyway.

Sorry, everyone, I shouldn't be dumping my problems on you."

"No need to apologize," Dillon said, seated at the head of the long table. "The plan that Tara came up with for you and Adrian to pretend to be in an exclusive relationship didn't work, so now you should go to plan B. I agree with Rico that getting those harassing conversations recorded will help."

"I can almost guarantee they will," Rico said, leaning back in his chair. "And I've got the perfect item you can wear without anyone, including the doctor, knowing his words are being recorded. It resembles a woman's necklace and all you have to do is touch it to begin taping. Piece of cake. Let's meet right before the doctor gets back in town and set things up."

Trinity smiled. "Okay. That sounds like a great plan."

"I had such a great time tonight, Adrian. Your family is super. Thanks for inviting me."

Adrian followed her through the door, closing it behind them. He had gotten angry when Trinity had told everyone what Belvedere had said to her, and he hadn't been able to get his anger back in check since. The man had a lot of damn nerve.

"Adrian?"

Upon hearing his name he glanced across the room. Trinity had already removed her jacket, taken off her boots and was plopping down on her sofa.

"Yes?"

"I was telling you how much I enjoyed myself tonight, but you weren't listening. You okay?"

"Yes, I'm fine," he lied, moving to join her on the sofa. Truth of the matter was, he wasn't okay. A part of him was still seething. He had a mind to forget about what Dillon had said and go over to Belvedere's place and do as

Bane had suggested and give him a good kick in the ass. How dare that man continue to try to make a move on his woman and...

It suddenly hit him solidly in the gut that Trinity wasn't *his woman*. However, for the past couple of nights she'd been his bed partner. He cringed at the sound of that. He'd had bed partners before, plenty of them, so why did classifying her in that category bother him?

She twisted around on the sofa to face him, tucking her legs beneath her. "No, I don't think you're fine. There's something bothering you, I can tell. You were even quiet on the drive back here, so tell me what's going on."

It was on the tip of his tongue to reassure her again that he was okay but he knew she wouldn't believe him. He decided to be honest. "Belvedere's phone call has me angry." He shook his head. "He has a lot of damn gall. And what's so sad is that he doesn't see anything wrong with his behavior, mainly because no one has yet to call him out on it. He feels he can get away with it. You should have told me about that call earlier, Trinity."

She frowned. "Why? It would only have ruined our evening. I regret mentioning it at all. The man was behaving as his usual asinine self."

Adrian stared at her, finally realizing the full impact of the crap she'd been going through for the past six months. This hadn't been just a few words exchanged now and then, but bull she'd had to put up with constantly.

He cupped her face in his hands. "Neither you nor any woman should have to put up with that. I don't just want Belvedere gone, but I want the top administrator of the hospital gone as well. The moment you went to him and complained, something should have been done."

"I agree, but that's politics, Adrian, not just at Denver Memorial but at a number of hospitals. That's how the game is played. Some people with money assume their wealth comes with power. The Belvederes evidently fall within that category. They are big philanthropists who support great causes. Only thing is, their gift comes with a price. Maybe not to the hospital who's grateful to get that new wing, but to innocent people…in this case women who are—doctors, nurses, aids. Women they can prey on sexually. Yes, there are laws against that sort of thing, but first the law has to be enforced."

She paused and then added, "I doubt it would have made any difference to Belvedere if I was married. A husband would not stand in the way of getting whatever he wanted. And I bet I'm not an isolated case. There were probably others before me. He's trying to hold my career hostage to get his way. Some other woman might feel forced to eventually give in to him. But not me. However, I know fighting him is useless, which is why I've completed paperwork for a transfer to another hospital."

Thunderstruck, Adrian's blood pounded fast and furious at his temples. "Transfer? You've applied for a transfer?"

"Yes."

His muscles tensed. "To another hospital here in Denver?"

"No. I don't know of any hospital in this city that the Belvedere name is not associated with somehow. I'm hoping to relocate to the east coast, closer to home."

He was quiet as he absorbed what she'd said. In a way he shouldn't be surprised. She'd told him more than once that she didn't like big cities and Denver hadn't really impressed her. All she'd been doing since moving here was putting up with crap. Still…

"When were you going to tell me about the transfer?" he asked. The thought that she had put in for one and hadn't mentioned it bothered him.

"I planned to tell you once I got word it went through.

There was no reason to tell you beforehand. I just put in the paperwork today."

No reason to tell him. Of course she would feel that way since all you are is a bed partner, man.

"But why today? Did something else happen that you haven't mentioned?" When she had left for work this morning she'd been in a good mood. He'd made certain of it.

She shrugged. "Nothing other than Belvedere being his usual narcissistic self. But he did something today that really got to me."

"What?"

She hesitated, as if trying to control her emotions. "I had patients to see, yet he wanted me to forget about their needs to go somewhere and have a cup of coffee with him. How selfish can one man be? I couldn't stand him as a man but after that conversation I no longer respected him as a doctor. It was then that I decided not to put up with it any longer."

"Just like that?"

"Yes, just like that."

He could appreciate her decision since no one—man or woman—should have to put up with a hostile work environment, especially when that environment was supposed to be about the business of caring for people.

"So, if you plan on leaving the hospital anyway, why did you lead Rico to believe you want to record one of those harassing conversations with Belvedere?"

"Because I do. The paperwork for the transfer will probably take a while to get approved. Once he finds out about it he might try blocking it or give me a low approval rating where no other hospital will take me. I can't let that happen. I need leverage and I will get it."

He heard the determination in her voice. She had worked hard for her medical degree. He of all people knew how hard that was since his twin, Aidan, had gone through the process. No person should have the right to tear down what it took another person more than eight years to build.

Adrian agreed that she needed peace of mind in her work, so she didn't have to worry about some crazy jerk trying to force her into his bed. The thought of her leaving Denver and moving on should have no bearing on him or his life whatsoever, but somehow it did.

At the moment, he didn't want to try to figure it out. All he knew was that she didn't need him anymore.

"Since you're moving to plan B, I guess that pretty much concludes plan A," he said, standing. He had been plan A.

She looked up at him, confused. "What do you mean?"

"You're going to expose Belvedere with that recording, so we don't have to pretend to be lovers anymore."

He watched her expression and knew the thought hadn't crossed her mind. She stood, sliding off the sofa in a fluid movement any man would appreciate. She wrapped her arms around his waist. "We stopped *pretending* to be lovers that night at your house, Adrian."

He felt the way her heart was beating, fast and powerful, a mirror of his own. And he saw the look in her eyes, glazed with desire. "Define our relationship, Trinity." He wanted her to establish her expectations.

She nervously licked her lips and his gaze followed the movement. A spike of heat hit him in the gut, making his erection throb. He wanted her and was, as usual, amazed at the intensity of his desire for her.

"It will be an affair with no promises or expectations, Adrian. I'm leaving Denver as soon as the transfer comes through and I won't look back. We're good together. You make me feel things I've never felt before. I want to get it all while I can. I figure the next few years of my life will involve working harder than ever to rebuild the momentum I've lost here. An involvement with anyone won't happen for a long time."

A fleeting smile touched her lips. "That means I need you to help me stock up on all the sex I can get. Think you can handle that?"

Oh, he could handle it, but...

Why did accepting her terms feel so difficult for him? Hadn't he presented the same terms—no promises or expectations—to a number of women? He didn't like being tied down, he liked dating, and he enjoyed the freedom of having to answer to no woman. And he definitely enjoyed sex. So why did her definition of what they would be sharing bother him? He should be overjoyed that she was a woman who thought the way he did.

He looked down at her, and knew he would accept whatever way she wanted things to be. "Yes, I can handle it."

"I knew you could."

She lowered her hands from his waist and cupped him through his pants. He didn't have to ask what she was doing because he knew. She was going after what she wanted, and he had no intention of stopping her.

She undressed him, intermittently placing kisses all over his body as each piece of clothing was removed. And then he undressed her.

"Make me scream, Adrian," she whispered when she stood in front of him totally naked.

"Baby, I intend to. All over the place."

He swept her into his arms and headed toward her bedroom.

Seventeen

"I am definitely going to miss this," Trinity said, collapsing on the broad expanse of Adrian's chest. The memory of a back-to-back orgasm was still vivid in her mind, its impact still strong on her body.

"Then don't go."

She somehow found the strength to raise her head and gaze into a pair of dark brown eyes. Although he had a serious look on his face, she knew he was joking. He had put his social life on hold while pretending to be her lover, and she knew the minute she left Denver it would be business as usual for him.

"You're just saying that because you know I intend to wear you out over the next few weeks," she said, leaning up to lick the underside of his jaw.

She watched him smile before he said, "I'd like to see you try."

Inwardly, she knew there was no way she could try and live to boast about it. The man had more stamina than a raging bull. He definitely knew how to make her scream.

Scream...

She had done that aplenty. It was a wonder her neighbors hadn't called the police. He shifted positions to cuddle her by tightening his arms around her and throwing his leg over hers. It was such an intimate position being spooned next to him. There was nothing like having his still engorged penis pressed against her backside.

She looked over her shoulder at him. "Tell me about your childhood with your cousins. I heard that you, Aidan, Bane and Bailey were a handful." She wouldn't mention that Dr. Belvedere had referred to them as little delinquents.

Adrian didn't say anything for the longest moment, and she began to wonder if he would answer when he told her in a low tone, "You don't know how often over the past eight to ten years that the four of us have probably apologized to Dillon, Ramsey…the entire family for our behavior during the time we lost our parents. That had to be the hardest thing we had to go through. One day they were here and the next day they were gone, and knowing we wouldn't see them again was too much for us.

"But Dillon and the others were there, trying to do what they could to make the pain easier to bear, but the pain went too deep. The state tried forcing Dillon to put us in the system, but he refused, and had to actually fight them in court."

He paused again. "That's one of the main reasons I work so hard now to make them proud of me, to show the family that their investment in my future, their undying love and commitment, didn't go to waste."

She heard the deep emotion in his voice and flipped onto her back to stare up at him. "Were the four of you *that* bad?"

"Probably worse than you can even imagine. We didn't do drugs or anything like that, just did a lot of mischievous deeds that got us into trouble with the law."

"Gangs?" she asked curiously.

He chuckled. "The four of us were our own gang and would take on anyone who messed with us. I truly don't know how Dillon dealt with us. Convincing Bane to leave home for the military was the best thing he could have done. And Bailey finally got tired of getting her mouth washed out with soap because of her filthy language."

"Dillon must be proud of the men and woman the four of you have become."

Adrian smiled. "He says he is, although he considers us works-in-progress. We're older, more mature and a lot smarter than way back then. But he probably can't help but get nervous whenever the four of us get together."

"Dillon seemed relaxed tonight."

"He was to a degree, probably because Aidan was missing. I figure it will be a while before he completely lets his guard down where the four of us are concerned."

"But I'm sure that day will come," she said with certainty. "Now I want to know about your college days. Did you have a lot of girlfriends?"

He chuckled. "Of course. But they could never be certain if it was really me or Aidan they were dating. We're identical and there's only one way to tell us apart."

She lifted a brow. "And which way is that?"

He eyed her as if trying to decide if she could be trusted with such valuable information. "Our hands."

"Your hands?"

"Yes." He held up his right hand. "I have this tiny scar here," he said, indicating the small mark right beneath his thumb. "I got this when I was a kid, trying to climb a tree. Before that, no one could tell us apart. Not even Dillon and Ramsey."

"So you played a lot of tricks on people."

"You know it. Basically all the time. Even freaked out our teachers. We liked dong that. I think the only people who could tell us apart without checking our hands were Bane and Bailey."

Then they talked about her childhood. She practically had him rolling in laughter when she told him how she'd tried to get rid of one of her brother's girlfriends that she didn't like. And she told him of the one and only time she'd gotten into trouble in school.

"You were a relatively good girl," he said.

"Still am. Don't you think I'm *good?*"

He grinned. "No argument out of me."

She returned his grin. "You're a softy."

"No," he said as his gaze suddenly darkened. "I'm hard. Feel me."

She did. Now his erection was poking her in the thigh. If anyone would have told her she would find herself in this position with a man a few months ago, she would not have believed them.

"You leave for work early in the morning—are you ready to go to sleep?"

"I should be ready, shouldn't I?"

"Yes."

She had shared his bed for three days straight now and she couldn't help wondering how things would be when she left Denver and he was no longer there to keep her warm at night. What would happen when those tingling sensations came and he wasn't there to satisfy them?

She felt his already hard penis thicken against her thigh. He'd practically answered the question for her. No, she wasn't ready to go to sleep and it seemed neither was he.

"Have I ever told you how much I love touching you?" he asked, running a hand over her breasts, caressing the tips of her nipples. The action caused a stirring in the pit of her stomach.

"I don't think that you have."

"Then I'm falling down on the job," he said, moving his hand away from her breasts to travel to the area between her thighs. She knew he would find her wet and ready.

"And speaking of *down.*" He shifted his body to place his head between her thighs. After spreading her legs and lifting her hips, his tongue began making love to her in slow, deep strokes.

He held tight to her hips, refusing to let them go. She groaned and as if he'd been waiting to hear that sound, he began flicking his tongue. She grabbed hold of his head to hold him there. *Yes, right there.*

She closed her eyes, taking in the sound of him, the feel of him. This had to be one of the most erotic things a man could do to a woman. And she was convinced no one could do it better than Adrian.

Her body was poised to go off the deep end, when suddenly Adrian released her hips, flipped her around, tilted her hips and entered her in one smooth thrust.

"I like doing it this way," he whispered, taking her in long, powerful strokes as he placed butterfly kisses along the back of her neck.

She liked doing it this way, too. Trinity cried out as spasms consumed her body. He kept going and going and she was the recipient of the most stimulating strokes known to womankind.

When he let out a deep, guttural growl, she felt him, the full essence of him, shoot into her. That's when she lost it and let out a deep, soul-wrenching scream of ecstasy.

Eventually he gathered her into his arms and pulled her to him. Their breathing labored, he cuddled her close to his chest. The last thing she remembered was the deep, husky sound of his voice whispering, "Now you can go to sleep, baby."

And she did.

Several days later, Adrian scanned the room, seeing eager expressions on the faces of his family members. Rico had called this meeting to give them an update. For the past year Rico's PI firm had been investigating the connection of four women—Portia, Lila, Clarice and Isabelle—to their great-grandfather, Raphel Westmoreland.

For the longest time the family had assumed their great-grandmother Gemma was their great-grandfather's only wife. However, it had been discovered during a genealogy search that before marrying Gemma, Raphel had been connected to four other women who'd been listed as his wives.

The mystery of Portia and Lila had been solved. They hadn't been wives but women Raphel had helped out of sticky situations. It was, however, discovered that the woman named Clarice had given birth to a son that Raphel had never known about. Upon Clarice's death in a train accident, that son was adopted by a woman by the name of Jeanette Outlaw. Rico's firm was still trying to locate any living relatives of the child Jeanette had adopted. The news Rico had just delivered was about the woman named Isabelle.

"So you're saying Raphel's only connection to Isabelle was that he came across her homeless and penniless? After she had a child out of wedlock and her parents kicked her out? He gave her a place to live?" Dillon asked.

"Yes. The child was not Raphel's. He allowed her to live at his place since he was not home most of the time while riding the herds. As soon as she got on her feet, she moved out. Eventually, Isabelle met someone. An older gentleman, a widower by the name of Hogan Nelson who had three children of his own. Isabelle and Hogan eventually married. Your grandfather Raphel was introduced to your grandmother Gemma by Isabelle. Gemma was Hogan and Isabelle's babysitter."

Megan nodded. "So that's why Gemma and Isabelle were from the same town of Percy, Nevada."

"Yes," Rico said, smiling at his wife. "It seems your great-grandfather had a reputation for coming to the aid of women in distress. A regular good guy. Of the four women, the only one he was romantically involved with was Clarice."

"Have you been able to find out anything about the family of Raphel and Clarice's son, Levy Outlaw?" Pam asked.

Rico shook his head. "Not yet. That's an ongoing investigation. We traced the man and his family to Detroit but haven't been able to pick up the trail from there."

A few moments later the meeting ended. Adrian was about to leave when Dillon stopped him.

"You okay?"

He smiled at his cousin. "Yes, Dil, I'm fine."

He nodded. "I talked to Thorn last night and he told me about Trinity putting in for a transfer. How do you feel about that?"

Adrian decided to be honest about it. "Not good. I knew she would eventually leave Denver, but she is being forced to leave and I don't like it one damn bit. Denver Memorial has not treated her fairly."

Dillon nodded. "No, they haven't."

Adrian ran a frustrated hand down his face. "I can't help wondering what happens when Trinity leaves. Who will Belvedere target next? He has to be stopped."

Trinity wished the days weren't passing so quickly. Two weeks were almost up and in a few days Casey Belvedere would be returning. She had hoped her transfer would have come through by now but it hadn't.

She had met with Rico and he had given her the necklace and had showed her how it worked. He'd stressed the importance of setting it to record the minute Belvedere began talking. He also said she shouldn't deliberately lead the doctor into any particular conversation. She didn't want to make it seem as if she was deliberately trapping him. It had to be obvious that he was the one initiating the unwanted conversations.

She stopped folding laundry when she received a text on her phone. She smiled when she saw it was from Adrian.

Want to go out to dinner? Millennium Place? ⌐

She texted him back.

Dinner at MP sounds nice.

Great. Pick you up around 7.

Trinity slid her phone back into the pocket of her jeans. Adrian had taken her at her word about wanting to be with him as much as possible. Every night they either slept at her place or she spent the night at his.

The more time she spent with him the more she discovered about him and the more she liked him. He hated broccoli and loved strawberry ice cream. Brown was his favorite color. In addition to mountain climbing, he enjoyed skiing and often joined his cousin Riley on the slopes each year.

Trinity glanced at her watch. Adrian said he would pick her up at seven, which would only give her an hour to get ready. Millennium Place was one of those swanky restaurants that usually required reservations well in advance. Evidently, Adrian had a connection, which didn't surprise her.

At seven o'clock Adrian rang her doorbell and after giving her outfit and makeup one last check in the full-length mirror, she answered the door, trying to ignore the tingling sensations in her stomach.

The sight of him almost took her breath away. He looked dashing in his dark suit. He handed her a red, long-stemmed rose. "Hi, beautiful. This is for you."

She accepted the gift as he came inside. "What's this for?"

"Just because," he said, smiling. "You look gorgeous."

"Thanks and thank you for the rose. And I happen to think you look gorgeous, as well."

He chuckled. "Ready to go? Dinner is awaiting this gorgeous couple."

Smiling, she said, "Yes, I'm ready."

She bit back the temptation to say *"for you always,"* and wondered why she would even think such a thing. She knew it wasn't possible.

Eighteen

Adrian held up his glass of champagne. "I propose a toast."

Trinity smiled and held up hers, as well. "To what?"

"Not to what but to whom. You."

She chuckled. "To me?"

"Yes, to you *and* to me. It was a month ago tonight we went out on our first date. Regardless of the reason, you must admit it ended pretty nicely. You have to admit it's been fun."

"Yes," she said. "It's been fun."

Their glasses clinked. As Adrian took a sip of the bubbly he recalled his conversation with Dillon. On the drive over to pick up Trinity he'd kept imagining how his life would be once she left town.

He placed his glass down and studied her. He'd made a slip a few days ago and asked her not to go. She hadn't thought he was serous. He had been serious. Unfortunately, he and Trinity didn't have the kind of relationship where he could ask her to stay.

Then change it.

He frowned, wondering where the heck that thought

had come from. Before he could dwell on it any longer, the sound of Trinity's voice broke into his thoughts.

"This is a beautiful place, Adrian. Dinner was fabulous. Thanks for bringing me here."

He smiled at her. "Glad you approve."

"I do. And the past two weeks with you have been wonderful, as well. I needed them."

He'd needed them, as well, for several reasons. His eyes had opened to a number of things. She had become very important to him. "Want to dance?"

"I'd love to."

As he led her onto the dance floor he thought of their other nights together. Lazy. Non-rushed. Just what the two of them needed. Usually on workdays they got together during the evenings. They would order out for dinner or settle in with grilled-cheese sandwiches. Once or twice he'd brought work from the office and while she stretched out on the sofa reading some medical journal or another, he would stretch out on the floor with his laptop.

He was aware of her every movement. She felt comfortable around him and he felt comfortable around her. She had allowed him into her space and he had allowed her into his. He'd never shared this kind of closeness with any woman. Frankly, he'd figured he never could. She'd proved him wrong.

And their mornings together had been equally special. He would wake up with her naked body pressed against his after a night of nearly nonstop lovemaking. Usually he woke before she did and would wait patiently for her eyes to open. And when they did, he welcomed her to a new day with a kiss meant to curl her toes.

That kiss would lead to other things, prompting them to christen the day in a wonderful way, a way that fueled his energy for the rest of the day.

And she would soon be leaving.

"How did the meeting with your family go?"

He had mentioned Rico's investigation, and this morning before they had parted he had told her that a meeting had been called. He gazed into her beautiful features as he held her in his arms on the dance floor. He told her everything that Rico had uncovered.

"At least now you know the part all four women played in your great-grandfather's life. I guess the next step is finding those other Westmorelands, the ones from the son Raphel never knew he had. The Outlaws."

"Yes. I think Raphel would want that. My great-grandfather went out of his way to help others. He was an extraordinary man."

"So is his great-grandson Adrian. You went out of you way to help me."

"For what good it did."

"It doesn't matter. You still did it. And I will always appreciate you for trying." She placed her head on his chest and he tightened his arms around her.

Moments later, she lifted her eyes to his and the combination of her beauty, her scent and the entrancing music from a live band made the sexual awareness between them even more potent. As if on cue, they moved closer. The feel of her hands on his shoulders sent heat spiraling through him.

The tips of her breasts hardened against his chest, something not even the material of his shirt could conceal. Wordlessly they danced, his gaze silently telling her just what he wanted, what he would be getting later.

To make sure she fully understood, he moved his fingertips down the curve of her spine. He drew slow circles in the spot he'd discovered was one of her erogenous zones. Whenever he placed a kiss in the small of her back she would come undone. Already he felt her trembling in his arms.

He leaned down, close to her ear. "Ready to leave?"

She answered on a breathless sigh. "Yes."

He led her off the dance floor.

Trinity didn't have to wonder what was happening to her. She was having an Adrian Westmoreland moment. Nothing new for her. But for some reason, tonight was more intense than ever before.

She could attribute it to a number of things. The romantic atmosphere of the restaurant, the delicious food they'd eaten or the handsome man who was whisking through traffic to get her home. From the moment Adrian had picked her up for dinner, he had been attentive, charming and more sexually appealing than any man had a right to be.

All through dinner she had watched him watching her. The buildup of sexual awareness had been slow and deliberate. She'd discovered Westmoreland men had a certain kind of charisma and there was nothing any woman could do about it. Except enjoy it.

And she had. All through dinner she had known she was the object of his fascination. He had captivated her with an appeal that wouldn't be denied. Now, as far as she was concerned, they couldn't get back to her place fast enough.

It was then that she noticed they weren't returning to her home. Otherwise, he would have gotten off the interstate exits ago. He was taking her to his place.

She glanced over at him, and as if reading her thoughts, he briefly took his gaze off the road. "I want you in *my* bed."

His words made her already hot body that much hotter. She gave him a smile. "Does it matter whose bed?"

"Tonight it does."

She was still pondering his response when he opened the door to his condo a few minutes later. Usually, whenever she visited Adrian's place, she took in the view of the majestic beauty of the surrounding mountains. But not tonight.

Tonight, her entire focus was on one man.

He closed the door behind them, locking them in. He beckoned her with his eyes, mesmerizing her. He was challenging her in a way she'd never been challenged before. And it wasn't all physical. Why was he going after the emotional, as well?

Before she could give that question any more thought, he began moving toward her in slow, deliberate steps. As she watched him, a rush of heat raced through her. The look in his eyes was intense, hypnotic, gripping.

When he stopped in front of her, undefinable feelings bombarded her. She'd never felt this way before, at least not to this degree. She reached out and pushed the jacket from his shoulders.

And then she kissed him all over his face while unbuttoning his shirt. An inner voice told her to slow down, but she couldn't. Their time together was limited. When her transfer was approved she would be leaving. Within hours, if she had her way. She'd already begun packing, telling herself the sooner Denver was behind her the better. But now she wasn't so sure. She had that one nagging doubt... only because of Adrian.

When she reached for his belt, he said, "Let me."

So she did, watching as he stripped off the rest of his clothes before he turned and stripped off hers. Then he carried her into the bedroom.

There was something about his lovemaking tonight that stirred everything inside her. His kisses were demanding, his hands strong yet gentle. His tongue licked every inch of her body, reducing her to a mass of trembling need.

When she thought she couldn't possibly endure any more of his foreplay and survive, he entered her, thrusting deeper than she thought possible. He looked down into her eyes and she felt something…she wasn't sure what. In response, she cupped his face in her hand. "Make me scream."

He did more than that. Before it was over, she'd clawed his back and left her teeth prints on his shoulder. She was totally undone. Out of control. His thrusts were powerful and her hips moved in rhythm with his strokes, in perfect sync.

Over and over he brought her to the brink of ecstasy, then he'd deliberately snatch her back. His finger inched up toward that particular area of her back and she let out a moan knowing what was about to come.

"Now!"

With his husky command, her body exploded and she ground against his manhood as she screamed his name. It seemed her scream spurred him to greater heights because his thrusts became even more forceful.

He threw his head back and his body began quivering with his own orgasm. She felt the thick richness of his release jutting through her entire body. She was suddenly stunned by the force of need that overtook her, made her come again as he once again carried her to great heights from this world and beyond.

Moments later when she slumped against him, weak as water, limp as a noodle, she knew her world would not be the same without him in it.

Nineteen

"You're looking rather well, Dr. Matthews."

Trinity's skin crawled. She'd known when she arrived at work this morning that her and Dr. Belvedere's paths would cross. This was his first day back at the hospital since returning to the city. She just hadn't expected him to approach her so soon. It wasn't even ten o'clock. She was wearing the necklace recorder and it was set.

"Thank you, Dr. Belvedere. I take it your trip to Texas went well."

"Of course it did. But what I want to know about is this foolishness I've heard. You've put in for a transfer?"

"Yes, sir, you heard correctly. More than once over the past six months you've made unwanted advances toward me. I've told you I'm not interested, and that I'm already involved with someone. Yet you refuse to accept my words. I feel I have no choice but to work at another hospital."

A smile touched his features. "Yes, you've made it clear that you're not interested in sleeping with me, but it doesn't matter what you want, Doctor. It's all about what I want, which is to engage in a sexual relationship with you. Only then will I be satisfied enough to let you continue your work here."

Trinity wanted him to make things perfectly clear…for the record. "Are you saying you will never let me do my job here unless I sleep with you?"

"That's precisely what I'm saying, Dr. Matthews. And it won't do you any good to report me. No one will say anything to me. They need that children's wing and my family is making sure they get it. You should consider our little tryst something for the cause. You'll be doing all those sick kiddies a favor."

"I refuse to believe there is no one here at the hospital who will put you in check."

He chuckled. "Believe it. It doesn't matter who you talk to. I am a Belvedere and I do as I please. Haven't you learned that yet?"

"I refuse to be sexually harassed, which is why I put in for that transfer."

"Unfortunately you won't be getting it. I talked to Dr. Fowler this morning and he agrees with me. Your transfer will be denied."

Anger flared within Trinity. "You can't do that. I am a good doctor."

"I can and I will. And as far as being a good doctor, show up at my place tonight and prove just how *good* you are. Seven o'clock sharp and don't be late. I'll even leave the door unlocked for you. Just find your way to my bedroom and come prepared to stay all night. I've already arranged for you to have tomorrow off. You're going to need it." Then he turned and walked away with a smug look on his face.

It took Trinity a while to gather her composure. Telling one of the other doctors that she wasn't feeling well and needed to leave for the rest of the day, she caught the elevator to the parking garage. As soon as she was inside her car she called Rico. "I think I have what we need to nail Dr. Belvedere."

* * *

Trinity called Adrian and he met her at Rico's office where the three of them listened to the recording of Belvedere's conversation with her. It took all of Adrian's effort to contain his anger.

"Well, you're right. This will nail him," Rico said, fighting back his anger, as well. "He'll willingly give you that transfer to keep this recording out of anyone's hands."

"But it shouldn't be that easy for him," Adrian snapped, unable to restrain the rage he felt. "What about other women after Trinity? How long will it take before he's hitting on another woman? Forcing her to do sexual favors against her will? Do you honestly think getting his hand spanked for coming on to Trinity will make much difference?"

Rico met Adrian's gaze. "No. But unless Trinity is willing to go public by filing a sexual harassment lawsuit, there's nothing else we can do."

Adrian turned to Trinity. "Are you willing to do that?"

She shook her head. "No, Adrian. At this point all I want is my transfer. I don't have the money to go against him and I could ruin my reputation and my medical career if I were to lose the case. I don't want to even imagine the legal fees. Even with this recording, I doubt fighting it will do any good. His family has too much power."

Adrian glanced over at Rico who shrugged. "The Belvederes do have power, Adrian. And it seems they have been allowed to get away with stuff for so long, it will merely be a matter of buying off certain people. I agree with Trinity, there is a risk she might be forced to stop practicing medicine while the case is resolved, which might take some time. Unless…"

Adrian's brow lifted. "Unless what?"

"Unless we called them out in such a way where they would have no choice but to make sure Belvedere never practices medicine again."

"Strip him of his medical license?" Trinity asked.

"Yes."

She sucked in a deep breath. "It won't happen. His family won't allow it. Right or wrong, they will still back him. In the end they will get what they want."

Trinity stood. "All I want is my transfer to be approved and after listening to that tape I'm certain the hospital administrators won't allow Dr. Belvedere to block it. If they do, then I'll go public."

"I never took you for a quitter, Trinity."

She lifted her chin. She'd known the moment Adrian walked into her house that he was still upset with her. After the meeting with Rico ended, he'd barely said two words.

"You think I'm a quitter because I won't take what Dr. Belvedere did public?"

"Yes. By not doing so you're letting him get away, letting him do the same thing to other women. You have the ability to stop him now."

"That's where you're wrong, Adrian. You heard what Rico said. Going against that family is useless. In the end—"

"You'll risk hurting your medical career. I know. I heard him. Is your career all you can think about?"

His question set a spark off within her. How dare he judge her? "No, it's not all I can think about, Adrian," she said, angry that he would think such a thing. "It's not about me but about the children."

"What children?"

"The sick kids who really need that wing the Belvederes are building. You heard what he said in that recording. If I make waves, they will withdraw their funding."

Adrian stared at her. "The way you're thinking is no better than those administrators at Denver Memorial. They are willing to turn a blind eye to what's going on to keep money rolling in."

"Yes, it's all politics, Adrian. That's the way it's played. It's not fair but—"

"It won't stop until someone takes a stand, Trinity. He was trying to force you into his bed. He expects you to show up at his place tonight. And then he has the gall to give you tomorrow off like he's doing you a damn favor. How can you let him get away with that?"

"He's not getting away with it."

"Yes, he is. All you're doing is demanding that he not block that transfer so you can haul ass from here."

Anger erupted within her. "Yes, I want to leave Denver. Why do you have a problem with that? If I make a fuss the hospital will lose a needed pediatric wing and I could have a ruined career. All you're thinking about is losing a bed partner, Adrian."

He took a step toward her. "You think that's all you are to me, Trinity? Well, you're wrong. I've fallen in love with you. I didn't realize it until I listened to that recording. As I sat there, all I could think about was that jerk disrespecting you. You are a woman whose body I've loved and cherished for the past month. But he only considers you a sex object for his own personal satisfaction."

"You've fallen in love with me?" she asked, not believing she'd heard him right.

"Yes. I hadn't planned to tell you since I know I'm not included in your dreams and goals. But even knowing that, I couldn't stop falling in love with you anyway. Imagine that." Without saying anything else he walked out the door.

Adrian was so angry he couldn't see straight. As far as he was concerned Casey Belvedere had crossed the line big time, and the idea of him getting away with it, or not getting the punishment he deserved, made even more rage flare through him

Trinity was such a dedicated doctor that her concern was for the children who needed that new wing. As far as Adrian was concerned, the Belvedere name didn't deserve to be attached to the hospital anyway. It wasn't as if they were the only people with money.

That last thought had ideas running through Adrian's head. He checked his watch. It was just a little after noon. He decided to run his idea by Dillon and hopefully things would take off from there.

"Adrian actually told you he's fallen in love with you?" Tara asked her sister. "Evidently you forgot to tell me a few things along the way. I wasn't aware things had gotten serious between the two of you."

Trinity sighed. She hadn't told her sister about becoming Adrian's real lover. "If by getting serious you mean sleeping together, then yes. That started weeks ago and we had an understanding. No promises and no expectations."

Trinity started from the beginning and told Tara everything. "So how could he fall in love with me? He knows I hate big cities. He knows I planned to leave Denver after I completed residency. He likes outdoorsy stuff and I don't. He—"

"Don't you know that opposites attract?" Tara asked her. "And when it comes to love, sometimes we fall in love with the person we least expect. Lord knows I had no intention of losing my heart to Thorn, and if you were to ask him, he probably felt the same way about me in the beginning."

Trinity couldn't imagine such a thing. First, she couldn't envision any woman not falling head-over-heels for her handsome brother-in-law. Second, Thorn adored Tara and Trinity refused to believe it hadn't always been that way.

"Well, I have no intention of falling in love with anyone

and I don't want any man to fall in love with me. My career in medicine is all I want."

"I used to think that way, too, at one time, especially after that incident with Derrick," Tara said. "Having a solid career is nice, but there's nothing like sharing your life with someone you can trust, someone you know will always have your back. There's no reason you can't have both, a career and the love of a good man."

"But I don't want both."

"Who are you trying to convince, Trinity? Me or yourself?"

Trinity nervously gnawed her bottom lip. Instead of answering Tara, she said, "I need to go. Canyon's wife, Keisha, offered to be at the meeting at the hospital in the morning and represent me. I need to call her to go over a few things."

"Okay. Take care of your business. And…Trinity?"

"Yes."

"Having a man love you has its merits. You loving him back is definitely a plus."

Adrian spent the rest of the day at the office making calls as he tried to pull his plan together. It wasn't as easy as he originally thought it would be. Most of his friends were in debt repaying student loans. That meant reaching out to family members who were known philanthropists such as Thorn, his cousin Delaney, whose husband was a sheikh, and their cousin Jared, who was a renowned divorce attorney representing a number of celebrities.

Adrian was about to get an international connection to call Delaney in the Middle East when the phone rang. "This is Adrian."

"I've got everything arranged and everyone can attend the meeting. We can meet at McKays," Dillon said.

Adrian glanced at his watch. "Can we make it at eight? I have somewhere to be at seven."

"Okay. Eight o'clock will work."

"Thanks, Dil. I appreciate it."

Adrian really meant it. Dillon had contacted the board members of the Westmoreland Foundation, a charity organization his family had established to honor the memory of his parents, aunt and uncle. Usually the foundation's main focuses were scholarships and cancer research. Dillon had arranged a meeting with everyone so Adrian could present a proposal to add a children's hospital wing to the list.

He glanced at his watch again and then stood to put on his jacket. It was a little after six. His seven o'clock meeting was one he didn't intend to miss.

At exactly seven o'clock, Adrian walked into Dr. Casey Belvedere's home. The man had left the door unlocked just as he'd told Trinity he would do. Adrian glanced around the lavishly decorated house. At any other time he would have paused to appreciate the décor, but not now and certainly not today.

"You're on time. I'm upstairs waiting," a voice called out.

Without responding, Adrian took off his jacket and neatly placed it across the arm of one of the chairs. He then took his time walking up the huge spiral staircase.

"I've been waiting on you," Belvedere said. "I'm going to give you a treat."

Adrian stepped into the bedroom and discovered Belvedere sprawled across the bed naked. The man's eyes almost popped out of his head when he saw Adrian, and he quickly jumped up and grabbed for his robe.

"What the hell are you doing here? You're trespassing. I'm calling the police."

Ignoring his threat, Adrian moved forward and said, "You disrespected *my* woman for the last time."

Before Belvedere could react, Adrian connected his fist to the man's jaw, sending the man falling backward onto the bed. Adrian then reached for Belvedere and gave him a hard jab in the stomach, followed by a brutal right hook to the side of his face. After a few more blows, he took the bottle of champagne chilling in the bucket and broke the bottle against the bedpost. He tossed the remaining liquid onto Belvedere's face to keep him from passing out.

"Go ahead and call the police—I dare you. If I have to deal with them, I'll make sure the next time I break every one of your damn fingers. Let's see how well you can perform surgery after that."

Adrian left, grabbing his jacket on the way out, and silently thanking Aidan for convincing him to take boxing classes in college.

Twenty

Trinity pulled herself up in bed and ran her fingers through her hair. She couldn't sleep. Her meeting with Keisha had taken its toll on her. They'd covered every legal aspect of the meeting they'd planned to spring on Dr. Belvedere and the hospital administration tomorrow. The element of surprise was on their side and Keisha intended to keep it that way.

Another reason Trinity couldn't sleep was that this was the first time in several weeks that she'd slept alone. She had gotten used to cuddling up to Adrian's warm, muscular body. He would hold her during the night while his chin rested on the crown of her head. She hadn't realized how safe and secure she'd felt while he was with her until now.

She glanced at the clock on her nightstand before easing out of bed. It was not even midnight yet. Keisha had instructed her not to go into work tomorrow. As her attorney, Keisha would call the hospital and request an appointment with the hospital administrator, asking that the hospital attorney, Dr. Fowler, and Dr. Belvedere be present. Just from talking to Keisha, Trinity could tell the woman was a shrewd attorney. Trinity couldn't wait to see how Keisha pulled things off.

When Trinity walked into her kitchen she realized how

empty the room seemed. Adrian had made his presence known in every room of her house and she was missing him like crazy.

If I'm feeling this way about him now, then how will I cope after moving miles and miles away from here?

"I'll cope," she muttered to herself as she set her coffeemaker into motion. "He's just a man."

Then a sharp pain hit her in the chest, right below her heart. He wasn't just a man. He was a man who loved her. A man who had been willing to let her go, to let her leave Denver to pursue her dreams and goals.

Sitting down at the kitchen table, she sipped her coffee, thinking of all the memories they'd made in this very room. Adrian cooking omelets in the middle of the night; them sharing a bowl of ice cream; them making love on this table, against the refrigerator, in the chair and on the counter when they should have been loading the dishwasher.

She knew all the other rooms in her house had similar memories, and those memories wouldn't end once she left Denver. They would remain with her permanently. At that moment she knew why.

She had fallen in love with him.

Trinity sighed as a single tear fell down her cheek. She tried to imagine life without Adrian and couldn't. No matter where she went or what she did, she would long for him, want to be with him, want to share her life with him. What Tara had said earlier was true. *Having a man love you has its merits, but you loving him back is definitely a plus.*

Wiping the tear from her eye, Trinity stood and headed for her bedroom. Adrian was angry with her. He thought she was a quitter. She intended to prove him wrong. This wasn't just about her. Those kids deserved better than a hospital wing from benefactors who routinely abused power.

After talking to Keisha and thinking about what Adrian had said, Trinity had changed her mind. It wasn't just about getting her transfer approved anymore. She knew that Dr. Belvedere had to go, and he could take Dr. Fowler and all those other hospital administrators who had turned a blind eye right along with him. If it meant she had to take them on, then she would do it because she knew she had Adrian backing her up. That meant everything to her.

She picked up the phone. It was late but Keisha had told her to call at any time since she would be up working on the logistics for tomorrow's meeting.

Trinity's conversation with Keisha lasted a few minutes. She quickly stripped off her nightgown, slid into a dress and was out the door.

Adrian was soaking his knuckles and thinking about Trinity. What would she say when she found out what he'd done to Belvedere tonight? As far as Adrian was concerned, the man had gotten just what he deserved. Every time Adrian remembered walking into that bedroom finding Belvedere naked and waiting for Trinity to arrive, Adrian wished he could have gotten in more punches.

He had no regrets about admitting that he loved Trinity. It had been as much a revelation to him as it was to her, but he did love her and the thought of her leaving Denver was a pain he knew he would have to bear. She didn't love him and her future plans did not include him. Now he understood how Aidan had felt when things had ended between him and Jillian. Evidently he and his twin were destined to be the recipients of broken hearts.

Aidan had called Adrian when he'd left Belvedere's place. His brother had been concerned when he felt Adrian's anger. Adrian had assured Aidan he was okay. He had handled some business he should have taken care of weeks ago.

The meeting with Dillon, his brothers and cousins had gone well and they'd unanimously agreed to shift some of

the donation dollars toward the hospital if the need arose.
Adrian knew from Canyon that Trinity was using Keisha
as her attorney and they planned to meet with Belvedere
and the hospital administrators tomorrow. Adrian would
do just about anything to be a fly on the wall at that meeting to see Belvedere in the hot seat trying to explain what
he'd said on that recording.

The police hadn't arrived to arrest Adrian, which meant
Belvedere had taken his threat to heart. Um, then again,
maybe not, Adrian thought when he heard the sound of
his doorbell. It was late and he wasn't expecting anyone.
If it was the police, he would deal with them. He had no
regrets about what he'd done to Belvedere. At this point,
he wasn't even concerned about Dillon finding out about
what he'd done.

He glanced out the peephole to make sure Belvedere
hadn't sent goons to work him over. His breath caught hard
in his chest. It was Trinity. Had Belvedere done something
crazy and sought some kind of revenge on her instead of
coming after him?

He quickly opened the door. "Trinity? Are you okay?"

A nervous smile framed her lips. "That depends on you,
Adrian."

Not sure what she meant by that, he moved aside. "Come
on in and let's talk."

Lordy, did Adrian always have to smell so nice? Trinity
could feel heat emitting from him. At least he was wearing clothes—jeans riding low on his hips. But he wasn't
wearing a shirt and it didn't take much for her to recall the
number of times she had licked that chest.

"Can I get you something to drink?"

She turned around and swallowed as her gaze took in all
of him. She must not have been thinking with a full deck
to even consider leaving him behind.

"Coffee, if you have it. I started on a cup at my place but never finished it."

"A cup of coffee coming up. I could use one myself. We can drink it in here or you can join me in the kitchen."

His kitchen held as many hot and steamy memories as her own. That might be a good place to start her groveling. "The kitchen is fine."

She followed him and, as usual, she appreciated how his backside filled out his jeans. She took a seat at the table. She knew her way around his kitchen as much as he knew his way around hers, although hers was a lot smaller.

Trinity noticed the magazine on the table, one that contained house floor plans and architectural designs. He had mentioned a couple of weeks ago that he would start building on his property in Westmoreland Country sometime next year. She picked up the magazine and browsed through it, noticing several plans he had highlighted.

He had started the coffeemaker and was leaning back against the counter staring at her. Instant attraction thickened her lungs and made it difficult to swallow. She broke eye contact with him. Moments later she looked back at him and he was still staring.

"Nice magazine," she somehow found the voice to say. "You're thinking of building your home sooner than planned?"

He shrugged massive shoulders. "After you leave I figured I needed to do something to keep myself busy for a while. I was thinking that might do it."

She didn't say anything as she looked back at one of the designs he had marked. "I see you marked a few."

"Yes. I marked a few."

When she glanced back at him he had turned to the counter to pour coffee into their cups. She let out a sigh of relief. She doubted she could handle staring into his penetrating dark gaze right now. It would be nice if he put on a shirt, but this was his house and he could do as he pleased. It wasn't his fault she had stocked up a lot of fantasies about his chest.

She turned back to the designs. All the ones he had highlighted were nice; most were double stories and huge. But then all the Westmorelands had huge homes on their properties.

"Here you go," he said, setting the cups of coffee on the table. That's when she noticed his knuckles. They were bruised.

She grabbed his arm, glancing up at him. "What happened to your hands?"

"Nothing."

She let go of his arm and he sat across from her at the table. Her forehead crunched into a frown. How could he say that nothing had happened when she could clearly see that something had?

"What happened to your hands, Adrian?" she asked again. "Did you injure yourself?"

A slight smile touched his features. "No, I did a little boxing."

She lifted a brow. "You can box?"

He nodded as he took a sip of his coffee. "Yes. Aidan and I took it up in college. We were both on Harvard's boxing team."

"Oh." She took a sip of her own coffee. "And you boxed today without any gloves?"

"Yes. I didn't have them with me."

Before she could ask him anything else, he had a question of his own. "So what's going on with you that depends on me, Trinity?"

She placed her coffee cup down, staring into those deep, dark, penetrating eyes. She hoped what she had to say didn't come too late. "Earlier today you said you have fallen in love with me."

He nodded slowly as he continued to hold her gaze. "Yes, I said it."

"You meant it?"

His lips firmed. "I've told you before that I never say anything I don't mean. Yes, I love you. To be honest with you, I didn't see it coming. I wasn't expecting to fall in love, and only realized the extent of my feelings today."

She nodded. What he'd just said was perfect. "In that case, hopefully you won't find what I'm about to tell you odd." She covered one of his hands with hers, being careful of his bruised knuckles. "I love you, too, Adrian. And to be quite honest, I didn't see it coming, I wasn't expecting it and only today—after you left—did I realize the full extent of my feelings."

She watched his entire body tense as he continued to stare into her eyes. Realizing he needed another affirmation, she tightened her hold on his hand and said, with all the love pouring from her heart, "I love you, Adrian Westmoreland."

She wasn't sure how he moved so quickly, but he was out of his chair and had pulled her into his lap before she could respond. Then he was kissing her as though he never intended to stop. A part of her hoped he didn't.

But eventually they had to come up for air. She cupped his face, fighting back tears. "I will remain in Denver with you. Not sure if I'll have a job after tomorrow, but I will be here with you."

"So you won't be leaving?" he asked as if he had to make sure he had heard her correctly.

Trinity smiled. "And leave my heart behind? No way." She paused. "You were right. The children at that hospital deserve a competent staff as much as they deserve a hospital wing. I've already talked to Keisha. I want more than just a guarantee that I'll get that transfer to another hospital. I want to clean house.

"So you might want to think about whether or not you want to have your name linked with mine. I plan to go public with everything Casey Belvedere has done unless he and the hospital administrators agree to leave voluntarily."

Adrian tightened his arms around her. "Don't worry about our names being linked. I am proud of your decision and support you one hundred percent. The entire Westmoreland family does." He then told her of the meeting he'd had with Dillon and his family earlier that day.

More tears came into her eyes as she realized that even when he hadn't known she loved him, he had gone to his family to do that for her. As she'd told him a few days ago, he was an extraordinary man just as Raphel had been.

"Don't worry about how tomorrow will go down. I will be there by your side."

She leaned up and placed a kiss on his lips. "Thank you."

He held her in his arms as if he knew that's what she needed. "When did you realize that you love me?" he asked her.

She looked up at him. "Tonight. When I woke up and you weren't there. I missed you, but I knew it was more than just the physical. I missed the mental, as well. The emotional. I also realized that even if I got the transfer I couldn't endure being separated from you. I knew I wanted a future with you as much as I wanted a career in medicine and that it didn't matter where I lived as long as we were together. You, Adrian Westmoreland, are my dream."

Adrian's features filled with so much emotion that his look almost brought tears to Trinity's eyes.

He crushed her to his chest, whispering, "I love you so damn much, Trinity. It scares me."

She tightened her arms around him and said softly, "Not as much as it scares me. But we'll be fine. Together we're going to make it."

Deep in her heart she knew that they would.

Twenty-One

The next morning Trinity glanced around the hospital's huge conference room. Keisha was seated on her left, Adrian on her right. Dillon sat beside Adrian and a man Keisha had introduced as Stan Harmer, the hospital commissioner of Colorado, sat beside Keisha. Mr. Harmer was responsible for the operations of all hospitals in the state and just happened to be in Denver when Adrian had called him that morning. Things worked out in Adrian's favor because it just so happened that the man was a huge fan of Thorn's.

"You okay?" Adrian asked Trinity.

"It would have been nice to have gotten a little more sleep last night."

He chuckled. "Baby, you got just what you asked for."

She smiled. Yes, she couldn't deny that.

At that moment the conference room door opened and a stocky man, probably Anthony Oats, the hospital's attorney, walked in, followed by Dr. Fowler, who almost stumbled when he recognized Stan Harmer. Both men uttered a quick, "Good morning," before hurrying to their seats.

Trinity noticed that Wendell Fowler refused to look at her. Instead, once seated, he bowed his head and said something to Anthony Oats who chuckled loudly and then glanced her way.

"Don't worry about what's going on across the table," Keisha whispered to Trinity. "They are playing mind games while trying to figure out what we might have other than your word against theirs. They are pretty confident you don't have anything."

Trinity nodded and when she glanced up she saw the man she had met last month, Roger Belvedere, Dr. Casey Belvedere's brother, enter the room. She was surprised to see him. She could tell by the others' expressions that she wasn't the only one.

"Why is Roger Belvedere attending our meeting?" Anthony Oats asked, standing. "This is a private hospital matter."

Keisha smiled sweetly. "Not really, Mr. Oats. And since it could possibly involve the completion of the hospital wing bearing his family's name, I felt it would be nice to include him. So I called this morning and invited him. Besides, there's a chance Mr. Belvedere might be our next governor," she added for good measure, mainly to flatter the man.

Roger Belvedere beamed, and Trinity knew he didn't have a clue what the meeting would be about. He took a seat at the table and glanced around the room. "Where's my brother?" he asked the chief of pediatrics, who suddenly seemed a little nervous.

Dr. Fowler cleared his throat a few times before answering. "He wasn't aware of this meeting until this morning. He wasn't scheduled to work today."

"I wonder why," Trinity heard Adrian mutter under his breath.

"I understand he needed to stop by his physician's office. It seems he was in some sort of accident last night."

Roger raised a brow. "Really? I didn't know that. It must

not have been too serious or he would have contacted the family."

At that moment, the conference room door opened and Casey Belvedere walked in at a slow pace. Trinity gasped, and she wasn't the only one. The man's face looked as though it had been hit by a truck.

Roger was out of his seat in a flash. "What the hell happened to you?" he asked his brother.

"Accident," Belvedere muttered through a swollen jaw. He then looked at everyone around the table. Trinity noticed that the moment he saw Adrian, fear leaped into his eyes.

Trinity wasn't the only one who noticed the reaction. Dillon noticed it, as well, and both his and Trinity's gazes shifted from Dr. Belvedere to Adrian, who managed to keep a straight face. Trinity suddenly knew the cause of Adrian's bruised knuckles and she had a feeling Dillon knew, as well. Adrian had gone boxing, all right, and there was no doubt in her mind with whom.

Dr. Belvedere looked over at Dr. Fowler. "What's going on here? Why was I called to this meeting on my day off? Who are all these people and what is Roger doing here?"

It was Keisha who spoke. "Please have a seat, Dr. Belvedere, so we can get started. I promise to explain everything."

He glared across the table at Keisha as he took a seat. And then the meeting began.

Casey Belvedere was furious. "Surely none of you are going to take the word of this resident over mine. It's apparent she's nothing more than an opportunist. Evidently Mr. Westmoreland doesn't have enough money for her, so she wants to go after my family's wealth."

It took every ounce of Trinity's control not to say anything while Belvedere made all sorts of derogatory comments about her character. Keisha would pat her on the thigh under the table, signaling her to keep her cool. Trinity in turn would do the same to Adrian. She swore she could hear the blood boiling inside him.

At the beginning, when Keisha had introduced everyone present, she had surprised Trinity by introducing Adrian as Trinity's fiancé and Dillon as a family friend.

"I agree with Dr. Belvedere," Anthony Oaks said, smiling. "Mr. Belvedere and his brother are stellar members of our community. It's unfortunate that Dr. Matthews has targeted their family for her little drama. Unless you have concrete proof of—"

"We do," Keisha said, smiling.

Trinity immediately saw surprise leap into both men's eyes.

"Just what kind of proof?" Roger Belvedere asked, indignation in his tone. "My family and I are proud of the family's name. As the eldest grandson of Langley and Melinda Belvedere, I don't intend for anyone to impugn our honor for financial gain."

"You tell them, Roger," Casey Belvedere said.

Keisha merely gave both men a smooth smile. "My client has kept a journal where she has recorded each and every incident…even those she reported to Dr. Fowler where nothing was done." Keisha slid the thick binder to the center of the table.

"And we're supposed to believe whatever she wrote in that?" Mr. Oats said, laughing as if the entire thing was a joke.

Keisha's gaze suddenly became razor sharp. "No. But I'm sure you will believe this," she said, placing a mini recorder in front of her. She clicked it on and the room grew silent as everyone listened, stunned.

Although he'd heard the recording before, listening to it fired up Adrian's blood over again. This was the first time

Dillon had heard it and Adrian could tell from his cousin's expression that his blood was fired up, as well.

"Turn that damn thing off!" Dr. Belvedere shouted. "That's not me, I tell you. They dubbed my voice."

Keisha smiled. "I figured you would claim that."

She then passed around the table a document on FBI letterhead. "I had your voice tested for authentication, Dr. Belvedere, and that is your voice. For the past six to eight months you have done nothing but create a hostile work environment for my client. We didn't have to request this meeting. We could have taken this recording straight to the media."

"But you didn't," Roger Belvedere said, looking at his brother in disgust. "That means you want a monetary settlement. How much? Name your price."

Adrian shook his head sadly. The Belvederes were used to buying their way out of situations. It was sickening. But they wouldn't be able to do that this time, at least not the way they expected. Keisha was good and she was going for blood.

Again Keisha smiled. "Our *price* just might surprise you."

Adrian leaned back in his chair and inwardly smiled. He reached beneath the table and gripped Trinity's hand in his, sending a silent message that things would be okay. The Belvederes would discover the hard way that this was one show they wouldn't be running.

Wordlessly, Adrian opened the door to his home and pulled Trinity into his arms. This had been a taxing day and he was glad to see it over.

Dr. Casey Belvedere would no longer be allowed to practice medicine. He was barred not only in the State of Colorado, but also in any other state, for three years. In addition, he would go through extensive therapy. The Belvedere name would be removed from the hospital wing, but their funding would remain intact.

Dr. Wendell Fowler had been relieved of his duties. In fact, Stan Harmer had pretty much fired him right there on the spot and indicated that Dr. Fowler would not be managing another medical facility in the State of Colorado. Further, sexual harassment training would be required of all hospital staff.

To top it off, a sexual harassment suit would be filed against Dr. Belvedere and the hospital. Roger Belvedere hadn't taken that well since it would be a scandal that would affect his campaign for governor. More details would be worked out.

The money Trinity would get if she settled out of court would be enough to build her own medical complex for children, right here in Denver. But first she had to get through her residency. Her transfer was approved right after the meeting by Stan Harmer, and she had her pick of any area hospital. The man had also said Colorado needed more doctors like her. Doctors with integrity who put their patients before their own selfish needs.

She'd been given a month off with pay to rest up mentally after the ordeal Dr. Belvedere had put her through. Keisha had refused to accept Roger Belvedere's suggestion that everything be handled privately and kept from the media. She had let him know that she would be calling the shots and they would be playing by her rules.

Now, Trinity gazed into Adrian's eyes and his love stirred sensations within her.

"I want you," he whispered as he proceeded to remove her clothes.

Then he removed his own clothes and carried her up the stairs to his bedroom. Standing her beside the bed, he kissed her, tenderly, thoroughly, full of the passion she had come to expect from him.

"I want to take you to your home in Florida," he told her softly, placing small kisses around her lips. "This weekend."

"Why?"

"Don't you think it's time I met your parents? Plus, I want your father to know all my intentions toward his daughter are honorable."

She tilted her head back to look up at him. "Are they?"

"Yes. I want to ask his permission to marry you."

Trinity's heart stopped beating as happiness raced through her. "You want to marry me?"

He chuckled. "Yes. I guess we'll have to get in line behind Stern and JoJo, though. But before the year ends, I want you to be Mrs. Adrian Westmoreland. No more pretenses of any kind. We're going for the real thing, making it legal."

He kissed her again. Tonight was theirs and she intended to scream it away.

Epilogue

"Stern, you may kiss your bride."

Cheers went up when Stern took JoJo in his arms. Sitting in the audience, Trinity had a hard time keeping a dry eye. JoJo looked beautiful and when she'd walked down the aisle toward Stern, Trinity could feel the love between them.

The wedding was held in the Rocky Mountains at Stern's hunting lodge. However, today, thanks to Riley's wife, Alpha, who was an event planner, the lodge had been transformed into a wedding paradise. It was totally breathtaking. Stern and JoJo had wanted an outdoor wedding and felt their favorite getaway spot was the perfect place. Trinity had to agree.

"Miss me?" a deep, male voice whispered in her ear as she stood at one of the buffet tables. Adrian and all of his Denver cousins and brothers had been groomsmen in the wedding.

Trinity turned and smiled. Then her smile was replaced with a frown. "Hey, wait a minute. You aren't Adrian."

The man quirked a brow, grinning. "You sure?"

Trinity grinned back. "Positive. So where is my husband-to-be?"

"He sent me to find you. Told me to tell you he's waiting down by the pond."

"Okay."

Trinity saw Aidan's eyes fill with emotion as he stared across the yard. She followed the direction of his gaze to where Pam and her three younger sisters stood. Trinity had met the women a few weeks ago when they'd come home to try on their bridal dresses. She thought Jillian, Nadia and Paige were beautiful, just like their older sister.

"Aidan? Is anything wrong?" Trinity asked him, concerned.

He looked back at her and gave her a small smile. "No, nothing's wrong. Excuse me for a minute." She watched as he quickly walked off.

It took Trinity longer than she expected to reach the pond. Several people had stopped to congratulate her on her engagement. Most had admired the gorgeous ring Adrian had placed on her finger a few months ago. They would be getting married in August in her hometown of Bunnell. They planned to live in Adrian's condo while their home in Westmoreland Country—Adrian's Cove—was under construction.

She found her intended, standing by the pond, waiting for her. He held open his arms and she raced to him, feeling as happy as any woman could be. He leaned down and kissed her.

"Happy?" he asked, smiling down at her.

"Very much so," she said returning his smile. And she truly meant it.

Once the details of the sexual harassment lawsuit had gone public, the Belvederes, not surprisingly, hired a high-profile attorney who tried to claim his client was innocent. That attempt fell through, however, when other women began coming forward with their own accusations of sexual harassment. So far there were a total of twelve in all. Keisha expected more.

Casey Belvedere was no longer practicing medicine, and Roger Belvedere had withdrawn his name as a gubernatorial candidate. Consumers and women's advocacy groups were boycotting all Belvedere dairy products. Needless to say, over the past few months, the family had taken a huge financial hit.

Adrian took Trinity's hand in his and they began walking around the pond. He needed a quiet moment with the woman he loved. The past three months had been hectic as hell. They had flown to Florida where he had asked Frank Matthews' permission to marry his daughter. His soon-to-be father-in-law had given it.

Now Adrian understood what Stern had been going through while waiting to marry JoJo. More than anything, Adrian couldn't wait for a minister to announce him and Trinity as husband and wife.

"Adrian?"

"Yes, sweetheart?"

"Is something going on with Aidan and one of Pam's sisters?" Trinity asked.

He gazed down at her. "What makes you think that?"

She shrugged and then told him what she'd witnessed earlier.

Adrian nodded. "Yes. He's in love with Jillian and has been for years. No one is supposed to know that he and Jillian once had a secret affair…especially not Pam and Dillon. Aidan and Jillian ended their affair last year."

Trinity stopped walking and raised a brow. "Why?"

He told her the little about the situation that he knew.

"Do you think they will work everything out and get back together?" Trinity asked softly.

"Yes," Adrian said with certainty.

Trinity glanced up at him. "How can you be so sure?"

Adrian stopped walking and wrapped his arms around Trinity. "I can feel his determination, and the only thing I've got to say is that Jillian better watch out. Aidan is coming after her and he's determined to get her back."

Not wanting to dwell on Aidan and his issues, Adrian kissed Trinity once, and planned on doing a whole lot more.

* * * * *

"I'm confused...

From what I've heard," Grace went on, "Cole was the workaholic, Dex, the playboy. Aren't you supposed to be the Hunter brother with a conscience?"

"I grew up," Wynn replied.

"Hardened up."

"And yet you're captivated by my charm."

Her lips twitched. "I wouldn't say that."

"So I dreamed that you came home with me three nights ago?"

"I was feeling self-indulgent. Guess we connected."

"In case you hadn't noticed, we still do."

"I can't regret the other night." She let out a breath. "But, I'm not interested in pursuing anything... rekindling any flames. It's not a good time."

Wynn felt his smile waver before firming back up. "I don't recall asking."

"So, that hand sliding toward my behind, pressing me against you...I kind of took that as a hint."

* * *

One Night, Second Chance
is part of The Hunter Pact series:
One powerful family, countless dark secrets

ONE NIGHT,
SECOND CHANCE

BY
ROBYN GRADY

MILLS & BOON

Published in Great Britain 2014
by Mills & Boon, an imprint of Harlequin (UK) Limited,
Eton House, 18-24 Paradise Road, Richmond, Surrey, TW9 1SR

© 2014 Robyn Grady

ISBN: 978 0 263 91461 0

51-0314

Harlequin (UK) Limited's policy is to use papers that are natural, renewable and recyclable products and made from wood grown in sustainable forests. The logging and manufacturing processes conform to the legal environmental regulations of the country of origin.

Printed and bound in Spain
by Blackprint CPI, Barcelona

Robyn Grady was first contracted by Mills & Boon in 2006. Her books feature regularly on bestsellers lists and at award ceremonies, including the National Readers' Choice Awards, the Booksellers' Best Awards, CataRomance Reviewers' Choice Awards and Australia's prestigious Romantic Book of the Year.

Robyn lives on Australia's gorgeous Sunshine Coast where she met and married her real-life hero. When she's not tapping out her next story, she enjoys the challenges of raising three very different daughters, going to the theater, reading on the beach and dreaming about bumping into Stephen King during a month-long Mediterranean cruise.

Robyn knows that writing romance is the best job on the planet and she loves to hear from her readers! You can keep up with news on her latest releases at www.robyngrady.com.

This book is dedicated to Holly Brooke.
I'm so very proud of you, baby. Aim for the stars!

Prologue

Turning her back on the wall-to-wall mirror, Grace Munroe unzipped and stepped out of her dress. She slipped off her heels—matching bra and briefs, too—before wrapping herself in a soft, scented towel. But when she reached the bathroom door, a chill rippled through her, pulling her up with a start.

She sucked down a breath—tried to get enough air.

I'm an adult. I want this.

So relax.

Let it go.

A moment later, she entered a room that was awash with the glow from a tall corner lamp. She crossed to the bed, drew back the covers and let the towel drop to her feet. She was slipping between the sheets when a silhouette filled the doorway and a different sensation took hold. She hadn't been in this kind of situation before—and never would be again. But right now, how she wanted this.

How she wanted *him*.

Moving forward, he shucked off his shirt, undid his belt. When he curled over her, the tip of his tongue rimmed one nipple and her senses flew into a spin.

His stubble grazed her as he murmured, "I'd like to know your name."

She didn't wince—only smiled.

"And I'd like us under this sheet."

This evening had begun with a walk to clear her thoughts; since returning to New York, she'd been plagued by memories and regrets.

Passing a piano bar, she was drawn by the strains of a baby grand and wandered in to take a seat. A man stopped beside her. Distinctly handsome, he filled out his tailored jacket in a way that turned women's heads. Still, Grace was ready to flick him off. She hadn't wanted company tonight.

To her surprise, he only shared an interesting detail about the tune being played before sipping his drink and moving on. But something curious about his smile left its mark on her. She felt a shift beneath her ribs—a pleasant tug—and her thinking did a one-eighty.

Calling him back, she asked if he'd like to join her. Ten minutes. She wasn't staying long. Slanting his head, he began to introduce himself, but quickly she held up a hand; if it was all the same to him, she'd rather not get into each other's stories. Each other's lives. She saw a faint line form between his brows before he agreed with a salute of his glass.

For twenty minutes or so, they each lost themselves in the piano man's music. At the end of the break, when she roused herself and bid him good-night, her stranger said he ought to leave, too. It seemed natural for them to walk together, discussing songs and sports, and then food and the theater. He was so easy to talk to and laugh with… There was almost something familiar about his smile, his voice. Then they were passing his building and, as if they'd known each other for years, he asked if she'd like to come up. Grace didn't feel obliged. Nor did she feel uncertain.

Now, in this bedroom with his mouth finding hers, she wasn't sorry, either. But this experience was so far from her norm. Was it progress or simply escape?

A year ago, she'd been in a relationship. Sam was a decorated firefighter who respected his parents—valued the community. Nothing was too much for his family or friends. He had loved her deeply and, one night, had proposed. Twelve months on, a big part of Grace still felt stuck in that time.

But not right now. Not one bit.

As her stranger's tongue pushed past her lips, the slow-working rhythm fed a hunger that stretched and yawned up inside of her. When he broke the kiss, rather than wane, the steady beating at her core only grew. She was attracted to this man in a way she couldn't explain—physically, intellectually…and on a different level, too. She would have liked to see him again. Unfortunately, that wasn't possible. This was all about impulse, sexual attraction—a fusion of combustible forces.

A one-night stand.

And that's how it needed to stay.

One

"Beautiful, isn't she?"

Wynn Hunter gave the older man standing beside him a wry grin. "Hate to tell you, but that bridesmaid's a little young for you."

"I would hope so." Brock Munroe's proud shoulders shucked back. "She's my daughter."

Wynn froze; his scalp tingled. Then he remembered to breathe. As his mind wheeled to fit all the pieces together, he swallowed and then pushed out the words. Brock had three daughters. Now it struck Wynn which one this was.

"That's *Grace*?"

"All grown up."

Brock didn't need to know just *how* grown up.

Had Wynn suspected the connection three nights ago, he would never have taken her back to his Upper East Side apartment—not so much out of respect for Brock, who was a friend of his father, Australian media mogul and head of Hunter Enterprises Guthrie Hunter, but because Wynn had despised Grace Munroe when they were kids. She'd made his blood boil. His teeth grind.

How could he have enjoyed the single best evening of sex in his life with that girl—er, woman?

"Grace gets her looks from her mother, like the other two," Brock went on as music and slow-spinning lights drifted around the Park Avenue ballroom, which was decked out for tonight's wedding reception. "Remember the vacation we all spent together? That Colorado Christmas sure was a special one."

Brock had met Guthrie as a Sydney University graduate vacationing at the newly opened Vail Resort. Over the years, they'd kept in touch. When the Munroes and Hunters had got together two decades later, Wynn had turned eight. Whenever he and his older brothers had built a snowman outside of the chalet the two families had shared, Grace and Wynn's younger sister Teagan had conspired to demolish it. Back then, Wynn's angel of a mother had still been alive. She'd explained that the six-year-olds had simply wanted to join in. Be included.

Now Wynn ran Hunter Publishing, the New York-based branch of Hunter Enterprises. Until recently, he had always prided himself on being an affable type. But that Christmas day, when Grace had tripped him up then doubled over with laughter as his forehead had smacked the snow—and the rock hidden underneath—he'd snapped. While she'd scurried inside, pigtails flying, Wynn's brother Cole had struggled to hold him back.

So many years had passed since then and yet, in all his life, Wynn doubted anyone had riled him more than that pug-nosed little brat.

But since then, her mousey pigtails had transformed into a shimmering wheat-gold fall. And her lolly-legs in kiddies' jeans had matured into smooth, endless limbs. He recalled that pest from long ago who had relentlessly poked and teased, and then remembered his mouth working over hers that amazing night they'd made love. When they'd struck up a conversation at that Upper East Side piano bar, Grace couldn't possibly have known who he was.

Could she?

"How's your father and that situation back in Australia?" Brock asked as Grace continued to dance with her partnered groomsman and other couples filled the floor. "We spoke a couple of months back. All that business about someone trying to kill him? Unbelievable." Brock crossed his tuxedo-clad arms and shook his head. "Are the authorities any closer to tracking down the lowlife responsible?"

With half an eye on Grace's hypnotic behind as she swayed around in that sexy red cocktail number, Wynn relayed some details.

"A couple of weeks after my father's vehicle was run off the road, someone tried to shoot him. Thankfully the gunman missed. When Dad's bodyguard chased him on foot, the guy ran out in front of a car. Didn't survive."

"But wasn't there another incident not long after that?"

"My father was assaulted again, yes." Remembering the phone call he'd received from a livid Cole, Wynn's chest tightened. "The police are on the case but my brother also hired a P.I. friend to help."

Brandon Powell and Cole went back to navy-cadet days. Now Brandon spent his time cruising around Sydney on a Harley and running his private-investigation and security agency. He was instinctive, thorough and, everyone agreed, the right man for the job.

As one song segued into another, the music tempo increased and the lights dimmed more. On the dance floor, Grace Munroe was limbering up. Her moves weren't provocative in the strictest sense of the word. Still, the way she arranged her arms and bumped those hips... Well, hell, she stood out. And Wynn saw that he wasn't alone in that impression; her first dance partner had been replaced by a guy who could barely keep his hands to himself.

Wynn downed the rest of his drink.

Wynn didn't think Grace had noticed him yet among the three hundred guests. Now that he was aware of their shared background, there was less than no reason to hang around until she did. It was way too uncomfortable.

Wynn gestured toward the exit and made his excuse to Brock "Better get going. Early meeting tomorrow."

The older man sucked his cheeks in. "On a Sunday? Then again, you must be run off your feet since Hunter Publishing acquired La Trobes two years ago. Huge distribution."

Brock was being kind. "We've also shut down four publications in as many years." As well as reducing leases on foreign and national bureaus.

"These are difficult times." Brock grunted. "Adapt or die. God knows, advertising's in the toilet, too."

Brock was the founding chairman of Munroe Select Advertising, a company with offices in Florida, California and New York. Whether members of the Munroe family helped run the firm, Wynn couldn't say. The night he and Grace had got together, they hadn't exchanged personal information…no phone numbers, employment details. Obviously no names. Now curiosity niggled and Wynn asked.

"Does Grace work for your company?"

"I'll let her tell you. She's on her way over."

Wynn's attention shot back to the floor. When Grace recognized him, her smile vanished. But she didn't turn tail and run. Instead, she carefully pressed back her bare shoulders and, tacking up a grin, continued over, weaving her way through the partying crowd.

A moment later, she placed a dainty hand on Brock's sleeve and craned to brush a kiss on his cheek. Then she turned her attention toward Wynn. With her head at an angle, her wheat-gold hair cascaded to one side. Wynn recalled the feel of that hair beneath his fingers. The firm slide of his skin over hers.

"I see you've found a friend," she said loud enough to be heard over the music.

Brock gave a cryptic smile. "You've met before."

Her focus on Wynn now, Grace's let's-keep-a-secret mask held up. "Really?"

"This is Wynn," her father said. "Guthrie Hunter's third boy."

Her entrancing eyes—a similar hue to her hair—blinked twice.

"Wynn?" she croaked. "Wynn *Hunter*?"

"We were reminiscing," Brock said, setting his empty champagne flute on a passing waiter's tray. "Remembering the time we all spent Christmas together in Colorado."

"That was a long time ago." Gathering herself, Grace pegged out one shapely leg and arched a teasing brow. "I don't suppose you build snowmen anymore?"

Wynn deadpanned. "Way too dangerous."

"Dangerous…" Her puzzled look cleared up after a moment. "Oh, I remember. You were out in the yard with your brothers that Christmas morning. You hit your head."

He rubbed the ridge near his temple. "Never did thank you for the scar."

"Why would you do that?"

Seriously?

"You tripped me."

"The way I recall it, you fell over your laces. You were always doing that."

When Wynn opened his mouth to disagree—six-year-old Grace had stuck out her boot, plain and simple—Brock stepped in.

"Grace has been friends with the bride since grade school," the older man offered.

"Jason and I were at university together in Sydney," Wynn replied, still wanting to set straight that other point.

"Linley and Jason have been a couple for three years," Grace said. "I've never heard either one mention you."

"We lost touch." Wynn added, "I didn't expect an invitation."

"Seems the world is full of surprises."

While Wynn held Grace's wry look, Brock picked up a less complicated thread.

"Wynn runs the print arm of Hunter Enterprises here in New York now." He asked Wynn, "Is Cole still in charge of your broadcasting wing in Australia?"

Wynn nodded. "Although he stepped back a bit. He's getting married."

"Cole was always so committed to the company. A workaholic, like his dad." Brock chuckled fondly. "Glad he's settling down. Just goes to show—there's someone for everyone."

It seemed that before he could catch himself, Brock slid a hesitant look his daughter's way. Grace's gaze immediately dropped. He made a point of evaluating the room before sending a friendly salute over to a circle of friends nearby.

"I see the Dilshans. Should go catch up." Brock kissed his daughter's cheek. "I'll leave you two to get reacquainted."

As Brock left, Wynn decided to let them both off the hook. As much as this meeting was awkward, their interactions three nights ago had felt remarkably right. Details of that time had also been private and, as far as he was concerned, would remain that way.

"Don't worry," he said, tipping a fraction closer. "I won't let on that you and I were already reintroduced."

She looked amused. "I didn't think you'd blurt out the fact that we picked each other up at a bar."

She really didn't pull any punches.

"Still don't want to get into each other's stories?" he asked.

"As it turns out, we already know each other, remember?"

"I didn't mean twenty years ago. I'm talking about now."

Her grin froze before she lifted her chin and replied. "Probably best that we don't."

He remembered her father's comment about there being a person for everyone and Grace's reaction. He recalled how she'd wanted to keep their conversation superficial that night. His bet? Grace Munroe had secrets.

None of his business. Hell, he had enough crap of his own going down in his life. Still, before they parted again, he was determined to clear something up.

"Tell me one thing," he said. "Did you have any idea who I was that night?"

She laughed. "There, see? You *do* have a sense of humor."

As she turned away, he reached and caught her wrist. An electric bolt shot up his arm as her hair flared out and her focus snapped back around. She almost looked frightened. Not his intention at all.

"Dance with me," he said.

Those honeyed eyes widened before she tilted her chin again. "I don't think so."

"You don't want the chance to trip me up again?"

She grinned. "Admit it. You were a clumsy kid."

"You were a brat."

"Be careful." She eyed the fingers circling her wrist. "You'll catch girl germs."

"I'm immune."

"Don't be so sure."

"Trust me. I'm sure."

He shepherded her toward the dance floor. A moment later, when he took her in his arms, Wynn had to admit that though he'd never liked little Gracie Munroe, he sure approved of the way this older version fit so well against him. Surrounded by other couples, he studied her exquisite but indolent face before pressing his palm firmly against the small of her back.

Dancing her around in a tight, intimate circle, he asked, "How you holding up?"

"Not nauseous…yet."

"No driving desire to curl your ankle around the back of mine and push?"

"I'll keep you informed."

He surrendered a grin. He just bet she would.

"Where's your mother tonight?"

Her cheeky smile faded. "Staying with my grandmother. She hasn't been well."

"Nothing serious, I hope."

"Pining. My grandfather passed away not long ago. He was Nan's rock." Her look softened more. "I remember my parents going to your mother's funeral a few years back."

His stomach gave a kick. Even now, memories of his father failing due to lack of sleep from his immeasurable loss left a lump in Wynn's throat the size of an egg. The word *saint* had been tailor-made for his mom. She would never be forgotten. Would always be missed.

But life had gone on.

"My father married again."

She nodded, and he remembered her parents had attended the wedding. "Is he happy?"

"I suppose."

A frown pinched her brow as she searched his eyes. "You're not convinced."

"My stepmother was one of my mother's best friend's daughters."

"Wow. Sounds complicated."

That was one way to put it.

Cole and Dex, Guthrie's second-oldest son, had labeled their father's second wife a gold digger, and worse. Wynn's motto had always been Right Is Right. But not everything about Eloise Hunter was black or white. Eloise was, after all, his youngest brother Tate's mom. With his father's stalker still on the loose, little Tate didn't need one ounce more trouble in his life, particularly not nasty gossip concerning one of his parents running around.

Out of all his siblings, Wynn loved Tate the best. There was a time when he'd imagined having a kid just like him one day.

Not anymore.

Wynn felt a tap on his shoulder. A shorter man stood waiting, straightening his bow tie, wearing a stupid grin.

"Mind if I cut in?" the man asked.

Wynn gave a curt smile. "Yeah, I do."

With pinpricks of light falling over the dance floor in slow motion, Grace tsked as he moved them along. "That wasn't polite."

Wynn only smiled.

"He's a friend," she explained.

What could he say? *Too bad.*

She looked at him more closely. "I'm confused. From what I've heard, Cole was the workaholic, Dex, the playboy. Aren't you supposed to be the Hunter brother with a conscience?"

"I grew up."

"Hardened up."

"And yet you're captivated by my charm."

Her lips twitched. "I wouldn't say that."

"So I dreamed that you came home with me three nights ago?"

She didn't blush. Not even close.

"I was feeling self-indulgent. Guess we connected."

"In case you hadn't noticed," his head angled closer, "we still do."

Her hand on his shoulder tightened even as she averted her gaze. "I've never been in that kind of situation before."

He admitted, "Neither have I."

"I can't regret the other night." She let out a breath. "But, I'm not interested in pursuing anything…rekindling any flames. It's not a good time."

He felt his smile waver before firming back up.

"I don't recall asking."

"So, that hand sliding toward my behind, pressing me in against the ridge in your pants… I kind of took that as a hint." Her smile was thin. "I'm not after a relationship, Wynn. Not right now. Not of any kind."

He'd asked her to dance to prove, well, something. Now he wasn't sure what. Three nights ago, he'd been attracted by her looks. Intrigued by her wit. Drawn by her touch. Frankly, she was right. The way he felt this minute wasn't a whole lot different from that.

However, Grace Munroe had made her wishes known. On a less primal level, he agreed. At the edge of the dance floor, he released her and stepped away.

"I'll let you get back to your party."

A look—was it respect?—faded up in her eyes. "Say hi to Teagan and your brothers for me."

"Will do."

Although these days the siblings rarely saw each other. But Cole was set to tie the knot soon with Australian television producer Taryn Quinn, which meant a family gathering complete with wily stepmother, stalked father and, inevitably, questions surrounding the altered state of Wynn's own personal life.

Until recently, he—not Cole or Dex—had been the brother destined for marriage. Of course, that was before the former love of his life, Heather Matthews, had informed the world that actually, she'd made other plans. When the bomb had hit, he'd slogged through the devastated stage, the angry phase. Now, he was comfortable just cruising along. So comfortable, in fact, he had no desire to ever lay open his heart to anyone again for any reason, sexy Grace Munroe included.

Wynn found the bride and groom, did the right thing and wished them nothing but happiness. On his way out of the room, which was thumping with music now, he bumped into Brock again. Wynn had a feeling it wasn't by accident.

"I see you shared a dance with my daughter," Brock said.

"For old time's sake."

"She might have told you…Grace left New York twelve months ago. She's staying on in Manhattan for a few days, getting together with friends." He mentioned the name of the prestigious hotel. "If you wanted to call in, see how she's doing… Well, I'd appreciate it. Might help keep some bad memories at bay." Brock lowered his voice. "She lost someone close to her recently."

"She mentioned her grandfather—"

"This was a person around her age." The older man's mouth twisted. "He was a firefighter. A good man. They were set to announce their engagement before the accident."

The floor tilted beneath Wynn's feet. Concentrating, he rubbed his temple—that scar.

"Grace was engaged?"

"As good as. The accident happened a year ago last week here in New York."

Wynn had believed Grace when she'd said that their night was a one-off—that she'd never gone home with a man before on a whim. Now the pieces fit. On that unfortunate anniversary, Grace had drowned out those memories by losing herself in Wynn's company. He wasn't upset by her actions; he understood them better than most. Hadn't he found solace—oblivion—in someone else's arms, too?

"She puts on a brave face." Brock threw a weary glance around the room. "But being here at one of her best friends' weddings, in front of so many others who know… She should have been married herself by now." Brock squared his heavy shoulders. "No one likes to be pitied. No one wants to be alone."

Brock wished Wynn the best with his make-believe meeting in the morning. Wynn was almost at the door when the music stopped and the DJ announced, "Calling all eligible ladies. Gather round. The bride is ready to throw her bouquet!"

Wynn cast a final glance back. He was interested to see that Grace hadn't positioned herself for the toss; she stood apart and well back from the rest.

A drumroll echoed out through the sound system. In her fluffy white gown, the beaming bride spun around. With an arm that belonged in the majors, she lobbed the weighty bunch well over her head. A collective gasp went up as the bouquet hurtled through the air, high over the outstretched arms of the nearest hopefuls. Over outliers' arms, as well. It kept flying and flying.

Straight toward Grace.

As the bouquet dropped from the ceiling, Grace realized at the last moment that she was in the direct line of fire. Rather than catch it, however, she stepped aside and petals smacked the polished floor near her feet. Then, as if wrenched by an invisible cord, the bouquet continued to slide. It stopped dead an inch from Wynn's shoes. The room stilled before all eyes shot from the flowers to Grace.

The romantically minded might have seen this curious event as an omen. Might have thought that the trajectory of the bouquet as it slid along the floor from Grace to Wynn meant they ought to get together. Only most guests here would know. Grace didn't want a fiancé.

She was still grieving the one she had lost.

As he and Grace stared at each other, anticipation vibrated off the walls and Wynn felt a stubborn something creak deep inside him. An awareness that had lain frozen and unfeeling these past months thawed a degree, and then a single icicle snapped and fell away from his soul.

Hunkering down, he collected the flowers. With their audience hushed and waiting, he headed back to Grace.

When he stopped less than an arm's distance away, he inspected the flowers—red and white roses with iridescent fern in between. But he didn't hand over the bouquet. Rather, he circled his arm around Grace's back and, in front of the spellbound crowd, slowly—deliberately—lowered his head over hers.

Two

As he drew her near, two things flashed through Grace's mind.

What in God's name is Wynn Hunter doing?

The other thought evaporated into a deep, drugging haze when the remembered heat of his mouth captured hers. At the same instant her limbs turned to rubber, her fingertips automatically wound into his lapels. Her toes curled and her core contracted, squeezing around a kernel of mindless want.

This man's kiss was spun from dreams. The hot, strong feel of him, the taste…his scent…

From the time she'd left his suite that night, she had wondered. The hours she'd spent in his bed had seemed so magical, perhaps she'd only dreamed them up. But this moment was real, and now she only wanted to experience it all again—his lips drifting over her breasts, his hands stroking, hips rocking.

When his lips gradually left hers, the burning feel of

him remained. With her eyes closed, she focused on the hard press of his chest against her bodice…her need to have him kiss her again. Then, from the depths of her kiss-induced fog, Grace heard a collective sigh go up in the room. With her head still whirling, she dragged open heavy eyes. Wynn's face was slanted over hers. He was smiling softly.

In a matter of seconds, he had made her forget about everything other than this. But the encounter three nights ago had been a mutually agreed upon, ultraprivate affair. This scene had been played out in front of an audience. Friends, and friends of friends, who knew what had happened last year.

Or thought that they knew.

Grace kept her unsteady voice hushed. "What are you doing?"

"Saying goodbye properly." With his arm still a strong band around her, he took a step back. "Are you all right to stand?"

She shook off more of her stupor. "Of course I can stand." But as she moved to disengage herself, she almost teetered.

With a knowing grin, he handed over the bouquet, which she mechanically accepted at the same time the DJ's voice boomed through the speakers.

"How about that, folks! What do you say? Is that our next bride-to-be?"

The applause was hesitant at first before the show of support went through the roof. Grace cringed at the attention. On another level, it also gave a measure of relief. Anything—including a huge misunderstanding—was better than the sea of pitying faces she'd had to endure that day.

"If you want," Wynn murmured, "I can stay longer."

With her free hand, she smoothed down her skirt—

and gathered the rest of her wits. "I'm sure you've done enough."

His gaze filtered over her face, lingering on her lips, still moist and buzzing from his kiss. Then, looking as hot as any Hollywood hunk, he turned and sauntered away.

A heartbeat later, the lights faded, music blared again and Amy Calhoun caught ahold of Grace's hand. As Amy dragged her to a relatively quiet corner, out of general view, her red ringlets looked set to combust with excitement.

"Who was *that*?" she cried.

Still lightheaded, Grace leaned back against the wall. "You don't want to know."

"I saw you two dancing. Did you only meet tonight? I mean, you don't have to say a word. I'm just curious, like friends are." Amy squeezed Grace's hand. "It's so good to see you happy."

"I look happy?" She felt spacey. Agitated.

In need of a cold shower.

"If you want to know, you look swept off your feet." The plump lips covering Amy's overbite twitched. "I actually thought that's what he'd do. Lift you up into his arms and carry you away."

Amy was an only child. She and Grace had grown up tight, spending practically every weekend at each other's places on Long Island—dressing up as princesses, enjoying the latest Disney films. Amy still lived and espoused a Cinderella mentality; a happily-ever-after would surely come if only a girl believed. An optimistic mindset was never a bad thing. However, with regard to this situation, Amy's sentimental nature was a bust.

"Wynn and I had met before tonight. It happened." Grace tossed the flowers aside on a table. "It's over."

"Okay." Amy's pearl chocker bobbed as she swallowed. "So, when you say *it* happened, you mean *it* as in…"

"As in intercourse. One night of amazing, mind-blowing, unforgettable sex." Grace groaned out a breath. God, it felt good to get that off her chest.

"Wow." Amy held her brow as if her head might be spinning. "Mind-blowing, huh? That's great. *Fantastic.* I'm just a little—"

"Shocked?"

"In a good way," Amy gave her a sympathetic look. "We've all been so worried."

As that familiar sick feeling welled up inside her, Grace flinched. "No one needs to be."

"I'm sure everyone knows that now. Sam was a great guy…a decorated firefighter from an awesome family. We all loved him. And he loved you—so much. But you needed something to push you to move on."

Those last words pulled Grace up.

But Wynn's invitation to this wedding was based on a lapsed friendship with the groom. He wasn't in the loop, and it was a stretch to think that someone had mentioned a bridesmaid's tragic personal situation over coffee and wedding cake.

Unless her father had said something.

Except the bouquet sliding from her feet across to his had been pure fluke. If not for that, he would never have had the opportunity to… How had he put it? Say goodbye properly. No way had he kissed her to simply show them all that she wasn't as fragile and alone as they might think.

And Wynn certainly wouldn't have swooped in to play superhero if he'd had any inkling of what had transpired the night of that accident a year ago. But the truth had to come out sometime. She only needed to find the right time.

Puzzle it out the right way.

Three days later, as his workday drew to a close, Wynn answered a conference call from his brothers on Skype.

"Bad time?"

Wynn smiled at Dex's laid-back expression and smooth voice. He was the epitome of a Hollywood producer ever since he'd taken over the family's movie unit in L.A.

"I have an easy four o'clock then I'm out of here," Wynn said.

"Off early, mate."

Skyping in from Sydney, Cole looked particularly tan after his sojourn with his fiancée Taryn Quinn on their yacht in the Pacific.

"Good to hear, bro," Dex said. "We all need time to chill."

"How's Dad?" Standing behind his chair, Wynn slipped one arm then the other into his jacket sleeves. That interview with Christopher Riggs—a job interview, and likely placement, based on a recommendation from Wynn's father—shouldn't take long. He'd get ready now to zip out the door as soon as he was done.

"No more attempts on his life since we spoke last," Cole replied, "and thank God for that."

"He's wondering if Tate should come home," Dex said.

"But Brandon thinks it's best to keep him out of harm's way," Cole explained, "at least until he can chase up some leads on that van."

Months back, during the stalker's last attack, Tate had almost been abducted along with his dad. Until the situation was sorted out and guilty parties thrown behind bars, the family had decided to place the youngest Hunter in a safer environment. Tate had spent time with the sweetheart/renegade of the family, Teagan, who lived in Seattle. And right now he was bunking down in Los Angeles with Dex. Tate had been happy with his movie-boss brother, and Dex had been happy with the boy's babysitter, Shelby Scott—in fact, she had recently become Dex's fiancée.

But now that there were leads on the van that had been

involved in that last assault, they might have a break in the case. Tate might soon be able to go home. Excellent.

"Brandon pinned down some snaps taken by a speed camera," Cole went on, "the same day Dad was attacked."

"Don't tell me after all this time he discovered the license plates were legit?" That they'd tracked down the assailant as easily as through a registration number.

Dex groaned. "Unfortunately, this creep isn't that stupid."

"But the traffic shots show the driver pulled over with a flat," Cole added.

"You have a description?" Wynn asked.

"Dark glasses, fake beard," Cole said. "Other than general height and weight, no help. But Brandon did a thorough survey of the area. A woman walking her Pomeranian remembers the van *and* the man. She also recalls him dropping his keys."

Dex took over. "She scooped them up. Before handing them back, she took note of the rental tag."

Leaning toward the screen, Wynn set both palms flat on the desk. "Weren't all the rental companies checked out?"

"The company concerned is a fly-by-nighter from another state," Dex explained.

"Brandon found the guy who ran it," Cole added. "Other than simply hiring out the car, he doesn't appear to be involved. But getting corresponding records was like pulling teeth."

"Until Brandon threatened to bring in the authorities, criminal as well as tax," Dex said. "The guy's got until tomorrow to cough up."

"Great work. So, Tate's staying with you in the meantime, Dex?"

"He and Shelby are as thick as thieves. He loves her cooking. I do, too. You should taste her cupcakes." Sitting back, ex-playboy Dex rested his hands on his stomach and licked his chops. "We're looking at taking the plunge some-time in the New Year. The wedding will most likely be in Mountain Ridge, Oklahoma, her hometown."

"Oh, I can see you now, riding up to the minister on matching steeds like something out of a '40s Western."

Wynn grinned at Cole's ribbing.

"Laugh if you dare," Dex said. "I bought a property that used to belong to Shelby's dad." Dex's tawny-colored gaze grew reflective. "One day we might settle out there for good."

"Away from the hype and glitter of Hollywood?" Wynn found that hard to believe.

"If it means being with Shelby," Dex assured them both, "I'd live in a tar shack."

Wynn was pleased for both brothers' happiness, even if he no longer possessed a romantic thought or inclina-tion in his body.

Barring the other night.

He felt for Grace and her situation. Covert glances and well-intentioned pity over past relationships that hadn't ended well... Painful to endure. Far better to give people something to really talk about. And so, with the entire room's eyes upon them, he'd kissed her—no half measures. After the shock had cleared, however, she'd looked ready to slap his face rather than thank him. It was a shame, be-cause after another taste of Grace Munroe's lips, he'd only wanted more.

Remembering that interview with Riggs, Wynn checked the time. "Guys, I need to sign off. Dad rang a couple of weeks back about giving a guy a job. Background in pub-lishing. Apparently great credentials and, quote, 'a finger on the pulse of solutions for challenges in this digital age.' Dad thought I could use him."

"Sounds great," Dex said. "Should help take some pres-sure off."

Wynn frowned. "I'm not under pressure." Or wouldn't be half so much when the merger deal he'd been working on was in the bag. For now, however, that arrangement was tightly under wraps—he hadn't even told his father about the merger plans.

"Well, it'll be strictly fun and games when you guys come out for the wedding." Pride shone from Cole's face. "You and Dex are my best men."

Wynn straightened. That was the first he'd heard of it. "I'm honored." Then his thoughts doubled back. "Can a groom have two best men?"

"It's the 21st century." Dex laughed. "You can do any damn thing you want."

"So, Wynn," Cole went on, "you're definitely coming?"

Dex's voice lowered. "You're okay after that breakup now, right?"

Wynn wanted to roll his eyes. He'd really hoped he'd get through this conversation without anyone bringing that up.

"*The breakup…*" He forced a grin. "Sounds like the title of some soppy book."

"Movie, actually," Dex countered.

"Well, you'll all be relieved to know that I've moved on."

"Mentally or physically?" Dex asked.

"Both."

"Really?" Cole said at the same time Dex asked, "Anyone we know?"

"As a matter of fact…remember Grace Munroe?"

Cole blinked twice. "You don't mean Brock Munroe's girl?"

"*Whoa.* I remember," Dex said. "The little horror who crushed on you that Christmas in Colorado when we were all kids."

"That's back to front." Wynn set them straight. "I wanted to crush her—under my heel."

"And now?" Dex asked.

"We caught up."

"So, we can put her name down beside yours for the wedding?" Cole prodded.

"I said I've moved on." Lifting his chin, Wynn adjusted his tie's Windsor knot. "No one's moving in."

In the past, these two had nudged each other, grinning over Wynn's plans to settle down sooner rather than later. Now Cole and Dex were the ones jabbed by Cupid's arrow and falling over themselves to commit while Wynn had welcomed the role of dedicated bachelor. Once bit and twice shy. He didn't need the aggravation.

The men signed off. Wynn could see his personal assistant Daphne Cranks down the hall trying to get his attention. She pushed her large-framed glasses up her nose before flicking her gaze toward a guest. A man dressed in an impeccable dark gray suit got up from his chair with an easy smile. Christopher Riggs was almost as tall as Wynn. He had a barrel chest like a buff character from a comic strip. When Wynn joined him, they shook hands, introduced themselves and headed for the boardroom.

"My father seems impressed by your credentials," Wynn said, pulling in his chair.

"He's a fascinating man."

"He worked hard to build Hunter Enterprises into the force it is today."

"I believe it was very much a local Australian concern when Guthrie took over from your grandfather."

"My father ran the company with my uncle for a short while. Two strong wills. Different ideas of how the place ought to run. I'm afraid it didn't work out." Wynn unbuttoned his jacket and sat back. "That was decades ago."

"Hopefully I'll have the chance to contribute something positive moving forward."

They discussed where the company was positioned at the moment, and went on to speak about publishing in general.

Christopher handed over his résumé and then volunteered information about his background. Guthrie had already mentioned that, until recently, Christopher's family had owned a notable magazine in Australia. Like so many businesses, the magazine had suffered in these harsh economic times. The Riggses had found a business partner who had buoyed the cash flow for a time before pulling the plug. The magazine had gone into receivership.

Christopher had a degree, a background in reporting and good references in marketing. Alongside that, he could talk rings around Wynn with regard to web presence statistics and methods, as well as social media strategies aimed at optimizing potential market share.

While they spoke, Wynn tried to look beyond the smooth exterior, deep into the man's clear mint-green eyes. No bad vibes. Christopher Riggs was the epitome of a composed professional. Even in his later years, Guthrie Hunter possessed an uncanny ability to sniff out true talent. Wynn could see Christopher well-placed in his marketing and tech team.

They discussed and then agreed on remuneration and benefits.

"Come in tomorrow." Wynn pushed to his feet. "Daphne can set you up in an office."

The men shook again and, with a bounce in his step, Christopher Riggs headed out.

After collecting his briefcase, Wynn came back into his private reception area. When he said good-night, Daphne held him up.

"These tickets arrived a few minutes ago." She gave him an embossed envelope. "A gift from the producer."

He was about to say that he wasn't interested in Broadway tonight—she was welcome to the tickets—but then he reconsidered.

Daphne was the most efficient personal assistant he'd

ever had. Always on top of things, constantly on his heels…
a bit of a puppy, he'd sometimes thought. Behind the Mr.
Magoo glasses and dull hairdo, she was probably attractive; however, from what he could gather, she was very
much single. He wasn't certain she even had friends. If he
left those tickets behind, chances were they'd be dropped
in the trash when five o'clock rolled around.

So he took the envelope as his thoughts swung to another
woman who was his assistant's opposite in every sense of
the word—except for the being single part.

Brock had mentioned Grace was in town for a few days.
Her hotel was around the corner. As he entered the elevator,
Wynn thought it over. Perhaps Grace had left New York by
now. And hadn't she made herself clear? She didn't regret
that night spent in his bed but she wasn't after an encore.
Grace didn't want to see him again.

As he slid the envelope into his inside breast pocket and
the elevator doors closed, Wynn hesitated, and then, remembering their last kiss, slowly grinned.

What the hell. He had nothing on tonight. Maybe he
could change her mind.

Three

Exiting the hotel elevator, Grace headed across the foyer and then pulled up with a start. Cutting a dynamite figure in a dark, tailored suit, Wynn Hunter stood at the reception counter, waiting to speak with someone behind the desk.

No need to assume he'd come to see her. There were a thousand other reasons he might be here tonight. Business. Friends. Another woman. An attractive, successful, single male like Wynn… Members of the opposite sex would flock to spend time with him.

She'd been on her way out to mull over a decision—whether or not to spend more time in New York before getting back to her job. Late last year she'd left New York to join a private practice in Florida as a speech-language pathologist. Providing tools to help both adults and children with communication disabilities was rewarding work. Just the other week, she'd got an update from a young mom who had needed additional support and advice on feeding her baby who'd been born with a cleft palate. The woman had wanted to let Grace know that the baby's first surgery, which included ear tubes to help with fluid buildup, had been a great success.

Grace had made good friends in Florida, too. Had a nice apartment in a great neighborhood. But she missed so much about New York—minus the memories surrounding Sam and his accident, of course, which seemed to pop up everywhere, constantly.

Except during that time she'd spent with Wynn.

Her lips still hummed and her body sang whenever she thought of the way they had kissed. She wasn't certain that, if she strolled over and started up a conversation with him now, one thing wouldn't lead to another. However, while the sex would be better than great, she'd already decided that their one-night stand should be left in the past. She wasn't ready to invite a man, and associated complications, into her life.

Best just to keep going without saying hi.

He seemed to wait until she was out in the open before rapping his knuckles on the counter and then absently turning around. In that instant, she felt his focus narrow and lock her in its sights. No choice now. She pulled up again.

He crossed over to her at a leisurely pace. People in his path naturally made way for him. In the three days since they'd spoken last, his raven's-wing hair had grown enough to lick his collar. The shadow on his jaw looked rougher, too. And his eyes seemed even darker—their message more tempting.

She remembered his raspy cheek grazing her flesh... the magic of his mouth on her thigh...his muscular frame bearing down again and again to meet her hips. And then he was standing in front of her and speaking in that deep, dreamy voice.

"You're on your way out?"

Willing her thumping heartbeat to slow, Grace nodded.
"And you? Here on business?"

"Your father mentioned you were staying here for a few
days." He waved an envelope. "I have tickets for a show.
We could catch a bite first."

He was here to see her?

"Wynn, I'd really like to, but—"

"You have another date?"

She shook her head.

"You've already eaten?"

No, but suddenly she could taste the rich fudge ice-
cream they'd devoured, eating off the same spoon that night
when they had both needed to cool down.

Grace pushed the image aside. "I'm sorry. This doesn't
work for me."

"Because it's not a good time."

For a relationship of any kind. She nodded. "That's
right."

He seemed to weigh that up before asking, "When are
you leaving New York?"

"I'm not sure. Soon."

"So, worst case scenario—we have a dog-awful time
tonight and you won't need to bump into me again for another twenty years."

It sounded so harmless. And maybe it was.

Brock Munroe was a devoted father to all three of his
daughters. He'd always been there, watching out for their
best interests—doing what he could to help. Did that include organizing some male company to help divert her
from unpleasant memories while she was back in town?

And if her father had gone so far as to suggest this get-
together, what else had Wynn and her dad discussed? Had
Sam been mentioned at all? To what extent? If Wynn had
spoken with her mother, the subject of her past boyfriend
would definitely have come up. Suzanne Munroe had

thought of Sam as a son—always would—and she took every opportunity to let others know it.

There'll never be another Sam.

"Wynn, did my father put you up to this?" she asked.

Wynn's chin kicked up a notch. "Brock did mention it might be nice for us to catch up again while you were in town."

Grace sighed.

"I like to think of my father's smile if he found out his plan here had worked, but—"

"Grace, I'm not here because your father suggested it."

"It's okay. Honest. I—"

He laughed. "Come on now. I'm here because I want to be." When she hesitated, he went on. "We don't have to go to the show. But you have to eat. I know a great place on Forty-second."

She paused. "What place?"

He named a restaurant that she knew and loved.

"Great food," he added.

She agreed. "I remember."

"Their chocolate *panna cotta* is sensational."

"The mushroom risotto, too."

Wincing, he held his stomach. "Personally, I'm starved. I skipped lunch."

"I grabbed an apple-pie melt off a truck."

"I love apple-pie melts."

When he sent her a slanted smile, her heart gave a kick and, next thing she knew, she was nodding.

"All right," she said.

"So, that's a yes? To dinner, or dinner and the show? It's an opening night musical. The scores are supposed to be amazing."

Then he mentioned the name of the lead actor. Who said no to that? Only she wasn't exactly dressed for the theater.

"I need to go up and change first," she said.

But then, his gaze sharpened—almost gleamed—and Grace took stock again. Was he debating whether or not to suggest a drink in her room before heading out? Given the conflagration the last time they'd been alone together, no matter how great the songs or the food, she guessed he wouldn't complain if they ordered room service and bunked down in her bedroom for the night.

She was reconsidering the whole deal when his expression cleared and he waved the envelope toward a lounge adjoining the lobby.

"I'll wait over there," he said. "Take your time."

As he headed off, Grace blinked and then eased into a smile. No inviting himself up or flirty innuendoes. Perfect. Except...

If Wynn wasn't here at her father's behest, or to test the air for some no-strings-attached sex, that made tonight about a mutually attracted couple who wanted to enjoy some time together. In other words, a date.

Her first in a year.

"Some like it steamy." As he walked alongside her, Wynn gave her a puzzled look. Grace indicated a billboard across the street. "There," she explained. "It's the name of a new movie."

Wynn grinned. "Sounds like something my brother would dream up."

She and Wynn were heading back to the hotel. They'd enjoyed their meal and the show had been fantastic.

During dinner, she'd caught up on all the Hunter news. Apparently Cole and Dex had been at loggerheads for years. When their father had decided to split the company among the kids, workaholic Cole had expected more from Dex than he'd thought Mr. Casual could give. Dex had been happy to get away on his own to California to head Hunter Productions, which, after some challenges, was now doing well.

Teagan had got out of the family business altogether. She'd followed brother Dex to the States and had forged a successful health and fitness business in Seattle. Grace decided she really ought to get in touch with her old friend again.

As for the show, the staging had been spectacular and singing amazing; more than once, Grace had had to swallow past the lump in her throat. And Wynn's company had been as intoxicating as ever. Despite her reservations, she was glad he'd convinced her to go out.

"I know Cole's getting married," she said as her attention shifted from the billboard to take in Wynn's classic profile. "But isn't Dex engaged, too? I'm sure I saw an announcement somewhere."

"I get to meet both Dex's and Cole's love interests in a couple of weeks. Cole's wedding's back home in Sydney."

In Australia? She remembered wondering about his accent that first night; she'd thought possibly English but hadn't wanted to get into backgrounds. "A Hunter wedding. Set to be the social event of the season, I bet."

Grunting, he flipped his jacket's hem back to slot both hands in his pockets. "I wouldn't count on that."

The Hunters were wealthy, well connected. When Guthrie had remarried a few years ago, her parents had attended. Grace's mother had come home gushing over the extravagance of the reception as well as the invitation list— sporting legends, business magnates, some of the biggest names in Hollywood today. But it sounded as if Cole and his bride-to-be might be planning a more private affair.

Grace was about to ask more when a raindrop landed on her nose. She checked out the sky. A second and third raindrop smacked her forehead and her chin. Then the starless sky seemed to split wide apart.

As the deluge hit, Grace yelped. Wynn caught her hand, hauling her out of the downpour and into the cozy alcove of a handy shopfront.

"It'll pass soon," he said with an authoritative voice that sounded as if he could command the weather rather than predict it.

With his hair dripping and features cast in soft-edged shadows, he looked so assured. So handsome. Was it possible for a man to be *too* masculine? Too take-me-now sexy?

As he flicked water from his hands, his focus shifted from the rain onto her. As if he'd read her thoughts, his gaze searched hers before he carefully reached for her cheek. But he only swept away the wet hair that was plastered over her nose, around her chin.

"Are you cold?" he asked.

She thought for a moment then feigned a shiver and nodded.

He maneuvered her to stand with her back to him. He held open his silk-lined, wool-blend jacket and cocooned her against a wall of muscle and heat. *Heavenly.* Then his strong arms folded across her and tugged her in super close.

Surrendering, Grace let her eyes drift shut. She might not want to get involved, but she was human and, damn, this felt good.

His stubble grazed her temple. "Warm now?"

Grinning, she wiggled back against him. "Not yet."

When his palms flattened against her belly, slowly ironing up before skimming back down, she bit her lip to contain the sigh. Then his hug tightened at the same time his fingers fanned and gradually spread lower. She let her head rock back and rest against his shoulder.

"Better?" he asked against her ear.

"Not yet," she lied.

"If we keep it up," he murmured, "we might need to explain ourselves to the police in that patrol car over there."

"We're not exactly causing a scene."

"Not yet."

He nuzzled down beneath her scarf and dropped a lingering kiss on the side of her throat as one hand coasted higher, over her ribs, coming to rest beneath the slope of her breast. When his thumb brushed her nipple, back and forth three times, she quivered all over.

She felt his chest expand before he turned her around. In the shadows, she caught a certain glimmer in his eyes. Then his gaze zeroed in on her mouth as his grip tightened on her shoulders.

"Grace, precisely how much do you want to heat up?"

Her heartbeat began to race. No denying—they shared a chemistry, a connection, like two magnets meant to lock whenever they crossed paths. She'd had fun this evening. She knew he had, too. And the way he was looking at her now—as if he could eat her...

On a purely primal level, she wanted the flames turned up to high. But if she weakened and slept with Wynn again tonight, how would she feel about herself in the morning? Perhaps simply satisfied. Or would she wish that she'd remembered her earlier stand?

She liked Wynn. She adored the delicious way he made her feel. Still, it was best to put on the brakes.

Sometimes when she thought about Sam, the years they'd spent together, the night that he had died—it all seemed like a lifetime ago and yet still so "now." Before she could truly move forward and think about starting something new, she needed to make sense of what had come before.

The loss.

Her guilt.

Lowering her gaze, Grace turned to face the street. The display featured in the shop window next to them caught her eye. They were sheltering from the rain in a bookshop doorway. The perfect in for a change of subject.

"Does Hunter Publishing own bookstores?" she asked.

Wynn combed long fingers back through his hair then

shook out the moisture as if trying to shake off his steamier thoughts.

"We handle magazines and newspapers," he told her, "not novels."

"Everyone's supposed to have at least one story in them," she murmured, thinking aloud.

She certainly had one. Nothing she wanted professionally published, of course. But she knew that committing unresolved feelings to paper could be therapeutic.

"Have you got a flight booked back home?" he asked as the rain continued to fall.

"Actually I was thinking of taking a little more time off."

Hands in his pockets, Wynn leaned back against the shop door. "How much time?"

"A couple of weeks." Another experienced therapist had just started with the practice. Grace's boss had said, although she was relatively new, if she needed a bit more time off, it shouldn't be a problem.

His eyes narrowed as he gave her a cryptic grin. "You should come to Cole's wedding with me."

She blinked twice. "You're not serious."

"I am serious."

"You want me to jump on a plane and travel halfway around the world with you, just like that?" She pulled a face. "That's crazy."

"Not crazy. You know all the old crowd. I already told my brothers that we caught up."

Her heart skipped a beat. Exactly how much had he told them? "What did they say?" she asked.

"They said you had a crush on me when you were six."

"When you were such a dweeb?"

"I was focused."

She teased, "Focused, but clumsy."

She could attest to the fact that he'd outgrown the clumsy phase.

"Cole suggested it earlier today. I brushed it off, but after tonight…" He pushed off from the door and stood up straight. "It'll be fun."

The idea of catching up with his family was certainly tempting. After that Christmas, she and Teagan had been pen pals for a long while. Then Tea had that accident and was in and out of hospital with a string of surgeries. Tea's letters had dwindled to the point where they'd finally lost touch.

But foremost a trip to Australia would mean spending loads of time with Wynn, which didn't add up to slowing things down or giving herself the time she still needed to work through and accept her past with Sam.

She waved the suggestion off. "You don't need me."

"That's right. I *want* you."

Such a simple yet complicated statement—it took her aback.

She tried to make light. "You must have a mile-long list of women to choose from."

His brows knitted. "You have that wrong. Dex was the playboy. Never me."

When a group of boisterous women walked by the alcove, he stepped forward to gauge the prewinter night sky.

"Rain's stopped," he said. "Let's go before we get caught again."

As they walked side by side past puddles shimmering with light from the neon signs and streetlamps, Wynn thought back.

By age ten, he'd had a handle on the concept of delayed gratification. If he needed the blue ribbon in swim squad, he put in time at the pool. If he wanted to win his father's approval, he studied until he excelled. Reward for effort was the motto upon which he'd built his life, professional as well as private.

Then Heather had walked away and that particular view on life had changed.

On the night he and Grace had met again, Wynn had seen what he'd wanted and decided simply to take it. A few minutes ago, with her bundled against him in those shadows, the same thousand-volt arc had crackled between them. For however long it lasted, he wanted to enjoy it. More than gut said Grace wanted that, too, even if she seemed conflicted.

Hell, if she had time off, why not come to Australia? He could show her some sights. They could share a few laughs. No one needed to get all heavy and "forever" about it. He wasn't out to replace her ex. He understood certain scars didn't heal.

Maybe it would make a difference if he let her know that.

"Should we have a nightcap?" he asked as they entered the relative quiet of her hotel lobby a few minutes later. "I found a nice spot in that lounge earlier. No piano though."

She continued on, heading for the elevators. "I have to get up early."

When she didn't elaborate, Wynn adjusted his plan. He'd say his piece when he said good-night at her door. At the elevators, however, she cut down that idea, too.

"It's been a great night," she said, after he'd hit the Up key. "But I think I'll say good-night here."

He was forming words to reply when he heard a woman's laugh—throaty, familiar. All the muscles in his stomach clenched tight a second before he tracked down the source. Engaged in conversation with a jet-set rock'n'roll type, Heather Matthews was strolling across a nearby stretch of marble tiles.

Wynn's heart dropped.

Over eight million people and New York could still be a freaking small world.

At the same time his ex glanced in his direction, the elevator pinged and the doors slid open. He shepherded Grace inside and stabbed a button. As the doors closed, the ice in his blood began to thaw and the space between collar and neck started to steam. It took a moment before he realized Grace was studying him.

"Inviting yourself up?" she drawled.

"I'll say good-night at the door."

"Because of that woman you want to avoid?" She hit a floor key. "Want to tell me who she is?"

His jaw clenched. "Not particularly."

She didn't probe, which he appreciated. Except, maybe it would help if Grace knew that he'd recently lost someone, too, though in a different way.

He tugged at his tie, loosening the knot that was pressing on his throat. "That woman and I…we were together for a few years. There was a time I thought we'd get married," he added. "Have a family. She didn't see it that way."

Her eyes rounded then filled with sympathy. The kind of pity Wynn abhorred and, he thought, Grace knew well.

"Wynn…I'm sorry."

"It's in the past." Drawing himself up to his full height, he shrugged. "I'm happy for Cole. For Dex, too. But I'm steering clear of that kind of—" heartache? "—commitment."

A bell pinged and the elevator doors opened. She stepped out, and then, with a look, let him know he could follow. She stopped outside a door midway down the corridor, flipped her key card over the sensor. When the light blinked on, she clicked open the door and, after an uncertain moment, faced him again. They were both damp from the rain. Drops still glistened in her hair.

"For what it's worth," she said, "I think your ex missed out."

Then she stepped forward and craned up on her toes. When her lips brushed his cheek, time seemed to wind down. She lingered there. If she was going to step away, she wasn't in too much of a hurry. She had to get up early. Had wanted to say good-night. But if he wasn't mistaken, this was his cue.

His hands cupped her shoulders. As her face angled up, his head dropped down. When his mouth claimed hers, he held off a beat before winding one arm around her back. He felt more than heard the whimper in her throat. A heart-beat later, she relaxed and then melted.

As his tongue pushed past her lips, a thick molten stream coursed through his veins. The delicious surge…that vis-ceral tug… And then her arms coiled around his neck and the connection started to sizzle.

He hadn't planned on taking Grace to bed tonight. He knew she hadn't planned this, either. But what could he say? Plans changed.

A muttering at his back seeped through the fog.

"For pity's sake, get a room."

Grace stiffened, and then pried herself away. Down the hall, a middle-aged couple were shaking their heads as they disappeared into a neighboring suite. Coming close again, Wynn slid a hand down her side.

Get a room.

"Maybe that's not such a bad idea," he murmured against her brow.

When she didn't respond, he drew back. A pulse was popping in her throat, but reason had returned to her eyes.

"Good night, Wynn."

"What about Sydney?"

"I'll let you know."

"Soon." He handed over a business card with his num-bers.

Before her soft smile disappeared behind the crack in the door, she agreed. "Yes, Wynn. Soon."

Four

The next morning, Wynn arrived at the office early.

By seven, he was downstairs, speaking with his editor-in-chief about a plagiarism claim that was causing the legal department major grief. An hour and a half later, he was heading back upstairs and thinking about Grace. They had parted amicably, to say the least. He thought there was a chance she might even take him up on the invitation to accompany him to Cole's wedding.

He'd give her a day, and then try her at the hotel. Or he could get her cell number from Brock. Even if she decided not to go to Sydney, he wanted to take her out again. By the time he got back to the States, she would have left New York and gone back to her life in Florida.

Wynn made his way past Daphne's vacant desk; his assistant was running a little late. A moment later, when he swung open his office door, he was called back—but not by Daphne. Christopher Riggs was striding up behind him, looking as enthusiastic as he had the previous day at his interview.

"Hey, Wynn." Christopher ran a hand through his hair, pushing a dark wave off his brow. "Daphne wasn't at her desk. I thought I'd take a chance and see if you were in."

Wynn flicked a glance at his watch. His next meeting— an important one—wasn't far off. But he could spare a few minutes.

As they moved inside his office, Christopher's expression sharpened when something on Wynn's desk caught his eye—the interconnecting silver L and T of a publishing logo. "La Trobes," he said.

Leaning back against the edge of the desk, Wynn crossed his arms. "Impress me with your knowledge."

"I know La Trobes's publications have a respectable share of the marketplace."

"Keeping in mind that print share is shrinking."

"But there are other, even greater opportunities outside of print, if they're harnessed properly. I've given a lot of thought to out-of-the-box strategies and the implementation of facilities for digital readers to be compatible with innovative applications."

For the next few minutes, Wynn listened to an extended analysis of the digital marketplace. Obviously this guy knew his stuff. But now wasn't the time to get into a full-blown discussion.

After a few more minutes of Christopher sharing his ideas, Wynn got up from the desk and interrupted. "I have a meeting. We'll talk later."

A muscle in Christopher's jaw jumped twice. He was pumped, ready to let loose with a thousand initiatives. But he quickly reined himself in.

"Of course," he said, backing up. "I'll get out of your hair."

Christopher was headed out when Daphne appeared at the open door.

"Oh, sorry to interrupt," Daphne said. "I didn't realize—"

As she backed up, her elbow smacked the jamb. When her trusty gold-plated pen jumped from her hand, Christopher swooped to rescue it. As he returned the pen, Wynn didn't miss the wink he sent its owner. He also noted Daphne's blush and her preoccupation as Christopher vacated the room.

Rousing herself, she nudged those glasses back up her nose and, in the navy blue dress reserved for Thursdays, moved forward. As Wynn dragged in his seat, Daphne lowered into her regular chair on the other side of his desk. So—head back in the game. First up, before that meeting, he needed to make some arrangements.

"I'm flying to Sydney Monday."

Daphne crossed her legs and scribbled on her pad. "Returning when?"

"Keep it open."

"I'll organize a car to the airport." She scrunched her pert nose. "Will you need accommodation?"

"We're all staying at the family home. Guthrie wants us all in one place leading up to the big day."

If Grace decided to join him, he'd make additional arrangements. Lots of them.

As Daphne took notes, her owlish, violet-blue eyes sparkled behind their lenses. He couldn't be sure, but he suspected his assistant was a romantic. She liked the thought of a wedding. Not so long ago, she had really liked Heather.

The two women had met several times. Daphne had commented on how carefree, beautiful and friendly his partner was. The morning after Heather had left him sitting alone in that restaurant, he'd returned to his apartment and had lain like a fallen redwood on his couch. He'd let his phone ring and ring. He didn't eat. Didn't drink. When an urgent knocking had forced him to his feet, he'd found Daphne standing, fretting in his doorway. Looking pale, she'd announced, "I've been calling all day." For the first time in their history, her tone had been heated. Concerned.

He had groaned out his story and had felt a little better for it. Afterward, she'd made coffee and a sandwich he couldn't taste. Then she'd simply sat alongside of him, keeping him company without prying or hassling about the meetings he'd missed. They hadn't spoken about that day since, but he wasn't sorry she'd appeared on his doorstep and had seen that shattered man. He trusted her without reservation. He knew she would always be there for him, as a top assistant, even as an unlikely friend.

Now, like every weekday, he and Daphne went through the day's schedule.

"Midmorning," Daphne said, "you have a meeting with digital strategists."

To make existing online sites more efficient and user-friendly while increasing cross-promotional links between Hunter Publishing's properties.

"At two, a consultation with the financial heads," she went on.

To get down to the pins and tacks of whether his proposed partial merger with another publisher—Episode Features—was as viable as he believed.

Daphne glanced at the polished-steel wall clock. "In a few minutes," she said, "a meeting with Paul Lumos."

Episode's CEO. They were both anxious to finalize outstanding sticking points. Neither man wanted leaks to either the public, employees or, in Wynn's case, his family.

Normally, walls didn't exist between Hunter father and son. This was an exception. During a recent phone conversation, Wynn had brought up the subject of mergers. Guthrie had cut the conversation down with a single statement. "Not interested." His father's business model was built around buyouts and takeovers. He didn't agree with handing over *any* controlling interest. Even in these challenging times, this giant oak would not bend. But with the regularity of print-run schedules cut in half, both Lumos and Wynn saw critical benefits in sharing overheads relating to factory and delivery costs.

As Brock Munroe had said: adapt or die.

Daphne was leaving the office when Wynn's private line announced an incoming call. His father. Sitting back, Wynn checked his watch. Lumos was due any moment. He'd need to make this brief.

"Checking in," Guthrie said. "Making sure we'll see you next week."

Smiling, Wynn sat back. "The flight's booked."

"I just got off the phone with Dex and Tate." His father pushed out a weary breath. "This place feels so empty without that boy's smile."

Wynn read his father's thoughts. *Did I do the right thing sending my youngest son away?* He'd had no choice.

"We all agreed. While there's any risk of Tate being caught up again in that trouble, it's best he stay somewhere safe."

It had also been agreed that *all* the Hunters should return home for Cole's wedding. Since that last incident, where father and child had very nearly been abducted, additional security had been arranged. On conference calls, the older Hunter brothers had discussed with Brandon Powell how to increase those measures these coming weeks.

"Any news on that car rental company's records?" Wynn asked.

"The license plate was a fake," Guthrie confirmed. "After hiring the van, the plates were switched and switched again before dropping it back. If that woman Brandon interviewed hadn't caught sight of the rental company's name on the keys, we'd be clueless. Now at least we have some kind of description of the man."

"Was a sketch artist brought in?"

"Should have something on that soon." Guthrie exhaled. "God help me, I want to know what's behind all this."

Wynn imagined his father standing by the giant arched window in the second-story master suite of his magnificent Sydney house—the estate that Wynn and his brothers had called home growing up. The frustration, the fury, must be eating him alive.

"We're getting closer, Dad." Hopefully soon his father would have his life back and Tate could go home to Sydney for good.

Wynn changed the subject.

"Christopher Riggs started today."

His father sounded sure-footed again. "That boy has good credentials. Christopher's father worked for me years ago. Later, he bought a low distribution magazine that he built up. A recent merger turned out to be a death sentence. The family's interests were swallowed up and spat out."

Wynn's stomach tightened. But his father couldn't know about his meetings with Lumos or his merger plans for Hunter Publishing.

"Christopher's father is a good friend," Guthrie continued. "Someone I would trust with my life. When Tobias and I had our falling out, it was Vincent Riggs I turned to. I wanted to fold—give my brother any damn thing he wanted if he agreed to stay and help run the company—it was our father's dying wish. But Vincent helped clear my head. Tobias and I did things differently. Thought differently. Still do. We would have ended up killing each other if he'd stayed on. I'll always be grateful to Vincent for making me see that. Giving his only son this opportunity is the least I can do."

Wynn was sitting back, rubbing the scar on his forehead

as he stared at the portrait of his father hanging on the wall. He couldn't imagine how betrayed Guthrie would feel when he found out he'd gone behind his back organizing that deal.

"You there, son?"

Wynn cleared his throat. "Yeah. Sorry. I have a meeting in five."

"I won't hold you up."

His father muttered a goodbye and Wynn pushed out of his chair. When his gaze found the La Trobes folder on his desk, he remembered Guthrie's words and his chest burned again. His father had spoken of how, in his dealings with Uncle Tobias, he'd needed to accept that sometimes the answer to a problem is: there is no answer.

And now, Wynn had no option, either. He had to pursue this merger deal. No matter the casualties or hard feelings—he needed to keep his corner of the Hunter empire strong.

Five

"Well, now, this is a surprise."

At the sound of Wynn's greeting and sight of his intrigued smile, the nerves in Grace's stomach knotted up. Wearing a white business shirt, which stretched nicely across his chest, a crimson tie and dark suit pants that fit his long, strong legs to perfection, he looked so incredibly tasty, her mouth wanted to water.

"I was out doing a few things," she replied as he crossed his large private reception area. "When I passed your building, I thought I might catch you before you left for the day."

When Grace had arrived, the assistant had let Wynn know he had a visitor. Now, as the young woman packed up for the day, pushing to her feet and securing a massive handbag over her shoulder, Grace noticed the interested—*or was that protective?*—glance she sent Wynn's way. Wearing serious glasses and a dress that had submitted to the press of an iron one too many times, the woman looked more suited to court dictation than boardroom infatuation. But wasn't it always the quiet ones?

A moment later, Grace was following Wynn into his spacious office suite.

To the left, black leather settees were arranged in a *U* formation around a low Perspex occasional table stacked with three neat piles of magazines and newspapers. A spotless fireplace was built into the oak-paneled wall. To one side of the mantle sat a framed copy of a well-known Hunter magazine—on the other hung an identically framed copy of the *New York Globe*, Hunter Publishing's primary newspaper; their offices were located on a lower floor. But what drew her attention most was the view of Midtown visible beyond those wall-to-wall windows. It never got old.

From this vantage point, gazing out over Times Square toward Rockefeller Center, she felt settled, warm—as if she were swaddled in a cashmere wrap.

She wandered over and set a palm against the cool glass. "I've missed this."

A few seconds later, Wynn's voice rumbled out from behind her.

"Growing up," he said, "I remember my father being away a lot. He had good people in key positions here in New York, but he wanted to keep an eagle eye on things himself. When he said he trusted me enough to take on that gatekeeping role, I almost fell out of my chair. I was twenty-three when I started my grooming here."

The deep, rich sound of his voice, the comfort of his body heat warming her back… She really needed to say her piece and get out of here before her knees got any weaker.

As she turned to face him, however, her blouse brushed his shirtfront and that weak-kneed feeling gripped her doubly tight. The message in his gaze wasn't difficult to read. She was a confident, intelligent woman who had her act together for the most part, yet she felt like a sieve full of warm putty whenever Wynn Hunter looked at her that way.

She moistened her lips. "I've decided not to go to Sydney."

His eyebrows knitted before his gaze dipped to her mouth, then combed over one cheek. She felt the appraisal like a touch.

"That's a shame." With a curious grin hooking one side of his mouth, he edged a little closer. "Sure I can't convince you?"

"If we arrive and stay there together... Well, I just don't want to give anyone the wrong idea."

"What idea is that? That we're a couple?"

"Yes, actually."

"And that would make you uncomfortable. Make you feel disloyal to your ex." He explained, "Your dad mentioned what happened last year. It must've been hard."

Her stomach began to churn in that sick way it did whenever someone said those words to her.

"I'm working through it," she told him, crossing to his desk and stopping to one side of the big, high-backed chair.

"No one has to know any background," he said.

"Your family will ask questions."

"Trust me." He followed her. "They'll only be jazzed about seeing you again. Particularly Teagan."

She exhaled. He never gave up. "Wynn, we've known each other five minutes." *This time.*

"I'd like to get to know you more."

When his fingertips feathered the back of her hand, she eased away around the other side of the chair. "I'm not ready for this."

"I'm talking about soaking up gobs of therapeutic, subtropical sunshine. Have you any idea how soft a koala's fur feels beneath your fingertips?"

She narrowed her eyes at him. "Not fair."

He moved around the chair to join her. When his fingers slipped around hers, she was infused with his heat.

She wanted to move away again. Tell him that he couldn't talk her around. Only these toasty feelings were getting harder to ignore. She could so easily give in to the urge, tip forward.

Let go.

"I lay awake last night," he said, moving closer. "I was thinking about our evening together. About putting the past in the past for a couple of weeks."

She remembered again how candidly he'd spoken about his ex. She'd seen it in the shadows of his eyes. He'd been badly hurt, too.

In some ways, he understood. And Grace understood him.

She couldn't fix it with Sam, but Wynn was here, in her present. He'd been nothing but thoughtful toward her. And he wasn't looking to set up house or anything drastic. He was merely suggesting that they make the most of the time they had left before she returned to Florida.

And, of course, he was right—she didn't have to divulge anything to his family that she didn't want to. That was her conscience getting in the way, holding her back—same way it had all these months.

When the pad of Wynn's thumb brushed her palm, her fingers twitched.

"If you won't see me again," he said, "could I ask you to do just one thing?"

"What's that?"

"Leave me with a kiss."

Her breath caught. He was looking at her so intently.

"Just one?" she asked.

He brought her close. "You decide."

The moment his mouth covered hers, longing flooded her every cell. The night before, she had lain awake, too, imagining he was there beside her, stroking and toying and pleasing her the way only Wynn seemed to know how. She'd reinvented the moment before she'd said good-night, but rather than closing the door, she'd grabbed his tie and dragged him inside.

Now, with his mouth working a slow-burn rhythm over hers and that hot pulse at her core beginning to throb, she felt boneless—beaten. *One kiss*. She didn't want to stop at just one. But she hadn't lost her mind completely. This wasn't the place or the time.

Breathless, she broke away. "Wynn, I need to go."

"I want you to stay." His lips grazed hers. "*You* want to stay."

"Anyone could come in."

He strode across the room, locked the door, strode back. No more words. He only brought her close, and as his mouth captured hers and his embrace tightened, suddenly time and place didn't matter.

He shifted his big hands and gripped her on either side of her waist. He slowly lifted her and as her feet left the floor, he made certain that he pressed her against him extra close. Then their mouths slipped apart and rather than looking up at him, now she was looking down.

When he sat her on the desk, his mouth found hers again—a scorching all-bets-are-off caress. His palms drove all the way down her back, and as his hands wedged under her behind, she blindly unbuttoned part of his shirt. Slipping a hand into the opening, she sighed at the feel of crisp hair matted over hard, steamy flesh.

One hand slipped out from beneath her, slicing down the back of her thigh until he gripped the back of that knee. As the kiss deepened, she wrenched at the knot of his tie. When collar buttons proved too stubborn, she tugged harder and they popped off. She unraveled the shirt from his shoulders at the same time he pushed against her, tilting her back, bringing her knee back, too.

When she lay flat on the desk, his mouth broke from hers. He shifted enough to peel the shirt off his back. As he moved forward, he pushed up her skirt. He positioned himself between her thighs and his mouth met hers again.

Arching up, she clutched at his chest while a big warm hand drove between them and found the front of her briefs. When she bucked, wanting more, the kiss intensified before two thick fingers slid lower between thin silk and warm skin. As he explored her slick folds, the pad of his thumb grazed the bead at the top of her cleft. She bit her lip to contain a sigh. *All those sizzling nerve endings.* Then he pressed that spot with just the right pressure and a burning arrow shot straight to her core.

She was clinging to his shoulders when he slipped his hand out from her briefs. She pushed up against him until she was sitting upright, her hands colliding with his in their race to unbutton her blouse. As he wrangled the sleeves off her shoulders, she scooted back more on the desk.

But then their eyes connected, and a hushed surreal moment passed. He drew down a breath and seemed to gather himself before he urged her back down. Finding her right leg, he raised it at an angle almost perpendicular to the desk. Taking his time, he slid off her high heel before his palms sailed down either side of her calf, her thigh. Then he slipped off the other heel and raised that leg, too. He dropped a lingering kiss on one instep and then repeated the caress on the other.

Holding her ankles on either side of his ears, he let his gaze travel all the way down her body. He studied her rumpled skirt and, higher, the swell of her breasts encased in two scraps of lace. Releasing her legs, he scooped one breast out from its cup. Between finger and thumb, he twirled the nipple, lightly plucked the tip. When the tingling, beautiful burn was almost too much to bear, she reached out, inviting him down.

His tongue circled her nipple, flicked around the edges, before teasing the tip. As his mouth covered the peak and he lightly sucked, she sighed and knotted her fingers in his hair. She murmured about how amazing he was—how incredible he made her feel—as the pulse in her womb beat stronger and the fuse linking pleasure to climax grew alarmingly short. She adored the suction, the careful graze of his teeth but, so much more now, she needed him to open her—to enter and to fill her.

He shifted his attention to scooping her other breast from the bra. As he turned his head and his mouth worked its magic there, his hands slid under her shoulders. When he drew her toward him, she was raised up and then off the desk to stand before him. His mouth left her nipple with a soft smacking sound before he unsnapped her bra and released her skirt's clasp. The skirt dropped at the same time she shrugged off her bra and he whipped open his belt, unzipped his pants and fell back into his big leather chair.

She was down to hold-up stockings and briefs. He tipped forward and two fingers slid under the elastic strips resting on each hip. He pressed a moist kiss high on her leg just shy of her sex before he dragged the silk triangle all the way down. The tip of his tongue drew a slow, moist path across her bikini line as a palm filed up over her belly, her abdomen and then high enough to weigh one breast. When his tongue trailed lower, fire shot through her body. Gripping the hand kneading her breast, she dropped her head to press kisses on each fingertip.

Reclining, he drew her along with him until she straddled his lap. She hadn't noticed until now but he'd already found a foil-wrapped condom. To give him room, she grabbed the back of the chair and pushed up on her knees—which relocated her sex at the level of his mouth.

As he rolled protection on, he dotted kisses on one side of her mound then the other. Then he guided her down until the tip of his length nudged at her opening and eased a little inside.

The rush was so direct, so entirely perfect, Grace shuddered from her crown to the tips of her still-stockinged feet. He held her in that position, hovering, as his lips trailed her throat and he told her how much he'd missed her, missed this. When she clasped his ears and planted her lips over his, he eased her down a little more.

He rotated her hips in a way that put pressure on an internal hot spot that already felt ready to combust. When he eased out and in again, deeper this time, a trail of effervescent sensations drifted through the expressways of her veins. Hands on her hips, he urged her up until the tip of his erection was cupped by her folds. Then he brought her down again, more firmly, filling her completely this time.

The slam hit her everywhere and all at once. Her walls squeezed at the same time her head dropped into his hair. She wanted to keep him there, buried deep inside of her. She needed to hold onto the fringes of this feeling that let her know she was already hanging so close to that edge. With each and every breath, the world dropped farther away. She'd become only the rhythm beating in her brain, ordering her movements, stoking those flames.

As his tempo increased, her breath came in snatches. When a thrust hit that hot spot again, she let go of the chair and pulled his face up to hers. Her fingers knotted in his hair as their tongues darted in and out.

And then his movements slowed to an intense, controlled grind. When his tongue probed deeper, everything started to close in.

As Wynn thrust forward, she flopped back, wrapping her legs around his hips. When he moved harder, faster, she couldn't hold on. The force of her orgasm threw her back more.

As she stiffened, he drew her toward him, his arms holding her like a vice. When his mouth closed over hers, it only pushed her higher. She came apart, every fiber, every thought. She felt as if she'd been released into the tightest, brightest place that had ever existed. Nothing could interrupt the energy, nothing could defuse the thrill. Nothing… except…

Except maybe…

She frowned.

That sound.

Who was knocking on the door?

With the throbs petering out, reality seeped back in. She was crouched over Wynn, naked but for stockings, one of which was pushed down below the knee. Wynn at least still had his pants on, even if they weren't covering what they normally would.

When the knock came again and a man called out, she looked to Wynn, who put a finger to her lips. A sound filtered back from the other side of the room—the knob rattling. With her eyes, she asked, *What do we do?* and he gave her a *don't worry* look. Then the rattling stopped.

After a long moment, he whispered, "Let's pretend that didn't happen—the interruption, I mean." He stole a deep kiss. "Not this."

When he leaned in close and flashed her his slanted smile again, she turned her head, let out a breath and gathered herself. The lights were so bright. Had the person at the door heard any telltale sighs or groans?

She held her damp brow. "We got carried away."

He was nibbling her shoulder. "Uh-huh." His mouth slid up her throat. "Let's do it again."

Pulling back, she gaped at him and almost laughed. "You're crazy."

"It's my office. My company." He dropped a kiss on her chin, on her jaw. "I can be crazy if I want."

He pulled her closer and she felt him still thick and rigid inside of her. She'd been so involved in her own responses, she hadn't thought about him, although now she got the impression he was dangerously close to climaxing, too. But what if that knocking came again? Wondering if someone was still hovering around out there wasn't so great for the mood.

As if reading her thoughts, he nodded toward a connecting door. "I have a suite through there I use if I've had a long day and feel too beat to drag myself home."

"Let me guess." She arched a brow. "There's a bed."

His lips grazed hers. "Coming right up."

Later, as she and Wynn lay in the adjoining suite's bed, her blood hummed with warmth, as if every drop were coated in soft golden light. She felt so high, she couldn't imagine enduring a less satisfied state. She wouldn't worry about whether this had been a dumb move or merely inevitable. Now that Wynn had finished to supreme satisfaction what had begun in his office, Grace only wanted to bask in the afterglow…although she did feel unsettled about one thing.

With his arm draped around her shoulders, Wynn was nuzzling her crown while Grace snuggled in and asked, "Any idea who knocked on the door?"

"Christopher Riggs. I put him on here at my father's recommendation. Guess he had something he wanted to share."

"Something urgent?"

"Right now, this takes priority."

When he leaned forward and grinned, she pushed up on an elbow. "It sounded urgent."

He lay back and cradled his head. "He's full of ideas. Good ones. But nothing that can't wait till tomorrow."

When Wynn rolled over and his mouth once again covered hers, thoughts of Christopher Riggs evaporated. All that mattered were the shimmering emotions wrapping around her body and her mind. She could lie here with Wynn like this all night, but she winced at the thought of slinking out of the building after dawn. He might not like it, either.

When his mouth gradually left hers, his strong arms bundled her closer still. "I'll book another ticket for Sydney."

Cupping his raspy jaw, she brushed her lips back and forth over his. "I haven't said yes yet."

"But you will," he said with a confidence that made her feel somehow safe.

Before they'd begun to make love outside in his office, yes, she had decided to change her mind and go with him. Naturally his family would be curious about her life, but she didn't need to answer any questions she felt uncomfortable with.

Wynn's hand trailed down over her hip. "And we could spend more time together," he murmured against her lips. "More time like this."

Mmm. So nice. "You've convinced me," she said, brushing her smile over his. "I'll go."

His dark eyes lit and his smile grew. "I'll let Cole know tomorrow. Teagan will be stoked, and you'll love Tate. I think he's the one I'm looking forward to seeing again most. Dad must be counting down the days."

Did Wynn mean *counting down the days to the wedding*, or, "Has Tate been away?"

He hesitated, frowned and then propped himself up. "There's been some trouble back home."

He relayed details surrounding the problems Guthrie Hunter had experienced with a stalker. Unbelievable, Hollywood thriller type stuff.

"Tate was with Dad the day he was assaulted," Wynn

said. "We all thought it best that he be removed from that situation until they catch the guy. He stayed with Teagan first. Now he's with Dex."

"But he's going back to Australia next week, right? So, the stalker's been caught?"

"Not yet."

The pieces of the puzzle began to slot into place. She thought back. "Last night, when I assumed your brother's wedding would be a huge event…"

"It was decided that a small and therefore more easily controlled ceremony would be wise."

"So where's the wedding being held?"

"At the family home. They have a huge mansion overlooking the harbor. Obviously security will be of the highest priority. We have a top gun in the security world on the job. Brandon Powell is the best."

"Does my dad know about all this?" She hadn't seen any reports in the news. Obviously the Hunters had worked to keep the whole ordeal as quiet as possible.

"We've tried to keep it out of the media, but our fathers have spoken about it. Brock and I touched on the subject the other night, too."

Clearly the problem was serious—serious enough for a father to ship his youngest halfway around the world. What lay behind it all?

Wynn eased out a breath. "It's been months since that last incident, and the investigation is still going strong. If anyone thought there was any possibility of danger, Tate wouldn't be coming home."

"So, he's staying home for good?"

Wynn hesitated. "Not decided yet." His hand wrapped around hers. "I'm looking forward to seeing all the family again together. It'll be good having you be a part of that, too."

An odd feeling crept into her stomach. The idea of some

psycho searching out Guthrie Hunter, intent on doing major harm… It chilled her to the bone. On the other hand, Wynn seemed so certain that everything was under control. Hopefully Brandon Powell would find some answers, and fast.

Six

Brock Munroe commuted to Manhattan from Long Island each weekday for work. However, rather than ask her father for a lift, Grace hired a car to drive herself to the French-inspired manor she'd once called home.

On returning to New York last week, Grace had, of course, arranged to drop by. That day she'd been welcomed by fifty of the family's closest friends. Everyone had been so careful not to mention Sam. Even her mother, perhaps his biggest fan, seemed to try. But Grace wouldn't run the risk of being swamped again. She'd decided that on subsequent visits, including this one, she'd show up unannounced.

Grace drove up the wide, graveled drive and took in the manicured lawns and the manor's grand provincial theme. A moment later, the Munroe's soaring front door was opened by a woman who had just joined the house staff earlier that year.

"Miss Munroe!" With a wide smile, the housekeeper

ushered her through. "Your mother will be pleased to see you."

"Thanks, Jenn." Grace stepped onto the white-oak hardwood flooring of the double-story foyer. Absorbing the familiar smells of cypress beams and jasmine-scented incense, she glanced around. "Where is she?"

"The sunroom. I need to consult on the dinner menu with your mother. I'll walk you through." Jenn headed down the hall. "Your sister's here."

"Tilly?"

The youngest Munroe girl was in her final year of high school. Popular as well as a brain, Tilly seemed to breeze through life, blithely knocking down whatever obstacle got in her way.

"Matilda's upstairs," Jenn said, "dancing to one of her routines, I expect." Pointing her rubber-soled toes, the housekeeper gave Grace a cheeky grin. "I learned dance when I was young." She looked ahead again. "Rochelle's here, too."

Grace's step faltered and she groaned. Guess she'd catch up with everyone, then.

A pattering of footfalls filtered down the hall before a little girl turned a corner and trundled into view, her mahogany curls bouncing in a cloud around her head. When Grace's five-year-old niece saw her, April squealed. Putting her head down, she ran in earnest, sending layers of play necklaces jangling and clinking around her neck. Laughing, Grace knelt and caught her niece as she ploughed into her open arms. April smacked a kiss on her cheek.

"The bell rang and Granma sent me." April held her aunt's face in tiny, dimpled hands. "We didn't know it'd be *you!*"

They rubbed noses. Then Grace pushed up to her full height and took her niece's hand.

"What've you been up to, princess?" Grace asked as they strolled on.

"Daddy's working hard. He has lots of people to fix."

"Your daddy's a surgeon. Very important job."

"Uh-huh. He's busy." Innocent brown eyes turned up to meet her aunt's. "Mommy says he has to stay away a while."

At the hospital? Or was Trey at a medical convention? No doubt, she'd hear the entire story from Rochelle soon—one more treat in her sister's chocolate box of "perfect married life" tales.

Nearing the sunroom, April skipped on ahead. "Gracie's here!" she called.

Looking exquisite in an apricot jersey dress, Suzanne Munroe pushed up from a white brocade sofa. Grace couldn't remember a time when her mother had looked anything other than exquisite. As a girl, Grace wanted to grow up to be just like her and had sought out her mother's approval in everything. If Mom suggested she tie ribbons in her hair, ribbons it would be. If her mother proposed singing lessons, Grace would do her best to reach those high notes. As she'd gotten older, she'd come to understand that she had her own identity and dreams to pursue.

The dynamics of their relationship had needed to change.

But apron strings made of steel weren't easy to break. As her mother crossed over, Grace imagined those same high-tensile tendrils reaching out to coil around her now. But at age twenty-six, whose fault was that—her mother's for not listening, or her own for not making herself heard?

Grace walked into an extra-long hug from her mother at the same time Suzanne Munroe instructed Jenn to come back with some suggestions for tonight's menu, which, she reminded the housekeeper, needed to be free of all nut and egg products. April was allergic. Then, pulling back, her mother gestured toward the stash of costume and kids' jewelry littering a coffee table. Lit by afternoon sunshine steaming in through a bank of picture windows, piles of red, green and yellow "diamonds" glittered like a children's book treasure.

Her mother explained. "April and I have been trying on our jewels."

Grace crouched beside April, who was holding up another bundle of necklaces in front of her pink pinafore bodice.

"When I was young, I loved dressing up," Grace told her niece.

"You had more costumes than regular clothes," her mom pointed out. "One minute you were a princess, then a mermaid...the next, a bride..."

On the surface, that last remark was harmless; however, Grace didn't miss the lamenting tone. The connection. Sam hadn't been the high-flying lawyer or doctor her upper-crust mother might have preferred for a son-in-law, but his family was extremely wealthy and, having saved two young boys from a raging inferno a couple of years ago, he'd been known as a hero. Before Sam's accident, how many times had her mother announced that she couldn't wait to see Grace in a white gown and veil? Couldn't wait for her to make them all happy as a bride?

"Your costumes...can I have the princess one?" April cupped the top of her head. "Does it have a crown?"

"That was a long time ago," Grace replied. It went way back to a time when she'd first known Wynn Hunter.

Her mother took Grace's hands. "I brought Nan back with me from Maine. She's been asking about you."

Grace remembered how frail her grandmother had looked three months ago, one hand resting on her husband's rose-strewn coffin, the other pressing a lace handkerchief to her cheek.

"How is she?" Grace asked.

"Still feeling lost." Her mother gave Grace a "you'd understand" look before flicking a glance toward the stairs. "She's napping."

"Nanna naps all the time," April lamented, slotting a multicarat "ruby" on her middle finger and then scooting off up the stairs, presumably to check.

"When she sees you," her mother went on, "I'm sure she'll perk up. You'll stay for dinner." She dropped her chin. "Now, I won't take no for an answer."

Grace was about to say that of course she'd stay—she also wanted to ask where Rochelle was hiding—but then two items resting on the mantle of the French limestone fireplace drew her attention and the words dried on her tongue. When her mother's attention shifted to the mantle, too, her shoulders slumped. Crossing to the fireplace, her mother studied the photos—one of Grandpa, the other of Sam.

"Last week, before you called in," her mother said, returning with Sam's photo in hand, "I put this away. Your father didn't think you needed reminding. Of course, I put it back out after you left." She smiled down at the picture and sighed. "He always looked so handsome in his uniform."

When she held the frame out to her, Grace automatically stepped away. Yes, Sam was kind and brave and handsome. He was a natural with kids, including April. But her father was right. She didn't need reminding. She lived with enough memories.

But she couldn't go back—change what had already played out. She could only move forward, and now seemed the time to let her mother know precisely that, and as plainly as she could.

"I'm going to Australia," Grace announced. "Leaving next week."

Her mother's brow pinched. "Why? With whom?"

"With Wynn Hunter."

While Grace's heart hammered against her ribs, her

mother blinked several times before a smile appeared, small and wry.

"Your father mentioned that he'd run into Wynn. But now, you're…what? Seeing each other?"

"His brother Cole's getting married in Sydney. Wynn asked if I'd like to go. It'll be nice to catch up with Teagan."

"I saw Wynn at his mother's funeral a few years back. At his father's subsequent wedding, too. He seemed to have grown into a fine young man." Her focus dipped to the photo again, and then she arched a brow. "Is it serious?"

Grace could truthfully admit, "Not serious at all."

"So, you're not having a…well," her voice dropped, "a relationship?"

Grace thought about it. "That would depend on your definition."

"I see. More a fling." Her mother's look was dry—*wounded*—as she crossed to slot the frame back on the mantle. "It's none of my business…." Then she took a breath and swung back around. "But, I'm sorry, Grace. I can't say I approve. Those types of affairs might seem like a harmless distraction. Except someone always gets hurt."

A movement near the stairs drew Grace's eye. Rochelle was wandering over. Her face was almost as pale as the white linen shirt she wore. With a fluid gait, her mother joined her.

"My God, Rochelle," Grace murmured, "what's wrong?"

When their mother asked, "Is April with Nan?" Rochelle found energy enough to nod and settle on the sofa. Sitting, too, Grace held her older sister's arm and examined her blotched complexion.

"Shell, you've been crying."

Rochelle shuddered out a defeated breath. "Trey's had an affair. He's gone."

The room seemed to tilt. Grace remembered April's comment about her daddy needing to stay away. So, he'd left the family home? Or had Rochelle kicked him out? But none of it made sense. Those two had the perfect marriage, the kind of union their parents held up as a shining example. The kind of relationship their mother wanted for all her girls. The kind of bond Grace had once tried to convince herself she'd had with Sam.

In the past, Rochelle's stories revolving around her sparkling life had grated. Still, Grace loved her sister. She adored her niece. Now, as tears filled Rochelle's desolate green eyes, Grace wanted to help if she could.

"Do you know the other woman?"

"A nurse. A friend." Rochelle set her vacant stare on the far wall. "I had no idea. She held April's hand while we all watched fireworks on Independence Day."

When a tear slid down Rochelle's cheek, Grace folded her sister in her arms; she couldn't imagine how dazed and sick to her stomach she must feel. And if Trey had confessed... Was the affair still on?

"Is Trey still seeing this woman?"

"Doesn't matter whether he is or not." Their mother's elegant fingers clutched her throat as she sniffed. "The damage is done."

Grace considered her mother's indignant look and made the leap: *this* was an example of a fling's dire consequences.

Another, younger voice boomed out across the room. "Yay! Gracie's here!"

With a hip-hop gait, Tilly entered the room. Given those shocks of black and burgundy hair, she might have stuck her finger in a power socket. Grace noted that Rochelle was swiping at her cheeks, putting on a brave face—the stoic Munroe way.

So, Tilly didn't know?

Tilly was blinking from one to the other. "What's up?"

Her mother busied herself tidying the jewels. "Everything's fine."

Tilly crossed her arms. "Doesn't look fine."

"Grace is staying for dinner." Taking control of the situation, as usual, their mother moved to slip an arm around her youngest daughter's waist. "Jenn can prepare a big roast with sweet potato rounds for appetizers. Oh, and how about a strawberry torte to finish?"

While Rochelle looked flattened, Tilly seemed confused and Grace couldn't help but recall: torte had been Sam's favorite.

When Brock Munroe arrived home that evening, Suzanne took him aside, presumably to relay the news regarding Trey's infidelity. During dinner, their father remained stony-faced, poor Nan and Rochelle barely spoke and Tilly quietly observed the whole scene. Their mother overcompensated with a slew of chatter—except when it came to the subject of Grace's visit to Sydney.

While her father patted her hand and said the trip sounded nice—he obviously didn't see a problem with regard to Guthrie Hunter's recent difficulties or her accompanying Wynn over there—the tension at the other end of the long table built.

After plates were cleared, Nan excused herself, April was put to bed and Grace decided some fresh air and alone time were in order.

She'd bought a notebook the day before. Now with that book and a rug tucked under one arm, she ventured out onto the back partly enclosed terrace, which overlooked the pool. She rested an elbow on the wicker chair's arm, tapped the pen against her chin and let her mind wind back. In these surroundings with her family—here and now seemed the best place to start.

Grace was a world away, adding to how events had unraveled the night of Sam's accident, when she was interrupted.

"What are you writing?"

Snapping back to the present, Grace focused on Rochelle, who had appeared beside a row of potted sculptured shrubs. She half fibbed. "Working on an exercise."

"For speech therapy?"

"It's definitely about getting a message clear."

Once she'd begun to jot down her thoughts, she'd experienced a kind of catharsis. Now she wondered why she hadn't thought to do this before.

"How're you feeling?" Grace asked, closing the notebook.

"Less shaken than I was earlier," Rochelle admitted. "April's eyes were itching before she nodded off."

"Allergies?"

"Maybe just tired. She's had a big day." She gestured toward a chair. "Can I join you?"

"I'd like that."

"I came from Tilly's room." Rochelle lowered into a chair. "She wanted to know what was wrong."

"You told her?"

"She might be seventeen but she's not a child. She said she'd come stay over the holidays if April and I needed company."

"Tilly's always been a good kid."

"And the only one in this family who Mom can't corral. That girl has the stubbornness of a mule."

"Of *ten* mules."

They both grinned before a distant look clouded Rochelle's eyes. Bowing her head, she studied her left hand. The enormous diamond on her third finger caught the artificial light, casting shifting prisms over her face.

"It's hard to believe it was all an illusion," Rochelle murmured. "That he doesn't really love me."

"Did Trey say that?"

"A person doesn't eat off another plate if he's happy

with the dish he has at home. This year, I wanted to try for another baby. Trey said to wait." Biting her lip, she let her head rock back. "I'm such an idiot."

"None of this is your fault. No one deserves that kind of betrayal."

"Mom didn't want Trey and I to get married. She thought he was a flirt. Women respond when he walks into a room." Rochelle's watery eyes blinked slowly as her mouth formed a bittersweet smile. "I felt lucky."

They sat in silence for a while, studying the shadows beyond the terrace, before Rochelle spoke again.

"I'm sorry I wasn't much of a help when Sam passed away. I liked him."

Yeah. "Everyone liked Sam."

"But you didn't love him, did you, Grace? Not deeply and with all your heart."

Grace froze as a surreal sensation swept through her body. She stared at her sister. "You knew?"

"He looked at you the same way I look at Trey—with adoration, and hope."

When Rochelle hugged herself, Grace threw one side of the rug over for her to share.

"If he hadn't died," Rochelle said, snuggling in, "do you think you'd have got married?"

"No." Grace shook her head. "Even if everyone else thought we should."

"I always wondered why Trey asked me."

"Maybe because you're smart and beautiful—"

"And filled with insecurities? You can't imagine how tiring it is, pretending everything's amazingly wonderful when you wonder if your husband thinks your hips are monstrous, or you're not witty enough, and it's a matter of time before someone finds out you're a big fat fraud."

Queen Rochelle had never thought she was good enough?

The stories about her fabulous life were all a front? Guess they weren't so different, after all.

"We all have insecurities," Grace admitted. "At some stage, we all pretend."

"All those late, long hours..." Rochelle's nostrils flared. "He's probably had other flings."

There was that word again. That jolt. But her situation with Wynn was a thousand times different from Rochelle's. No cheating was involved—although in some ways they were each still attached to other people: her to Sam's memory, and Wynn to his beautiful ex.

Wynn had said that woman was in his past and yet she'd seen the emotion in his eyes. His ex had broken it off. Had she cheated on him the way Trey had cheated on Rochelle? Sam would never have done such a thing. Wynn, either.

Surely not.

"When are you leaving for Australia?" Rochelle asked.

Grace was still shivering from that last thought. "Monday. Mom's not pleased about it."

"Daddy thinks it's a good idea. I do, too. It's been years but I liked Wynn Hunter, even if he seemed a little intense."

"He's still intense, but in a different, steady-simmer kind of way. There's something about him, Shell. Something... hypnotic." Grace's smile wavered. "Almost dangerous."

"Different from Sam, then?" Rochelle joked.

"In pretty much every way."

When Grace shifted, the notebook slipped. Rochelle caught it and handed it back. Thinking about the secret contained within those pages, Grace ran a fingertip over the cover. What would her family say if they knew the whole story? Given Wynn's past, what would *he* say?

"I'm still not one hundred percent sure about going to Sydney," she admitted. "Cole's getting married. Apparently Dex is besotted with his fiancée. Cupid's shooting arrows all over the place where the Hunters are concerned."

She thought of her friend Amy and her bubbling enthusiasm over Wynn's kiss the previous weekend.

"I know the kind of atmosphere weddings create," Grace said. "Everyone's in love with the idea of being in love, and I'm over fending off other people's expectations."

"I'm not the one to give advice here but, Gracie, don't worry about what anyone thinks. You're a different person from the girl who started dating Sam. Hell, I'm different from the person who fell head over heels seven years ago for Trey. Back then, I felt giddy—so happy. Now I feel as if I've fallen in some deep, dark pit."

Grace's heart squeezed for her sister. It had been hard losing Sam, but he wasn't the father of her child. Regardless of this bombshell, Rochelle had loved her husband. Still, Rochelle could find comfort in the knowledge that people cared about her, and would look after both her and April, no matter what.

Grace held her sister's gaze. "You'll be okay. You know that, right?"

"Yeah. I know." Finding a brave smile, Rochelle leaned her head on her little sister's shoulder. "We both will."

Seven

The following week, the Qantas airbus Grace and Wynn had boarded in New York landed safely at Sydney Airport. With luggage collected, the pair jumped into a luxury rental vehicle and headed for the Hunter mansion. Travelling over connecting roads with the convertible's soft top down, Grace sighed at the picture-perfect views.

Sydney's heart was its harbor, an enormous, mirror-blue expanse that linked town and suburbs via fleets of green-and-yellow ferries. Built on the capital's northeastern tip, the giant shells of the world-famous Sydney Opera House reflected the majesty of a city whose mix of skyscrapers and parkland said "smart and proud and new." The mint-fresh air and southern-hemisphere sunshine left Grace feeling clean and alive, even after a twenty-odd hour flight.

She'd been a little anxious over whether Wynn's wedding-focused family might cast rose petals in their path, or if that crazy stalker situation would prove to be less contained than Wynn hoped and believed; if some madman wanted to harm

Wynn's father, what better time to creep out from the shadows than when the entire family was together and off guard.

But with a warm breeze pulling through her hair and the promise of nothing but relaxation, mixed with some sight-seeing adventures, she was feeling good about her decision. Nevertheless, when the BMW swung into the Hunter mansion's massive circular drive, Grace found herself drawing down a deep breath.

A member of the house staff answered the door and they were shown to a lounge room that was filled with people. An older silver-haired man, whom Grace recognized as Guthrie Hunter, stepped forward and put his arms around Wynn in a brief but affectionate man-hug before stepping back to assess his son's face.

"You look well, Wynn."

"You, too."

Grace heard relief in Wynn's voice; given those escalating threats on his father's life, no doubt he expected the wear to show.

And then all eyes were on her. Grace tacked up her smile at the same time Wynn introduced her.

"Everyone, meet Grace Munroe." Grinning, he cocked a brow. "Or, should I say, meet her again?"

An attractive woman around Grace's age romped up to hug her, long and tight. With thick blond hair pulled back in a ponytail, she smelled of oatmeal shampoo. Her tanned arms were strong, her body superfit and lean in her hot pink exercise singlet. Grace let loose a laugh and pulled back.

"Teagan, you need to be on the cover of your own health and fitness magazine!"

"Blame the day job." Teagan mock flexed a biceps. "I can't wait to catch up on all your news." She slid a knowing glance Wynn's way. "That is, if my dear brother will let you out of his sight for a minute."

Grace waited for Wynn to somehow brush the remark

aside. Instead he looped an arm around her waist and gave everyone a lopsided smile—a kind of confirmation. Which felt nice, but also wrong. She hadn't wanted to give anyone that impression. They weren't dating. Or at least they didn't have any long-term agendas, and she didn't want to have to fend off any open speculation that they did.

But then Wynn gave her a squeeze and she read the message in his eyes. *Relax.* Guess she was looking uptight. Overreacting.

A man stepped up, acknowledging her with an easy smile and tip of his head. He had hair dark and glossy like Wynn's, classically chiseled features and ocean-green eyes...

"You, I recognize," Grace exclaimed. "Cole, right?"

"The pigtails are gone," Cole joked, "but you haven't lost that cheeky grin." He beckoned someone over—a stunning woman with a waterfall of dark hair and eyes only for this man. She held out a hand—slender and manicured.

"I'm Taryn, Cole's blushing bride-to-be." Her Australian accent was pitch-perfect and welcoming. "We're so glad you could both make it."

"Wynn's excited about being here for the wedding, seeing everyone," Grace admitted. "I am, too."

Another man sauntered up. This brother's hair was sun-streaked, and his expression was open for all who cared to see. Those tawny eyes—like a lion's—were unmistakable.

"I'm Dex," he said, "Let me introduce you to the love of my life."

Laughing, a statuesque redhead dressed in modest denim cut-offs stepped up and shook Grace's hand heartily. "Shelby Scott. Pleased to meet you."

Grace detected a hint of a twang. "Texas?"

"I was born in a real nice place in Oklahoma," Shelby said with pride.

"Mountain Ridge," Dex added. "Ranch country. You

should see her in a pair of spurs." With his strong arms linked around her, Shelby angled to give him a censoring look. Dex only snatched a kiss that lingered until a boy with Dex's same tawny-colored eyes and wearing a bright red T-shirt, broke through the wall of adults.

"Are you going to marry Wynn?" The boy's shoulders bobbed up and down. "All my brothers are getting hitched."

Dex ruffled the boy's hair. "Hey, buddy, rein it in a little. We don't want to scare Grace off just yet."

It seemed like a room full of curious eyes slid back toward Grace as the boy considered, and then asked again. "Well, are you?"

Wynn hunkered down. "Tate, when Grace and I first met, she was around your age. Crazy, huh?"

Shoving his hands into the back pockets of his shorts, Tate eyed Grace as if he truly did think it was mad, but also interesting. "I like dinosaurs," he told her. "Do you?"

Kneeling down, Grace tried to think. "I don't know any."

"That's okay." When Tate smiled, Grace saw he'd lost a tooth. "I have lots. I'll show you."

Taking her hand, Tate yanked but his father stopped him short. "Son, our latest guest hasn't met all the family yet."

Another woman—a *very* pregnant woman—entered the room. Her high cheekbones and large, thickly-lashed eyes bespoke classic beauty—or would have if not for the grimace, which seemed to have something to do with the way she held the small of her back. This must be Eloise, Grace thought. Wynn's stepmother, although she looked young enough to be a sister.

"I swear, if I don't have this child soon," Eloise said, "I'll collapse. I can't carry this twenty-pound bowling ball around inside of me much longer."

As Eloise ambled nearer, Cole's shoulders inched up. Taryn slipped an arm through her fiancé's, as if reminding him she was there, a support. Grace wondered.

What's that all about?

Stopping before the newly arrived couple, Eloise dredged up a put-upon smile and Wynn stepped forward to brush a kiss on his stepmom's cheek. As he drew away, Eloise looked to Grace as if she expected the same greeting from her. Grace only nodded hello before saying, "Thanks for having me in your home," and then, "Can I ask—do you know what you're having?"

"I've prayed for a daughter. Every woman wants one." Eloise's gaze flicked to Teagan, who was squatting, tying Tate's shoelace. "*Another* daughter, I mean." She set her weight on her other leg. "After that long trip, you both must need a good lie down. Your old room's all ready for you, honey," she said to Wynn.

"Barbecue's happening around five," Cole added.

"I'll bring a dinosaur," Tate said.

A moment later, Wynn was ushering Grace up a grand staircase, then down a corridor that led to a separate wing of the house. His "room" looked more like a penthouse suite. Standing in the center of the enormous space, which included a king-size bed, Grace set her hands on her hips.

"You had all this to yourself growing up?" she asked.

"Doesn't mean I sat around, bathing in milk and ringing the butler's bell."

"No?" She turned to face him.

"I worked very hard at my studies and sport."

She wandered over. "Wanna show me your trophies?"

"I wanna show you something."

His arms circled her and his mouth covered hers. It was a stirring kiss. Warm and good and…somehow different. Must be because of the surroundings. As his lips left hers, she let her eyes drift open and memories of the Hunters and that Colorado Christmas came flooding back. One memory in particular. She pressed her lips together to cover a laugh.

"I can still see you gnashing your teeth over that snowman's hat not sitting straight."

He pretended to scowl. "Because you and Teagan kept messing with it when my back was turned."

She didn't cover her laugh this time. "You were so darn easy to stir."

When she bopped his nose, he jerked to take a bite at that finger. "You were lucky I remained a gentleman."

"I don't remember you behaving in a gentlemanly fashion. You'd go all stiff and mutter that I needed a good spanking."

His lips came close to graze up the slope of her throat. "I'm feeling and thinking the same thing now."

While his tongue tickled her earlobe, the zipper on the back of her dress whirred down. She felt the cool air, and then a warm palm slid in over her skin before skating down toward her rear. Closing her eyes, Grace let her head rock back.

"I thought we were going to rest before dinner," she said, "not play."

"Either way, we need to get out of these clothes."

He slid the dress off one shoulder, she handled the other shoulder, and the dress fell to the floor.

Since that evening in his office, they'd seen each other regularly. Whenever they got together, inevitably they would end up in bed, exploring each other's bodies, discovering what the other liked best, and then finding new ways to top that. Like that thing his mouth was doing now to the lower sweep of her neck. The gentle tug of his teeth on her skin felt light and yet deep enough to ignite a set of nerve endings directly connected to her core.

But today they'd been travelling around the clock. Her body was pleading for a warm shower and some rest.

She stepped out of the dress pooled around her ankles and headed for the dresser, stopping twice to slip off each shoe while unfastening her heavy necklace. Laying the necklace on top of the dresser, she caught Wynn's reflection in the mirror. His gaze was dark and fixed upon her hips, the back of her briefs. He didn't look tired at all.

When he slipped off his shoes and moved up behind her, Grace's insides began to squeeze. His palms sailed over her bare shoulders, down her arms. Leaning back against his muscled heat, she breathed in his musky scent as two sets of fingers drew lines across her ribs before arrowing down, running light grooves over her belly to her briefs. He plucked at the elastic and murmured, "These need to come off."

As his fingers dived lower to comb and lightly tug at her curls, liquid heat filled her.

For comfort's sake, she hadn't worn a bra on the flight. In the mirror, through half-lidded eyes she watched him scoop up a breast with one hand while, lower, his other worked beneath her briefs. When he lightly pinched and rolled her nipple, she shivered, sighed and let her head drop to one side. The palm covering her mound urged her closer, pushing her bottom back to mold against him.

Then, knees bending, he began to slide down. She savored the feel of his defined abdomen, his chest and then chin, riding lower down her spine. When she felt his breath warm the small of her back, a finger hooked into the rear of her briefs and the silk was eased down to her knees. He dropped a lazy kiss on a hip then the slope of her bare behind. At the same time, the stroking between her legs delved deeper, slipping a little inside of her. She couldn't see his reflection in the mirror anymore—she only felt his mouth as it explored one side of her tush before trailing across the small of her back to sample the other side.

When his lips traveled lower and he kissed the sensitive area under the curve of one cheek, she held on to the dresser for support. Between her thighs, his fingertip rode up until he grazed and circled that sensitive nub. When he applied perfect pressure to the spot, stars shot off in her head before falling in a tingling, fire-tipped rain. She brought up one knee. Her briefs dropped from that leg before falling to rest around the other ankle. Pushing to his feet, he turned her around.

As his teeth danced down the column of her throat and his hands cupped her rear—lifting her at the same time they scooped her in—she gripped his shoulders. Steamy heat came through the fabric of his shirt to warm her palms. She brushed her wicked grin through his hair.

"Am I the only one getting undressed here?"

He paused. "Well, now, that could work."

He backed up a few steps while his gaze drank her in. Feeling desirable—and a little vulnerable—she leaned back against the dresser as his chest expanded on a deeply satisfied breath.

"You're perfect," he said. "I could stand here and just look at you all day."

Her cheeks were burning, not because she was embarrassed but because his words, the honesty in his voice, touched her in a way that left her wanting to please and tease him this much all the time.

With his focus glued on her, he backed up until his legs met the bed. After he threw back the covers and sat on the edge of the mattress, he beckoned her with a single curl of a finger. He wanted her to walk over and, given the glimmer in his eyes, he wanted her to take her time.

She took a breath and set one foot in front of the other; the closer she got, the more his dark eyes gleamed. When she was close enough, he reached to cup her neck and draw her down.

Her hair fell forward as her lips touched his. The contact was teasing—deliberately light. Her tongue rimmed the upper and lower seam of his mouth before she nipped his bottom lip and gently sucked. That's when his mouth took hers. As a strong arm coiled around her back, drawing her toward him more, she let her lips slide down and away from his at the same time she lowered to kneel at his feet.

She was positioned between his opened thighs, her mouth inches away from his chest. Taking her time, she released a shirt button, two and then three. Each time, she twirled her tongue over the newly exposed skin.

She pulled the shirttails out from his jeans, and when his shirt lay wide open and the bronzed planes of his chest and stomach were completely revealed, she started on his pants. With him leaning back, his arms supporting his weight, she flicked the snap, unzipped his fly. As she tugged at his jeans, her head dropped down.

Her tongue drew a lazy circle around his navel before she dotted moist kisses along the trail of hair that led to his boxer briefs. When she grazed her teeth over the bulge waiting there, his chest gave an appreciative rumble and he leaned back more, propping his weight on his elbows. Her fingers curled inside his briefs.

She dug out his engorged shaft and whirled a finger around the naked tip before her head lowered and her mouth covered him—barely an inch. Gripping his length at its base, her fist squeezed up as her mouth came down. Relishing the taste of him—the scent—she repeated the move again and again, taking her time, building the heat. He started to curl his pelvis up each time she came down while she squeezed him harder, took him deeper.

Too soon, he was sweeping her up and over, so that she lay flat on the bed. He whipped the shirt off his back and then retrieved a condom from his wallet, all before she could say she wasn't finished with him yet. When he tore open the foil, she took the condom and rolled the rubber all the way on. After ditching the jeans, he came back to kiss her, first thoroughly and then in one hungry, savoring snatch after another.

They were tangled up around each other, breathing ragged and energy pumped, when he urged her onto her side and pressed in against her—his front to her back. As he nuzzled the side of her neck, he drew her leg back over his and entered her in a "no prisoners" kind of way.

When he slid her leg back more, she stretched and ground against him. His thigh felt like a steel pylon. His chest was a slab of thermal rock. She grazed her cheek against his biceps as he held her and moved, setting up a rhythm that fed the pulse thumping in her throat and in her womb.

With his palm pressed against her belly, his fingers toyed with her curls. With each sweep, he grazed that uber-sensitive nub. The contact was maddening—drugging and delicious. When she was balanced on a precipice, oh-so ready to let go, he used his weight to tip her over.

Her leg uncoiled from around his thigh and her knee dug into the mattress at the same time her cheek pressed against the pillow. Settling in behind her, he began moving again, his pace faster now—fast enough for the front of his thighs to slap the backs of hers. This different angle changed the way that he filled her, placing a different pressure on a sensitive spot inside. The pleasure was so fragile and yet fierce—too exquisite to get her whirling mind around.

As his thrusts went deeper, he slid a palm under her belly to lift and press her closer. A searing heat compressed her core. A few more thrusts and she cried out as her fingers curled into the sheet and contractions swept in.

A heartbeat later, he gripped her hips and his strangled growl of release filled her ears.

Eight

"We don't have to go down," Wynn murmured as he bundled her close. "Go back to sleep."

After making love in his former bedroom, he and Grace had crashed. When his watch alarm had beeped a moment ago, he'd been stirred from a vivid dream—and Wynn rarely dreamed.

They were kids again, back in Colorado that Christmas long ago. There was a snowman with a screwy felt hat, and Wynn's scar was a fresh wound on his brow. Rather than blame an annoying brat for the gash, Wynn wondered if he'd tripped over his lace. He'd gone on to invite Grace—a lively, pretty thing—back to his parents' home in Australia.

"My brain feels full of cottonwool," Grace murmured against his chest as she tangled her leg around his. Her toes tickled the back of his knee. "But everyone's expecting us."

Inhaling the remnants of floral perfume mixed with the more alluring scent of *woman,* he kissed her crown. "They'll understand."

She glanced up. A line formed between her brows as she pushed hair away from her face. "We're not spending all our time here, right?"

"You mean in bed?"

She grinned. "In Sydney, dummy."

"I do have a surprise or two planned."

"Then I want to spend as much time as I can with Teagan while we're here." Grace shifted to lean up against the headboard of the bed. Her hair was mussed and still flopped over one side of her brow. "Do you know if she's seeing anyone? Anyone special?"

"Dex said he thought that she might be. But the man who catches our Ms. Independence will need to be darn determined."

She concurred. "Doesn't work until a girl wants to be caught."

"Like this?"

Craning up, he exacted one very thorough kiss that he didn't want to end.

When his mouth finally left hers, her breathing was heavier. The sheet had slipped from under her arms. Sliding down, he took a warm nipple deep into his mouth. His tongue was teasing the tip and his hand was snaking down over her belly when she gathered herself and pushed at his shoulders.

"I need a shower."

He spoke around the nipple. "You really don't."

Grace eased off the mattress and he lost possession of that breast. Then she was on her feet, standing in front of him with fists on her hips, as if that could put him off. He would have hooked her around her waist and brought her back—only he had a better idea.

Pushing up on an elbow, he cradled his cheek in his palm and nudged his chin. "Bathroom's that way."

Her eyes narrowed as if she suspected he might suddenly pounce, but he only smiled.

Two minutes later, Grace had the shower running and Wynn was swinging open the glass door to join her. When she turned to face him—her hair wet and rivulets of foam trailing over her body—her expression was not surprised. As he stepped in, she threaded slippery arms up and around his neck. With her breasts sliding and brushing against his ribs, she grazed her lips up his throat to his chin.

"You are so predictable," she said.

Grinning, he reached for the soap. "Don't bet on it."

"It's about time!"

Standing alongside of Wynn in the Hunter mansion's manicured backyard, Grace tracked down the source of the remark.

Inside an extravagant pavilion, two house staff flipped and prodded food grilling on a barbecue. A third attendant, carrying a drinks tray, was headed for the resort-style bar. Music played—a current hit from the U.K.—while a half dozen people splashed around in an enormous pool. Australian time put the hour at six o'clock, but the sun's heat and angle said they had a couple more hours of daylight yet to enjoy.

Grace heard the male voice that had greeted them earlier call again from the pool. "We were getting ready to come up and drag you two out of bed," Dex said as he splashed water in their direction.

Grace's cheeks heated, but it was a harmless remark. No one knew what she and Wynn had gotten up to. Even if they had guessed, they were all adults, with one exception.

In the pool, Tate was balanced on Cole's shoulders. He had his legs wrapped around his big brother's neck and was kicking in excitement. With a grin, Grace wondered where the dinosaurs were.

"Wynn!" the little boy called out. "I got a beach ball. We're in teams. You're with me!"

"Us against those two clowns?" Wynn called back, making a face as he gestured toward Cole and Dex. "Hardly seems fair."

Wynn wore a pair of square-leg black trunks that, along with his impressive upper body and long, strong legs, made Grace want to pounce on him again. She wore a bikini the color of the pool water with a matching resort-style dress cover. Now, the arm around her waist brought her closer as he asked, "Are you game?"

To splash around in that enormous pool with four boys?

Taryn was already out of the water, wringing her long dark hair, and Shelby was wading up the last of the arced pool stairs, right behind her. Teagan must be around somewhere, too.

"I have a feeling a lot of splashing and dunking is about to go down." She pinched his scratchy chin. "I'll go hang with the girls."

She craned up to catch his light kiss before returning her attention to the women. Shelby was motioning her over.

As Wynn ran up to the pool edge and did a cannonball, creating one hell of a splash, Grace accepted a glass of juice from the help and joined Shelby and Taryn near an extravagant outdoor setting.

Grace eyed Taryn's tan and smiled. "Wynn mentioned you and Cole had been off sailing."

Taryn wrapped a towel around her hips and folded herself into a chair. "A leisurely sweep around some Pacific islands." She sighed. "Pure heaven."

"When are you going again?" Shelby asked, grabbing a plastic flute of orange juice off the table before reclining into a chair.

"If all goes according to plan, we'll be able to fit it in just after the wedding." Taryn sent an adoring look over to where her fiancé was spiking a ball at Wynn. "Cole wants to start a family straightaway. Me, too."

Shelby leaned across and wrapped an arm around her future sister-in-law. "That's fabulous, hon."

Grace didn't feel she knew Taryn well enough to hug her. She saluted with her glass of juice instead.

Taryn cocked a brow Shelby's way. "Am I imagining it, or is Dex coming across as clucky, too?"

"Since looking after Tate these past weeks, he can't stop talking about having kids. We're really gonna miss that little guy if Guthrie decides he can stay." She sent Grace an apologetic look. "Sorry. We're leaving you out, running off at the mouth here."

Grace waved the apology away. She'd anticipated talk focusing on happily-ever-afters and babies. "I'm really glad for you both."

"Cole says you all knew each other as kids," Taryn said.

Grace glanced toward the pool. The three older brothers were play-wrestling, strong bodies glistening, muscles rippling, while Tate sat on the pool's edge, laughing and clapping his hands.

Grace admitted, "We've all changed a lot since then. I didn't recognize Wynn."

Leaning forward, Shelby straightened her bikini-top tie. Dex's fiancée had a presence—tall with striking features; she might have been a catwalk model rather than the nanny Dex had employed when he'd needed a sitter for Tate.

"They sure are big boys now," Shelby said. "What was Wynn like twenty years ago?"

"Earnest. Intense. He certainly didn't like girls. At least he didn't like me."

"And you?" Taryn asked. "Did you think he was cute even back then?"

"I had a tiny crush," Grace admitted. "A couple of times

I pinched his arm and ran away. The way he remembers it though, I harbored evil plans to ruin his life."

Taryn laughed. "True love," she said, while Shelby exclaimed, "It was meant to be, just like Dex and me. When we met, I was so off men. We took a long route round, but now I can't imagine life without him."

"I thought Cole was an arrogant jerk. He was so, my way or the highway." When Taryn came back from a memory that made her cheeks glow, she asked Grace, "How did you and Wynn meet up again?"

Grace cleared her throat and reinvented the truth.

"At a wedding," she said. "We talked, danced. He was leaving when the bride threw the bouquet. The flowers landed at my feet then skated across the floor right up to him. He brought them back and kissed me right in front of the crowd."

The words were out before Grace could think twice; she hadn't meant to reveal so much. Now Shelby was swooning while Taryn swirled her drink.

"A sentimental streak runs deep in the Hunter boys," Taryn said, "no matter how much they try to hide it at first. No question, they're all into family."

Grace focused on Wynn again. His arms out, he was encouraging Tate to dive back into the pool. *Yes*, she thought. If he ever got over the ex, Wynn would do well with a family of his own at some stage, and perhaps Taryn and Shelby were wondering if it might be with her. Still, this conversation didn't make Grace feel as uncomfortable as she'd thought it might. Rather she felt included—part of the club—even if the gist wasn't relevant to her.

While the three women discussed plans for the wedding as well as Taryn's dress, which sounded amazing, Grace spotted Teagan emerging from the house. Looking superfit in a black and neon-orange tankini, Teagan glanced around. Rising from her chair, Grace excused herself and waved her friend's way.

"What say we fill up some water bombs," Teagan said as Grace moved closer. "We can set off a full-scale attack."

Grace laughed. "You mean against the guys in the pool?"

"Who else?" Teagan took a fruit skewer from the nearby table filled with food. "I still can't believe you're here and Cole's getting married." Teagan's eyes sparkled. "It would be nosey to ask whether you and Wynn are headed that way, wouldn't it? It's just so bizarre thinking of you two together."

Grace's stomach gave a kick. "We're not really together, Tea. Not in the way, say, Shelby is with Dex."

"Oh. Sure." Teagan waved her skewer. "Nothing wrong with cool and casual. Totally understand."

Grace wasn't sure that she did.

She and Teagan hadn't communicated since those pen-pal letters years ago. Even so, Grace now felt that same connection—the trust. It seemed like only yesterday they had shared and talked about everything. Grace wanted to fill her friend in a little on her previous relationship but it wasn't for everyone's ears.

While the others were occupied with wedding talk, she told Teagan about Sam—what a great guy he'd been, how he'd died and how she should have let him go much sooner. She omitted what had transpired thirty minutes before the accident. No one knew the truth about that; she hadn't even written it down in her notebook yet. She finished by saying that whatever she and Wynn shared, it was with a view to having fun in the now rather than till death do them part.

"I'm in a similar kind of relationship," Teagan admitted. "On the surface, we're great together. Underneath, it's complicated."

"Is he coming to the wedding?"

"No. Like I said. Complicated." Teagan slid a grape off

the skewer. "He comes from a big family. His brothers and sisters are all already married. Damon is eager to follow in his siblings' footsteps, which includes heaps of kids."

"How many kids?"

"He's mentioned six."

Grace let out a long whistle. "I was thinking maybe three."

"Maybe none."

Grace's head went back. A couple having a half dozen children wasn't that common nowadays, was it? But none? Was it because Teagan thought it was too soon to be discussing having a family with this man? Maybe his many family members could be nosey and interfering.

Teagan was about to say more when Guthrie and Eloise strolled out of the house. As Guthrie helped his wife into a chair near the pool, Teagan nudged Grace.

"I should go see if they need anything."

Grace was about to follow when a pair of cold, strong arms coiled around her, hauling her back against a hard, equally chilly chest. Yelping, she jumped and tried to spin around, but Wynn wouldn't let go.

"Struggle is futile," he said while his sister laughed.

"Told you," Teagan said. "You should have bombed him while you had the chance."

Two hours later, Tate was in bed and Guthrie stood at the head of the outdoor table, preparing to say a few words. His smile was sincere, but also weary, as if he'd been on a long journey and knew that soon he could rest.

"I don't need to tell anyone how pleased I am to have you all together, to see you happy, particularly, of course, Cole and the soon-to-be bride, our dear Taryn."

While Cole lifted Taryn's hand to his mouth for a kiss, the rest of the gathering put their hands together in a light round of applause.

"Next Sunday will be a special day," Guthrie went on. "I've taken measures to be certain nothing is, well, spoiled." He lowered back into his chair. "Brandon is still working hard to track down information that will lead to the unmasking of the unknown parties who have caused us so much grief these past months. I want you all to be assured that security will be the top priority on the day."

"We've kept the announcement from the press," Cole said. "The invitation list is at bare-bones."

"No red carpet and blowing of horns," Dex pointed out, linking his arm through Shelby's.

"So, who did make the cut?" Teagan asked.

"You guys, of course," Cole said. "Taryn's aunt and a handful of our closest friends."

Wynn remembered Cole mentioning that Taryn's aunt was the only family she had.

"Your Aunt Leeanne and Uncle Stuart." Guthrie began his own list.

"Your sister and her husband? Nice," Teagan said. "We haven't seen them in ages."

"Talbot and Sarah," Guthrie continued, which raised a few eyebrows; until recently, when the attacks had started, the two older Hunter brothers hadn't spoken in years. "And Talbot's son."

Dex sat up. "Slow down. Talbot doesn't have any kids."

Flinching, Eloise pushed lightly on the top of her pregnant belly. "Seems one's worked his way out from the woodwork."

While Guthrie bowed his head as if restraining himself from reacting to the snide remark, Wynn got his mind around the statement—Uncle Talbot had a son? Was he the result of a previous relationship, or had Talbot at some stage strayed from the marriage bed?

Cole's comment was supportive. "I look forward to meeting him."

Guthrie sent a grateful smile. "There are a few people from Hunter Broadcasting. A couple of family friends." He flicked a look Wynn's way before addressing the table again. "Including a longtime friend and his wife, the Riggses."

Wynn sat up. Christopher Riggs's parents? Guess he'd be fielding questions relating to how their boy was doing in New York, not that there was much to report at this early stage.

Dex brought the conversation back to a more serious subject. "So, no new leads on the case?"

"Whoever's responsible," Guthrie said, "seems to have vanished off the face of the earth."

"And hopefully," Eloise added, "that'll be the end of that."

Cole growled. "I won't give up looking for that SOB until he's caught. Neither will Brandon."

Shelby agreed. "If you don't finish it, these kinds of things have an ugly habit of creeping back into your lives." She and Dex shared a look.

Taryn spoke up. "Sometimes troublemakers move to another country. Some simply pass away."

Grace's stomach was knotted as she listened intently to all the back and forths.

If she were Taryn, she would pray for that last scenario. Not only would Taryn want the wedding to unfold without a hitch. She'd want her future children to be immune to these kinds of dangers. All the Hunters wanted to keep Tate free from the possibility of coming to any future harm. One day soon, God willing, Taryn and Cole would have children of their own. Dex and Shelby, too. How could any one of them feel relaxed about having their son or daughter visit this home or spend time with their grandfather with this maniac still on the loose?

Wynn's ex must be grateful she didn't have to deal with

that dilemma. He had said that once he'd wanted to have a family with her. Although now Wynn was steering clear of commitment, which suited this situation just fine.

Wynn reached for her hand.

"You okay?" he said only loud enough for her to hear. The others were still discussing the stalker. "You really don't have to worry," he went on. "I don't know if we'll ever get to the bottom of all this, but those first three incidents were close together. After all this time, I don't think we'll hear from him again."

"So you'd be okay with Tate coming back here to stay?"

Wynn blinked. "He's not my son to say."

"If it were your son," she asked, "what would you do?"

Wynn's jaw tightened as he gave a tight grin. "That's a question I doubt I'll ever need to answer."

Grace watched as a recent-model pickup, boasting the name of a construction firm on its side panel, drove up to the Hunter estate and two privately uniformed men stepped forward to check it at the gate. At the side entrance, which led to the Hunters' vast manicured back lawn, another man waited, constantly running his eye over the zone.

Grace quietly took it all in while waiting for Wynn by their rental car parked on the drive. They'd stayed on for two days, picnicking, boating and generally catching up with his family. She'd been made to feel so welcome; she'd enjoyed every minute, particularly her chance to chill with Teagan, though Tea's idea of relaxation was a ten-mile jog followed by a protein shake. The words cheesecake and alcohol weren't in her vocabulary.

Apparently neither was "kids." Not that Teagan had brought that subject up again.

This morning Wynn had told her it was time to unveil his vacation surprise. They were in for a bit of a drive, he'd explained, but that was all part of the experience.

At breakfast, she and Wynn had said farewell for now to the rest of the clan. A moment ago, packed and about to jump in the car, Wynn had asked if she could wait a second while he gave his little brother another goodbye hug; Guthrie and Cole were in the side yard, teaching Tate to throw a pass.

From the side yard, Taryn spotted her and wandered over.

"The guys are sure enjoying being all together again," Taryn said as she joined her. Wynn had taken the ball and was executing a controlled toss to Tate. Taryn laughed. "You might need to go over and physically drag him away if you want to be on the road by noon."

"I don't mind." Grace straightened her hat; the sun Down Under had a real bite. "This is his time, not mine. I think he misses seeing Tate more than he knows."

"Tate is everyone's favorite, particularly when we all came so close to losing him that day."

Grace shuddered at the thought of seeing a loved one assaulted and then barely escaping an abduction. She couldn't imagine how a child would interpret and internalize all that. As if reading her thoughts, Taryn explained.

"He's spoken with counselors and doesn't appear to have nightmares, thank God. Cole was pretty shaken up over it, though. Not long after that incident, Cole took Tate to a park to toss a ball, like they're doing now. When Cole took his eyes off him for a minute, Tate vanished."

Grace held her sick stomach. "But Cole must have found him."

"Safe and sound. Cole told me later those few moments turned his world upside down. For the first time he understood what he truly wanted from life."

Grace surmised. "A family of his own."

"To protect. To love." Watching her fiancé swing Tate up onto his shoulders, happiness shone in Taryn's eyes.

"Not long after that ordeal, with Brandon Powell on the case, we set sail and got away for a few weeks. That time only brought me and Cole closer together. There hasn't been any trouble since."

"So, maybe Eloise is right," Grace said. "Perhaps the stalker's given up, gone away."

"Doesn't mean the Hunters will give up their search. Whoever's responsible needs to be behind bars."

Eloise appeared in the side yard. Guthrie crossed over to offer a chair to his pregnant wife. Grace couldn't help but notice Cole's reaction to his stepmother's appearance. He seemed to stiffen and his expression cooled before he swung Tate down from his shoulders. When Tate ran to join his mother and father, both Cole and Wynn headed over, too.

Although the men were well out of earshot, Taryn lowered her voice. "I'm sure you've guessed. Eloise isn't Cole's favorite person."

"Wynn mentioned something about how Cole and Dex think she married their father for his money."

"If only that were the worst of it."

Before Taryn could say more, Cole and Wynn were upon them. Cole acknowledged Grace with a big smile before leveling his hands on Taryn's hips and stealing a quick kiss. "What say we see how things are going out back?"

"Sounds good," Taryn replied.

Wynn opened the passenger door of their rental car for Grace. "We'll see you guys in a couple of days."

A moment later, when the convertible passed through the opened gates, both security guards threw them casual salutes. Grace wondered if they were wearing guns, and then whether they would need to use them while they were on this assignment. But everyone seemed so confident. All this security was only a precaution.

Wynn changed gears then reached to hold her hand.

"Ready for an adventure?"

Grace sat straighter and looked ahead.

"Maestro, lead the way."

Nine

By the time they reached the Blue Mountains west of Sydney, Grace had put her questions and concerns regarding the wedding's security out of her mind. Instead, as she slid out of the passenger seat, she focused on the magnificent retreat where Wynn had booked accommodation. With the sash windows and gothic-inspired pointed arches, the hotel reminded her of the Elephant Tea Rooms in London. Then there were the pure, eucalyptus-scented air and serene, top-of-the-world views…

And apparently Wynn had something even more amazing planned.

At the hotel reception counter, a man around Wynn's age lowered his magazine as they approached.

"Morning," the man said. "You have a reservation, sir?"

Wynn gave his name and the man—Mick, according to his badge—studied his computer screen.

"You don't appear to have a booking, Mr. Hunter."

Wynn's eyebrows hiked. "Look again."

A few seconds later, Mick shook his head. "We do have a room available. Ground floor. No view, I'm afraid."

When Wynn's expression hardened and he pulled out his cell phone, Grace cast a look around. A few guests were mulling over brochures. A few more were headed out the door to sight-see, she assumed. She looked back at Mick, who gave her a thin smile before Wynn disconnected. His voice was low and unyielding.

"My assistant assures me a reservation was made. She received a confirmation for a deluxe suite with views. She spoke with you personally, Mick."

Rubbing a palm over his shirt, Mick analyzed the screen again, and then his shoulders bounced with a "can't help you" shrug. "I apologize, sir."

Wynn rapped a set of fingertips on the counter. "Is your manager in?"

A little girl, around April's age, had wandered out from a room adjoining the reception area. She tugged on Mick's sleeve. "Daddy, wanna help me color?"

Mick called the manager before combing a palm over his daughter's wispy fair hair. "Hang on, peaches."

After a three-hour drive, Grace was simply happy to be here. She didn't care what kind of room they had. She certainly didn't want to upset that little girl.

Setting a forearm on the counter, Mick leaned closer. "I can do a great deal on that room, but all the suites are taken."

Another man strolled out. Introducing himself as the manager, he enquired, "Is there a problem?"

As Mick explained and Wynn put his objection forward, Grace stepped back. The manager was apologetic. Then, when he realized who Wynn was—the Hunter family was legendary in Australia—he was doubly so. When Mick got tongue-tied—he couldn't explain the missing email or botched booking—the little girl crept back and hid behind

that door. Her chocolate-brown eyes were wide. She had
no idea what the problem was, why her daddy was upset.

Wynn saw her too and held up his hands. "Don't worry,"
he said. "We'll take that room."

"I'm so sorry, Mr. Hunter," the manager said again.

Wynn took the key card. When they reached their com-
pact double room on the ground floor, Grace was curious.

Wynn dropped his cell phone on a table. "Not what I
had in mind."

"You weren't happy."

"I'm not a fan of incompetence."

"You wanted to tell them both that."

"I think I had a right."

"But you didn't." She moved over. "Why not?"

He shrugged. "No point."

"It was because of that little girl, wasn't it? You saw her
watching so you dropped it."

"It wasn't that big of a deal, Grace."

Grinning, she trailed a fingertip around his scratchy
jaw. "You backed off."

He narrowed his eyes at her. "You like a man who backs
down?"

"For those kinds of reasons, absolutely." She circled her
finger around the warm hollow at the base of his throat.
"You can be quite chivalrous, do you know that?"

"As opposed to what you thought of me as a kid." His
hands skimmed down her sides. "You didn't think that I was
behaving in a gentlemanly fashion back then, remember?"

"Except whenever I teased you, no matter how much you
wanted to belt me, you always walked away."

His lips twitched as he moved in closer. "I remember at
least one time when Cole needed to hold me back."

Standing on her toes, she brushed the tip of her nose
against his. "Face it, Wynn Hunter. You're one of the good
guys."

"Uh-uh." He angled his head to nip her lower lip. "I'm bad to the bone."

Before she let him kiss her, she admitted, "But in a very good way."

Two hours later, Grace was gazing upon the most incredible site she could ever have imagined. And this place was used for wedding ceremonies? *Wow.*

Wynn had bought tickets for a tour of the Lucas Cave, the most popular of the three hundred forty million-year-old Jenolan Caves, which were within walking distance of the hotel. After climbing hundreds of steps, they entered an anteroom and then the Cathedral Chamber, which soared to a staggering fifty-four meters at its highest point. It reminded her of that scene out of *The Adventures of Tom Sawyer.*

Grace instantly forgot the muscle burn from the climb as she stood in the midst of such amazing limestone formations. Some looked like stained glass windows. The guide pointed out a limestone bell tower and a pulpit, too.

The chamber could accommodate up to one hundred guests and the acoustics were apparently perfect; orchestras and a local Aboriginal band regularly entertained audiences here. When the guide wanted to show how disorientating the caves could become without electricity, she turned out the lights. As they were dropped into darkness, Grace gripped Wynn's arm while he chuckled and held her tight.

Farther along the flights of narrow stairs that wove through the caverns, the temperature dropped and they were introduced to formations that looked like sheets of white lace, as well as ribbons of stalactites that flared with reddish-orange hues. In another cave, pure white calcite formations looked like icicles dripping from the ceiling and snow-dusted firs sprouting up from the ground.

When they emerged from the cave and were greeted by

warm sunshine again, they walked hand in hand around the fern-bordered Blue Lake, which was, indeed, a heavenly, untouched deep blue. They spotted a platypus; Grace stood spellbound as the mammal, which looked like a cross between a duck and an otter, wiggled around the bank, foraging for food. As they approached a group of wallabies, she expected them all to hop away. One actually let her brush a palm over its supersoft fur and look into those liquid black eyes. Later, however, she was more than a little hesitant, skirting around the frozen, guarded posture of a dragon lizard.

She flicked on her phone's camera, snapped a few shots of the wildlife and sent them straight through to April via her mom's cell. Grace got a reply back a minute later. April wanted to know if her auntie could bring home a wallaby.

Back at the hotel, she and Wynn showered and changed for dinner at a nearby first-class restaurant. Thankfully there weren't any hiccups with reservations this time.

They were halfway through their meal when conversation turned to work. Wynn had asked about her studies.

"Before getting my masters," she said, "I had dreams of starting my own practice."

"What does a person need to study to get a license for speech therapy?"

"Speech-language pathology. I learned about anatomy, physiology, the development of the areas of the body involved in language, speech and swallowing."

"Did you say swallowing?"

"People don't tend to realize how important it is."

He grinned. "I've always been a fan."

Setting down his cutlery, Wynn reached for his glass. He'd chosen a wine produced in Victoria—an exquisite light white. After forking more of the creamy scalloped potato into her mouth, Grace picked up the thread of their conversation.

"We studied the nature of disorders, acoustics, as well as the psychological side of things. Then we explored how to evaluate and treat problems."

"I knew a boy who stuttered. Aaron Fenway could barely get his name out. It must have been tough. But it didn't seem to faze him. He was always top of the class at math."

"Sounds like my younger sister. A head for figures."

"Aaron owns a huge dot-com now."

"Bruce Willis and Nicole Kidman stuttered. Winston Churchill and Shaquille O'Neal, too."

"I'm trying to imagine anyone being brave enough to tease Shaquille."

"Apparently, when Shaquille was a kid, he'd sit in class, sweating over whether the teacher would ask him a question. He knew he wouldn't be able to get the words out."

"Must make you feel good, helping." Wynn set down his glass. "The business I'm in doesn't have that kind of reputation, I'm afraid."

"News needs to be told. It's a noble profession."

"It can be. Lots of challenges ahead of us there, though. More and more readers are getting their news off the Net."

"So, what's the future?"

"Keep our eyes open to all the options. Change is the one constant. We need to look at cutting costs on the print side. Factory and distribution overheads. I'm talking with someone at the moment."

"To share those costs?"

"More than that. We're looking to merge parts of our companies."

"Ooh, sounds very highflier."

"And very confidential. Not even my father knows."

She studied his expression and put down her fork. "You don't look as if you're punching the air about telling him."

"Guthrie's idea of building success is to buy out the opposition or run them out of business. He doesn't *merge*."

"Isn't that your decision? You run Hunter Publishing now."

"For things to go smoothly, I need his approval." He pushed his plate aside. "And I need it soon. Better to explain face-to-face."

"Sometime this week?" He nodded. "Maybe keep it for after the wedding."

"My thoughts exactly."

After the meal, the young waitress served coffee and asked if they'd enjoyed the tours.

"I saw you this afternoon," the waitress explained, "wandering back from the Grand Arch."

Grace well remembered the Arch. According to the guide, while that particular cave had collapsed many centuries ago, the giant rock arch of the original structure remained—a truly awe-inspiring sight.

Grace sighed. "It was all amazing."

"Did anyone mention the ghosts?" the waitress asked, setting down the cups.

Wynn's lips twitched. "We missed that tour."

But Grace remembered seeing a mysteries and ghosts tour outlined on a brochure.

"There's evidence of strange things happening down there—photographs and videos." The waitress lowered her voice. "There's even supposed to be a ghost living right here, in this restaurant."

"Does she float around the town, as well," Wynn asked, "rattling her teapot?"

"If she does," the waitress said, "don't worry. She's friendly."

Later, when Grace and Wynn were back at their hotel and entering their room, Wynn suddenly grabbed her from behind, around the waist. Grace's heart leapt to the ceiling before, spinning around, she smacked his shoulder and, heart pounding, turned on the lights. Why did guys think stuff like that was funny? It wasn't—or at least not when she'd imagined the sound of footfalls following them up the street. She might have heard a teapot rattle, too.

"You're such a child."

He laughed as she strode off. "Oh, *I'm* a child? Will we leave on a night-light tonight?"

"I'd love to see how smart you'd be if a ghost sailed through that door right now and poured cold tea all over your head."

He followed her. "So you believe all that haunted house woo-ha." Lashing an arm around her middle, he growled against her lips, "Good thing I'm here to protect you."

Refusing to grin, she set her palms on his chest, which seemed to have grown harder and broader since the last time they'd made this kind of contact.

"I have an open mind. I can also look after myself."

"Just letting you know," he said, lowering his head to nuzzle her neck, "I'm here if you need me." He nuzzled lower. "For anything." His hand curved over her behind. "Anything at all."

Her eyes had drifted shut. Damn the man. She couldn't stay mad.

"You want to help?" she asked.

"Want me to order a medium? Organize a séance? Sprinkle some salt on the threshold?"

She grabbed his shirt and tugged him toward the cozy double bed. "You're going to help me with a whole lot more than that."

Ten

"Promise me one thing," Grace said.

Wynn squeezed her hand. "Anything?"

"No stunt today like the one you pulled at that other wedding."

When she and Wynn had returned from their magical stay at the Blue Mountains with a hundred snaps and a thousand memories, the final preparations for Cole and Taryn's big day were in full swing. They'd watched the extensive back lawn and gardens being pruned to perfection. A giant fairy-tale marquee had shot up and the furnishings had been arranged both inside and out.

Now Grace looked around at the marquee's ceiling draped with white silk swags and the fountains of flowers, as the sixty or so guests took their seats on either side of a red-carpeted aisle.

Beside her, Wynn wore a tuxedo in a way that would impress James Bond. Now, responding to her request that he behave himself, he sent her a wicked grin and stage whispered, "No surprise kiss in front of the multitudes? Why? Can't handle it?"

She tugged his ear. "Mister, I can handle anything you care to dish out."

"Except letting people know that there might be more."

"More of what?"

"More to us."

That took her aback. What did he mean *more*? They were here in Australia, doing exactly as he'd suggested: relaxing and enjoying themselves. There wasn't any *more* to it.

Or she was reading too much into his words. That tease was more likely a warning that she shouldn't become too complacent. He just might shock the crowd again. She had news for him.

"Just remember whose show this is, okay?"

"Yep." The corners of his smoldering eyes crinkled. "Can't handle it."

When he leaned closer, she put on a business-only face and dusted imaginary lint from his broad shoulders. "Time you went and joined your brothers at the altar."

He gave her a curious look. "You think so?"

She hesitated before laughing. He was acting so strangely today.

"You look amazing in that dress," he said.

"You told me," she grinned. "Maybe ten times."

He tipped close and took a light but lingering kiss that brought a mist to her eyes. His warm palm curved around her cheek. "You'll be here when I get back?"

She wanted to laugh again, but his gaze was suddenly so serious.

"Yes," she said and softly smiled. "I'll be right here. I promise."

On Wynn's way to the platform where Cole and Dex waited, Guthrie pulled him aside to introduce a couple who seemed familiar, in more ways than one.

"Son, you remember Vincent and Kirsty Riggs," Guthrie said with his father-of-the-groom smile firmly in place.

"Of course." Wynn shook Vincent's hand and nodded a greeting at the wife. "Nice to see you both again."

Mr. Riggs's expression was humble. "Christopher's so pleased that you've allowed him this chance in New York."

"I'm sure he'll be an asset to the company," Wynn replied.

"We should catch up after the ceremony," Vincent went on. "I'd like to know what you have in store for him."

"But right now," Mrs. Riggs said, nodding at the altar, "you have an important job to do."

"Guthrie mentioned that Dex will be joining his older brother soon," Vincent said, "tying the knot."

When Vincent flicked a glance Grace's way and waited for some kind of response, Wynn only grinned and replied, "It's true. Dex will soon be a married man. Another reason to celebrate." Wynn bowed off. "Please excuse me."

Strolling up to the platform, Wynn concentrated on the task ahead. He and Dex were to stand beside the oldest Hunter brother as he took this important step in his life. But another related thought kept knocking around in his brain.

After that initial hiccup with their booking, he and Grace had enjoyed every second of their time away in the mountains. They'd explored, eaten out, talked a lot and when they weren't otherwise engaged, made love. He had assumed the constant physical desire would, in some way, slack off. Anything but. His need to feel her curled up around him, have his mouth working together with hers, had been a constant. He understood sexual attraction, but he and Grace seemed to have created their own higher meaning.

Ever since he'd been here, when he and Cole and Dex sat down at the end of the day with a beer, he listened to their banter about how much they looked forward to settling down, and the ache he'd suffered after that bust-up with Heather had begun to fester again. In the past, whenever he'd looked ahead, Heather had been there, standing alongside him. But seeing Grace tonight in that knockout strapless red gown with the sweetest of all sweetheart necklines, silver bangles jangling on both wrists and her eyes filled with sass and life…

He didn't want a relationship, and yet he and Grace were doing a darn fine imitation of having one. A moment ago, after he'd hinted at perhaps wanting more, for just a second, he'd meant it. But he didn't need to go down that track again. Why rock a perfectly happy boat?

He was nearing the platform when another guest stopped him—a tall, well-built man in his twenties.

"You're Wynn, right?" the man asked.

"We've met?"

"I'm Sebastian Styles."

Wynn thought back and then apologized. "No light bulb, I'm afraid."

"Talbot's son."

Wynn had known to expect his long-lost cousin today, but no one had passed on a name. And while the brothers had speculated, no one seemed to know the story behind this surprise addition to the Hunter line. Which wasn't a problem. Sebastian Styles was family now and more than welcome.

As the men shook hands, Wynn confirmed, "Good to meet you."

"I wasn't sure whether Guthrie had explained my sudden arrival on the scene."

"Only that you'd caught up with your father."

The rest really wasn't any of Wynn's business. He glanced toward the platform—he needed to take his place alongside his brothers right now.

"I've heard plenty about you," Sebastian was saying,

"and your brothers. Can I join you for a drink after the ceremony?"

"I look forward to it."

Wynn skirted around the front section of chairs, which were filling with guests, and came to stand alongside Dex—three Hunter brothers all in a row.

Assuming the apparently obligatory "hands clasped in front" stance, he asked the others, "We set to go?"

Dex dug into a breast pocket and flicked out a clean white handkerchief for Cole. "For when the perspiration starts coursing down your face."

"I'm not nervous." Cole straightened his bow tie. "This is the best day of my life."

"When you know it's right, you know," Dex said, and the two older brothers bumped shoulders before remembering themselves. They were happy, settled. Wynn was not.

Oh, for pity's sake.

"I wish you two would stop going all goofy on me," Wynn growled. "I thought you'd know by now—I'm over that other stuff."

"Grace is a special woman," Cole said sagely.

Dex followed up with, "You two give off some pretty intense sparks. As long as you're both having fun. Right, Cole?"

But Cole's attention was elsewhere. He straightened his tie again.

"My master of ceremonies just gave the signal. Taryn's ready to come out." Cole sent his brothers a fortifying wink. "See you on the other side, boys."

Grace was figuring out the seating arrangements.

The only person she recognized in the first row, which was set aside for family, was a put-upon Eloise, who was draped in yellow chiffon and nursing a baby bump that looked more like a balloon ready to pop. Teagan was a bridesmaid and Tate, a page boy. Shelby wasn't anywhere to be seen. Without Wynn to sit beside, Grace didn't want to crash. Perhaps she ought to sit more toward the middle—neutral territory.

She was deciding on a row when, looking breathtaking in a glamorous single-shoulder, emerald-green gown, Shelby came rushing up.

"You're sitting with me," she said, indicating the second row before continuing on her way. "I'll be back in a shake. Just want to give one of the best men a big kiss for good luck."

Lowering onto the outermost chair of the row Shelby had indicated, Grace was perusing the leather-bound order of service when a man appeared at her side—the man Grace had seen Wynn speak with before taking his place beside his brothers on the platform.

"Is there room for one more?" the man asked.

He had a presence about him, Grace decided, which complemented his smooth baritone and kind hazel-colored eyes.

"Of course." Grace moved over.

Settling in, the man rubbed both palms down his suit's thighs before he glanced at her. "I'm feeling a little out of the circle."

She returned his awkward smile. "Me, too."

"I'm Sebastian Styles, by the way. The long-lost cousin."

"Grace Munroe." She added, "Third brother's date."

"I didn't feel as if I should intrude today. It's such a private affair. Smaller guest list than I'd even imagined."

It wasn't her place to ask how much Sebastian knew about the stalker business, so she merely agreed with his last point.

"At first, I declined the invite," Sebastian said. "But Talbot and, apparently, Guthrie insisted."

She nodded toward a couple in the front row. "Are they your parents?"

"That's Leeanne—Talbot and Guthrie's sister—and her husband, Stuart Somersby. Sitting alongside them are Josh and Naomi, their grown kids."

From this vantage point, Josh looked to be in his early twenties with sandy-colored hair and strong Hunter features, including a hawkish nose. Biting her lip she was so excited, Naomi was younger and extremely attractive. Her tumble of pale blond hair was dotted with diamantés.

Perhaps having heard her name, Leeanne—a slender, stylish brunette—glanced over her shoulder and wiggled her fingers, *hi*. Sebastian and Grace wiggled back before he nodded toward a magnificent display of flowers where two men were discussing some obviously serious matter.

"That's Talbot, my father, speaking with Guthrie."

"Neither one looks happy."

"I'm guessing it's about the security. My father was none too pleased about being frisked so thoroughly at the door." Sebastian's brow creased before he hung his head and smiled. "My father. Still sounds weird."

"I know everyone's looking forward to meeting you." She turned a little toward him. "Do you have a partner?"

His expression changed before he straightened in his seat. "No. Nothing like that."

The music morphed into a moving tune that Cole and Taryn had chosen to kick off this all-important part of the day. When the bride appeared, on the arm of the woman who must be her Aunt Vi, a rush of happy tears sprang to Grace's eyes. Who didn't love a wedding?

Shelby appeared and Sebastian and Grace both shifted one seat over in the row.

Pressing a palm to her heart, Shelby whispered to them both. "What a gorgeous dress. She's the most beautiful bride I've ever seen."

Then Tate, in a tiny tux, and Teagan and another brides-maid started off down the aisle and Grace sat back.

This was bound to be an amazing day.

Hours after the ceremony, during the reception that was also held inside the marquee, Grace caught a glimpse of Teagan. She stood behind a massive, decorative column, a cell phone pressed to her ear. Biting a nail, she looked upset enough to cry.

The music filtered through the sound system, drawing lots of couples onto the dance floor. Grace had just finished speaking with a couple—Christopher Riggs's parents, as a matter of fact—lovely people who seemed pleased their son was moving forward with his life in New York.

Grace had been ready to join Wynn, who appeared to be enjoying his conversation with his new cousin. Now, Grace hurried over to Teagan.

"You're upset," she said as Teagan disconnected her call.

"That guy I've been telling you about…" Teagan tacked up a weak smile. "He's missing me."

Grace let out a sigh of relief. That wasn't bad. That was *sweet*. Grace had wanted to learn more about Teagan's guy but when her friend hadn't brought the subject up again, Grace didn't want to prod.

Now she said, "Looks like you're missing him, too."

Beneath the marquee's slow-spinning lights, Teagan's gaze grew distant and her jaw tensed, as if she were try-ing to keep from frowning.

"Guess I've gotten used to having him around. Except… I can't see things working out between us. Not in the long term."

"Because he wants lots of children?"

Teagan nodded.

Teagan's guy sounded a lot like Sam, Grace thought.

Difference was that Teagan obviously cared deeply for this man in the way a future wife should.

"So, he's proposed?" Grace asked.

"Not yet. And I don't want him to. Like I said, it's complicated. I was going to talk with you more about it, but…"

"You don't have to explain—"

"I want to." She took Grace's champagne flute and downed half the glass—a big deal, given that Teagan didn't usually drink.

After a visible shudder, Teagan handed the glass back. "That accident I had all those years ago…"

They'd spoken about that, too, these past days. "You were in and out of hospital."

"I missed so much school. Mom and Dad tried to make it up to me. I had every material thing a girl would wish for. I think they knew pretty much from the start. I found out later." Her lips pressed together and, staring off at the people dancing, she blinked several times. "I can't have children."

The words hung in the air between them before Grace's heart sank to her knees. She gripped her friend's hand. She'd never dream for one minute…

"Oh, Tea…"

"It's okay," she said quickly. "I'm used to the idea. There's plenty of other things in life to keep a person focused and busy."

"Maybe if you spoke to him. There are options."

"Sure. Great ones. But you'd have to meet him, Grace. I look at him and know he's destined to have boys with his strong chin and the same sparkling blue eyes." Her wistful expression hardened. "He deserves everything he wants from life."

"Speak with him," Grace implored.

Teagan's chin lifted even as she smiled. "I'm fine with who I am. I don't want anyone's pity. I've had enough of that in my life. I certainly don't want to put him in a position where he feels he has to choose."

Between marrying the woman he loved and marrying someone else who could bear his children?

Grace remembered those hours she and Teagan had spent as kids playing with baby dolls, pretending to feed and rock and diaper change. Grace took for granted that when she was happily settled and tried to get pregnant, she wouldn't have trouble. Of course, adoption and surrogates had proven wonderful alternatives for so many couples who couldn't conceive. Although Teagan said she was used to the idea of being unable to conceive, something in her eyes said that this minute, she found acceptance hard.

When the music faded, both women's attentions were drawn by some commotion playing out on the marquee's platform. Taryn was getting ready to toss her bouquet. So Grace put her conversation with Teagan aside. If her friend ever wanted to talk more, Grace would be available, even from halfway around the world.

Having composed herself, Teagan tipped her head toward the gathering and put on a brave face. "Are you having a go?"

"Last time I was involved with a bouquet, I got way more than I bargained for."

Teagan grinned. Grace had told her about that kiss at the reception.

"I'm rooting for Shelby," Teagan said. "But I'll help make up the numbers."

When Teagan and the other eligible women were positioned on the dance floor, Taryn spun around and then threw her bouquet. The flowers sailed a few yards before Shelby, using her height advantage, snatched them out of the air. As people cheered, Dex marched up to her. Pride shining from his face, he dipped his fiancée in a dramatic pose before kissing her. All the wedding crowd sighed, including Grace.

Those two seemed so right for each other. It was as if all their edges and emotions were two halves of a whole.

At first, Grace had been hesitant about coming to Australia, to this event. She'd worried she might need to defend the fact that she and Wynn weren't serious the way Cole and Taryn were. The way people had assumed she and Sam had been.

And yet, with all these sentimental feelings surrounding her now, Grace felt as if she were falling into that very trap herself. In these couple of weeks, she felt so connected to Wynn.

From the platform, the DJ asked the women to move aside. Cole was preparing to throw the bride's garter.

Wynn stood at the back of the pack. When he caught sight of her, he sent over a wave an instant before Dex grabbed both his brother's arms and, fooling around, struggled to hold them behind Wynn's back. Grace laughed even as her chest tightened. Like the bouquet, tradition said that the person who caught the garter was meant to marry next. Dex would want to catch the garter and slip it on his fiancée's leg. But, as he wrangled free of Dex's hold and prepared to leap, Wynn seemed just as determined. A competitive spirit.

Or something more?

Teagan joined her. No one would guess that she'd been close to tears a few minutes ago.

"Look at those brothers of mine." When Dex tried to body block Wynn, Wynn elbowed his way in front again and Teagan laughed. "I've never seen Wynn have so much fun as he has this trip. These past months, whenever we've spoken on the phone, he's been so distant." Teagan wound her arm through Grace's. "Then you came along."

Grace looked at her twice. Right there was the kind of

comment she hadn't wanted to deal with during this trip. Wynn had lost the woman he had wanted to marry. Grace hadn't wanted to come across as anyone's replacement. She was still working through her own past.

And yet, something inside her had shifted. Something had changed.

Up on the stage, the groom knelt before his new bride and slipped the garter off her leg. As he held it above his head, the bullpen erupted with calls to begin.

The DJ revved them up more. "Guys, are you ready?"

A roar went up, the groom about-faced, and then the garter went flying at the same time as Wynn's heels grew wings. He caught the garter on a single finger. Feet back on the ground, he accepted slaps on the back from his peers. Meanwhile, out of the corner of her eye, she noticed Tate scooting through the pack and climbing the steps to the platform. He'd been having a blast dancing up there most of the night.

Wynn ambled over to her and dropped to one knee. The room hushed and all eyes fell upon them. Grace shrank back. This all had a familiar ring to it.

"Heel up here," Wynn demanded and slapped his raised thigh.

And have everyone ask later whether they'd set a date? That was going too far. She shook her head.

He sent her a devilish smile. "Guess I could always wear it as a headband." When he widened the garter and threatened to fit it around his crown, the crowd exploded with laughter. "You can't disappoint everyone." His voice lowered and gaze deepened. "Don't disappoint me."

The DJ stepped in, egging her on, and the crowd got on board. Wynn's expression wasn't teasing now. It was… solemn.

Grace's heart was booming in her chest, in her ears. This display was sending the wrong message.

Or was it just a bit of fun? With all the room smiling at them, she couldn't help but smile herself.

She placed one shoe on his knee. He slipped the garter up over her toes to just above the knee and then, holding her gaze with his, pushed to his feet. Rather than applaud, their audience was hushed. Were the guests aware of the energy pulsating between the two of them?

"Know what this calls for?" he asked.

She felt almost giddy. "A modest bow?"

Of course, his arms wound around her, and when his lips touched hers, any urge she might have had to push away, tell him to behave, faded into longing. She hadn't wanted to be the center of attention. She didn't want people to peg her into yet another hole. And yet…

Sensations gathered, vibrating through her body and spilling out like ripples from the sweetest sounding bell. For the slightest fragment in time, she believed that the fireworks going off in her mind and through her blood were so powerful that they physically shook the room.

Then a different reality struck, and the crowd began to scream.

Eleven

The force from the blast almost knocked Wynn over.

With the noise from the explosion ringing in his ears, he spun around. A piece of debris smacked his cheek as a haze of dark smoke erupted from somewhere near the platform. He remembered who had been standing there a second earlier and his stomach crashed to his knees.

He turned to Grace. "Get out of here. *Run!*"

With a hacking cough, she gripped his arm. "Tate's over there."

He knew it. He spun her around.

"Go!"

He headed toward the smoke by the platform, at the same time checking out the rest of the area. Guests smeared with dust and debris were charging toward the exit. He couldn't see Cole or Dex but, glancing over his shoulder, he caught sight of Taryn and Shelby helping Grace outside. Chances were his brothers were somewhere searching in this smoke, too.

With sparks spitting against his face, his nostrils burning and surrounded by the smell of his own singed hair, he leapt onto the platform. A pint-size silhouette—Tate?—stood frozen off to one side. If he'd been knocked down, he was on his feet again now. He'd be disorientated, possibly injured.

Wynn was bolting across when another explosion went off—different from the first. It was the electrical equipment shorting. Catching fire. Flames spewed out from the area where the DJ had set up. Heat radiated from the fire, searing Wynn's back as Tate's smudged, frightened face appeared in the smoke. His little hands were covering his ears. His eyes were clamped shut. Lunging, Wynn heaved Tate up against his chest, holding him close with one arm.

He was jumping off the creaking platform when Brandon materialized out of the chaos, holding an extinguisher. Brandon acknowledged Tate before disappearing back into the haze.

A moment later, Wynn was out in the sunshine, legs pumping toward the house where many of the startled guests had gathered. Security men were herding them back. Teagan was on her cell, presumably to emergency services, although he was certain one of Brandon's men would have sent up the alarm already. Teagan was also consoling Eloise, who was visibly shaken. When Teagan saw Tate, she covered her mouth to catch a gasp of relief. Dropping her phone, she put out her arms.

As Wynn passed the boy over, he did a quick check. Tate's little dress shirt was gray from the smoke, but Wynn didn't see any blood. The child's eyes were still closed, his face slack. Poor kid must have fainted.

While Teagan cradled Tate, Eloise seemed to emerge from her stupor. She brought both Teagan and Tate close, hugging them as much as her belly would allow. Wynn spun away, searching for Grace. And then, familiar arms were around him and she was saying, "Thank God you're out. Thank God you're safe."

He pulled her back, looked into her eyes. Grace was shaken but unhurt.

The screams of sirens bled in over the noise of the fire that had eaten through the marquee's ceiling. He gripped her arms. "I'm going back in."

As he pulled away, she tried to hold him back. Her eyes were as wide as saucers. They said, *Please, please, don't go.* During that beat in time, he remembered her ex had been a firefighter; if he had died in an accident, Wynn guessed it had been a blaze. But today he had no choice.

He couldn't see his father anywhere. Cole and Dex must be inside that trap, too. Engines were on their way, but there were extinguishers in there; Brandon had gone through safety procedures thoroughly with them before the guests had arrived and now his team needed help.

As Wynn sprinted back through the entrance, shock subsided into rage. When they found whoever was responsible, he wanted just five minutes alone with the son of a bitch. He wanted a fight?

This meant war.

"This time yesterday, champagne corks were flying down there." Grace turned from the window as Wynn entered the bedroom. "Hard to believe it's all cordoned off now with police tape."

Brandon Powell and his team, along with Wynn and his brothers, had extinguished the majority of flames before emergency services had arrived. Consequently, most of the marquee still stood, but the air outside reeked with the stench of charred debris. As Wynn joined her, Grace turned again to the view. This side of the crime scene tape, Brandon stood, arms crossed, as he spoke with a detective. A few feet away from them lay a bunch of flowers—Taryn's bouquet?—dirty and trampled.

"Teagan's with Tate." Wynn's arms wound around her middle as he pressed his chest snug against her back. "I can't believe he came out of it all with nothing more than a couple of scratches." He rested his chin on her crown. "He can't remember anything between the time I caught the garter and when he came to outside."

"Will he ever remember?"

"No one knows."

Hearing the screams and feeling the heat of the flames again, Grace winced and, pressing back against Wynn more, hugged his arms all the tighter. She hoped Tate never remembered.

Wynn turned her around to face him. "Cole followed up on his guests. Other than still being a little shell-shocked, everyone's fine."

"I guess the authorities will be in touch with them all."

"Brandon, too. If anyone saw anything that didn't fit, it'll come out. No one's going to let up until we track down whoever's responsible. In the meantime, Dad's been offered protective custody. He's considering it."

The Hunter clan had spent the night in a nearby hotel with security. After the grounds and house had been swept by the bomb team and cleared, they'd returned this morning. But questions remained: Would that madman try to strike again here? When? How?

The public was curious, too.

"Is the media still out front?" she asked.

"It's news," he groaned, before leading her to the bed and coaxing her to lie down next to him. Studying her expression, he brushed some hair away from her cheek.

"Did you get ahold of your family?" he asked.

"Mom says she wants me back right away."

"I'll speak with your father myself. Pass on my apologies."

"This isn't your fault."

"I'm still responsible. Cole doesn't want Taryn anywhere near this place. He's stepped up the security at the Hunter Broadcasting building, too."

"And Dex?"

"He wants Tate to go back to L.A. with him and Shelby. Makes sense, but Tate is clinging to his mom." He cursed. "Christ, this is a mess."

"And you?"

He held her chin and told her firmly, "I agree with your mother. I need to get you out of here."

He brushed his lips over hers and it didn't matter what had gone before—she felt nothing but safe.

"Did you get an update from Brandon?" she asked.

"He's adamant that every workman and hospitality person was checked coming in and going out. They've bagged some evidence that'll help determine the sophistication of the device, although bets are it was small and crude. No suspicion of high-grade explosive material."

He pressed a soft kiss to her brow. The warm tingles fell away as he pushed up off the bed and onto his feet.

"We have seats booked on an evening flight to New York," he said, moving to pour a glass of water from a carafe. "And you'll be flying on to Florida a few days after that."

It was a statement. And she did need to get back to Florida. She'd just expected to be here a couple more days. It was all ending so quickly.

"I've told Teagan we need to keep in touch," she said. "Either she'll come out to the East Coast or I'll visit her in Seattle."

He moved to the window to gaze out over the debris in silence.

She swung her feet over the edge of the mattress onto the floor. If she was ever going to know, she might as well ask now.

"What was she like?"

"What was who like?"

"The woman in that hotel foyer that night." *The woman you used to love. Perhaps still love.* "What was her name?"

When he faced her, his jaw was tight. She thought he was going to say he didn't want to talk about her, not ever. But then his chin lifted and clearly, calmly, he said, "Her name is Heather Matthews."

Grace crossed over to join him at the window. "I met Sam at a local baseball game. I dropped my hot dog. He offered to buy me another one."

Wynn considered her for a long moment.

"I met Heather at a gallery opening. She's a photographer. Inventive. Artistic. My perfect foil." He frowned to himself. "That's what I'd thought."

"Sam asked for my number," she said. "He asked me out the next week. A movie and hamburger afterward. Not long after that, I met his parents and he met mine."

"Cole and Dex were the devout bachelors," he said. "Too busy with other things to worry about that kind of commitment. But me..."

"You proposed."

"After two years."

"Sam and I were together for five years before..."

"He asked you to be his wife. And you said yes."

They were talking so openly, feeding off each other's stories. Now she opened her mouth to correct him. She hadn't accepted Sam's proposal. She'd turned him down. But the words stuck in her throat. If she admitted that—told him the truth about that, wouldn't he view her as another Heather? A woman who gave a man in love some hope only to wrench it away.

What would he think about her if he knew the rest of the story?

He set his glass on the window ledge and held her. "I didn't lose what you lost. *How* you lost."

Her stomach turned over. If he only knew…

"It was hard for you, too. Although…" She said the rest before she could stop herself. "Heather was only being honest with you."

He cocked his head as his mouth twisted into an uncertain grin. "Are you defending her?"

Grace was defending herself.

"The truth is," he said, "that when we met, I had industry connections. Two years on, she didn't need them anymore."

The urge swelled up inside Grace like a big bubble of hot air. She had to be honest with him, even if he could never understand.

"Wynn, I need to tell you something."

His face warmed with a smile that she imagined he kept only for her. "You don't need to tell me anything."

"I do."

"If it's something more about Sam, you don't have to explain. That explosion, those flames—yesterday would have shaken you up maybe more than any of us. I was cut when Heather and I broke up, but I didn't lose her in a fire—"

"Wynn, Sam didn't die in a fire."

His brows snapped together. "He was a firefighter." She nodded. "When your father mentioned an accident, I assumed…"

"Sam died in a car crash."

She wanted to tell him more, tell him everything, how she'd felt about Sam, how the years they'd spent together as a couple had just seemed to pass and drift by. She wanted to tell him about the secret that she had yet to describe even in that notebook. But now she couldn't bear to think of how quickly that thoughtful look Wynn was sharing with her now would turn into a sneer.

He led her over to a sofa. They sat together, his arm around her, her cheek resting against his chest. After a time, he dropped a kiss on her brow and asked, "Will you be okay alone for a while? I need to speak with my father. I need to get something off my chest before we leave."

"About that merger deal?" she asked.

"I'm not looking forward to it. Especially not after yesterday."

She held his hand. "You'll still be his son."

He sent her a crooked grin. "Fingers crossed."

Wynn found Eloise reclining on a chaise lounge, lamenting over the images in a swimwear catalogue. Seeing him, she seemed to deflate even more.

"Honey, could you bring me some ice tea from the bar?" She fanned herself with the catalogue. "I feel so parched. Must be all that ash floatin' around."

Wynn dropped some ice in a highball glass and then filled it from a pitcher in the bar fridge. Handing it over, he asked, "Where's Dad?"

"In his study, last I heard, worrying over insurance."

Soon, he'd be worrying about even more than that.

Wynn turned to leave, but Eloise called him back. She had a certain look on her face. He thought it might be sincerity.

"Wynn, I need to thank you."

Was this about how he'd rescued Tate from the burning marquee? He waved it off. "You've already done that."

Everybody had, but no one needed to. In his place, anyone would have done the same.

Eloise dragged herself to a sitting position. "I want to thank you for supporting us—my family. Supporting *me*."

Her chin went down and her gaze dropped. "I'm ashamed to say, I haven't always deserved it."

"There's no need to—"

"No. There is." Her palm caressed her big belly. "I may not be a fairy-tale mother, but I do love Tate. With him being away so much this year, with us almost losing him yesterday…" Her eyes glistened and her mouth formed what Wynn knew was a genuine smile. "I don't know what I'd do without you all."

Wynn allowed a smile of his own before he headed out. In a place he rarely visited, he knew the truth: some time ago, Eloise had propositioned Cole. Before this stalker trouble had begun, Tate had lived here in Sydney. Cole had had the benefit of seeing their father and Tate regularly, but he also had to contend with those issues surrounding his stepmother. Not pleasant.

Wynn arrived at his father's study and knocked on the door. He waited before knocking again. When there was no response, he opened the door and edged inside. Guthrie sat in a corner, staring into space. His hair looked grayer and thinner. The frustration and despair showed in every line on his face. As Wynn drew nearer, his father roused himself—even tried to paste on a smile.

"Take a seat, son."

"I wanted to let you know," Wynn began, "Grace and I are flying out this evening."

"Understood. Only sensible."

"If there's anything I can do… If you need me to come back for any reason—"

"You need to get back to New York. They'll be missing you there."

Wynn rubbed the scar on his temple. "There's a lot going on. Lots of industry changes."

"How do they put it? The death of print. We simply need

to find ways to work around it. Diversify. Make sure we're the last man standing."

"Actually, I have something in the pipeline. Something I'm afraid you won't like."

A keen look flashed in his father's eyes. "Go on."

"I've had discussions with Paul Lumos from Episode Features. My attorneys have drafted up a merger agreement."

His father's face hardened, but he didn't seem surprised. "You went behind my back."

"You assigned me to run our publishing operations in New York. I'm doing what I feel is best. Frankly, I don't see any option. Together, Hunter Enterprises and EF can save on overheads that are threatening to kill us both. And I want to act now. Eighteen months down the track, it could be too late."

"You know, it's not the way I do business."

"Then, I'm sorry, but you need to change."

"I'm too old to change."

"Which is why you put me in charge."

Pushing to his feet, Guthrie crossed to the window, which overlooked the peaceful southern side of the property. As boys, Wynn and his brothers had pitched balls there, and roughhoused with Foxy, their terrier who had long since passed on. Wynn's mother had always brought out freshly made lemonade. She'd never gotten involved with the business side of things. Her talent had lain in cementing family values, keeping their nucleus safe and strong. When she'd passed away, the momentum of everything surrounding her had begun to warp—to keel off balance.

His father had remarried, then had needed heart surgery. The company had been split up among "the boys," and the siblings had gone off to live thousands of miles apart. Wynn's decision to mount this merger was just another turn in the road.

He waited for his father to argue more or, hopefully, see reason and acquiesce.

Guthrie turned to face him. "Now I have something I need to say."

Wynn sat down. "Go ahead."

"Christopher Riggs…"

Wynn waited. "What about Christopher?"

Guthrie pushed out a weary breath. "Vincent Riggs and I were having lunch a couple of months ago. His son joined us. Of course, I'd met Christopher before, but he's grown into such a focused man. Afterward, Vincent confirmed that Chris was extremely thorough—a dog with a bone when he got his teeth into a task. His background is investigative reporting."

When his father seemed to clam up, Wynn urged him on.

"I know Christopher's background." What was it that Guthrie wanted to say?

One of his father's hands clenched at his side. "I employed him," Guthrie said. "I gave him a job."

"You mean you had *me* give him a job."

"Son, I gave him the task of being my eyes and ears in New York."

Wynn sat back. He didn't like the feeling rippling up his spine.

"Why would you need him to do that?"

Before he'd finished asking, however, Wynn had guessed the answer. The righteous look on his father's face confirmed it. And then all the chips began to stack up. His insides curled into a tight, sick ball.

"Despite your objections to a merger, you suspected." Wynn ground out. "You knew I'd go ahead and put the deal together."

When Guthrie nodded, Wynn's pulse rate spiked before

he bowed forward, holding his spinning head in his hands. His throat convulsed. He had to swallow twice before he could speak.

"You hired that man to *spy* on me?"

"You mentioned mergers months ago. I needed to know what was going on." He moved closer. "Christopher admires you. It took a good deal to convince him."

"I'm sure a fat transfer into his checking account helped."

"I knew, out of all my boys, you would have the most trouble accepting why I would need to do something like this."

Understatement. Wynn felt it like a blunt ax landing on the back of his neck. "Who else have you got over in New York, sharpening their knives, waiting for the chance to stab me in the back?"

"This was a special circumstance. I needed to be able to step in. Defuse anything before promises were made I couldn't keep."

"Do Cole or Dex know?"

"No one knows."

Wynn swallowed against the bile rising at the back of his throat. His lip curled. "Guess we're even."

"We can move on from this."

"Until the next time you decide to go behind my back."

"Or you behind mine."

"I could go ahead without your approval," Wynn pointed out. He had the necessary authority.

His father slowly shook his head in warning. "You don't want to try that."

Wynn shot to his feet and headed for the door.

His father called after him. "You're more like me than you know."

"Yeah. We're both suckers." He slammed the door behind him.

He was striding down the hall when he ran into Dex.

"What the hell is wrong with you?" Dex asked, physically stopping Wynn as he tried to push around him.

"It's between me and the old man."

"Whatever it is, it couldn't be any worse than what we all went through yesterday."

"It's up there."

Wynn told Dex everything—about the merger plan, about the lowlife corporate spy, Christopher freaking Riggs. When Wynn had finished, his brother looked uncomfortable. Dex ran a hand through his hair.

"Geez, I wonder if he's ever sent anyone over to spy on me."

He'd needed his sons to take over the reins. None of them was perfect, but at least each brother was nothing but loyal to the family.

"He'd be better off sending someone to spy on his wife," Wynn growled under his breath. "If he thinks I betrayed him organizing a company merger, what the hell would he think of Eloise throwing herself at Cole, and God knows how many others?"

Dex gripped Wynn's arm and hissed, *"Shut up."*

"Why?" Wynn shook himself free. "You know the story better than me."

Dex was looking over his shoulder. Wynn paused and then an ice-cold sensation crept down his spine. He shut his eyes and spat out a curse at the same time his father's strained voice came from behind.

"Seems everyone knew the story but me."

With a sick feeling curdling inside, Wynn edged around. His father stood a few yards away. Leaning against the wall as if for support, his skin had a deathly pallor.

Wynn felt his own blood pressure drop. *What the hell have I done?*

From behind, he heard footfalls sounding on the polished wooden floor. As he stared at his father, he heard Cole exclaim, "Eloise's water just broke. Dad, she's having the baby."

Twelve

Grace was headed downstairs when she heard a commotion. A woman was crying out as if she were in pain. Grace clutched the rail. What the hell was going on? Had that maniac stalker somehow struck again?

Below her in the vast foyer, Teagan appeared. Wynn's sister was helping Eloise to the front door. The older woman supported the weight of her big belly with both hands. Her stance was stooped and the grimace on the beautifully made-up face pointed to only one thing.

Grace fled down the stairs. She had not expected to be around for this. Wynn would want to stay longer now. It wasn't every day a person got to meet their new little brother or sister.

"Is there anything I can do?" Grace asked as she reached Teagan.

At that moment, Cole appeared. Rushing up, he let them know, "I just told Dad. He's on his way."

Eloise groaned, a guttural, involuntary, in-labor sound.

"Oh, *God*. We need to hurry." After another grimace, she started to pant.

"You'll be fine," Teagan told her. "Just try to relax. And nice deep breaths."

"I'll bring the car up," Cole said, flinging open one half of the double doors. "And where the hell is Dex?"

Suddenly Guthrie was there. The older man's expression was harried but not excited. His pallor, his shuffling gait...Wynn's father looked almost stricken. Wynn, who was coming up behind him, didn't look much better.

As Guthrie and Teagan escorted poor ambling Eloise out the door, Grace crossed over to Wynn. Worried, she cupped his bristled cheek.

"You look like you're ready to collapse."

He waited until everyone else was out the door, out of earshot, before he replied in a gravelly voice.

"I spoke with my father."

About the merger deal. "Guess he took the news badly."

Under her palm, a muscle in his jaw flexed twice. "He already knew."

Confused, she shook her head. "How?"

"And now he knows something else," Wynn muttered before wincing and rubbing his brow as if massaging the mother of all headaches. "I'm the world's biggest ass. I should have kept my freaking mouth shut," he groaned, clamping his eyes shut.

Grace tried to make sense of what he was saying but couldn't. "Wynn, Eloise is having the baby. You're going to be a brother again very soon."

He was shaking his head as if he wanted to block something out. Either they were staying or returning to New York. But if they were going to make that flight, they needed to think about getting to the airport.

"I opened my stupid mouth and now—" Resigned, he

exhaled and shrugged his broad shoulders. "Guess now I have to live with it."

Grace's heart was thumping high in her chest. "Wynn, please tell me what you're talking about."

His gaze—vacant and resigned now—met hers. He tried to tack up a tired smile. "There's no point dragging you into all this. You can't help. No one can."

As he grabbed her hand and they headed up the stairs, it took Grace all her willpower not to grill him again. But he was right. Whatever had happened between Wynn and his father, she couldn't help, no matter how much she might like to.

She and Wynn shared a certain spark. Aside from yesterday's near tragedy, these past days had been fun. But they were two individuals who had agreed to come together for a short time to enjoy a diversion. With bombs going off, things had gotten complicated enough. She shouldn't expect to get any more involved.

More to the point…Wynn clearly didn't want her involvement, either.

Later that evening, as Grace followed Wynn into Eloise's private hospital suite, she wished she were someplace else.

He'd decided they should stay and cancelled the flights. A couple of hours ago, when they'd received word that Eloise had given birth and both mother and child were doing well, Wynn had seemed less than enthusiastic.

Looking around the hospital suite now, the first thing Grace saw was a big white teddy bear with pink balloons and a sign that read, It's a Girl. Sitting up in bed, wearing a midnight blue nightgown set, Eloise looked radiant as she gazed down at her sleeping baby, who was wrapped in a pale pink blanket. Despite her complaints about being uncomfortable and "over it," she obviously adored this child.

While Shelby and Taryn were close enough to sigh over

the miniature fingers and that perfect baby face, Wynn's back remained glued to the wall. Dex looked uncomfortable, too. Guthrie stood on the opposite side of the room by a window, gazing upon the family scene from afar. No smile. Certainly he'd been through a lot these past hours, but Grace couldn't keep Wynn's earlier comment from her thoughts.

And now he knows something else.

Before coming to the hospital, she and Wynn, along with Dex and Shelby, had spent a quiet time with Tate. Wynn hadn't provided any more information about what had transpired between father and son that afternoon. She had vowed not to dig any more than she already had. But this situation, seeing Wynn so distant and cold, was cutting her to the quick.

Eloise was running a gentle fingertip around the baby's plump cheek. "Isn't she a honey? In fact, Honey would be a fine name." She glanced across at her husband. "Guthrie, darlin', you haven't had a hold. You know she looks just like you."

Wynn flinched. Muttering "Excuse me," he headed out the door.

Grace found him at the far end of the corridor. He seemed oblivious to the activity buzzing around him—nurses checking trays, mothers being wheeled to birthing suites. Gripping the wall behind his back, he looked haunted, as if he'd met a monster from his worst nightmare. She strode up to him.

Wynn wiped a palm down his face. Then, taking her arm, he led her into a small unoccupied waiting room.

Sitting together, he inhaled a fortifying breath.

"I didn't mean for him to hear," he began to explain. "I was blowing off steam. He must have followed me out of the study. I had no idea he was coming up behind me."

Blowing off steam. Grace's scalp began to tingle. "You mean your father? What did you say, Wynn?

"I said if anyone needed to be spied on, it was his wife." He angled toward her. "Can't you guess the reason Cole would rather avoid his beautiful, attention-seeking step-mother?"

When a thought crept in, too vile to contemplate, Grace shivered. She felt too stunned to breathe.

"Are you sure?"

"One holiday here in Australia, Eloise cornered Cole. Dex walked in and witnessed the tail end. Eloise had been trying to kiss Cole, caress him. She'd been drinking...." Wynn shuddered. "I never wanted to believe it. Now my father can't even look at me, or his wife, or his baby. After keeping it quiet all this time, Cole will be pissed when he finds out that Dad knows. He never wanted to be the bearer of that news. And Tate…"

Cringing, Wynn held his head in his hands. After a long tense moment, he sat back. His expression blistered with contempt.

"If I were Guthrie, I'd want to know. I'd want to know everything, straight up." He hung his head and then coughed out a humorless laugh. "You're probably thinking I wanted to give as good as I got."

That he'd meant to hurt his father through Eloise the same way he'd been hurt by Heather? God, no.

"I think there are times when lines get blurred."

"Between truth and deception? I'm not that naive." He found a grin. "Neither are you."

"I said that sometimes lines blur. Sometimes a person can unintentionally, well, *mislead*. Mislead themselves."

He thought about it and finally nodded. "Sure. I've convinced myself of things that turned out to be a lie."

"Me, too." She pulled down a breath. "The night Sam died," she said, "he proposed to me."

Wynn groaned and reached out to squeeze her hand with such tenderness, Grace could barely stand it.

"Wynn…" She swallowed. "I said no."

Wynn's expression stilled before doubt faded up to gleam in his eyes. "But…you *loved* Sam."

"I did love Sam." Her throat convulsed. "But more like a friend."

His brows swooped down. The grip on her hand tightened and then grew slack. "I'm confused."

"Sam and I dated for years. Everyone expected us to marry one day. I don't know if we started out in the same place and I grew in another direction, or if I was just too young to understand what I was getting myself into." Feeling heat burn her cheeks, she took a breath. "One minute we were kids, having fun. The next, people were asking when we were planning our big day."

Grace waited as the information sank in and Wynn slowly nodded.

"So, you turned Sam down," Wynn said, "he left, upset I imagine. And you never saw him again."

He paused and his eyes narrowed. "Did Sam say anything before he went?"

"Like what?"

"Like, I wish I was dead."

She recoiled. *Oh, God.* "Don't say that."

"But that's what's behind this confession, isn't it? What you've been thinking all these months after his accident. That you might have pushed him to it."

"I couldn't stop him from charging off," she explained, "getting in his truck. When I got word of the crash…"

The same raw regrets wound through her mind again. *If only I'd told him sooner. If only he hadn't taken the news so hard. If only I could have loved him the way that he'd loved me.*

"I never wanted to hurt Sam." She hesitated. "I'm not sure that Heather ever wanted to hurt you, either."

Wynn's face broke with a sardonic grin. "Hell, that's part of the attraction here, isn't it? Part of our bond. Only I didn't know it until now. Sam's tortured soul might be gone but I'm still here. You can't ask Sam just how bad it was, but you can ask me."

Before she could deny it, or admit he was right, Wynn went on.

"Well, I can tell you that the hours after Heather left me were the worst in my life. Jesus, I didn't *want* a life. My world was black, meaningless, and I couldn't see a way past it. So, if you're after some kind of absolution from me, I'm sorry, Grace. I just can't give it."

A tear spilled down her cheek. Wynn didn't have to forgive her. She hadn't expected that he would. The question was: would she ever forgive herself?

"I wish I could go back," she said. "Somehow make it right."

"There's no way back. All we can do is move forward. Call the truth the truth when we see it." He reached for her hand. "Avoid making the same mistakes."

Those words seemed to echo in her ears.

"That first night we met again," he went on after a moment, "we were clear on what we wanted. What we didn't want."

Grace remembered. She'd told him, *I'm not after a relationship...of any kind.*

"I'd always wanted a family of my own," he said. "When Tate came along, I decided I wanted a kid just like him." Taking a breath, he seemed to gather himself as he sat up straighter. "I don't want that anymore. None of it. I don't want to worry about infidelity or divorce or seeing my children every other weekend. I don't want permanent. No broken hearts. That's the God's honest truth."

A sound near the door drew their attention. A man walked in. His hair was rumpled like his shirt, but his smile was clear and wide; it spread more when he saw them sitting there.

"Hey, I have a boy!" he exclaimed as if he'd known them for years. "He's one hundred percent healthy." The man held his nose, as if he were trying to stem tears of joy. "He even looks like me. Same wing nut ears."

As the man headed for the coffee machine, Grace noticed someone else standing in the doorway. His head was hanging and a plastic dinosaur lay on its side near his sneakers. As she pushed to her feet, Wynn strode over and swung his little brother up on his hip.

"What are you doing here all by yourself, little man?"

"I ran down." Tate laid his head on Wynn's shoulder. "Teagan's coming."

A second later, Teagan appeared. She ruffled Tate's hair. "You're as fast as a cat, you know that?"

Putting on a brave face, Wynn hitched Tate higher. "Your baby sister's cute, huh?"

Tate rubbed a finger under his nose. "I guess."

Teagan dropped a kiss on Tate's cheek. "Doesn't mean we won't all love you just the same."

When Wynn pressed his lips to his brother's brow, a rush of emotion filled Grace's chest. Once he'd wanted a little boy just like Tate, but not anymore. At that wedding in New York, she'd told him that she wasn't after a relationship. She'd been clear. That had been *her* truth.

But now…

She didn't want to worry about infidelity or divorce, either. But one day she did want to get married. One day she wanted a child. A husband and family of her own. And she wanted to be closer to the family she had. She wanted to be near at hand to support Rochelle and April through the hard times ahead. Foremost, she wanted to truly get over the past, not just play at it. She thought she might finally be getting there.

No surprise. As much as that might hurt now, that meant a future without Wynn.

Thirteen

Two days after Eloise gave birth, Grace and Wynn landed back in New York. Wynn said she could stay at his place before she went back to Florida. She kept mum about her decision not to return there for good. Rather she said that she'd stay on with him an extra couple of nights.

He wanted to negotiate and they settled on five nights; after that explosion, they'd cut their stay in Australia short anyway. He'd have to make appearances at the office, he said. But Grace figured, with evenings all their own, five days would be enough for a proper goodbye.

When they arrived from the airport at Wynn's apartment, Grace headed for the attached bathroom where she ditched her travel clothes and slipped on a bathrobe. A few minutes later, she found Wynn, minus his shirt, standing in the middle of the master suite. He was studying his cell phone as if it might hold some answers.

"That was Cole," he said, looking up. "Apparently since we left, my father hasn't come out of his study."

Grace edged closer. Before leaving for the airport, Wynn had told his brother about his ill-timed slip regarding Eloise. "Does your stepmother know that Guthrie knows?"

"If she doesn't yet, my guess is she will soon." With a mirthless grin, Wynn rubbed his jaw. "My father's not the type to let a conflict go unresolved."

His young wife had sexually propositioned his oldest son—a humiliating kick in the gut. Guthrie would have suffered a complete loss of faith in Eloise—in his marriage. Still, some relationships could be repaired.

"Do you think they'll work it out?" she asked.

"Christ, I hope so. For the kids' sake."

That brand new baby, Honey, and, of course, Tate. When she and Wynn had left the Hunter mansion, his little brother had clung to Teagan's hand, a toy dinosaur clamped under his other arm. His chin had wobbled. He'd tried so hard not to cry.

"How's Tate?" she asked.

"Cole said he's missing us."

Missing Wynn. The Hunters didn't all get together often. Studies had proven that children benefited in so many ways from regular contact with extended family. That situation made her decision about being closer to her own family not only clearer but also vital. She'd made friends in Florida, in and outside of the practice. But when she'd left New York a year ago, Florida had merely been a means to escape.

She'd licked her wounds long enough. It was time to come home and, perhaps, start up her own practice. Years ago, when she'd decided on her college degree, that was the original plan. But she didn't want Wynn to think her decision to come home to stay, whenever he found out, had anything to do with *him*. It didn't. He'd told her—and in plain terms—he wasn't after "permanent." So, no need to further complicate this time together with info that didn't concern him. Wynn wouldn't want complications, either.

Now when he lifted her wrist and his mouth brushed the skin, a stream of longing tingled through her system. For these remaining days, she had every intention of acting on that physical desire. Then she would set those feelings aside. It made no sense to hang on to those emotions and fall in love with someone who would never love her back.

His arm wound around her at the same time his lips met hers. He kissed her until she was giddy and kneading his bare chest. By the time his lips left hers, her limbs were limp. This might not be forever but it was real and comforting and, for now, utterly right.

He swung her up into his arms and carried her over to the bed. When they lay naked on the sheet, he kissed her again—lazy and deep. Then his mouth made love to each of her breasts, her belly and then her thighs. She was coiling a leg around his hip, getting ready for his incredible icing on their cake, when he shifted and maneuvered her over onto one side.

The warm ruts of his abdomen met her back at the same time his tongue traveled in a mesmerizing line between her shoulder blades and up one side of her neck. As his palm sailed over her hip toward her navel, then her sex, her heightened physical need rushed to heat her blood. He explored her, delving and stroking until mad desire quivered and twisted inside of her.

Then he moved again, swinging her over. With her straddling him, he shifted her into position, aligned himself, and then thrust up, forcefully enough to send air hissing back through her teeth. Unsteady, she tipped forward, planting both palms on his pecs before his hands gripped her hips and she gave herself over to the heat and magic of his skill.

The strokes grew deeper, stronger, until each time he filled her, she pushed back and told herself never in her lifetime would she ever feel this good again. She'd never felt so connected, had never felt closer to anyone, to anything—

Her climax hit at the same time Wynn groaned and dragged her off him. Her fingers and toes were still curling when, out of breath, he gathered her close and buried his face in her hair. He ground out the words.

"I forgot."

Forgot what?

Then her eyes sprang open. She'd forgotten, too. They hadn't used protection. But he hadn't spilled inside of her.

"You pulled away in time," she said.

Which didn't mean a whole lot. Even with contraception, no one was a hundred percent safe. Every freshman knew a couple should never rely on withdrawal.

"We both got carried away," he said, urging her closer.

So true. But, no matter how carried away they'd both gotten, this was inexcusable.

"Wynn, that can never happen again."

He pressed a kiss to her brow. "You read my mind."

Which ought to have been the right response. No thinking person wanted an unplanned pregnancy, particularly between two people who had zero intention of spending their lifetimes together. And yet there was a part of her that felt—*disappointment?* Or, more simply, a sense of sadness.

One day she would find Mr. Right. Have a family. But she wasn't so sure about Wynn anymore. He was fun to be around. On so many levels he was caring, thoughtful. He was a good brother. An excellent lover.

But, deep at his core, Wynn could be cynical. Even bitter. He didn't believe in love—not for himself, in any case.

And it wasn't her place to convince him.

"In Greek mythology, Prometheus had returned the gift of fire to mankind. As far as Zeus was concerned, he'd overreached. The immortal was sentenced to an eternity of torment. A lifetime in hell."

Hunching into her winter coat, Grace listened in as a

local explained the story behind the famous Rockefeller Center statue to his tourist friend. Then he related how an engineer from Cleveland was contracted in the winter of 1936 to build a temporary ice-skating rink that had become a permanent fixture. Sometimes a bold idea panned out.

Sometimes it didn't.

Beside her, Wynn was on a call. Each time he spoke, vaporous clouds puffed out from his mouth. His black wool overcoat made his tall, muscular frame look even more enticing. When his gaze jumped across to her and he sent her a slanted smile, heat swam all the way through to her bones.

This afternoon, they'd strolled along Fifth Avenue, checking out the window displays at Saks, listening to carolers; Wynn's favorite Christmas song was "Winter Wonderland," and hers was "Silver Bells." No pressure. And yet, oftentimes Grace caught herself wondering where the two of them would be next holiday season—or five seasons from now.

Wynn finished the call and, with an apology, pulled her close.

"I'm taking you home, out of the cold," he said. "We can wrap presents." His lips grazed her cheek. "Do some *un*wrapping, too." His mouth grazed hers again. "I'll call Daphne and tell her I'm not coming back into the office."

"But you have a meeting about the merger this afternoon."

"That was Lumos. He postponed." He stole another feathery kiss. "I'm all yours."

Hand in hand, they headed down the Channel Gardens, a pedestrian street that linked to Fifth Avenue.

"Did you ever hear back from Christopher Riggs?" she asked, as the sound of carolers and the smell of roasting chestnuts wafted around them.

She'd been floored when Wynn had explained how

Guthrie had employed Riggs as a plant to feed back information regarding the possibility of a merger.

"Not a word," he said. "I figure, since he hasn't shown up at the office since I got back to town, my father must have gotten in touch and told him that his services were no longer needed."

"But you're going ahead with the merger. What if your father won't agree?"

"Then I'll have to reconsider my position here." He shoved his hands deeper into his coat pockets. "Times have changed. Are still changing, and fast. Business needs to keep ahead. I know a merger is the right way to go, and I can't twiddle my thumbs about it. I have to act now. If Hunter Publishing ever goes down, it won't be because I was a coward and didn't push forward."

So, he was willing to step down from his role at Hunter Publishing? She hoped this stalemate between father and son wouldn't come to that. And yet she saw in Wynn's expression now something that told her he wouldn't back down. Not because he was being stubborn but because he thought he was right. Typical Wynn.

But what was the alternative? He was convinced his company needed to evolve in order to survive and, hopefully, grow. If he couldn't make this deal happen—if a drastic change wasn't made—to his mind, he'd be knowingly committing corporate suicide.

She shunted those thoughts aside as he wrapped an arm around her waist.

"So," he leaned in toward her, "about that unwrapping…"

Her stomach swooped. He knew very well what day it was. Their agreement had been for her to stay at his place five nights. She'd made plans and, however much it cut her up inside, she needed to stick to them.

"I'm staying at Rochelle and April's tonight. We're putting a new star on their tree." Her heart squeezed for her sister and niece's situation. "Trey's not coming home for Christmas."

"Poor kid." His mouth tightened. "Another marriage bites the dust."

Grace understood the attitude, but his tone made her wince. He'd had his heart broken. Hell, Grace had broken someone's heart, too. But a man and a woman *could* build a happy life together. If they met at the right time, if they shared similar values, were prepared to commit—if they believed in their love, in their future, marriage could absolutely work out.

"So, you're staying at your sister's place tonight."

She nodded. "Flying to Florida tomorrow."

To formally resign and make arrangements to sublet her apartment there. In the New Year she would be back in New York and find a new door to hang her speech therapist sign on.

"But you'll be spending Christmas with your family, won't you?" he said as they turned onto Fifth Avenue.

"I thought I'd fly back up a couple of days beforehand." And stay—at her parents' home initially—until she found a place of her own.

"An invitation came through this morning," he said. "A Christmas Eve masquerade ball. All monies raised go to the Robin Hood Foundation."

Grace knew the charity. She supported their work helping all kinds of people in need. But she couldn't accept Wynn's invitation.

"You go." He would be generous with his donation either way. "I've already let my family know. I'm staying in with them Christmas Eve."

"You can change your mind."

"No, Wynn. I can't."

He didn't respond other than to tighten his grip on her hand.

When they passed a window display featuring a well-dressed snowman, she tried to edge the uneasiness aside. She wanted to enjoy what little time they had left together.

"Whenever I see a snowman," she said, "I think of that Christmas in Colorado."

When he didn't reply, she glanced across at him. Preoccupied, he was looking dead ahead. Fitting a smile into her voice, she tried again.

"You were the snottiest boy I'd ever met. You were always so serious."

"I've been thinking," he said. "This doesn't have to end. You and me. Not completely. I could fly down to Florida. You'll be up here to see family. And we can always get away again. Maybe to the Bahamas next time."

Grace hung her head.

She'd anticipated this moment. Wynn didn't want to say goodbye. Not completely. But *she* didn't want to risk this affair going on any longer. Every day she felt herself drawn all the more. Breaking off now, for good, was hard. One of the most difficult things she'd ever had to do.

But how much more difficult would it be if they went on and on until she had to admit to herself, and to Wynn, she wanted more. It might not have started out that way but, ultimately, she would be after a commitment that he couldn't give.

He thought they could get away again sometime…

She tried to keep her tone light. "I don't think that'll work."

His frown was quickly interrupted by a persuasive smile. "Sure it can."

"No, Wynn." *I'm sorry.* "It can't."

When he stopped walking, she stopped, too. His gaze had narrowed on hers, as if he were contemplating the best way to convince her. To *win*. Finally, his chin kicked up and he took her other hand, too.

"Let's go home and we'll talk—"

"Your apartment isn't my home, Wynn, it's yours. I was only a guest." She hadn't even unpacked her bags properly.

"You can come and stay any time you like," he said.

"For how long? One month? One year? As long as it's not permanent, right?"

Her heart was thumping against her ribs. As she drew her hand from his, his brow creased even more.

"Where did all that come from?"

"We had an agreement. We extended it. Now it's over."

"Just like that?"

"Tell me the alternative."

He shrugged. "We go on seeing each other."

"When we can. Until it ends."

Her throat was aching. She didn't want to have this discussion. Wynn had been burned—now he was staying the hell away from those flames. His choice. But she had to do what was best for her. She had to protect her heart. She had to get on with her life.

Her phone rang. Needing a time out, Grace drew her cell from her bag and answered.

"I wanted you to know," Rochelle began, sounding concise but also breathy. "It was scary at the time, but everything's fine now."

Grace pushed a finger against her ear to block the noise of nearby traffic as Wynn, hands back in pockets, frowned off into the distance.

"What was scary?" she asked.

"April was admitted to the hospital this morning."

Grace's heart dropped. She pressed the phone harder to her ear.

"What for? What happened?"

"She was on a play date," Rochelle said. "Cindy's mother knew about the allergies. No nuts. Not a hint. Apparently an older sister had a friend over who'd brought some cookies…"

Rochelle explained that when April had begun to wheeze and complain of a stomachache, the mother had called Rochelle right away. April's knapsack always carried an epinephrine auto-injector in case of just this kind of emergency. Her niece had spent the next few hours in the E.R. of a local hospital under observation. Sometimes there was a second reaction hours later. Not this time, thank God.

"We're at Mom and Dad's now," Rochelle finished.

"I'll come straight over."

"You don't have to do that. I just wanted you to know." Rochelle paused. "But if you can make it, I know April would love to see you. Me, too."

When Grace disconnected, Wynn's expression had eased into mild concern. He cupped her cheek.

"Everything okay?"

Grace passed on Rochelle's news. "I need to go and give them both a big hug."

Wynn strode to the curb and hailed a cab in record time. But when he opened the back passenger-side door, Grace set a hand on his chest.

"You don't need to come," she said.

"Of course I'll come."

An avalanche of emotion swelled, poised to crash over the edge. She shook her head. "Please. Don't."

As traffic streamed by one side of them and pedestrians pushed past on the other, Wynn's gaze probed hers. For a moment, she thought he was going to insist and then she would have to find even more strength to stay firm when all she really wanted to do was surrender and let him comfort her. But that was only delaying the inevitable.

His look eventually faded beneath a glint of understanding. She could almost feel awareness melt over him, and see the consequences of "what comes next" pop into his head. In his heart, Wynn knew this was best.

"What about your bags?" he asked.

"I'll arrange to have them picked up."

"No. I'll send them on. I've got your father's address."

Leaning in through the passenger doorway, he spoke to the driver. "The lady's in a hurry," he said before stepping back.

On suddenly shaky legs, she slid into the cab. Before Wynn could close the door, she angled to peer up at him.

"I really did have the best time," she said.

His jaw flexed and nostrils flared before his shoulders came down and he nodded. "Me, too."

And then it was done. The door closed. The cab pulled away from the curb and she rode out of Wynn Hunter's life for good.

Fourteen

The next day, Wynn sat in his office, staring blankly at an email message his father had sent. He'd read it countless times.

Son, you have my blessing.

His eyes stinging, Wynn's focus shifted to the final merger document waiting on his desk. All the *i*'s were dotted. Every *t* crossed. Bean counters were happy and public-relations folks were beaming over the positive spin they could generate. In an hour, signatures would be down and the deal would be done.

Thank God.

He had his father's consent, but did he really have his approval? Did Guthrie understand that his son had acted only in the best interests of Hunter Publishing? Of the family? Which brought to mind that other predicament. The issue surrounding his father's marriage. The question of infidelity. Of trust. And desire.

He glared at his cell phone and finally broke. A moment later, he was waiting for Grace to pick up. When the phone continued to ring, he thought back and analyzed the situation.

There was no reason for her to be upset with him. After her niece's allergic reaction scare, Grace had been told that the little girl was home and fully recovered. Nevertheless, naturally he'd wanted to jump in that cab and keep her company—offer his support.

Yes, he'd wanted her to come to that charity ball Christmas Eve. If at all possible, he'd wanted her to stay a few more nights. Sure, the vacation was over but he wanted to see her again. Way more than he could have ever imagined. He cared for Grace a great deal.

Enough to continue to push the point?

He hadn't changed his mind about relationships, particularly after pondering the future of his father's second marriage. And it seemed Grace hadn't changed her mind about not wanting a serious relationship, either. Yesterday she'd been blunt. They'd had an arrangement. Now it was over. She didn't want the tie.

The line connected. Grace said hello.

"Hi." He cleared his throat. "Just making sure your niece is okay."

"April's fine. Thank God."

He closed his eyes. Just her voice… The withdrawal factor after only twenty-four hours was even worse than he'd thought.

"Did your bags get to your parents' address?"

"Yes. Thanks. I really appreciate it."

A few seconds of silence passed before he asked the question. "So, you're leaving for Florida today?"

"On my way to the airport now."

Wynn paused to indulge in a vision: him jumping in a cab and cutting her off at the pass. Crazy-ass stuff. Better to simply let her know his thoughts. His—*feelings*.

"Wynn, you there?"

"I'm here."

"I need to pay the driver. I'm at the airport."

"Oh. When's your flight?"

"Soon."

He heard a muffled voice—the driver, Wynn presumed.

"Sorry," she said. "I really have to go."

The line went dead. Wynn dropped the phone from his ear and rewound the brief conversation in his head. Then he stared at that merger contract again. He was about to sit back, rub his brow, when his cell phone chimed. Jerking forward, he snatched it up.

"Grace?"

A familiar voice came down the line. "Hey, buddy."

Wynn slumped. "Hey, Cole."

"Before I start, I want you to know that no one, including Dad, blames you for the fallout from your slip last week."

Cold comfort.

"Where is he with it?" Wynn grunted. "Filing for divorce?"

"*No*. He and Eloise have spoken. Are speaking."

Well, that was something.

"I'll keep you up to date," Cole said.

If only he could take it back. Of course, he didn't condone Eloise's behavior. He simply hadn't wanted to be the unwitting messenger, particularly when things in Sydney were crap enough for his father as it was.

"How's the investigation going?" Wynn asked.

"No one's easing up. Surveillance footage hasn't turned up any leads. Crime investigation is still tracking down possible links with the device's components. They're looking into DNA."

"And Brandon?"

"Everyone's in his sights, even his own men."

Off the job, Brandon Powell exuded a laid-back air, but beneath the cool sat a steely nerve. With his black belt in martial arts, a man would have to be nuts to pick a fight with that guy.

"Is there still a battery of security guards around the place?" Wynn asked.

"Twenty-four seven."

"And Tate?"

"When Tate begged to stay with his parents a bit longer, Dex and Shelby stayed on, too. Tate knows his parents are either avoiding each other or quarrelling. We all try to shelter him from it as much as we can, but Eloise isn't good with conflict."

Cole was being kind there.

Wynn was concerned about Tate coping with this situation, but none of this could be good for that baby—his half sister—either.

Wynn loosened his tie. Thank God he'd never have to go through anything like this. This whole situation sucked so bad, discussing it made him feel physically ill.

"I have something to ask," Cole said.

"Anything."

"Could you have Tate come for Christmas?"

Wynn blinked several times. "Where exactly is this coming from? How's Tate going to take that?"

"Tate's the one asking."

"And he asked to stay with me? Not Dex or Teagan or you?"

"He must want to spread the love. Or maybe he feels particularly safe with you. The way you rescued him that day—"

"He doesn't remember that."

"Maybe he does." Cole took a breath. "Can I put him on a flight next week?"

"Of course." *If that's what Tate really wants.* "Let me know the details when they're locked in." Dates, times, and obviously Tate would need a chaperone on the flight.

There were two beats of silence before Cole asked, "How's Grace?"

Wynn explained yesterday's conversation—how she wanted to end it and how he had complied.

Cole grunted. "How do you feel about that?"

"I feel…well, pretty crappy about it, actually."

"Because?"

He needed to ask? "Because we had a good time together."

"And?"

"And, I *like* her. But, Cole, she's right. We had an arrangement."

"What's that?"

Wynn hesitated a moment and then spilled it all—about Grace's ex, his proposal, the accident and how she wasn't interested in getting serious with anyone right now.

"What about you?" Cole asked.

"Of course, I was on board."

"Because of your bust-up with Heather."

Wynn ran his fingers through his hair. This wasn't rocket science. "Yes, because of my bust-up. I planned to marry the woman."

"Now you plan to stay single."

"Yes, sir, I do."

"And you told Grace that."

Wynn narrowed his eyes. "I told her. But you're missing the point. Cole, *she* was the one who wanted to end it."

"Smart girl."

Wynn cocked a brow. "I think I should feel insulted."

"Ask yourself something, and answer it truthfully. Are you falling in love with Grace Munroe?"

Wynn opened his mouth and then shut it again before he decided on a defense. "Just because you're happily married now—"

"Wynn, it doesn't have to be Grace, but I'd hate to see you lose someone meant for you because you're too damn stubborn and stuck to see what's right in front of your nose."

When they disconnected, Wynn was hot around the gills. Cole didn't understand. Wynn didn't need anyone second-guessing his life, his decisions, or telling him what he should or should not feel.

Five minutes on, Wynn had cooled down, not that it made him feel any better. His relationship with his father had been resurrected. The merger deal would go through. And yet, with all that he had…irrespective of all that "being right"…none of it seemed to matter alongside one simple, complicated truth.

He'd lost Grace.

Fifteen

A few days after Grace had flown down to Florida to resign her position, she was back in New York for the holidays. Back in New York to stay, although she had yet to find
a place of her own. Not that Wynn could know any of that.

When he sent a text to say his little brother was visiting for the holidays, naturally Grace was curious. Were
Guthrie, Eloise and the baby here in the States, too? She
doubted it. She'd responded, How cool! Tate would always
have a very special place in her heart. Then a second text
had mentioned that Tate loved to visit Rockefeller Center—
every day at around two.

She knew she probably shouldn't. But she decided to
go anyway.

Five minutes ago, she'd arrived at the Center and immediately spotted her boys. Dressed for chilly weather, the
Hunter brothers were checking out skaters, laughing whenever Santa slid around with a conga line of kids hanging
off the back of his red suit. The giant tree towered over the

crowd, rewarding everyone with glowing, festive thoughts. Like streams of sparkling atoms filling the air, on Christmas Eve, magic seemed to be everywhere.

As if he sensed her nearby, Wynn pulled up tall and scanned the crowd. When their gazes connected, a spark zapped all the way up her spine. His expression shut down before a smile tugged the corners of his beautiful mouth.

He didn't call her over. Rather he simply waited, drinking her in as if he worried that, should he look away, she might disappear. Then Tate tugged his brother's windbreaker and his little red beanie tipped back. Wynn crouched down.

Tate seemed to know that his big brother was distracted. When he spotted her, Tate jumped into the air, so high she thought his feet must have grown springs. Wynn placed a hand on his shoulder, but Tate refused to calm down. Grace heard his squeals for her to join them.

He was such a good kid, going through such a hard time. His family might have wealth but, no doubt, he would trade everything, and in a heartbeat, for a safe and settled home.

As she came closer, Tate broke away. In a bright blue parka and boots, he scampered up and flung his arms around her hips.

"This is a really big city," Tate said, still hugging her tight. "You found us anyway." He pulled back and looked up with the familiar tawny-colored eyes that stole her heart away. "The Empire State Building has a hundred and two stories."

She laughed. "Pretty high, huh?"

"Didja see the snowman in that window?" He pointed toward the avenue before he flapped his arms against his thighs and shrugged. "Santa's coming tonight. We need to finish the tree."

Wynn had strolled up. "And we need to get to bed before those reindeer swing their bells on into New York."

Grace's stomach fluttered at the sound of his voice—the

white flash of his smile. She had to dig her hands deeper into her pockets to stop them from reaching out.

"Mommy takes my picture when I put cookies out for Santa, but Wynn's gonna do it this year."

When Tate took his brother's leather-gloved hand, the picture, its setting, just seemed to fit.

Grace schooled her features. She was getting misty, damn it.

"Not going to that masquerade ball?" she asked Wynn.

"They have my donation." He winked at his little brother. "Tate and I have important things to do."

Tate gave a big nod. "Can Grace come over?"

Wynn arched a brow. "I think she already has plans."

"I'm staying with my parents," she told Tate. "My sisters will be there tonight. My niece, too. April's almost your age."

Tate's mouth hooked to one side, not in a happy way. "A girl?"

"Like Honey," Wynn said, "only older." Then he checked out the sky, which was heavy with the promise of snow. "We were getting ready to go for a hot chocolate—"

"Oh, sure," she slipped in. "I won't hold you up."

"I like mine with marshmallows on top," Tate said. "Wynn likes chocolate curls."

Grace jerked a thumb toward the street. "I really have to go. But I have something for you, Tate." She drew a wrapped gift from beneath her coat. Accepting it, Tate looked to Wynn. "He can open it now," she said.

Tate peeled the wrapping and eased out the gift. His legs seemed to buckle before he whooped with delight.

"A Yankees triceratops! His horn goes right through the cap!" Tate gave her an earnest look. "Santa can't beat this."

Grace held her throat. Her heart felt so full and at the same time so empty. She wished she could stay longer. But a fast, clean break would be best.

"After the holidays, Wynn's gonna take me to his office." Tate tugged his brother's coat. "Can I go see the skaters?"

"Sure, pal." When Tate was out of earshot, Wynn stepped closer. His gaze swept over her face, lingered on her lips.

"You look great," he said.

"You look—relaxed. Did your father come out with Tate?"

"Cole chaperoned him over on the flight. Tate had asked if he could come out."

Wynn didn't need to explain more. Grace thought she understood.

"Dad let me know he was okay with the merger going through," he went on.

"*Wow.* That's great. Congratulations."

"He and Eloise are trying to work things out."

She eased out a grateful breath. "I'll pray that they do."

He looked back at Tate standing a short distance away, checking out Santa, who was performing one very fine axel jump.

"It's good having Tate over," he said, "even if the circumstances aren't the best."

"Any progress on who was behind that explosion?"

"Not yet. But I'm sure they'll find something soon." He adjusted one leather glove then the other. "Dex and Shelby are flying over tomorrow afternoon. They're staying with her father in Oklahoma tonight. In fact, Mr. Scott is flying out here with them."

"A real family affair."

"He and Tate got to be chums when Dex took him out there for a stay."

"What are Cole and Taryn doing tomorrow?"

"Visiting Dad and the new baby. And Eloise, I suppose."

Awkward. "And Teagan? Is she flying out to be with Tate, too?"

"She says she isn't. When I spoke to her, I got the feeling it might have something to do with a man."

The man who wanted a big family? "Did she sound okay?"

"She sounded preoccupied."

As soon as she left here, Grace decided, she'd phone Teagan. She hoped her friend hadn't broken up with the guy she'd been seeing. If he was in love with her, and Teagan felt the same way, there had to be a way to sort everything out.

"I was wondering," Wynn said, crossing his arms, "whether you might like to come over tomorrow, too. I know you'd have all the traditional stuff in the morning with your family. And lunch. But if you're free for dinner, Tate would love to have you over. Dex and Shelby, too."

As he made the invitation, the ache in Grace's throat grew and grew. But she'd been prepared for something like this. Wynn didn't give in easily. Neither did she.

Over these past few days, with being away from Wynn and missing him so much, she'd come to a solid conclusion. She loved this man. Loved most everything about him. But she wasn't about to do anything foolish like admit it and set herself up for a gigantic fall. She'd seen firsthand how a move like that could destroy a person.

"Thanks for the invite," she said, proud of herself for holding his gaze. "But I can't. I'm sorry."

"No. It's fine. *I'm* sorry. Just had to ask. You know. For Tate."

Tate was gazing up at the big tree in wonder, holding his new dinosaur under his arm. So cute and innocent.

She swallowed.

God, her throat was tight. Clogged.

She really had to go.

"I'll just say goodbye," she said.

Wynn tried to smile. "You've only been here a minute."

She began to skirt her way around him.

"Stay a little longer," he said.

"I have to go."

"Grace." He caught her arm and her eyes finally locked with his. A soft smile touched the corners of his mouth. "Grace. I don't want to lose you."

She held her stomach. How blunt did she need to be? "Wynn, you don't want what I want."

"I want you."

"And I want *love.*"

Her heart was thumping in her ears. She felt weak and emotional and, hell, it was *true*. And now, in a single heart-beat, it was out.

She watched understanding sink in and then resistance darken his eyes. Meanwhile, Tate had run back and was tugging on his big brother's coat again.

"Wynn, where's the hot chocolate shop? I'm cold."

Grace crouched down. She prayed Tate didn't see that she was trembling or that tears edged her eyes.

"You'll have a great Christmas with everyone, won't you, hon?"

"Are you gonna come, too?" Tate asked.

"Afraid not," she said.

Tate studied the Yankees dinosaur she'd given him. "Well," he said, "maybe next time."

When she looked up at Wynn, he was taking Tate's hand.

"Come on, buddy," he said. "Don't want that hot choco-late going cold."

They started off and then Wynn stopped, turned back around.

"Have a good day tomorrow, Grace," he said.

Forcing a smile, she nodded but couldn't say the words. *Merry Christmas.*
Happy New Year.

It was past eight that night when Grace edged inside the room her niece used whenever she stayed at Grandma and

Grandpa's. The night-light was on, casting stars around the ceiling and walls.

"Is she asleep?" she whispered.

With a children's Christmas book closed on her lap, Rochelle had been gazing at her daughter.

"I thought I'd need to read *'Twas the Night Before Christmas* at least twice through." Rochelle eased to her feet. "April was counting sugar plums after the third verse." Crossing over, Rochelle saw the notebook Grace held. "You're working on exercises tonight?"

"Not the kind you think."

The women tiptoed out of the room. Downstairs, their mother was finalizing tomorrow's menu with Jenn. Dad would be reading in his chair. Tilly was out with friends, due home soon, or at least not late.

Grace led Rochelle into her room. The fire she'd lit earlier was crackling with low yellow flames while snow piled up on the windowpane outside. A gift she'd bought April that afternoon lay on the bed. When she and Rochelle sat on the quilt, Grace rapped her knuckles against the notebook's cover.

"I had something I needed to work through," Grace explained. "I thought writing it all down might help. It's about Sam." She bowed her head. "A year after the funeral, I still felt responsible."

"Because you didn't love him?"

"The night Sam died, he asked me to marry him." Everyone knew that he had planned to sometime very soon. "Rochelle, I said no. I turned him away."

Rochelle froze. "Okay, wait. You think he took his own life, or maybe he was so upset that he lost control of the vehicle?"

"Not anymore." Wincing, Grace gripped the book. "I mean, I don't know."

"He'd just gotten off a long shift. It was deemed an accident."

Grace finished for her. "Authorities surmised he'd fallen asleep at the wheel. But I couldn't put it to rest."

"So you kept it bottled up inside of you all this time?" Rochelle's hand covered hers. "Grace, you're not responsible for what happened to Sam. Just like I'm not responsible for Trey's actions."

"Yeah. I know, but…"

"Sam was taken away from us too soon. We were all lucky to have known him. But you can't change the past, and you can't change how you feel. If Sam were here now, he'd want you to let it go and really get on with your life."

Grace expelled a breath. Of course, Rochelle was right. Tonight, missing Wynn and wondering about the future, Grace had only needed to hear it, and from someone she trusted, despite any past sisterly spats.

That story finished, Grace slid the notebook into her bedside drawer and then eyed the velvet box containing April's gift. "What time's Trey collecting April tomorrow?"

"He isn't. Says it'll be too awkward for her." Rochelle rolled her eyes. "Makes me all the more determined. This Christmas is going to be extra special—with plenty of family and love to go around. Every kid deserves that."

Grace picked up April's gift and flipped open the lid. A huge crystal ring shone out. "Think she'll like it?"

"April?" Rochelle gave a low whistle. "Heck, I want it myself."

Grace cut the paper while Rochelle ripped off some tape.

"Have you heard from Wynn?" Rochelle asked, pressing a glossy pink bow on top.

Grace had confided in Rochelle about that afternoon when she'd called after April's allergy scare. She spilled all about her tormented feelings toward Wynn as well as her decision to stay clear. To protect her heart.

"I saw him today." Grace set aside the wrapped gift. "His little brother's out for the holidays."

"I thought you said you two were through."

"We are. But Tate asked to see me. After all that kid's been through, I wasn't going to stand him up."

"Oh, Grace, are you sure you want to end it? You had such a great time in Australia."

"Aside from the explosion."

"Aside from that." Rochelle leaned forward. "The way you feel about each other...the things he says and does..."

"Are all *incredible*. Addictive is the word. But Wynn isn't interested in strings." She fell back on the bed and stared at the ceiling. "He doesn't want the hassle."

"He might change his mind."

No. "I need to get on with my life."

Grace's cheeks were hot, her throat thick. She sucked down a breath and, determined, pulled herself up. She was moving on.

"For now," she said, calm again, "that means helping you bring Santa's presents in from the garage." Swiping April's gift from the quilt, she headed for the door. "One extra-special Christmas coming up."

Wynn jingled the ornament at the overdecorated tree, which was set up in a prime corner of his apartment's living room.

"This is the very last bell."

Tate pointed to a spot on a lower branch. "Here."

After securing the bell in place, Wynn pushed to his feet, flicked a switch and the tree's colored lights blinked on, flashing red and green and blue.

Tate squealed. "We did it!"

"Of course we did! We can do *anything*."

They jumped into a "dice roll" move and finished with a noisy high five.

"Now, we need to put out those cookies for Santa," Wynn said, shepherding Tate toward the open-plan kitchen.

"And take a picture to send to Mommy."

Tate dropped some red tinsel on the special Santa plate while Wynn broke open a new batch of cookies. When the milk was poured, they moved to the dining table and set the snack up. They took a photo and sent it through to Australia. Within seconds, they got a reply.

Looks delicious! Love you, baby.

Tate read the message ten times over. When he said, "Send it to Grace," Wynn hesitated. He'd sent her a couple of messages during the week and when she'd shown up that afternoon at the rink, frankly, he'd almost begged her to stay. And then things had gone a little far afield. At first he hadn't been sure what she'd said. He'd only known the word *love* was involved.

She'd put it out there. What she'd wanted had changed. Or shifted one hell of a lot forward. At Cole's wedding, before that explosion, he might have been swayed. Knowing he was at least in part responsible for the possibility of his father's marriage ending—knowing the added crap this small boy would need to endure if that union ultimately broke down for good… Why the hell would he, would anyone, knowingly risk that much? When things went south, it just freaking *hurt* too much.

His jaw clenched tight and he lowered the phone. "How about we send the snap to Grace in the morning?"

Hopefully, with everything else happening and their visitors arriving, Tate would forget about it.

"Won't Grace like the picture?"

"Well, sure. She'd love it. It's just getting late. She's probably already in bed."

"She could still find it in the morning when she wakes up."

"Which is why we ought to send it then."

"We might forget."

"No way."

Tate blinked. "Please, Wynn."

Wynn took in his brother's uncertain expression, the mistrust building in his eyes. "You're right," he said, thumbing a few keys. "There. Sent."

They waited. No reply came through. But Wynn simply explained, "See. Told you she'd be asleep by now. We should be, too."

Picking up Tate, he swirled him through the air until his brother was giggling madly. Then they moved to the guest bathroom, where Tate brushed his teeth. After Wynn had bundled his brother into bed, he saw the distant look in Tate's eyes. Was he thinking of his home?

"Do you miss your Mom, Tate?"

He fluffed the covers. "Daddy, too. But I'm kinda used to it."

"Being away?"

Tate nodded. "I had lots of fun with Dex and Shelby. With Teagan and Damon, too."

"Damon's Tea's friend, right?"

"He likes Tea a lot. Like you and Grace. They hold hands and laugh."

Wynn cleared the thickness from his throat. "Sounds good."

Tate's head slanted sideways on the pillow. "Why didn't Grace want to come home with us?"

"It's Christmas Eve. Grace is with her family."

Tate flashed a gappy grin. "I'm glad I'm here with you."

"Things must seem a little…mixed up back home."

"That's not why I wanted to come. I thought you'd be lonely. I thought we could hang."

Wynn smiled but then sobered. "Why did you think I'd be lonely?"

Tate frowned but didn't say anything.

"Things aren't as good as they could be back home," Wynn said. "But you need to remember that everyone loves you very much—your parents, your brothers, Tea. Me. Family's very important."

"If that's right, Wynn, why don't you want a little boy of your own?"

Wynn stopped breathing. "Why would you say that?"

"You said so. You don't want to have a son like me, or family, or anything."

"Did you hear that at the hospital?"

"Tea wanted something hot to drink. I ran ahead. You and Grace were there, talking." He fluffed the covers again. "It's okay. I don't want to be a dad, either. Kids only get in the way. Mommies only ever sleep or cry." His voice lowered. "Mommy says it's all your fault. Don't know why."

Wynn did. If he'd kept his big mouth shut, Guthrie wouldn't have overheard his bleating to Dex about Eloise coming on to Cole.

Tate pushed out a sigh. "I'm pretty sure it's my fault though. That's the other reason we should have Christmas together. No one else has to feel mad or sad when we're around."

It felt as if a giant hand was squeezing the life from his windpipe. Tate thought it was *his* fault?

Wynn's voice cracked as he said, "I'm so sorry about what's happening at home." He'd never been more sorry about anything in his life.

"Aw, Wynn. Don't cry." Tate reached to cup his big brother's face. "You're perfect."

A serrated knife twisted high in Wynn's gut. He ran a hand over his little brother's head. So soft and sweet and unreservedly worthwhile. His own childhood had been great. He'd known he was loved and adored by both parents. That's why he'd been so sure about having a family of his own. Then Heather had done him in and all of that no longer mattered. Except...

Now, looking deeper, that *hadn't* changed. In this moment, that dream seemed like the only thing that *did* matter. What the hell was the point of being here if he couldn't be with the person that he—?

That he what exactly? Just how deeply did he feel about Grace?

"I want you to know that if ever I had a boy of my own," he croaked out, "I'd want him to be just like you."

"That's not what you said. You said if you never had a family of your own, you wouldn't miss it."

"You're wrong." Drawing back, Wynn shook his head. "No. *I* was wrong. I was sad and confused. I haven't, well, been myself lately. But I do want a son."

Tate touched his big brother's cheek. "I think Grace is mad at you, too."

"I don't blame her." Wynn found Tate's hand on his cheek and set his jaw to stem the emotion. "We're just going to have to fix it, is all."

"Do you think that we can?"

"Of course we can. Remember?" Wynn smiled. "You and I can do anything."

Sixteen

Early the next morning, with all the presents opened, April was twirling around the Munroe's twelve-foot tree showing off the new pink princess costume that Santa had brought. There were coloring books and puzzles and a bike with training wheels, too. Grace liked to think her niece's favorite gift was the big crystal ring she'd received from her aunt. When she'd opened the box, April's eyes had bugged out. The ring hadn't left her finger since.

Now Grace sat on a couch sampling a perfume that Tilly had hoped she would like—sweet and sassy, just like her younger sister. Her father stood by the window that overlooked the vast backyard and, beyond that, a park. Children had constructed a snowman there—hardly anything new for this time of year. Still, this morning the sight created a giant lump in Grace's throat.

Wynn and that long-ago Christmas were in her thoughts constantly. After seeing him with Tate yesterday, she'd barely been able to sleep. She imagined she heard his laugh.

She closed her eyes and saw his sexy, slanted smile. She felt so filled with memories, she wondered if her family could see them mirrored in her eyes. Smell them on her skin.

April twirled over and presented a large gold and crimson Christmas bonbon.

"I'll let you win," April said.

Grace grabbed an end and angled her wrist just so, but when April tugged hard, the gold paper ripped and she won the prize—a green party hat and tiny baby doll.

Rochelle was checking out the foot spa Grace had given her. "My toes can't wait to use this," she said, wiggling her slippered feet.

"And I can't wait to wear these." Her mom was showing off a silk scarf and sapphire drop earrings.

Grace forged her way through a sea of crumpled paper to join her dad. He had three new ties slung around his neck.

"More snow's on the way," he said, surveying the low, gray sky.

April's voice came from behind. "Didn't stop Santa last night. Mommy, can I ride my bike?"

Rochelle was studying the titles on a CD, a gift from Tillie who, earphones in, was tapping her foot to a tune belting out of her new iPod.

"It might be too slippery." Rochelle pushed up and crossed over to the duo parked by the window. Then she poked her nose closer to the pane. "That's a mighty fine looking snowman."

April squealed. "Can I go see?"

Grace turned around and tapped April's tiara. "I'll take you. I want to see him, too." She crouched before her niece. "But our guy looks as if he's missing a hat and pipe."

"That's my job." Grandpa headed off. "I put them away in the same place every year."

She and April pulled on their boots, shrugged into coats and worked their fingers into mittens or gloves. April took the hat from Grandpa, Grace the pipe, and together they headed out down a shoveled path rimmed with glistening snow. As they passed through the side gate, April scooted on ahead.

"Be careful!" Grace called out. "Don't slip. You don't want to get your princess skirt wet."

When Grace caught up, April was skipping about the snowman.

"He's so tall!" Her niece held out the hat. "I'll put it on."

Grace lifted April high and she very carefully positioned the battered fedora on the snowman's head. When Grace put April down, the little girl stood back. With her mittened hands clasped under her chin, she inspected her work.

"It's crooked."

"I think it lends him character."

"What's that?"

"It means snowmen are more fun when their hats don't sit straight."

But if Wynn were here, Grace thought, he would want to straighten it, too.

"You can do the pipe." Examining the snowman, April tilted her head and her beanie's pink pom-poms swung around her neck. "Put it in crooked."

Grace slid the pipe in on one side of the snowman's mouth, and then flicked it up a tad.

April danced around the snowman again, her pink princess skirt floating out above her leggings while she sang. Then she stopped and trudged closer to their man.

"Something's up there." April pointed. "On his broom." She gasped. "Presents!"

Grace trod around and looked. Sure enough, two wrapped gifts were dangling from the rear of the snowman's broom. She leaned in closer. Were they tied to shoelaces?

"Whatever they are, we should leave them be." Grace

took April's hand as she reached for the gifts. "They don't belong to us."

"They do, too. Santa left them." April glanced around. "Maybe he left more."

"They're for decoration."

April wouldn't listen. Only her eyes appeared to be working—they were wide, amazed. Grace sighed. If April was disappointed when those boxes ended up being empty, perhaps Aunt Gracie could leave something special out here later to compensate.

Grace untied the gifts and handed them over. April would accept only one.

"That one's for you," April said.

Grace peeled off her wrapping while she kept an eye on April. They both got to their boxes at the same time and flipped open the lids. April let out a sigh filled with wonder.

"It a Christmas watch!"

When April tried to slide the white leather band off its looped holder, Grace helped. April slipped the oversize watch over one mitten, and then held her arm out to admire it.

"It has a Christmas tree," April murmured.

"And Christmas balls at the ends of the hands."

"What about yours?"

Wondering now if they ought not to have opened the boxes—clearly these were meant for someone else, perhaps the neighbors—Grace examined her watch face. "Mine has a snowman—" she blinked, looked harder "—with a crooked hat."

"Why did Santa leave them out here?"

Grace was about to admit she had no idea when a voice replied for her.

"He wanted to let us know that it's time to count our blessings—past, present and, hopefully, future."

On suddenly wobbly legs, Grace turned around while April crept forward.

"Gracie, someone's standing behind our snowman."

Wynn stepped into view. He wore a black sweater and windbreaker and pale blue jeans. With his dark hair ruffling in the breeze, he'd never looked so handsome.

When April whispered *"Who is he?"* Grace was brought back to the moment and replied, "I think he must be lost."

Wynn stepped forward and his one-in-a-million energy radiated out. The wind was cool and yet she might have been standing on a hot plate.

"I don't feel lost. Not anymore." He glanced at the sky. "Snow's coming—any minute, I reckon."

Smooth. He was after an invitation. "I'd invite you in, but—"

"I brought someone with me," he cut in, and nodded toward a vehicle Grace hadn't noticed until now. Tate was waiting by the hood. All bundled up for the weather, he arced an arm over his head, waving.

April tugged her aunt's jacket. "Do you know him? Is he nice? Can I say hi?"

Wynn answered April. "I'm sure he'd like that."

Still, April looked to her aunt with pleading eyes. Giving in, Grace straightened April's beanie.

"Sure. Go ahead."

Her tiny boots crunching in the snow, April trundled away. When she stopped before Tate, April hesitated before extending her hand to give him a look at what Santa had left.

Grace had put it together. "You built this snowman."

"Me and Tate."

"How did you know I'd come out to have a look?"

"I'd like to think I know you pretty well."

When he edged closer and reached out, Grace was ready to push him away—no matter how much she might want to, she wouldn't change her mind about rebooting their affair. But he only gestured at the watch.

"You like it?" he asked. "They're matching *his* and *hers*."

As in *you* and *me?* "You're not going to get that watch back from April."

His crooked grin said, of course not. "Tate brought a gift especially for your niece."

Near the vehicle, Tate was holding the watch, inspecting the face, while April ogled a necklace decorated with huge sparkling blue and clear "jewels." The two kids began to talk, and then laugh.

"That's a good sound," Wynn said. "Reminds me of when we were kids."

"I don't remember you laughing very often."

"Perhaps because I expected too much."

She crossed her arms over her coat. "I don't expect too much." She only knew what she needed. What she'd accept.

She didn't want to sound harsh but neither would she back down. What they had shared had been a wonderful but also brief journey. He wanted the fun times to go on. She'd made herself a promise. She needed to get on with her life. And Wynn didn't want to be a part of that. Not in the long term.

Wynn was studying the snowman. "Tate and I had a talk last night. It opened my eyes to a lot of things. Honesty can slog you between the eyes," Wynn said. "But we get back up. A couple of months ago, my truth was that I needed some release. Some fun. A connection. I found that with you. And I found a lot more."

Nearby, snow crunched as if someone had fallen, and then a little cry ripped out. A few feet away, Tate lay face down. Without missing a beat, April shot out her hand. Tate wrenched himself up and then they set off, running around again.

"I wonder if they'll remember this day," she said, watching as the kids stopped to pat together two snowballs.

"My bet is, as clearly as I remember that day in Colorado when I tripped over my lace."

She narrowed her eyes at him. "After all these years, now you remember it that way?"

"I remember that I'd agonized over whether or not to give you a gift."

"A poke in the eye?"

"A bunch of flowers, plastic, lifted from a vase in one of the chalet's back rooms. But then I thought you might want to hug me or something gross like that, and it seemed easier to pretend I didn't like you."

Her smile faded. "We're not kids playing games anymore."

"No. We're not."

He leaned forward just as a snowball smashed against his shoulder. Tate stood a short distance away; given his expression, he didn't know whether to run or laugh or fastball another one. Beside him, April's pom-poms were dancing around her neck, she was giggling that hard. She pitched her baby snowball and bolted in the other direction. Tate followed.

Grinning, Wynn swiped snow off his jacket. "Naughty and nice."

"Is Tate missing his folks?"

"He knows they're arguing. He's not sure why. He thinks it's his fault. Well, his and mine. That's why he wanted to come over from Sydney. So we pariahs could hang together."

Her heart clutched and twisted. "That's so sad."

"We'll work through it, me and Tate—and the rest of the family. Sometime in the New Year, I'm going back to... well, face it all."

Grace cast a glance toward the house. Her father was

peering out the window again. She thought of all the food and warmth and company inside that house. She could hear Tate and April playing some game together and, after listening to what poor Tate was going through, it seemed wrong not to ask.

"Wynn, would you and Tate like to have breakfast with us?"

His somber expression faded into a soft smile. "We'd like that very much. There's something else I'd like even more." His eyes searched hers. *"You."*

She shivered with longing, with need, but she wanted more than "just for now," and she refused to feel guilty because of it.

"Wynn, we don't need to go through this again."

"We really do."

The knot high in her stomach wrenched tighter. He was making this so hard. "I want a family of my own, Wynn. Don't you get it?"

"Me, too. So, we need to get married. The sooner the better."

She'd come to terms with him showing up unannounced, organizing the snowman, the gifts. But this? A proposal? She wanted to be hopeful, excited. But a man didn't change his mind about something like that overnight.

"I didn't believe it," he went on, "that it could happen that fast. Falling in love, I mean."

Her back went up. "I can't help how I feel."

"Not you. *Me.*" His gloved hand slid around the back of her waist. "I love you," he said, and then broke out into a big smile. "Damn, that felt good."

Time seemed to stop. She set her palm against his chest to steady herself as her head began to spin.

"This isn't happening," she said.

"Close your eyes and I'll prove that it is."

When his mouth slanted over hers, her eyes automatically drifted shut and, in an instant, she was filled up with his warmth—with his strength. And then the kiss deepened and a million tiny stars showered down through her system—her head and her belly. Most of all, her heart. When he drew her closer, she stood on the toes of her boots and curled her arms around the padded collar at his neck. He tilted his head at a greater angle and urged her closer with a palm on her back until they were pressed together like two pages in a book.

When his lips finally left hers, she couldn't shake herself from the daze. His face was close and had a contented expression. In his eyes she saw every shade of "I'm certain." And the way he was holding her... No matter what she said, he wasn't about to let her go.

"I love you, Grace. The kind of love that can't take no for an answer. The kind that just has to win out."

While deepest emotion prickled behind her eyes, snow began to fall, dusting their hair and their shoulders. A snowflake landed on the tip of his nose at the same time a hot tear rolled down her cheek.

"Marry me," he said in a low, steady voice. "Be my wife. My love forever."

She swallowed deeply. Tried to speak.

"This isn't a rebound, is it?" she asked.

He only grinned. "Not a chance. I want you to have my name. Grace Hunter. Mrs. Wynn Hunter. I want to have babies with you and work through all those ups and downs families face. The challenges and triumphs that will make us even stronger."

Two little voices drifted over.

"He's gonna kiss her again."

"Gracie's gonna be a princess bride."

When she and Wynn both looked over, the kids darted away. Wynn's voice rumbled near her ear. "Smart kids."

He kissed her again, working it until she was mindless,

boneless—completely, unreservedly his. When his mouth gradually left her, she had to grip his windbreaker while her brain tried again to catch up.

"Can you see the future?" he asked. "Me in a tuxedo, Dex and Cole standing at my side. Your father is walking you down the aisle and our guests are sighing, you look so beautiful. So happy."

A breath caught in her throat. And then she realized. He was right. She could see it, too. Their families were there—all of them.

"Tate will be a ring bearer," she murmured, as another drop slid down her cheek, "and April the flower girl."

"And?"

"And…" She cupped his jaw then ran fingers over that faint scar on his temple. He was waiting for her answer. It seemed the *only* choice.

"I love you," she said. "I can't wait to marry you."

The snow was falling harder, catching on his lashes, in the stubble on his jaw, and as he kissed her again, everything in their world—everything in her heart—felt incredible. Amazing. Just the way it ought to.

"Would you believe," he said as his lips slipped from hers, "I don't have a ring."

A little hand tugged Grace's coat. One of April's mittens was off and she was offering up her crystal solitaire.

Grace laughed she was so touched, and Wynn cocked his head. "Wow. April, are you sure? That looks like a lot of carats."

Tate held April's hand. "I'll get her another one."

A call came from the house—it was Grace's father telling everyone to come in. When Tate looked up at his brother, Wynn said, "Go ahead, buddy."

As they watched the young couple trot toward the path, Grace linked her arms around her fiancé's neck.

"Guess we ought to go in, too," she said. "Snow's coming down pretty fast."

"Let it snow," he said. "I *love* the snow. I love you." Cupping her cheek, he smiled adoringly into her eyes. "Today all my Christmases have come at once."

Epilogue

Meanwhile in Seattle...

Crouched on her bathroom floor, Teagan Hunter hugged herself tight, and then groaning, doubled over more. Her stomach was filled with barbed wire knots, but the pain went way beyond physical. It was memories. It was regrets. They circled her thoughts like a pack of vultures waiting to drop.

The High Tea Gym had barely seen her all week, and that had to change. She had a business to run, bills to pay, staff to supervise and clients to inspire. But then those vultures swooped again and Teagan only had the strength to lower her brow to her knee.

Her determined side said this was a case of mind over matter. She'd be fine. She would endure. No. She would *flourish*. God knew, up until now, she'd coped with a lot in her life. Still, she couldn't shake another voice gnawing at her ear, telling her that what she had lost this time was immeasurable—impossible to have, or try to protect, ever again.

As she dragged herself into the kitchen, her cell phone sounded on the counter. It could be Cole with some news about their father's ongoing stalker situation, she thought. But, checking the ID, tears sprang to her eyes. Her finger itched to swipe the screen, accept the call. But what if she lost it and broke down?

Finally, she pushed the phone aside and crossed to the pantry. She forced down a protein shake—vanilla with blueberries, usually her favorite, although this morning it went down like gobs of tasteless sludge. After tying her shoes, she stretched her calves while trying to project positive thoughts for the coming day. Thought dictated behavior, which in turn determined mood. Picking yourself up and moving forward was without question the best way.

And yet this minute she only wanted to curl up and cry.

When her phone sounded again, Teagan set her hands over her ears and headed for her rowing machine. She didn't have any answers for Damon. He would simply have to accept it. She didn't want to—couldn't bear to—see him ever again.

Three days ago, she'd sat behind her desk and had calmly passed on her decision. His eyes had gone wide. Then an amused smile had flickered at one side of the mouth she had come to adore. But when she'd stood her ground—had asked him to leave—his jaw had tensed and his brows had drawn together.

"Tell me what's going on, Tea," he'd said. "I won't leave until you do."

Now, as she positioned herself on the machine, strapped in her feet, grabbed the ropes and eased into the flow—sliding forward, easing back, pushing with her legs, holding in her belly…already firm and flat and *empty*—

She dropped the handles. The ropes flew back and, shaking, she covered her face. She'd already cried so much, surely she was done, and yet the salty streams coursing down her cheeks wouldn't stop.

It must pass *sometime*—the constant praying and begging that she could have that chance again. Because she didn't know how much longer she could bear it…the images from that night when her greatest dream came true had turned into a nightmare. It all seemed so pointless, so gut-wrenchingly cruel. She'd been told she would never conceive. She'd learned to live with that fact. She'd pushed on and had come to accept it.

But how could she ever accept that she'd miscarried a child—Damon's baby—because now…

Nothing in the world seemed to matter.

* * * * *

*If you liked Wynn's story, don't miss a single novel
in* THE HUNTER PACT *series from
Robyn Grady:
LOSING CONTROL
TEMPTATION ON HIS TERMS
All available now!*

A sneaky peek at next month...

Desire™

PASSIONATE AND DRAMATIC LOVE STORIES

My wish list for next month's titles...

In stores from 21st March 2014:

- ❏ One Good Cowboy – Catherine Mann
- & His Lover's Little Secret – Andrea Laurence
- ❏ The Black Sheep's Inheritance – Maureen Child
- & A Not-So-Innocent Seduction – Janice Maynard
- ❏ Wanting What She Can't Have – Yvonne Lindsay
- & Once Pregnant, Twice Shy – Red Garnier

Available at WHSmith, Tesco, Asda, Eason, Amazon and Apple

Just can't wait?

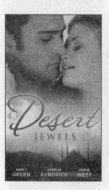
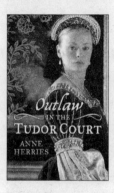

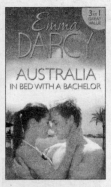
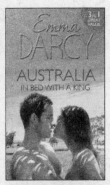
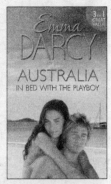

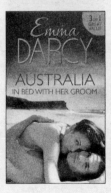

Discover more romance at

www.millsandboon.co.uk

- ❤ WIN great prizes in our exclusive competitions
- ❤ BUY new titles before they hit the shops
- ❤ BROWSE new books and REVIEW your favourites
- ❤ SAVE on new books with the Mills & Boon® Bookclub™
- ❤ DISCOVER new authors

PLUS, to chat about your favourite reads, get the latest news and find special offers:

- Find us on facebook.com/millsandboon
- Follow us on twitter.com/millsandboonuk
- ❤ Sign up to our newsletter at millsandboon.co.uk

The World of Mills & Boon®

There's a Mills & Boon® series that's perfect for you. We publish ten series and, with new titles every month, you never have to wait long for your favourite to come along.

By Request
Relive the romance with the best of the best
12 stories every month

Cherish™
Experience the ultimate rush of falling in love
12 new stories every month

Desire™
Passionate and dramatic love stories
6 new stories every month

nocturne™
An exhilarating underworld of dark desires
Up to 3 new stories every month

M&B/WORLD4a